Praise for Let's █████

'Just delicious . . . a gorgeous love █████
Marian █████

'The absolute pinnacle of romcoms; Laura Wood delivers another incredible, sweeping love story. Utterly stunning, hopeful and bitingly funny. I am starstruck by Cynthie and Jack's romance'
Lizzie Huxley-Jones

'Sparky and terrific fun – a charming twist on a fake dating romance with two starry leads you'll end up falling for yourself'
Justin Myers

'I truly, truly adored *Let's Make a Scene* . . . I embarrassed myself giggling, sighing and crying my way through it, and couldn't put it down. This book is absolutely glorious'
Lucy Vine

'I loved *Let's Make a Scene* so so much! Argh, it was a total delight! I took ages to read it on purpose because I did not want it to end. Laura has delivered an absolute masterclass of a romcom and this story is sheer perfection'
Hannah Doyle

'Laura Wood is quite possibly now my favourite romcom author, and *Let's Make a Scene* is a perfect mix of hilarity and slow burn delicious sex appeal'
Rebecca Ryan

'Featuring some of the hottest kiss scenes I've ever read and filled with the kind of yearning that will send hopeless romantics swooning, *Let's Make a Scene* is laugh-out-loud funny, unapologetically heartfelt and everything a romcom should be'
Catherine Walsh

'The most delicious, indulgent, funny and emotionally charged romcom I have read in a long time – it ranks up there with my favourite ever romances'
Cressida McLaughlin

Praise for Laura Wood

'I fell in love with Laura Wood's writing when I read *Under Your Spell*'
Julia Quinn

'I absolutely adored *Under Your Spell* the sweetest,
sexiest, funniest romance. It was such a treat!'
Marian Keyes

'*Under Your Spell* is a hilarious, touching and relatable
story that should become a touchstone for readers
navigating the ups and downs of life, love and work'
The Bookseller

'So witty and smart. I am thoroughly under Laura Wood's spell'
Hannah Grace

'A fabulously engrossing read! With wit and charm, Laura Wood
creates a magical world readers will want to dig into. *Under Your
Spell*'s epic sisterhood, healing journey and slow burn romance
beautifully demonstrate how love can rock you to your core'
Christina Lauren

'Capturing the deep dreaminess of summer, this is a book bursting with
great love and laughter, and at its heart is a trio of sisters you'll never
forget. For any fans of Emily Henry, this is a romantic read supreme'
Stylist

'I loved this so much … like Taylor Jenkins Reid combined with
pure Emily Henry romance joy. I have loved Laura Wood's books
for years but this is my favourite of all her books. Go buy!'
Ella Risbridger

'A note-perfect romcom featuring a heroine to root for, a hero to swoon
over and a sexy, tender and funny story that I never wanted to end. Fans
of Emily Henry and Mhairi McFarlane will adore *Under Your Spell*'
Sarra Manning, *Red* Magazine

Laura Wood is an author and an academic. Her debut adult novel, *Under Your Spell*, has sold into seventeen languages. *Let's Make a Scene* is her second romance book for adults. She is also a bestselling and acclaimed author of children's and young adult novels. Laura has a PhD in nineteenth century literature, and lives in Warwickshire with her husband and their dog, Bea. You can visit lauraclarewood.com and follow her on Instagram @lauracwood.

Also by Laura Wood

Under Your Spell

LAURA WOOD

Let's Make A Scene

**SIMON &
SCHUSTER**

London · New York · Amsterdam/Antwerp · Sydney/Melbourne · Toronto · New Delhi

First published in Great Britain by Simon & Schuster UK Ltd, 2025

1 3 5 7 9 10 8 6 4 2

Simon & Schuster UK Ltd
1st Floor
222 Gray's Inn Road
London WC1X 8HB

Simon & Schuster Australia, Sydney
Simon & Schuster India, New Delhi

www.simonandschuster.co.uk
www.simonandschuster.com.au
www.simonandschuster.co.in

The authorised representative in the EEA is Simon & Schuster Netherlands BV,
Herculesplein 96, 3584 AA Utrecht, Netherlands. info@simonandschuster.nl

A CIP catalogue record for this book is available from the British Library

Paperback ISBN: 978-1-3985-2979-3
eBook ISBN: 978-1-3985-2980-9
Audio ISBN: 978-1-3985-2981-6

This book is a work of fiction. Names, characters, places and incidents are either a product of the author's imagination or are used fictitiously. Any resemblance to actual people living or dead, events or locales is entirely coincidental.

Typeset in Bembo by M Rules
Printed and Bound in the UK using 100% Renewable Electricity at CPI Group (UK) Ltd

MIX
Paper | Supporting
responsible forestry
FSC
www.fsc.org   FSC® C013604

For my fellow tender-hearted introverts who are feeling sad and overwhelmed. I hope this book is the friend to you that it has been to me. I hope in these pages you find joy and escapism and a safe space to feel all your feelings.

I hope you know that we like you very much, just as you are.

Chapter One

Cynthie

I am ninety per cent certain that my personal trainer is trying to kill me, but if she's truly homicidal she'll have to get in line: the list of people who want me dead is currently pretty long.

'Stop crying like a little baby and give me five more!' Petra yells.

'I'm not crying,' I pant, clinging to what little dignity I have left as I crawl across my exercise mat. 'I am *sweating*. I think my *eyeballs* are sweating. Is that even possible?' I take a deep, shuddering breath. 'Physiologically speaking, I mean.'

'I am not here for a science lesson about your sweaty body!' Petra snaps out. 'I am here to make you strong! Right now you are not strong, you are weak and limp! Like a worm! Or the leaf of lettuce!'

Every sentence out of Petra's mouth is punctuated so emphatically with an exclamation mark that I can almost see them floating through the air towards me, though that could be the delirium brought on by how knackered I am.

Standing over me in her hot-pink Lycra workout gear, she looks and sounds like the meanest cheerleader in the world. Petra is small and blond, with a bouncing ponytail and perfect white teeth: a tiny Serbian prom queen with the dark, shrivelled heart of Wednesday

Addams. I love her. At least, I do when she's not actively trying to destroy me.

Over the speakers, Mary Poppins sings peppily about spoonfuls of sugar. Petra's obsessive love for Julie Andrews is extremely intense, and today it was her turn to choose the music. While I would not previously have considered Julie's oeuvre to be the obvious soundtrack to a workout, I have to admit she does have some bangers.

I attempt to curl my body into another of the impossible crunches Petra wants. 'It hurts,' I whimper.

'Life is pain, princess.' Petra is unmoved.

'Hey,' I say, like a hostage trying to forge a human connection with their captor, 'I love that film.'

She frowns. 'What film?'

'"Life is pain, princess",' I repeat. 'Isn't that a quote from *The Princess Bride*?'

'Oh.' Petra tilts her head to the side and nods. 'Yes, I have seen that film. I like best the giant rat.'

Of course the woman is on the side of the rodents of unusual size.

'I suppose you were team Darth Vader, too,' I grumble, falling back against the floor, my jelly-like limbs splayed around me, refusing to move any further.

'His cape is excellent,' she says with approval, before nudging at my leg with her foot. 'Now we will do the light weights.'

I groan, which only makes her smile widen – like a shark showing off all its teeth.

'We do the jabs and the uppercuts and you pretend you are punching *that man* in the face.'

I don't need to ask her which man she means.

'Okay,' I agree, letting her drag me to my feet.

Once I'm standing with the weights in my hands, I mirror her stance and start moving my arms, putting some snap into the jab-cross movements.

'You can do better than this!' Petra is fired up, bouncing on the balls of her feet. 'You hit him in the face! You hit him in the mouth! Go for the groin! You break that asshole's nose!'

'Yeah,' I pant, arms flailing everywhere as 'The Lonely Goatherd' blasts out at top volume. 'Fuck him.'

'That's right.' She nods, 'Louder!'

'FUCK HIM!' I yell, twisting my fists, imagining the punches landing on Shawn Hardy's stupid, handsome face.

Petra cheers and lets loose a string of Serbian profanities.

'What does that mean?' I ask, when I come to rest with my hands on my hips, sucking in deep gulps of air.

Petra considers this for a moment. 'It is like . . . I hope the thunder from the sky fucks you until you are dead.'

I blink.

'We Serbs are very good at cursing,' she adds proudly.

'Clearly.'

'We are done for today. Make sure you drink the water and stretch.' With a flick of her ponytail, Petra moves to stop the music, cutting Julie off mid-yodel.

'It is better,' Petra concedes, as I guzzle from my water bottle. 'Maybe you will not be total embarrassment after all.'

I start to stretch my hamstrings. 'I don't know . . .' I feel a flutter of nervous energy. 'I've never done proper combat training like this before. It's going to be intense – so many classes in martial arts *and* weapons. I'm going to have an axe to wield.'

'Nice.' Petra takes a swig from her own bottle. 'Will you also get to wear a cape?'

She looks so hopeful that I say, 'Probably.' And now I know exactly what to get her for Christmas.

'But they want a more muscular look,' I continue, flexing my bicep, which is certainly more of an event than it was a few weeks ago. 'I've still got a way to go.'

I've been putting in a lot of hours with Petra lately, which has been fine with me. Until this scandal blows over, there's no way I'm voluntarily leaving the house, so my home gym has been a place to burn off some of my rage.

When I first bought my place in LA, I didn't give much thought to the large exercise space in the basement, even though the realtor had been in raptures about it. As Petra would be the first to point out, I am neither a natural or an enthusiastic athlete.

I was much more interested in the bright, sunny kitchen, and in the rooms that weren't just big empty glass boxes, but felt a little familiar given the 1920's English-Revival style of the building. An LA mansion was hardly a two-bedroom semi in Wiltshire, but it felt a lot closer to home than some of the properties I'd been looking at.

After spending over twenty years plotting to get as far away from the place as possible, it was a real kick in the teeth to find myself feeling homesick.

Anyway, it turned out the realtor had been right all along and I was extremely grateful for the slick, kitted-out room that I had once referred to as 'the dungeon'. Preparing for my next role in a big comic-book-hero franchise has been the perfect distraction from the disaster that is my life.

Perhaps disaster is the wrong word. Catastrophe? No, what's worse than a catastrophe? It sounds like the Serbs could just about do justice to the absolute bin fire of the past month.

It's been four weeks now since the news of my affair with Shawn Hardy hit the tabloids. Four weeks of relentless attention, of paparazzi camped outside the door, of increasingly hysterical headlines, of earnest think-pieces, of tweets and letters and emails ranging from 'I'm very disappointed in you' to 'I wish you were dead'. I've been called a slut, a whore, a scarlet woman (a fun throw-back). There's even been an SNL skit about it – so I hear, anyway. I haven't seen it because Hannah confiscated all my devices after I spent the first week curled up under a blanket, crying and subsisting entirely on ice cream.

'If you leave it to melt, you can just drink it straight from the carton,' I had told her, wild-eyed and sugar-drunk. 'The tub is already cup shaped and there's no washing up. It's the perfect method. Do you think people know about this?'

'You don't even do your own washing up,' Hannah had replied sharply, wrenching my phone from the birdlike claw my hand had formed around it thanks to hours of doom-scrolling.

As if the memory has summoned her, Hannah hustles into the room.

'Oh, good, you're done,' she says. 'Gayle is here, and she wants a word.'

My agent turning up unannounced . . . This can't be good.

'Do I have time to grab a quick shower first?' I ask. Petra may be able to work out and develop a delicate, aesthetic glow, but I am tomato-red and my hair is scrunched into a sweaty ball. This is in stark contrast to Hannah, who looks chic in a drapey black linen jumpsuit. She's all perfect flicks of black eyeliner, glowing golden skin and cut-glass cheekbones, courtesy of her Bangladeshi mum and her Italian dad – a genetic combination so winning that she absolutely could have made it as a model if she wasn't – and I quote – 'unable to be in a photo without blinking, and deeply dedicated to carbohydrates.'

'Of course,' Hannah replies hastily, because, as I said, the picture is not a pretty one. 'I'll set Gayle up with a coffee.'

'I'll be quick,' I promise, and bidding goodbye to Petra I run upstairs, shower and change into a pair of yoga pants and a stretchy cashmere jumper.

(It seems to me that when you're heartbroken and your reputation is circling the drain, you can't be expected to wear anything that doesn't have an elasticated waistband. The fact that I bother with a bra at all is an indication of my innate professionalism.)

'There she is!' Gayle greets me when I make my way back down to the living room. 'Darling, you look gorgeous.'

Considering the last time Gayle saw me I was hyperventilating into an empty crisp packet (Who has paper bags in the house these days?) I'm sure my current appearance is indeed an improvement.

Hannah and Gayle sit side by side on the horseshoe-shaped, pink velvet sofa that has been my cozy little depression-themed, trash-panda nest in recent weeks – probably not the vision my interior designer had in mind – but that is currently respectably tidy. There are barely any chocolate bar wrappers and crumpled tissues stuffed down the sides of the cushions.

Gayle Salt is one of the most formidable agents in the world, representing a whole roster of movie stars both in the UK and here in the States. When she took me on thirteen years ago it felt like a miracle, and most days it still does. She looks and dresses like Iris Apfel but with improbably red hair, commands any room she walks into, and has a career that has spanned over fifty years (though she remains extremely vague about her age beyond telling me 'Darling, I was the merest child when I started out! Practically a foetus!') She drops names through conversation like confetti, but does so without affectation: she simply knows *everyone*.

'There's good news and bad news,' she says now, direct as always.

My eyes flicker over to Hannah. The woman has been my best friend since we were in nappies, and I can usually read her like a book. Now, however, her expression is a strange mixture of anxiety and excitement.

I lower myself into a chair facing the sofa, and pick up the coffee that Hannah has made.

'Okay,' I say. 'Let's hear it.'

'The bad news', Gayle says it quickly, like she's ripping off a plaster, 'is that the studio has dropped you from *Iron Maiden*.'

I thought I was braced for whatever was coming, but I was

wrong. It turns out that what I had considered rock bottom still left me with further to fall.

'They've . . . what?' I ask. My coffee cup shakes perilously in my suddenly numb fingers.

Gayle shrugs. 'It's a family franchise. They don't like the press you've been getting.'

'But . . . we have a contract,' I say weakly. I can't believe this is happening. My work is the only thing that's been keeping me going. Or, at least, *preparing* for the work has kept me going. I haven't wanted to tell Gayle that the thought of being on set, of actually filming, fills me with a sense of rising dread.

'They say you've violated the morality clause.' Gayle sounds impatient. 'It's bullshit, but fuck 'em. If they haven't got the balls to stand behind you now, then you don't want to be working with them.'

'The morality clause,' I say dully. 'Because of the affair.'

'I wish you'd stop calling it an affair!' Hannah cuts in, furious.

'Why?' I sigh. 'It *was* an affair. Shawn is married.'

'But he told you he was separated.' Hannah is practically vibrating with anger. 'He told you there were lawyers involved. That it had been over for years.'

'And I was stupid enough to believe him.' I knuckle my eyes, too tired to deal with another wave of guilt and regret. 'I should have known better. I should have . . . Well, there are a lot of things I should have done, but I didn't.' I exhale a shaky breath. 'So that's it? Just like that, I'm out?'

Gayle sits forward, and there's a sparkle in her eye. 'Ask me about the good news.'

'What's the good news?'

'Jasmine Gallow got in touch with me,' Gayle says, and I feel a flicker of interest. Jasmine co-directed my first film, and she's the one who hooked me up with Gayle in the first place. I loved working with her.

'Does she have a new project?' I ask.

'Of sorts,' is Gayle's cryptic response. She nods to Hannah, who slides an iPad across the coffee table between us. Cued up on the screen is a video. I hit play.

I'm surprised when I see my own face. It's a trailer for a film – a period romance – but it's not a film I have any memory of making.

'What is this?' I murmur.

'Just watch,' Gayle says tranquilly.

When Jack Turner-Jones' face fills the screen, I almost drop the tablet. 'I— What?' I manage.

It takes me a moment to realize that the trailer has been made by splicing together scenes from other films that I've done: a small but well received adaptation of *Northanger Abbey*, some snippets from a fantasy film where I played a tragic princess, and the one that started it all, *A Lady of Quality*. They've skimmed a bunch of stuff from *Blood/Lust*, Jack's vampire show, too – mostly the historical flashbacks.

As the music swells, the words '*A Lady of Quality 2*: Coming Soon' roll across the famous scene of the two of us kissing in the original. I feel my stomach tighten.

There's a long moment of silence. When I look at the women in front of me, they are both watching me with anticipation.

'I don't understand,' I say slowly.

'So, as you know, several years ago *Lady* went up on Netflix.' Gayle drums her long, dagger-sharp nails against her silk-clad knee. 'And its popularity has gone from strength to strength. We're talking cult-classic at this point. The numbers are really impressive, and interest from the sixteen to twenty-four demographic has gone through the roof. It's all over social media: there are hundreds of these homemade trailers, mock ups of movie posters, fan art . . . and that moment from the MTV awards has gone viral *again*.' The glint is back in her eye. 'There's an online petition calling for a sequel that has over one hundred thousand signatures. No one can predict when these things are going to happen, when an old title gets a new lease of life, but it's gaining very serious momentum. People are paying attention.'

'We made this thirteen years ago,' I say. 'Are you suggesting that Jasmine wants to make . . . a sequel?'

'I'm saying that the funding's in place,' Gayle sounds delighted, and well she might – everyone knows that funding a project can take years of shaky negotiations, false starts and disappointments.

'Netflix wants the sequel, and Jasmine's had a script knocking around for years. Frankly, the only thing that's been holding the idea back is you: you got too big, too busy. Without Cynthie Taylor, there is no movie.' She leans forward. 'But the script is great, Cyn. Really, something special. And a hole just opened up in your schedule.'

'They want to make it *now*?' I'm trying to keep up.

'In two months, when you were due to start working on *Iron Maiden*.' Gayle is brisk.

'That is insane,' I say flatly. 'There's no way.'

'It's not as wild as it sounds,' Gayle jumps in. 'Like I say, the script's been doing the rounds for a while. They want to use most of the original cast and crew – that's part of the draw, so there's no messing around convincing producers that this guy or that gal are the right choice. The scheduling has fallen into place like you wouldn't believe. The original locations in the UK are available and they'll shoot the rest on the same lot in the studio outside London. I swear, it's like the universe is behind this movie. Even Logan is on board.'

'Logan?' I frown. 'I thought he was doing the next Marvel movie?'

Logan Gallow is Jasmine Gallow's twin brother. *A Lady of Quality* was the first and last film they ever directed together and the experience was . . . interesting. Logan went on to direct a bunch of action blockbusters, while Jasmine's sporadic output has been much more arthouse.

'Wait.' The final piece of the puzzle slips into place. I blame my muddled brain for the fact it's taken this long. I look at Hannah, and she gazes innocently off to the side, careful not to meet my eye. 'What about Jack?'

Saying his name makes my stomach hurt again.

If I hadn't been looking for it, I don't think I would have noticed Gayle's infinitesimal hesitation. 'That's the best part. He's just wrapped the latest series on his show,' she says brightly. 'If you're in, he's in.'

I absolutely cannot make a film with Jack Turner-Jones. I can't even be in the same room with Jack Turner-Jones.

Thirteen years ago we swore we'd never see each other again. It's a promise we've managed to keep.

I close my eyes.

Apparently, that's about to change.

Chapter Two

Cynthie

'There's more,' Gayle says.

'Of course there is,' I murmur, rubbing my temples, a tension headache brewing. Because naturally it can't end there, with the reappearance of my mortal enemy. *Obviously*, there has to be some further catch – a scene where I have to roll around in jam before being chased by a swarm of angry bees, perhaps.

That actually sounds preferable to working with Jack again.

'The funding for the film comes with a couple of . . . stipulations.' The way Gayle breezes over the words has me on high alert.

'What sort of stipulations?'

'Nothing too daunting.' Gayle sips demurely at her latte. 'In fact, everything should work in our favour.'

'Just tell me.'

Gayle runs her finger around the rim of the china coffee cup, suddenly coy. 'Alongside the film, the producers are interested in pursuing another project: a documentary.'

'A documentary?' I'm going to have to stop parroting everything she says back to her, but the situation just keeps getting more and more bizarre. Perhaps this is all a hallucination, and back in the real world I'm still lying on my exercise mat,

Petra cackling gleefully over the unconscious, dehydrated husk of my body.

'An all-access, behind-the-scenes look at the filming process. The whole cast and crew back together after thirteen years to make a second-chance romance, you and Jack reuniting on-screen after all this time, reminiscing about the original *Lady*, the movie that launched your careers. And the whole production is being driven by a wave of new, young fan interest ... It's a great angle,' Gayle continues, and there's excitement in her words. She's fired up about this. 'You know how much content people consume now; the studios simply can't keep up. This is a two-for-one for them, double the exposure for us. Win-win.'

I narrow my eyes, suspicious. 'The film is a second-chance romance?'

Gayle waves an airy hand. 'I mean, the first movie ended happily, so the conflict in the sequel obviously comes from the fact that events have separated the young lovers in the interim. This film is about them reuniting: older, wiser, a little more jaded. It's called *A Woman of Fire*, and it's gorgeous stuff, Cyn. Gorgeous! Think *Persuasion* meets *The Notebook*. A total swoon!'

My suspicions are not allayed. In fact, I can almost hear warning sirens wailing in the distance. 'So ... the *film* is about a second chance between the characters,' I say carefully.

Gayle doesn't blink but Hannah looks increasingly shifty. She's always been a shit poker player.

'Well,' – Gayle leans forward, places her coffee cup down with a decisive clink – 'now we come on to the other stipulation. Naturally, the angle of the movie *did* get the folks at the studio thinking. Former lovers reuniting ... a second chance at romance ... young love rekindled ...' She trails off suggestively.

My stomach drops as I see exactly where this has been heading all along. 'If you're talking about me and Jack then I'll remind you that there was never any romance the *first* time around. It was all a publicity set-up. In fact,' – my breath is coming quicker now – 'I can't believe you're even bringing this up when you know how bad things were between the two of us.'

'Now, now,' Gayle chides. '*You* know that the public perception was a very different thing, so you can't blame anyone involved in making the film for thinking it's a neat spin that'll draw the crowds.' Her eyes are shrewd behind her thick, red-framed glasses. 'What's a little pretend romance between co-workers? They just want you to do a few appearances, get your picture taken together, stir things up. And you can protest all you like, but even you can't deny the chemistry the pair of you had on-screen.' She fans her face with her hand. 'You can't fake that kind of heat.'

'It's called acting,' I insist. 'We absolutely hated each other.'

'And that was the whole story, was it?' Gayle lifts her brows, and it's my turn to look away.

'Anyway,' she continues after a moment of weighty silence. 'The two of you did a great job playing things up for the cameras once before … Why not do it again? You're both professionals; you know how to handle something like this.' She fixes me with a sudden, penetrating look, her easy charm dropping away to give me a glimpse of the hard-boiled dame beneath. 'Frankly, Cyn, we need to do something for your image. If we don't act now then *Iron Maiden* could be just the start of our problems. I'm offering you a lifeline here.'

'Okay, just so I'm clear.' I briefly close my eyes, letting the facts settle. 'Not only am I supposed to make a sequel to a film from thirteen years ago with a man I can't stand, but he and I are required to pretend we're in a romantic relationship … in front of a documentary crew that is following our every move.'

Gayle nods.

'Let me ask you a question.' I sit forward, resting my elbows on my knees, my chin in my hand as I scan her face. 'Are you high right now?'

Gayle hoots. 'I mean, I've had my morning edible, but you know I gave up the hard stuff years ago. California sober, darling! I get your hesitation, but if you give it a little thought, I think you'll realize what a no-brainer this is.' She gets to her feet, the chunky beaded necklaces she wears clacking wildly.

'I can't believe Jack would agree to this!' I blurt.

Gayle's face softens. 'Of course he did! You're Cynthie Taylor. Any man would be lucky to have a relationship with you – even a fake one. You're a brilliant, beautiful force of a woman, and a once-in-a-generation talent.' She shakes her head, her lip curling in distaste. 'Shawn Hardy did a number on you, that weaselly little shit, and I'd like to smack him right in the face, but he's *not* going to derail your career. Not while I have breath in my body.'

Easy tears spring to my eyes, and I try my best to blink them away.

'I've already sent Hannah a copy of the script.' Gayle grabs her voluminous Hermes handbag. 'I'm going to give you time to read it, to process things, and then we'll talk again. I'm off for lunch with Leo.' She rolls her eyes. 'The man is so needy.'

On this note, Gayle breezes out, leaving Hannah and I alone.

'What . . . the . . . fuck?' I say finally.

Hannah lets out a wheeze of laughter. 'I know,' she agrees, curling her feet up beside her on the sofa.

'I don't even understand what just happened.' I shake my head. 'I can't believe Gayle thinks this is a good idea. I can't believe *anyone* thinks this is a good idea.'

'Welllll . . .' Hannah trails off.

'*You* think I should do this?'

Hannah hesitates for a moment, and then she sits forward, pushing her hands through her hair in an impatient gesture. 'Okay. Do you want softly-softly, or is it finally time for hard talk?'

What I want is to squeeze my eyes shut, to find a blanket and curl up under it, to hide from the whole world, but Hannah is looking at me expectantly.

It could have been a huge mistake, all those years ago, hiring my best friend as my assistant. There are a million ways it should have blown up in our faces, but it didn't. It has never felt like Hannah works for me. It's like it has always been, since we were kids: we're a team, partners in crime, Cynthie and Hannah against the world.

I might be the one who stands in front of the camera, but Hannah is with me every step of the way; she undertakes every practical aspect of the job, organizes my entire life and keeps me sane. I couldn't do what I do without her, and we both know it. I trust her more than anyone else on the planet, and that is the *only* reason I'm going to listen to what she has to say, even if I begin to suspect that Gayle hasn't been the only one hitting the edibles.

'Fine,' I huff. 'Hard talk, let's go.'

Hannah sends me a long, measuring look, her lips pursed, as though she's working out exactly what I can handle. Eventually, she gives a satisfied nod, and it's clear I've passed some sort of test.

'Okay.' Picking up the iPad again, she taps the screen a few times and turns it to face me.

SAINT OR CYNNER? The headline screams in giant letters, and I groan.

'I am going to let you read this article,' Hannah says firmly, 'because we both know it's bullshit, and we are capable of detaching a bad, fabricated story that is written to attract clicks, from the reality of this situation. Right?'

'Right,' I repeat, but the word is shakier than I'd like.

After another second of hesitation, Hannah hands me the tablet so that I can read the whole thing.

It's been four weeks since Saint Cyn was caught on camera with her very married director Shawn Hardy, the article begins, gleefully.

I cringe. I didn't think it was possible, but Saint Cyn – the most awful nickname in the world – has become even worse now that it's being used in this smirky, ironic fashion. Underneath the opening paragraphs are the grainy pictures of Shawn and I – the ones that blew up my whole life. I'm practically wrapped around him, his hands are on my ass, our faces fused together. The fact that we were – I thought – in private, was apparently irrelevant. Neither of us had seen or heard the drone camera overhead.

I feel a wave of nausea at the sight of the photos. The caption underneath reads: *Saint Cyn's wicked deeds! Cynthie Taylor, 33, and Shawn Hardy indulge in a passionate clinch.*

It's hardly the first time I've seen the images, but I find myself examining them again like a detective scrutinizing shots of a grisly crime scene. It feels as though I'm looking at someone else. I wish the woman in the pictures had known what a colossal mistake she was making.

Taylor hasn't been seen in public since the story of the red-hot fling leaked, and for good reason. The article continues. While Hardy (who allegedly broke off the affair) has made a public apology to his wife, grovelling hard in a movingly honest interview with *GQ*, Taylor's camp has been suspiciously silent, leading to speculation that the woman scorned is not taking her very public dumping well. Perhaps last week's announcement that Hardy's wife – former model, Karyn, 30, – is four months pregnant with the couple's second child, has contributed to Taylor's troubles.

'Yeah, do you think?' I murmur. I gaze at the recent photo of Shawn and his wife at a launch event for her wellness line. She is beautiful, glowing, and he cups a protective hand over her stomach, looking down at her with immense tenderness. This is the marriage he told me had been over for years. He must have known she was pregnant when we were together. I can feel the bile rise in my throat as I force myself to keep reading.

> While many of us were shocked by this turn of events, others were quick to point out that the English rose and former sweetheart of the big screen has always had a taste for the bad boys – most famously when she was in an on-again-off-again relationship with serial womanizer Theo Eliott years before he settled down.

'Shit,' I exclaim. 'They're dragging Theo into this mess now?' I look up at Hannah who is watching me with sympathy in her eyes. 'I need to call him,' I mutter, making a mental note to do so later.

Theo and I split up a long time ago and now he's one of my closest friends. When the story first broke, he sent me a giant chocolate fudge cake from my favourite bakery with the words FUCK THAT GUY piped beautifully on the top in swirling vanilla frosting. I laughed and cried at the same time and ate the cake out of the box with my hands like a bear. It wasn't my finest moment, but then I hadn't been having many of them lately.

I drag my attention back to the device in my hand.

> With rumours swirling that Taylor is about to be dropped from her next big Hollywood project, it looks like the turbulent times are far from over. Sources close to the starlet have hinted that her isolation may not be down to the affair alone – there's talk that this erratic behaviour is part of a wider pattern, and friends and family are urging Taylor to seek help for substance abuse. Whatever the case, it's rare that the public sees such a dramatic fall from grace

unfolding in real time. It just goes to show – you really don't know
what goes on behind closed doors, and even the most squeaky-
clean of celebrities might be hiding a dark side.

I sit for a moment with the iPad in my lap. I'm sure that I should
be feeling something right now, but I don't. I don't feel anything,
there's just a tingling in my fingers, and a distant buzzing noise in
my ears.

'Cyn?' Hannah says, and she gets up, comes to crouch down
beside me and takes my hands in hers. Her fingers are warm . . . or
maybe that means mine are cold.

Hannah bites her lip. 'Please, please don't shut down. I'm not
showing you this to upset you. I'm showing you because it's time
to stop letting that shitbag stomp all over the life you've built. This?
This is so far from the truth it's crazy. You can't let such stupid lies
hurt you. You need to get up. You need to fight back now.'

Her words are soft, but they're stirring. They reach through all
this crackling anxiety. She's right. I look down at the article, and
there it is again – the candle-flicker of anger, the tiniest spark of
rage. I grab on to it.

I may have made some extraordinarily shitty choices, but that
can't be everything I am. After all this time, all this work . . . I can't
let this be what it comes to: me slinking off into the shadows while
Shawn Hardy faces absolutely zero consequences.

'It's bullshit.' I don't realize I've said the words until Hannah
squeezes my hand.

'Yes!' she exclaims. 'It is *absolutely* bullshit. So let's do something
about it.'

'Okay,' I say, and then I try the word again, firmer this time.
'Okay.'

Hannah stands, her smile is sharp. 'Good.' Tapping her fingers
across the screen she passes the tablet back to me one more time.

Now, there's another face staring out at me. Jack Turner-Jones.

It's a recent red-carpet snap, and he's standing, relaxed, one hand in his pocket, laughing at something.

He is undeniably gorgeous. More gorgeous now, even, than he was thirteen years ago. He's filled out for his role in *Blood/Lust*, packing on the muscle and broadening in the shoulders. Where he used to be clean-shaven, he now sports an attractive shadow of scruff along his square jaw. His light brown hair is swept back, a little longer than it used to be, and his eyes – a vivid, arctic blue – have tiny crinkles at the corners that didn't used to be there. He looks happy.

'I just can't believe ... Jack?' I don't take my eyes off the picture, unthinkingly touching my finger to his face. 'You really think this plan of Gayle's is the right move?'

'I do.' Hannah moves back to her seat, crosses her legs. 'Let me tell you why.' She's got her organized voice on, and I wouldn't be at all surprised if she considered a PowerPoint presentation to go with this particular pep-talk before deciding she didn't want to overwhelm me. I bet there were pie-charts.

'For better or worse, your image has always been the unimpeach-able, English rose. Classy, understated, wholesome.' She ticks the words off on her fingers. 'It's an image that we've built your brand on, one that people recognize.'

I nod here, because I'm not stupid: you can't be in this business for longer than five minutes without understanding that public perception is everything. The real Cynthie Taylor has very little to do with what the fans and the press see. I may not particularly like the image Hannah is talking about, but that doesn't mean I haven't used it to my advantage. Together with Gayle and a whole team of publicists we've carefully crafted this persona over the years. It sounds cynical, I know, but I prefer to think of it as business.

'It's exactly why the press have jumped all over this scandal with so much glee, and why it's not dying down.' Hannah gestures to the iPad. 'Staying out of sight isn't working, because they're building stories around that, filling the space with more nonsense. What we need is for them to see you happy, healthy, thriving.'

'I get that,' I say, nodding slowly, 'but is now a good time to be seen out with another man? I mean, isn't there a danger it will feed into the idea of me as some sort of . . . maneater?' I grimace. I hate having to think like this.

'That's why Jack is the perfect solution,' Hannah says earnestly. 'He's not some random guy. He is – as far as they know, anyway – *the* guy. The first guy. The one that got away. Gayle is right that the press will go nuts for this.'

I turn this over in my mind. It's starting to make a worrying amount of sense.

'And,' Hannah continues, 'instead of them getting the picture they want – the one of you looking sad and harried in your dirty tracksuit . . .' The look she gives me here is pointed.

'This is very nice athleisure wear!' I protest.

' . . . they get a picture of you looking happy with an insanely handsome man,' she continues blithely, ignoring me. 'One who has been carrying a torch for you, for thirteen years, because you're so damn wonderful that he *never got over you*.'

'Hmmmm,' I murmur. 'Yes, I do quite like that part.' I frown. 'Except for the fact that it's Jack. Why does it have to be Jack?' The words come out on a whine.

'Maybe he's not so bad anymore,' Hannah says diplomatically. 'Thirteen years is a long time.'

'Not long enough,' I mutter, staring down once more at the picture of him, at those crinkling blue eyes. My heart beats a little bit harder.

Because of hatred, I tell myself.

'There are some upsides you haven't considered,' Hannah says.

'Like what?'

'The idea is to get the whole cast and crew back together, so that means working with one jerk you hate, but a lot of people you really, really love.'

I hadn't even thought of that. Jack's presence aside, making *A Lady of Quality* was one of the most fun and important experiences of my life.

'And,' Hannah says, leaning forward, eyes enormous. 'The script is absolutely fucking brilliant. You're going to be thanking your lucky stars they let you out of your *Iron Maiden* contract.'

'Really?' I sound dubious.

'It's on there.' Hannah gestures to the tablet in my hand. 'Read it and see for yourself. But, honestly, Cyn, Gayle isn't just blowing smoke ... This could be really good for you.'

'Fine, I'll read it,' I say, 'but I'm not making any promises.'

Hannah smirks. 'I'll make you another coffee.'

I curl up in the chair, arranging a cushion behind my back and taking one last, long look at the photo of Jack.

One thing is for certain: if Jack Turner-Jones is going to make a reappearance, my life is about to get even more complicated.

THEN

THIRTEEN YEARS EARLIER

Chapter Three

Cynthie

I am not, not, *not* about to be late for my first ever table read. It cannot happen, I will not allow it. I sit, thrumming with anxiety at the top of the bus as it crawls along Piccadilly, stuck in an endless stream of traffic. It's late summer and approximately a million degrees in central London. I run a clammy hand over the crumpled linen of my skirt. Hannah and I went through every single item in our combined wardrobes before settling on the pretty, floral-patterned skirt and black T-shirt. At the time, I thought the outfit struck a sort-of boho-artist feeling, but after the long, hot journey it looks more like I'm wearing an old dishrag. At least the black T-shirt should hide how sweaty I am.

I can also *feel* my hair expanding outwards, the humidity creating havoc with my thick, not-quite-straight, not-quite-wavy locks. I close my eyes for a brief moment, wondering for the hundredth time what possessed me to have it all cut off.

Well, I know what possessed me – it was the misguided belief that I would look like Audrey Tautou: elfin, chic, *French*. I thought I'd be fricking *Amelie,* and people would describe me using words like 'gamine', before offering me elegant, skinny cigarettes which I would then smoke without coughing while sharing my thoughts on existentialism.

(In this scenario I understood existentialism because of my haircut.)

Instead of this, my hair is an awkward frizzy triangle that is threatening to take over the whole world.

And the bus still isn't moving.

Shit. Shit. Shit.

I hesitate for another long moment, and then reach up and press the bell. I'll walk the rest of the way, and by walk, I mean run. It's not too far. I've still got – I look at my watch, wince – seven minutes.

Flinging myself from the bus doors the second they open, I start sprinting down the road in what I hope is the right direction. I have the map that I printed out with directions clutched in my sweaty fist, and I gaze up at the improbably tall buildings looking for a road name. Bloody London, with its bloody looming architecture and a million pedestrians striding confidently along like they know exactly where everything is.

By the time I reach the swanky hotel where the table read is happening, I am wheezing and my enormous hair is now also damp and sticking out in a variety of wild tufts around my face. But I'm here, I made it. With about five seconds to spare.

I've never fully appreciated the phrase 'he looked down his nose at me' before, but that's exactly what the man behind the reception desk does. I swipe at my sticky face and smile brightly.

'Hello.' I try to get my breathing under control, because I currently sound like someone squeezing an asthmatic accordion. 'I'm here for the table read. *A Lady of Quality*?' when he says nothing, I blink. 'The ... film?' The word comes out quavering, because, honestly, if this whole thing is some sort of extended break from reality, it would still be less weird than the situation I believe myself to be in: attending a table read for an actual, real film of which I – Cynthie Taylor – am the star.

'There you are,' a voice says, and I recognize the woman bustling towards me with a clipboard as Marion, the first assistant director. I met her at the audition I attended, but I haven't seen her in person since they offered me the part.

'Hi,' I exhale. 'Sorry, the bus got stuck in traffic and—'

Marion flicks her steely blue gaze over me, and her brow furrows. 'Why did you get the bus?' she asks. 'We could have sent a car.'

'Oh,' I flounder. 'I didn't know that was an option.'

Her brows pinch tighter. 'Jasmine put you in touch with Gayle, right?' Marion speaks the same way that she moves: briskly, economically, like she's a busy woman who doesn't have time for any nonsense.

'Yes.' I swallow, still barely able to comprehend that *the* Gayle Salt wants to represent me. 'I mean, I haven't actually spoken to Gayle ... Ms Salt. I've been dealing with one of her assistants. We haven't sorted out all the paperwork; it's been a bit of a whirlwind. I only got the call two days ago—'

'Well, get on with it.' Marion takes me by the arm and begins steering me through the gilded lobby towards a corridor. Despite being slightly taller, I have to jog beside her like a show pony to keep up. A short, sturdy woman in her late-fifties, with a cap of light silver hair, she has the energy of a person who could single-handedly run a small empire, never mind a film crew. 'You need to have an agent and manager in place as soon as possible.' Her face softens for a fraction of a second. 'Make sure you have a team that works for *you*. The film business is like the Wild West and you need people looking out for your interests.'

'I will,' I say fervently. The idea that I have *interests* is – in itself – thrilling.

'Good. Here we are.' She stops outside a polished wooden door with a brass sign that discreetly indicates it is a meeting room.

'I thought I could just freshen up a bit fir—' I start, but she's already opening the door and thrusting me inside.

'Found her,' Marion says loudly, which effectively cuts off the gentle hum of chatter that was filling the air, and all eyes turn in our direction.

Oh, god. So many eyes. The room is crowded with people, clustered in small groups around its edges as they help themselves to tea and coffee. In the middle of the space a number of tables are arranged in a large square.

I try again to smooth my skirt, with little effect. 'Hi, everyone.' I lift my hand in a feeble wave.

'Cynthie, there you are.' Jasmine Gallow comes towards me, and I feel a flicker of relief. Even though Jasmine doesn't emote a lot of warmth, I've had a sense from the beginning that she's somehow on my side. I want, with a borderline unhinged intensity, to impress her.

Jasmine is slim and tall with pale, elegant hands that drift about when she talks. Despite the heat of the day, she is dressed top to toe in black. Her ice blond hair is pulled tightly back from her narrow face. She's just over thirty, with a quiet air of authority. She smells faintly of cigarettes and sandalwood perfume.

Her grey eyes drift over me, only the slightest thinning of her mouth confirming that my appearance is . . . not great.

'Let me introduce you to everyone,' she says, and unlike Marion she doesn't take my arm, only moves forward, safe in the knowledge I will follow right behind. 'We've kept it pretty small,' she says. 'Cast, directors, producers are here along with Marnie from casting, and a couple of the department heads.'

She moves around the room, introducing me in a flurry of names that I make sure to repeat, burning them into my brain. I've met hardly anyone in here before. When the actress who was supposed to be playing the lead withdrew last-minute because of scheduling conflicts, the Gallow siblings decided to place an open casting call and it was through this unusual route that I ended up here.

The audition process was hasty, and I'd almost talked myself out of applying several times, finally recording a monologue on Hannah's dad's video camera. Hannah and I did a good-luck ritual over my clunky laptop, which involved smudging the keyboard with sage before pressing send on the video file. It stank out my room for a week, and my dad attempted to have an awkward conversation with me about drug use. As he and I rarely exchange more than a few words despite living in the same house, this came as something of a surprise.

I didn't expect a call-back. The only acting experience I have is a handful of stage roles in amateur productions, and a single voice-over gig for a toothpaste advert, which up to this point I considered the height of glamour. I scrimped and saved for the best part of a year in order to attend an intensive six-week acting class in London last summer, but it wasn't the A-Star-Is-Born experience I'd been hoping for. Still, when I read the pages – or *sides*, as I now know they are called – for the audition, I immediately fell in love with Emilia, the protagonist of *A Lady of Quality*. Even that tiny glimpse into her character sparked something inside me.

It was something the Gallow siblings and Marnie the casting director must have seen too, because they invited me to London to audition in person. Hannah and I fell into hysterics after the phone call, and she suggested we spoke only in Regency English until the audition so I could get into character. (This ultimately prompted my dad – clearly exhausted from his previous effort – to leave a pamphlet about Narcotics Anonymous on the kitchen counter.)

Immediately after the solo audition, I was called back for a chemistry read.

Speaking of which . . .

'And of course you remember Jack,' Jasmine says.

Jack Turner-Jones is as heart-stoppingly gorgeous as the last time I saw him. When I first walked into the audition room and saw him standing there, my insides all temporarily rearranged themselves, as if I was falling from a great height, and today I get a repeat performance.

He's tall, lean, with snapping blue eyes, and light brown hair that's cut short at the sides but longer on top. He wears dark jeans and a dark T-shirt, a pair of black Ray-Bans tucked into the collar. There's a braided leather bracelet around his wrist, and he's wearing expensive trainers that have been carelessly worn in. His teeth, when he smiles at Jasmine, are perfectly straight, his posture relaxed. Everything about him screams that he belongs in this room.

The smile he gives Jasmine drops a little, and his eyes widen as he takes in my tragic haircut, but he recovers quickly.

'Cynthie, hi.' His voice is cool with just the right touch of gravel.

'Nice to see you again.' I nod, trying my best to look unaffected.

In truth, Jack was part of the reason I summoned the courage to send in my audition tape. As the son of two of the biggest legends of stage and screen – Max Jones and Caroline Turner – perhaps it was no surprise he ended up following in their footsteps.

I first saw him perform when I bought a cheap ticket to the Royal Shakespeare Company theatre in Stratford-Upon-Avon to watch a production of *Love's Labour's Lost*. Jack had been playing Berowne, and I was captivated by his performance, scouring the programme for information about him. At twenty-two, he'd just graduated from the Royal Academy of Dramatic Art and was already playing lead roles with the RSC – it was impressive, and envy overtook lust as I watched him prowl the stage, the audience hanging on his every word.

The following year, he had a small role in a BBC adaptation of *A Tale of Two Cities* which thrust him more firmly into the limelight.

'You too,' he says now. 'Did you have a good journey?' It's a polite question, delivered in his posh-boy, private-school voice.

'Bit of a nightmare, actually,' I admit, the jitter of nerves making me chatty. 'The trains were all late because it's hot, which I don't even get. I mean, snow on the tracks – sure, but how can it be too sunny for the trains to run on time?' I shake my head. 'The *most*

British problem. You know, we have a special "fallen leaves" time-table where I live, too? Like it's simply unimaginable that we could find an efficient solution to deal with the leaves that fall off the same trees at the same time every single year.'

He looks a bit startled by this breathless rant. 'I think it's something to do with the rails expanding in the heat,' he says finally.

'Ah,' I reply. 'Yeah, that makes sense.' There's an awkward silence (hard to believe when I am providing all this classic train timetable chat). 'So, I guess you're ready to get going,' I say finally, gesturing to the table.

He nods. 'It feels like it's been a long time coming. For me, anyway. Bit of a whirlwind for you.' Although his expression is mild, there's a tension in his voice that wasn't there before.

'Mmm, that's an understatement,' I agree.

'The chemistry read went well, though,' Jack says, and for some reason I feel more like he's trying to reassure himself than me.

The chemistry read had actually passed in a blur, almost an out-of-body experience. They had us go through a couple of scenes together several times, while Jasmine or Logan said cryptic things like, 'Let's try that again but ... give us something different this time.'

In the beginning, I was thrown by Jack's presence, but soon I stopped seeing Jack at all. Instead, he was Edward, the standoffish younger brother of the man Emilia was supposed to marry. After the first few minutes I lost myself in it. The thrill of slipping into a different character, the fun of performing: the pure joy of it. When the audition ended, I'd lost all sense of time and place. The way I had to peel myself out of Emilia's thoughts and feelings was almost unnerving, as if the room around me was coming slowly back into focus.

Clearly it *had* gone well ... well enough for them to offer me the part. I only wish imposter syndrome wasn't currently hitting me quite so hard.

'Yes,' I reply. 'I think so – it's all a bit of a haze. I guess my adrenaline was working overtime.'

He frowns at this. 'But you're prepared for today, right? I mean, you're ready to jump in?'

I fix a bright smile on my face. 'Oh, absolutely,' I say, even as my stomach ties itself in knots.

Hannah once described me as 'embarrassingly confident', which, when you think about it, is obviously not a compliment, but it is largely accurate. I've always loved to be at the centre of things. For my whole life I've dreamed of acting professionally, have chased that improbable dream in every way I could manage, fuelled by a frankly insane level of self-belief. Finally, the moment has arrived. I'm being offered what I've always wanted . . . and for the first time, I wonder if I can actually pull it off.

'Right.' Jasmine claps her hands together, breaking through my reverie. 'Now that everyone's here, let's get started, shall we?'

Deep breath. I guess we're about to find out.

Chapter Four

Jack

We take our places, sitting behind the cards printed with our names. I'm next to Cynthie, and I watch the way she touches the script in front of her with something like reverence.

I run my eyes over her, still bewildered by her presence. And her god-awful haircut.

She's not a quiet person, fidgeting at my side, crossing and un-crossing her legs. I think she's trying to hide her nerves, but the way her eyes dart around the room gives her away, as if she wants to take it all in, but only in tiny bite-sized pieces so that no one guesses she's looking. I catch the sweet, citrus scent of her perfume as she leans over to grab a bottle of water, and it hits me like a punch to the gut.

A Lady of Quality is supposed to be the next step on a career path that has been carefully planned since I was practically in the womb, and I'm trying hard not to panic that the whole enterprise is suddenly at the mercy of an untrained, undisciplined wild card.

Even if she smells great and is quite interesting to look at.

She blows at a strand of hair that's fallen in her eyes and offers me a rueful grin. 'It feels like the first day of school,' she says, her voice low, as she leans towards me.

I try to shake off the jittery feeling that I get around her – like I've just necked a quadruple espresso and I can feel my heartbeat in my fingertips. 'I need to focus,' I say aloud. The words come out too hard, a reprimand, and from the way she moves abruptly away from me, I know I sounded rude.

'I just ... I have a process.' I try again, but my nerves are taking over, mixing with the heady swirl of her perfume to smother me, and I'm flustered, so rather than an explanation, it sounds like another brush off.

'Oh, sure,' Cynthie replies lightly. 'A process. Got to have a process. Absolutely.' She gnaws on her bottom lip, and my eyes linger there, on her pretty mouth.

Pretty mouth?

Jesus, I need to get a grip. I let out a slow exhale. I can do this; I can use this. It's got to be a good thing that I find the woman playing Emilia moderately attractive, right? In fact, that's probably what this is – me committing to the role. It's actually *extremely professional* of me to be distracted by her mouth.

Sure.

When Jasmine and Logan told me they were going to do open auditions after Mia pulled out at the last-minute, I was conflicted. On the one hand, I know how easy it is for a production to collapse at the eleventh hour, but I wasn't convinced by the argument that bringing in someone untested would add a 'dynamic edge' to the film. Not when that person had absolutely zero training.

The chemistry read was not a reassuring experience. Cynthie had come in, crackling with an energy that left me feeling like I'd been struck by lightning. Or hit by a truck. Or trampled by a herd of wildebeest. Basically, that scene in *The Lion King* that traumatized an entire generation? That was what meeting Cynthie Taylor felt like. We'd run through the pages several times and she was uninhibited, playful – reading the same line in totally different ways. Some of it was unhinged, some of it worked – I think – but all in all it was like trying to act with a tornado.

It might have been fun, if it wasn't for the fact that said tornado holds my entire career in her hands.

With a sigh, I drag my attention back to the work in front of me, to Edward, and the situation he finds himself in: in love with the woman who is due to marry his brother. Torn between duty and desire. I close my eyes, let everything else fall away as I sink into familiar techniques, drummed into me over years and years. Pulling on memories that spark the same emotions, I breathe deeply and let the character settle over me.

When I open my eyes again, Cynthie is watching me. She looks away, a hint of pink crawling along her cheekbones.

I pull the script towards me and take a pen from the bag at my feet. Both of my parents have been – if not actually impressed – then at least lukewarm about this project, which is a huge improvement on their usual attitude towards my life. The pen was an unexpected gift from my dad in honour of starting work on my first feature film, and for a moment the weight of it is almost unbearable in my hand.

Glancing up I find Cynthie side-eyeing me again, and something in her expression has me even more on edge.

'You're supposed to write down the notes they give you,' I say defensively.

Her eyes widen. 'I know.' She reaches into the tote bag slung over the back of her chair and takes out a clear plastic pencil case. 'I just didn't realize we needed a solid gold fountain pen to do it.' She pulls out a biro with a chewed cap, and I feel heat rise to my own cheeks.

I make myself feel better by giving her a look that my sister, Lee, once described as my 'Mr Darcy sneer'. (It's handy for an actor to have several Mr Darcy expressions in his arsenal, and I've perfected this one. I'm also great at looking standoffish at parties.)

Cynthie's spine stiffens, but she doesn't say anything.

'Okay.' Logan breaks in from his position at the head of the table. He gets to his feet. 'Let's kick things off. You've all met now, but we'll do brief introductions before we get started. Obviously you know me. I'm Logan Gallow, co-director.' He grins, and shoves a hand through his streaky blond hair.

If I didn't already know that Logan and Jasmine were twins, I would be unlikely to guess they were from the same gene pool at all. It's not just their appearances that are different, but their personalities seem almost comically at odds with one another. Logan is currently wearing a bright red Hawaiian shirt and a pair of board shorts. He's a director in his thirties but he dresses like a twenty-year-old Californian stoner. He talks as loudly as he dresses and laughs easily, head thrown back, always the life of the party.

Jasmine is much more self-contained, hard to read. She swathes herself in black, and has the look of a woman who carries a copy of *The Bell Jar* around and has a lot of thoughts on deconstructionism. Honestly, she makes me nervous. I have a horrible feeling she sees right through me.

'I'm excited to get to work on this film, which is my third full-length feature,' Logan continues. 'But this project also gives me an opportunity to work with my darling sister for the first time *and* on her directorial debut.' Here, he bats his lashes at Jasmine who rolls her eyes in response. 'At least,' he carries on, 'this is the first *official* time we've made a film together. Let's just say there are some epic movies featuring a cast of Sylvanian Families, knocking around at our mum and dad's house.'

When this gets a laugh, Logan's smile widens. 'Listen, those fuzzy little rabbits went through some dark shit. Jassy kept having them bump each other off. There was an entire storyline about their bakery selling poisoned pies.'

'It was a scathing exploration of consumerism and the capitalist agenda,' Jasmine says, and it's not clear if she's joking. If any child was going to use fuzzy little rabbits to make stark political commentary, I can believe it would be a young Jasmine Gallow.

'Anyway, back to business. I'm Jasmine.' She lifts her hand but remains seated, and Logan flops back into his chair beside her. 'I'm co-directing, but I'm also here in my capacity as the writer.' She places her hand on top of the script in front of her in an unconscious gesture of possession.

The script is brilliant. Subtle, sensitive, romantic. When my agent, Mike, sent it to me, I knew instantly that we'd found the elusive project that was going to launch the next phase of my career. It's tough to find a romance where the male lead isn't just a prop but a well-drawn, interesting character in his own right. It was why I agreed to take a risk on a pair of relatively unknown directors ... before that lack of experience extended to include my co-star as well.

I glance at Cynthie again, but she's watching Jasmine with a rapt expression.

We move around the table, everyone briefly introducing themselves. The world of filmmaking is so small that I know most of the people here already. The fact that my on-screen parents are being played by Rufus Tait and Hattie Prince is both a blessing and a curse. They're great actors, but they've also known me since I was in nappies.

Trying to project the image of a capable leading man is more difficult when your fellow cast member can share hilarious stories about your three-year-old self running naked around their garden. Not to mention that my every move will be reported back to my parents. Max Jones and Caroline Turner have spies everywhere.

When it's Cynthie's turn, she flashes a wide smile. 'I'm Cynthie Taylor,' she says. 'I'll be playing the part of Emilia, and I can't really believe I'm here.' She laughs, delighted, and an answering chuckle runs around the table, the rest of the cast emanating goodwill. I wonder if any of them share my reservations.

She takes a deep breath, 'I know I'll have some serious catching up to do, but I'm going to work very hard to do justice to this amazing character and her story.'

'Thank you, Cynthie.' Jasmine nods. 'We're all grateful that you stepped in at the last-minute.'

Finally, it's my turn. The last to go.

'I'm Jack,' I say, and I'm utterly confident that you'd never know from the way I speak or the way I sit that I'm anxious at all – I've been faking my way through things like this for a long time.

Looking around the room, I decide it's better to acknowledge that I've grown up with these people, than to pretend otherwise. ' ... though most of you already know that,' I add ruefully. My mouth tugs up as I glance at Hattie. She lifts her hand to her chest, a pantomime performance of a proud parent, and – again – there's a ripple of laughter. Apart from Cynthie, I notice, who looks vaguely pissed off.

'I'll be playing the role of Edward, and I'm sure I speak for everyone when I say that Jasmine's script is something special. I'm excited that we have the opportunity to bring her vision to life. With the incredible team Jasmine and Logan have put together, I'm confident we'll be able to do justice to her words.'

'Hear, hear,' Rufus calls, and he gives me a nod of approval.

'Thank you for that, Jack,' Jasmine says, and I swear there's a touch of warmth in her usually impassive face.

She turns to Marion, who picks up her clipboard.

'So, today is going to be a relaxed read-through of the entire script,' Marion says, running her eyes over her notes. 'Starting Monday we'll have a full week of rehearsals at Shepperton studios which will include time with the movement coach and choreographer, as well as costume fittings. You'll each be getting your individual schedules over the next couple of days. The following week we'll head to Cornwall to begin the location shoot. Jack and Cynthie will be the only cast members needed on site for the entire four weeks.'

Cynthie slides a look at me here, and I can't work out if the thought of four weeks stranded in rural Cornwall with her sounds thrilling or disastrous.

'All other cast members will be coming and going based on need and availability,' Marion continues briskly. 'My team and I have worked hard to make sure these changeovers run smoothly, so if there are any problems, you need to come to me as soon as possible. The budget is squeezed and we're on a tight schedule here, so trust me when I tell you, you're about to be organized within an inch of your lives.' There's a gleam in her eyes that says she's relishing the idea.

'Perfect.' Logan claps his hands together. 'Let's get started.'

There's an excited hum of agreement from the rest of us, an instant where we're poised right on the edge of something – the start of the process, the moment when things finally become real.

We settle into the read-through, with Marion reading out all of the stage directions. The first scene is between me and Simon – the actor playing my brother, John – and it goes smoothly enough. Occasionally, Logan or Jasmine will cut in with a note. I can feel myself settling into the work, finding the rhythm of the dialogue.

That all changes when we get to Cynthie's first scene. To begin with she misses her cue.

'Sorry, sorry,' she says, unable to hide how flustered she is.

'It's no problem,' Jasmine replies. 'Let's take it from the top.'

Marion reads the direction, and this time Cynthie comes in at the right time. Unfortunately, by her second line she's tripping over her words.

'No problem,' Logan says lightly. 'That's what today is for. We'll start again.'

Cynthie's face is pink, but she nods. She flubs the lines again, but on her third attempt she manages to get through the first page of the scene.

When she jumps in early, speaking over her scene partner – the actress playing her maid – she apologizes once more.

My eyes drift over to meet Logan's.

Cynthie takes a deep breath. 'Okay,' she says almost to herself, and she glances up at Jasmine, offers a small, tremulous smile. 'Sorry, I'm a bit more nervous than I thought. I'll get it.'

'Of course you will,' Hattie leaps in, quick to soothe.

Jasmine nods. 'Just take your time.'

'Let's go from "My lady, you know you can't go out like that",' Logan says, and again his eyes flicker to meet mine.

We pick up the scene once more, and Cynthie gets through it without any further incident. Unfortunately, she also gets through it without a single ounce of emotion.

This continues for the rest of the read-through. Cynthie is no longer tripping on her lines or missing cues, but her delivery is wooden. If anything, the first scene between the two of us is even worse than what came before. I'm beginning to miss the tornado who stormed in to audition, because this is painful – like playing against someone with the rich interior life of a boiled potato.

'So let's pause here and unpack this scene,' Jasmine calls, breaking in. 'Emilia and Edward are strangers, but it's clear there's an instant click, a spark of attraction between them.'

I glance at Cynthie who looks more like she's about to throw up her breakfast than fall in love with me.

'Although the audience knows that Edward is John's brother, Emilia and Edward have no idea of the circumstances around them so you need to be careful that you're playing in *that* moment, that reality,' Jasmine continues.

'There needs to be more heat,' Logan breaks in impatiently. 'A sexual charge.'

Jasmine lets out a hiss of annoyance. 'It's not *Girls Gone Wild*, Lo. It's Regency England.'

Logan crosses his arms. 'Oh, sorry, I forgot that *no one* in Regency England had sex.'

'There can be a . . . sensuality to it,' Jasmine concedes, and I swear Cynthie is turning green around the edges. 'But for now, let's focus on the immediate emotional connection. The conversation flows.' She clicks her fingers several times. 'It's sparkling; they banter and it's fun. That's key here – there needs to be a . . . quickness.'

I nod, scribbling notes over the pages in front of me, as if I can fix this. 'So it's the rhythm of it, and there's a moment of recognition between them.'

'Right, right.' Jasmine nods; she looks expectantly at Cynthie. 'Does that feel good to you, Cynthie?'

Cynthie's eyes dip to her script. She swallows. 'I . . .' She hesitates, looks between me and Jasmine. 'Sure.'

It's hardly an enthusiastic response, but it's something, and when we continue the scene it is marginally better.

We push forward, but you can feel tension creeping into the room. It's not just my scenes with Cynthie that are the problem; it's as if the hesitance, the self-consciousness has seeped in to affect everyone. We limp towards the end and when the whole, painful experience finishes there's a weak round of applause that manages to sound sarcastic.

Oh, god.

This is so far from how I wanted today to go. I watch Hattie and Rufus exchange a glance, and I can only guess what Mum and Dad are going to hear about this train wreck.

Everyone stands, gathering their things and getting ready to go. There's a quiet hum of chatter, and I gesture to Logan to meet me in one of the smaller meeting rooms off to the side. He nods.

By the time he reaches me, I'm pacing back and forth. Anxiety is a fist around my heart. I play through every terrible moment of the last couple of hours, wincing over how badly we butchered the material.

'I know, I know,' Logan says, already holding up his hands in surrender.

'That was a disaster,' I say flatly, too riled up to hit a diplomatic note.

Logan winces. 'Disaster is a bit strong . . . We knew there would be teething problems—'

'Teething problems?' I snap, panic rippling through me. 'I can't believe that anyone thought this was a good idea. We need a professional in the role. Someone who actually knows what they're doing. The schedule is tight as it is; we've only got a week before filming starts! We have to cast somebody who can jump straight in.'

'I'll admit it wasn't great,' Logan concedes, 'and you know there was a lot of back and forth on the casting decisions – you're not the only one with doubts here – but we need to at least give it a chance.'

'Christ.' I rub my forehead. I can practically hear the scathing reviews, the slow, death rattle of my career, over before it really began. 'There's inexperienced and then there's this . . . I don't think she's got so much as an A-level in drama. What the hell is Cynthie Taylor *doing* here? You need to get rid of her as soon as possible.'

Logan doesn't reply, and when I look over at him, he's watching the door with a rictus grin in place.

Even before I turn, I know precisely what I'll see, but my stomach still rolls over at the sight of Cynthie standing in the doorway, eyes wide and face pale as a ghost as she stares at me.

'Cynthie . . .' I start, unsure how I'm going to finish the sentence.

I don't know if it's a good thing or a bad one that she doesn't give me the chance, turning on her heel and tearing out the room.

Chapter Five

Jack

'Shit,' I say succinctly.

'Er . . . bit of an understatement. I think you'd better go and deal with that,' Logan replies.

I scrub my hands over my face, indulging in one long, frustrated groan before running out the door to chase after Cynthie.

Unfortunately, there's no sign of her in the meeting room where the others are gathering their stuff, and saying their goodbyes.

'Have you seen Cynthie?' I ask Marion.

'She just left,' Marion replies. 'I told her we'd call her a cab, but she said something about the bus . . .'

I'm on the move before she can finish the sentence, calling my goodbyes over my shoulder.

'Ah, chasing after the girl,' I hear Rufus say cheerfully behind me. 'I can't say I blame him. She's a looker, isn't she? Even with the awful haircut.'

I head back through the hotel as quickly as I can and out onto the crowded street. There's no sign of Cynthie, and I hesitate, unsure which way to turn, but as I glance down the road, I spot the tousled mess of her hair in the distance.

'Cynthie,' I shout, and several heads turn. Not hers, though. I hurry after her and call her name again. I'm a lot taller than she is, so it's not hard to catch up, and when I'm right behind her I realize she's not ignoring me, not on purpose anyway – she has headphones in.

I say her name again, and when I get no response, I reach out, gently touching her elbow.

She turns sharply, the tote bag on her shoulder swinging with her and socking me in the stomach with plenty of momentum. Her hands are raised in what looks like a comedy karate chop pose, and if all the air hadn't just been knocked out of me, I might have laughed. As it is I let out a rusty wheeze.

'Oh,' she says coolly, 'it's you.' She pulls her headphones out of her ears, and I'm hit with a blast of Kelly Clarkson, before she stuffs the headphones in her bag.

'I didn't hear you over my righteously-angry-women playlist.' She gives me a pointed look.

'Fair enough.' I nod, and I lift my hand to the back of my neck. Now that I've found her, I'm not sure what to say. 'Er, can we … talk?'

She crosses her arms. 'I'm not sure that's a good idea.'

'Please?' I gesture to a nearby coffee shop. 'Let me buy you a coffee?'

She stares at me and my gaze drops to her mouth when her lips purse. My body temperature kicks up, presumably because it's hot as hell out here. Finally, she gives a stiff nod. 'You can buy me a cup of tea. Milk no sugar. But only because London prices are criminal and I'm thirsty.'

'Tea, sure.' I agree quickly, ushering her through the door and off the hot, noisy street.

The coffee shop is fairly empty, and – thankfully – hums with the sound of air conditioning. 'You go find a seat,' I say. 'I'll grab us some drinks.'

Again, she hesitates, but then to my relief, she stomps off to sit in one of the booths. I grin weakly at the girl behind the counter and order a tea and a large coffee with an extra shot of espresso. Hopefully the caffeine will inspire me – I currently have no idea what I'm going to say.

Regardless of what I flung at Logan in the heat of the moment, I know that they're not going to push to recast Cynthie . . . not after one table read, no matter how disastrous it was. I have to work with her, and that's going to be hard enough without any added animosity. Given that she's currently glaring at me across a coffee shop, with enough ice in her gaze to lower the temperature in the already chilled place by several degrees, I'm about to have my work cut out for me.

But, hey, I can be charming.

'One tea,' I say, placing the cup down in front of her with a smile.

'Thanks,' she murmurs, not looking at me.

I slide into the seat across from her. 'So—' I start.

'Believe me, I know exactly what you're going to say,' she interrupts.

'You do?' I ask, relieved, because broaching the subject of what she'd overheard me say to Logan is a bit of a minefield. I'm happy to let her take the lead, then I can add in a bit of grovelling and we can leave here on good, professional terms.

'You think I'm a disaster, that I'm going to mess this all up.' She looks into her cup of tea.

'Errr,' I flounder, because actually yes, I do think that, but I'm supposed to be smoothing things over between us. 'That's not—'

'That *is* what you said, isn't it?' She looks up then, her eyes boring into mine.

'Well, yes, but—'

'I know it's tough, having someone so inexperienced brought in,' she continues, as if I haven't spoken, and her tone is agitated. 'But instead of behaving like an arrogant jerk, you could have offered to help; you could have been supportive. We could work *together . . .*'

Even though she is basically saying the things I was going to say to her, I find myself bristling at her tone.

'You don't seem to realize or care that this is actually a huge deal for me,' Cynthie carries on, and there's a flash of hurt in her eyes. 'This part, this opportunity is a dream come true. Do you think I *want* to mess it up?'

Guilt nips at me with sharp little teeth. 'I'll admit that it was unfortunate . . .' I begin again, trying to be careful with my words.

'*Unfortunate,*' she scoffs.

' . . . that you overheard what you did,' I push on, 'but we need to be professional about this. Listen, I'm not trying to be cruel, but if you want to be in this business you have to toughen up. Learn to take a bit of criticism.'

I'm vaguely horrified to hear myself parroting my father, but god, if anyone ever needed this advice, it's Cynthie Taylor. She has to have a thicker skin than this because what I said was nothing compared to the shit she's going to hear. I could tell her some horror stories about the type of soul-crushing feedback I've had – and that's just from the people I share DNA with. She's trying to break into a world of critics and back-stabbers, one full of people who would absolutely love to see her fail. It's not for the faint of heart. Better she learns that lesson now.

'Oh, sorry.' She tilts her head, with a look of wide-eyed confusion. 'Is this you being *professional*? I must have missed the part where professionals bad-mouth their co-star to the director and try to get them sacked. That doesn't sound like a professional to me. It sounds like a spoilt prima donna.'

A muscle in my jaw starts to tic.

'Because, trust me,' she continues, 'you've made yourself very clear. You want me off this film, but it's too late. I'm not going anywhere so you're going to have to get over yourself and your giant ego and deal with it.'

'I *am* dealing with it,' I say through gritted teeth. 'I tried to apologize—'

'Really?' She cuts me off again. 'Because I don't remember that part.'

'Because you won't let me finish a sentence!' The words come out too loud, but she only smirks, pouncing on my exasperation like it's a delicious treat.

'Oh! I'm sorry for interrupting your apology,' she says, sweet as cyanide. 'Please,' she gestures with her hand, 'carry on. I'd *love* to hear it. At length.'

And then, she actually bats her eyelashes at me, which I don't think I've seen a human do in real life before.

Any guilt I was feeling is quickly evaporating, as the insults pile up and it's clear that she's enjoying my discomfort. I came into this coffee shop perfectly prepared to grovel, but with every passing moment I want to be the one to watch *her* squirm. I'd absolutely love to be the bigger person here, but her taunts are enough to demolish all my good intentions.

Two can play this game.

I lean forward, sincerity in every line of my face. 'I'm sorry,' I start.

I don't think she realizes that she's leaning towards me, too, that her posture has softened, mirroring mine, that I'm reeling her in so easily.

'I'm sorry . . .' I say again, pausing, keeping my expression earnest and open '. . . that you overheard a private conversation. I hope you learned a valuable lesson about eavesdropping.'

She blinks as the words settle between us, then snaps back, almost knocking over her tea.

'You— I— that—' she splutters and I take a sip of my coffee. It tastes like victory.

Cynthie narrows her eyes. '"A valuable lesson about eavesdropping",' she repeats, finally, each word carefully enunciated in what I would guess is an imitation of my accent. 'Well, that's quite the apology. I suppose I shouldn't expect better from an entitled twat who speaks like a Victorian ghost.'

My pulse leaps in my throat. Cynthie's cheeks are flushed, her hazel eyes glittering.

'I'm just saying . . .' I sling my arm over the back of the booth, and keep my tone deliberately conversational, allowing a nice condescending note to creep in. 'Instead of focussing on a little criticism that wasn't actually meant for you to hear, you should be focussed on the job at hand. Then you might not make so many mistakes,' I add, kindly, and temper leaps in her eyes.

'I *am* focussed on the job, you tremendous dickhead. *I'm* not afraid of hard work, which is good, seeing as I'm going to be working much harder than you,' she says. 'Because you're right about one thing. I am trying to catch up. I don't even have an A-level in drama' – she puts little finger quotes around the words and rolls her eyes – 'because not all of us were born with a silver spoon in our mouths. Some of us had to leave school and get a job instead of a full fucking ride to RADA. Some of us had to scrimp and save, and pursue our dreams any way we could. And some of us, *some of us*,' she repeats, her voice shaking with fury, 'got the part because of raw, natural talent and not because of who our mummy and daddy are.'

'What did you just say?' The words are a growl low in my throat.

'You heard me.' She lifts her chin, the picture of disdain. 'You're so convinced it's me that's the problem, but at least I got here on my own merits. Can you really say the same? Do you think if it wasn't for your parents you'd have all these doors opening for you? Would you be playing Edward? Or could the part have gone to someone else, someone better?'

It's like she's digging her fingers into an open wound. I can only stare at her.

Finally, I let out a bitter laugh. 'I'm not the one who's out of my depth, sweetheart. This isn't an after-school musical where you can *find yourself* through the power of performance and discover that the real gift was the friends you made along the way. There are hundreds of people's jobs and millions of pounds riding on the success of this film. You fuck up, and there are real consequences. You think *I'm* arrogant?' I run my eyes over her in a lazy examination. 'Take a look in the mirror.'

She puts her palms flat on the table and levers herself up so that she's leaning over, crowding into my space. Her perfume is a silk ribbon wrapping around my throat, but her expression promises only cold, calculated murder. This close, I can see the tiny flecks of green in her eyes. Her chest rises and falls and I can hear the ragged intake of her breath.

She's not the only one who is furious. Anger is a snarling, snapping thing inside me. I want to sink my teeth into her.

'*You*', she says, her voice a husky accusation, 'are the worst person I have ever met. I can't wait to shove my success in your boyband-reject face.' Her laugh holds an edge of mania as she slides out of the booth. 'We'll see who's out of their depth, won't we? Nepotism can only get you so far, Jack.'

The way her mouth curls around my name makes something tighten in my stomach, but I ignore the sensation, getting to my feet, looming over her. 'Good luck with that,' I sneer. 'Or should I say *break a leg*? Sincerely. Break both of them. Then maybe we'll actually get to cast a real actor.'

'I'd like to break your *neck*.' Cynthie's smile is wide and wicked and she steps in close to me, close enough that I can feel the heat from her body brushing up against mine.

'Well, look at that,' I rumble. 'We're finally on the same page.'

She treats me to one last smouldering look of disdain, then without another word, she whirls away, a tiny tempest about to unleash herself on the streets of London.

My heart clatters. There's so much adrenaline crashing inside me, I feel like I've jumped out of an airplane into crocodile-infested waters. So much for smoothing things over. We're going into the first week of the most important project of my career so far . . . and it looks like Cynthie Taylor and I are officially at war.

NOW

THIRTEEN YEARS LATER

Chapter Six

Jack

'Are you sure this shirt is good?' I ask, standing in front of the phone screen and turning around.

'Mate, it's a white shirt. I don't know what sort of feedback you want from me.' Nico's voice rings from the tinny speaker. My best friend sounds suspiciously close to laughter.

'Yeah.' I roll my shoulders, trying to ease some of the tension there. 'I guess you're right.' I cast another look over my reflection in the mirror. 'Why am I so panicked?' I wonder aloud.

'Errr, I think it's because you're about to try and convince Cynthie Taylor to be your fake girlfriend,' Nico pipes up, and he's not even trying to hold back the laughter now. 'You are the luckiest guy in the whole fucking world. *Imagine* having Cynthie Taylor as your girlfriend.'

'It's not like it would be the first time,' I murmur.

'I always forget that part.' Nico hesitates, 'But ... that wasn't real either, right? Didn't you guys hate each other?' He stares off thoughtfully into the distance. 'Now that I think about it, didn't you refer to her as "Satan's Bride"?'

I clear my throat. 'That was a long time ago. A lot has changed since then.' *I hope.*

'Sure.' Nico peers out at me from the phone. He looks tired, maybe a bit pale, but I suppose it is late in London. 'I've got to go, anyway. Hot date.'

'Isn't it almost midnight there?' I ask, reaching for my watch and buckling it round my wrist.

Nico just smiles, that crooked smile that seems to win over an ever-changing roster of beautiful women. 'The perfect time for a date.'

I huff a laugh. 'Right. Don't let me keep you.'

'Don't get so wound up about this,' Nico says. 'I know there's a lot going on, but remember . . . she needs you more than you need her. And the shirt looks good.'

'Yeah?' I dust down my front. 'Okay. I'll let you know how it goes. Have a good night.'

'I will.' Nico grins. 'Oh, and roll your sleeves up. Women love that. Trust me, it's a whole thing. Like Victorian ladies and their ankles.'

He ends the call on this bizarre note, and I'm left alone in the quiet of the hotel suite.

I should have let my agent come along. Mike was adamant that he should be here, but my instinct told me that Cynthie would be more comfortable in this incredibly awkward situation if it was just me. Now I'm second-guessing myself. What if asking her to meet me alone in my hotel comes off as creepy? Oh god. I have done that, haven't I? I've lured her here to my hotel room to discuss business: the notorious move of the Hollywood pervert. I'm a *lurer*.

Turning to look back in the mirror again, I take a breath. My own perfectly normal reflection stares back, perhaps a little dazed around the eyes.

I'm not a lurer, I'm the picture of respectability. I chose the shirt and the tailored soft grey trousers because they have a business-meeting vibe. It seems like that is the way to handle the situation: it's a simple business arrangement. We don't need to bring our history or – God forbid – *feelings* into it. It's going to be cool, considered and nothing like it was before.

Shit, these things are so awkward.

If I had a pound for every time I've been asked to establish a fake relationship with Cynthie Taylor for the benefit of the press, I'd have two pounds, which isn't a lot but it's pretty wild that it's happened twice. I hope this part goes better than it did last time, at least.

I wince at the memory, still looking in the mirror, and decide to follow Nico's advice and roll up my sleeves. Yes, this is fine. Relaxed but still professional.

I move from the bedroom of the large suite through to the living room where the meeting will take place. I've already had room service send up an assortment of cold drinks and a fruit plate. At a loss, I wander around the room like a caged animal, glancing down at my watch a couple more times.

Finally, I stand, looking out the floor-to-ceiling window with its impressive view over the city. Even after spending so much time here the past few years, I still get a buzz out of seeing LA laid out like this. If she were here, my mother would snort derisively and quote Fran Leibowitz in ringing tones: 'Darling, Los Angeles is just a large city-like area surrounding the Beverly Hills Hotel.' But I can appreciate the sprawl. This place still holds that edge of Hollywood glamour for me.

There's a knock and I start, glance at my watch again. Right on time.

I take a deep breath and move to the door, checking through the peephole. I don't see Cynthie, but I do recognize the woman standing there.

I open the door and smile. 'Hey, Hannah.'

It's been years, but Cynthie's best friend doesn't look too different – a more polished, more expensive version of the quiet, funny girl I knew, the one with the watchful eyes.

'Hi, Jack,' she says, running her gaze over me in a much more overt assessment. I step back from the door and spin slowly in a circle, arms outstretched.

'Unarmed,' I say, and when I come back to face her, she's smiling, just a little.

'Good to know.' Her voice is dry. She peeps over my shoulder. 'Just you?' she asks.

'Yeah.'

She glances off to the side, and that's when I realize there's someone standing next to her, out of my line of sight. If Hannah's expressive eyebrow movement is anything to go by, some sort of silent communication passes between the two of them, and then Hannah nods.

'Cool,' she says. 'I'll be down at the bar. Just buzz if you need me.'

She wiggles her fingers and then turns and walks away. There's a pause, and then a small, platinum blond woman in a baseball cap and sunglasses appears in the doorway. It takes me a second to realize it's Cynthie.

My heart bumps – one slow, solid rolling over in my chest. I clear my throat, step back and gesture inside with my hand.

'Thanks,' she mutters, already striding in, pulling off the hat and the wig, which she throws down on the sofa behind us. She removes her sunglasses and turns to face me, shaking out her long, golden-brown hair.

There's a moment of hesitation as she finally looks at me, the tiniest hitch in her movement.

'Hi,' she says softly. 'Sorry about that. Getting out the house has been a bit of an ordeal. The paparazzi . . .' she trails off.

'Of course,' I reply. I can hardly pretend to be ignorant of her circumstances – not only is the story plastered far and wide, it's the whole reason we're here in the first place.

We stand for a beat, watching each other. I haven't seen her in person for a long time, though her face has followed me everywhere. The career she's built over the last thirteen years has been – until recently – a fairytale climb to the top: coming out of nowhere and building to an Oscar nomination, two Golden Globe wins, an impressive list of roles in solid, critically-acclaimed movies that any actor would envy.

In fact, Cynthie is exactly where I once thought I'd be by now, and that thought stirs up a lot of confusing emotions.

The changes in her are more obvious than the ones in Hannah. Gone is any trace of the awkwardness she carried at twenty. Her face is almost impossibly perfect: a luminous peaches and cream complexion, thickly lashed hazel eyes, the sort of rosebud mouth old Hollywood went wild for. My gaze snags there for a moment, while something long-buried sizzles to life in my blood. Her hair falls in a long silky sheet, dark and glossy shot through with caramel and honey. She even stands differently. The Cynthie I knew was all restless energy, but now she has a stillness about her that makes her hard to read. You used to be able to see everything she thought written all over her face.

At least I could whenever she looked at me.

You have to really pay attention to see the tiredness around her eyes, the shadows there. I know it's been a bad time for her, and for a second she looks so small and vulnerable that I have a very strong and inappropriate desire to pull her into my arms and tell her everything will be okay.

I try to remind myself that I know better than to be taken in by the damsel in distress look – if anyone is aware of what Cynthie is truly capable of, it's me. Sure, she looks delicate but I know the truth: she's not delicate like a flower; she's delicate like a scalpel – and twice as sharp.

'You look well, Jack,' she says, rigidly polite, and I realize that I've been staring at her like a creep. *So much for dispelling the lurer vibes.*

I lift my hand to the back of my neck. 'Thanks, so do you. Why don't we sit down?'

She sinks onto the sofa, picking up her wig and untangling a knot in it before laying it across the back of her seat. Her face is a carefully controlled blank. I round the coffee table and sit in the chair across from her, grabbing a bottle of water from the tray in the centre.

'Do you want something to drink?' I ask. 'I can call down for some tea?'

'Water's great,' she says, but makes no move to take anything from the tray.

I twist the top off my water bottle, then twist it back on. I would love to be able to think of anything to say right now. Literally anything. What a perfect time for my brain to start playing 'Girl From Ipanema' elevator music.

'Thank you for flying in for this,' Cynthie says, breaking the awkward silence. 'I know it's a . . . strange situation.'

'Sure.' I nod. 'No problem.' Then after another pause, I add, 'It *is* strange. I don't know how to start this conversation. It's been a long time.'

Talk about an understatement. I meet her eyes, and for a second it's all there, spilling between us. Everything that happened thirteen years ago. All the things we never talked about. The moment stretches, the air buzzing with a tension so thick I can practically see it.

She blinks, her eyes slide away from mine, and it's both a relief and a disappointment. My body feels hectic – pulse quickening, temperature rising – and I shift in my seat, trying to settle myself.

Even after all this time, being around Cynthie Taylor still feels like clutching a live wire. I guess some things never change.

Cynthie makes a humming noise in her throat. She looks down

at her hands which are clasped neatly in her lap. 'You don't live in LA then?' she says finally, glancing around at the hotel room.

'No. The show I'm in films in New York so I have a place there, and then I'm usually in London for the rest of the year.'

She nods. 'It's been a while since I've been back to England,' she says. 'It will be strange to film there again.'

'Does that mean you want to do the movie?' I try to keep the words neutral.

She hesitates. 'The script is good,' she says finally.

'Really good,' I agree. The script was what hooked me in the first place, though when I read it, I thought there was a better chance of hell freezing over than of us ever making it. There was no way Cyn would sign on.

'And working with Jasmine would be great,' she hedges.

'Jasmine and Logan directing together again,' I huff out a laugh. 'It'll either be brilliant or a total disaster.'

A smile tugs at Cynthie's mouth. 'Entertaining, at least.'

'Oh sure,' I agree. 'They were always that.'

We lapse into silence again.

'So,' I say, 'if you're considering taking the role, I guess that means you've given some thought to the studio's stipulations.'

'The documentary,' she turns her big eyes on me, 'and ... you and me.'

'Right.' I take a swig of water, and when I put the bottle down, I notice Cynthie's gaze dart from my throat to linger on my forearms. Her cheeks take on a tinge of pink. It looks like Nico was right. She frowns, as though annoyed.

'Well,' I continue, suddenly amused. 'It's not like we haven't been here before.'

Her eyes narrow at the laughter in my voice.

'I believe last time, you said something about preferring to lose certain parts of your anatomy to being in a relationship with me,'

Cynthie says tartly, and for the first time I catch a glimpse of her, the real her, underneath the layers of cool elegance.

'You weren't exactly turning cartwheels over the idea yourself,' I point out. 'It's no use acting like I was the only problem.'

She huffs, glares at me for a moment. I swear, I don't mean to do it, but I feel my smile widen like a challenge.

She shoots suddenly to her feet and starts to pace around the sofa. There's more colour in her face now, a flush climbing up her neck. It seems I can still get under her skin; it's so easy to slip back to what we were. Maybe that's the problem.

'This is stupid,' she mutters. 'This whole situation is stupid. You and I . . .' She shoots me a look that is almost venomous.

'We barely survived last time,' I finish. I'd be lying if I said I didn't share her concerns.

'*You* barely survived,' she tosses her hair. 'Because *I* almost murdered you.'

'I don't know about murder,' I muse. 'Though I do recall you had someone in wardrobe whip up a worryingly accurate voodoo doll.'

'Ha!' Cynthie gives a shout of laughter, falls back onto the sofa with her head in her hands. 'I forgot about that.' Her voice is muffled.

'Oh?' I lift a brow. 'And here was me thinking you'd probably spent the last couple of days sticking it with pins.'

She sighs. 'I'm sorry. Not about the voodoo doll, which you fully deserved,' she adds quickly. 'But about this . . . today. I know why everyone thinks *I* should do this, but I have no idea why you'd even consider it. I'm not sure if you've noticed, but I'm absolutely toxic, just about the most hated person on the planet right now.'

'Oh, come on. Barely even top five.' I lean back, cross my arms.

She scowls. 'You're not taking this seriously.'

'I am, actually,' I relent and gentle my voice. 'I can give you three excellent reasons why I'm considering this. First,' – I count off on my fingers – 'the script is incredible, and the team behind it are too.'

'On that we can agree,' Cynthie says cautiously.

'Second . . .' I pause and take a breath here. 'I don't know how much you know about the show I'm in? *Blood/Lust*?'

She nods slowly. 'I've heard of it.'

'Okay, well, we just finished up season five and the ending for my character is . . . ambiguous. We're negotiating a new contract right now, and there's a possibility they'll decide not to bring me back.' I try not to wince.

In the past I'd rather have died than show her any kind of vulnerability, but if I want things to be different this time around, then I know I need to change our dynamic.

'I don't want that to happen,' I say finally, keeping the explanation brief. 'I love the show, I want to make more of it. Signing on to this film will help with my visibility, but me and you in the press' – I gesture between us – 'I'm not going to lie, that will give me a huge publicity bump right when I need it most.'

She only watches me carefully for a moment. 'Okay,' she says slowly. 'I can see that making sense.'

I was worried that she'd be offended by my less than chivalrous reasons for helping her out, but if anything she finally looks more comfortable.

Her shoulders come down a couple of inches. She grabs a bottle of water to sip, while she thinks this over. Then, she picks up a triangle of watermelon from the fruit plate in front of her and nibbles on it with a murmur of appreciation. Her tongue flicks out to catch a bead of pale pink juice left on her lip.

All the blood in my body rushes immediately to my groin.

'What's the third thing?' she asks.

'Hmm?' I manage, dragging my eyes away from her mouth and shifting awkwardly in my chair.

'The third thing,' Cynthie says. 'You said you had three excellent reasons for doing this.'

'Oh,' I laugh a little too loud, willing my body to calm the fuck down. 'That's easy. It's you. I think you're an incredible actor, and I'd love the chance to work with you again.'

Cynthie scoffs. '*You* think I'm an incredible actor?'

I wince at the disbelief in her tone. Jesus, twenty-four-year-old me really was a tremendous ass. 'Yes,' I say, leaving it at that, but filling the word with as much sincerity as I can.

She crosses her arms, clearly not convinced. She taps her foot against the plush carpet.

'Right,' she says, finally. '*If* I agreed to this . . . I think we'd need to come up with some rules.'

Chapter Seven

Cynthie

'Rules?' he asks, and he leans forward again, resting those perfect forearms of his on his knees while I try not to stare at him, to keep my body as still as possible. Baby pronghorn antelopes do that to avoid being eaten by coyotes. I know because I watched a documentary about it from my depression nest last week. I'm going full baby antelope on this situation. There's no way lust is sinking its coyote teeth into me.

'Yes, rules.' I clear my throat, scrambling to stay on track. 'Let's assume that I believe at least *some* of what you're saying and you have your own reasons for doing this. How do you picture it working? There will be a documentary crew following us around so it's going to have to be convincing.' I can hear the anxiety bleeding into my own words at this.

He only nods calmly, like he's been giving it some thought. 'The way I see it, we have a couple of months before filming starts, when we can schedule some public events so that we enter the documentary as an established couple.'

'Public events?'

'Dates,' he clarifies. 'Where we get our picture taken. Just a couple, nothing too out there. Dinner, drinks, whatever. The sooner the press pick up on the story, the better for both of us, I guess.'

I nod. That, at least, is true. I still don't know how much I can trust him, but his explanation about *Blood/Lust* made sense. I actually feel better knowing that he, too, has ulterior motives for agreeing to this charade. If he's driven by self-interest, it must mean he's not going to mess with me just for the fun of it . . . right?

'So by the time we come to film, we'll be more comfortable together, have a better sense of back story,' Jack continues. 'We'll know how we want to play it. We pulled this off once before and in worse circumstances.'

'I don't know,' I sigh. 'The circumstances seem pretty dire to me.'

'At least we don't want to actively destroy each other this time.'

'The jury is still out on that,' I mutter.

Instead of looking annoyed, his mouth pulls up. 'Fair enough.'

Which isn't really a reassuring answer. I take a moment to look at him again, to try and cut through the thick cloud of pheromones that must be wrapped around him if my tap-dancing heartbeat is anything to go by. He seems genuine enough, those silver-blue eyes focussed steadily on mine, but he's always been a very good actor.

Jesus, this whole thing would be a lot easier if he didn't look like he was about to pose for the cover of *GQ*. When I walked through the door into this hotel room, his handsomeness was like an attack, a swift one-two punch to any defences I thought I had built up. For a moment my mind went blank, like the world turning white after a devastating explosion. After that cleared, my first impulse was to imagine peeling the crisp white shirt he's wearing from his big, muscular body.

Which is . . . not ideal.

Last time I saw him I was twenty and basically just a walking bag of hormones, so being a horny little demon around the man, despite my low, low opinion of him, was somewhat understandable, but now I'm a mature, independent, adult woman. At least I am when I'm not drinking ice cream and living in my pyjamas. I'm certainly old enough, and wise enough, to know that Jack Turner-Jones is a terrible idea dressed up in a nicely fitted pair of trousers.

Still, my entire body is having some sort of episode. I watched him drink water like it was happening in slow motion and being soundtracked by Barry White. His collar is unbuttoned and there's a small triangle of golden skin on display. If I pressed my thumb there, to that divot, I'd feel his pulse beating.

I remind myself that I hate this man, that we are mortal enemies.

'I'd want some sort of paperwork,' I say, trying to sound firm. 'An NDA. Something to make sure that this arrangement stays . . . private.'

'We didn't do anything like that last time.'

'Things are different now,' I reply. 'It's not like the last time.'

The air thickens again. Our history hangs between us, a swirling, technicolour mess of emotions that I can't even begin to pick through. I hadn't anticipated how overwhelming it would be, past and present colliding like this. It's been thirteen years since the last time we were in a room together, but in some ways it feels as though no time has passed at all.

'I'm not disagreeing with you.' Jack holds up his hand in a conciliatory gesture. 'But it wouldn't do either of us any good if the details of this plan were made public.'

'Mutually assured destruction?' I lift my brows. 'Hardly a promising basis for a relationship, even a fake one.'

'And an NDA is?' Jack counters.

I only shrug. How could I explain to him – even if I wanted to – just how royally screwed I've been by someone I trusted? Gayle and Hannah might have come up with a plan to salvage my career, but it involves me putting my faith in someone who has never made a secret of how little he thinks of me. I reach for my bottle of water, willing my expression to remain neutral, not wanting to show a flicker of the fear and anxiety that are a constant presence in my life right now.

Jack's eyes narrow. 'Look,' he says, and his voice is gruff, 'all I meant was that I'm not going to do anything to fuck you over. You might not believe that' – his fingers run impatiently through his hair, pushing it into an artful disarray that only makes him look more appealing – 'but it's the truth. If an NDA will make you feel safer, then I have no problem with it. Tell Gayle to have the lawyers draw up whatever she likes and I'll sign it.'

I press my lips together and nod. I don't know why his words make me feel tearful, I mean, apart from the fact that absolutely *everything* makes me feel tearful at the moment. When the news about me and Shawn first broke, I was numb; I barely felt anything for weeks. Now, it's as if all those feelings are catching up with me. I'm stuck inside a snow globe that someone has shaken up and there are sparkly little emotions flying everywhere.

Jack clears his throat. 'You're right that this isn't like last time,' he says. 'We can do it differently. You can be in charge here, Cynthie. No one's going to make you do anything you don't want to do,' he finishes softly.

Oh, no. I absolutely cannot cope with Jack Turner-Jones being kind to me. If he's behaving like a half-decent person, I must be a truly pitiful creature.

I straighten my spine, flip my hair back over my shoulder. 'Which is exactly why I suggested the rules.' I make my voice crisp, all business.

'Right.' He nods. 'So apart from the paperwork, what did you have in mind?'

I blink. I hadn't really got past the paperwork part. Honestly, the whole idea seems so demented that I'm not sure where to start.

'We keep the circle tight,' I say finally. 'Only the people close to us know that this isn't real. As far as the rest of the world is concerned, we're together.'

'Sure.' Jack nods. 'That makes sense.'

'So no . . .' – I hesitate, and he frowns – 'No seeing other people,' I finish on a rush. It would be beyond disastrous if the next big news story became about Jack cheating on me.

'That's fine with me,' he says, then it's his turn to pause. 'Is there anyone else you're . . .' he trails off.

'No!' I exclaim, vehemently. 'It would just be you. Only you.'

Something flares in his eyes at that, but he looks down at his hands, hiding whatever emotion he feels.

'No seeing other people.' He clears his throat. 'Any other rules?'

'None that I can think of right now.'

'I think we should have one about touching,' Jack says matter-of-factly, and my mouth dries.

'Touching?'

Again, he nods, his expression serious. 'If the point is to have our picture taken then I guess we're going to have to be fairly tactile with each other.'

'Sure,' I agree.

He's sitting across from me. There's a coffee table and several feet of clear air between us; he hasn't laid one finger on me since I entered this room, and I already feel like my body is coming apart. The thought of being tactile with him is . . . Well, 'dangerous' is the word my brain supplies.

But we're actors. We're going to be in a film together. I can hold hands with him without having a total meltdown, right? I just need to be professional.

Some of my discomfort must show because that earnest furrow appears between Jack's eyes again. 'The biggest difference this time around is that we'll handle it like adults,' he says. 'Loads of communication, very clear boundaries.'

Why does Jack Turner-Jones talking about boundaries make me want to squirm in my seat? I am such a mess. Is a man talking about behaving with basic respect really doing it for me? Apparently so. God, the bar is on the fucking floor these days.

'Everything can be agreed in advance,' he continues evenly. 'I won't touch you without asking. No surprises.'

At those words, my eyes fly to Jack's and he's gone very still. Perhaps he's doing the baby antelope thing too, but I can see what's happening in his head as clearly as if it were being projected on a screen in front of the two of us. It's the same thing that's happening in mine.

My fingers tighten around the arm of my chair as a hundred remembered moments flash through my mind. The memories clash together, hot and vivid and angry, and I feel my heartbeat accelerate. There's a bead of sweat making its way down my back. Jack's jaw clenches and I watch the muscles tic.

'No surprises,' I repeat.

Jack looks away, breaking eye contact, and the air rushes back into the room. He rubs his fingers absently across the left side of his chest. I draw in a long, cool breath. Is it possible to drown in sexual tension? Is that even what this is? It feels more like a medical catastrophe. Maybe I'm not hopelessly attracted to my worst enemy. Maybe I just have the plague. Fingers crossed.

'If there's anything else you need to make this work, you can just tell me.' His voice has dipped, a rougher timbre to it that vibrates through my bones. I don't know whether to be relieved or worried that I'm obviously not the only one affected by whatever is going on. 'It's important that you feel comfortable.'

'Fine,' I say at last, because deep down I knew I was going to agree to this before I even walked through his door. My reputation is in shreds but my career is too important to me. This is how I'm going to get my life back on track, and the fact that Jack hasn't been *utterly* awful about it is a surprising bonus.

'I'll probably regret this, but what the hell.' I exhale slowly, lift my water bottle in a toast. 'Things can hardly get worse. Why not throw a fake relationship with my nemesis into the mix? Let's do it.'

'Not a rousing display of enthusiasm, but I'll take it.' Jack lifts his bottle and clinks it against mine. 'To a new chapter,' he says, but as the words leave his mouth, I find myself wondering if a new chapter is even possible, or if the story of the two of us was written thirteen years ago.

THEN

THIRTEEN YEARS EARLIER

Chapter Eight

Cynthie

As we rattle down the long gravel drive towards Alveston Hall, Hannah lets out a low whistle. 'Holy shit, this place is amazing.'

I look out the rain-streaked windshield of my old Ford Fiesta, and I have to agree. Even in this miserable weather, the building is beautiful: U-shaped and three-storeys high, built out of the local limestone with tall, white-framed windows, glossy greenery crawling cheerfully up the walls.

'It used to be a rectory, apparently,' I say, having memorized the details on the website. I'm so excited about this whole adventure that I devoured all the information I could find.

'A rectory?' Hannah wrinkles her nose. 'Like for a vicar?'

'I think rectors and vicars are different,' I say vaguely, because that hadn't been covered on the history page of the site.

'Either way, it's massive. All these Regency books about the poor son joining the Church, and they were living in mansions like this.' She shakes her head in dismay. 'And now I can't even afford a studio flat in Chippenham.'

'Yes,' I agree, 'you are truly the most tragic spinster of them all.'

'Shut up.' Hannah nudges me as I manoeuvre the car into a parking space, next to several much nicer, shinier vehicles.

I turn off the ignition and we both sit for a moment, looking up at the beautiful Georgian building.

'Are we really doing this?' I ask, not for the first time. 'It could be such a disaster.'

Hannah's hand comes up to rub my shoulder. 'It's not going to be a disaster. You're just being too hard on yourself. You said rehearsals went well.'

'I said they went *better*,' I amend. 'Which isn't saying anything, because the only way they could have been worse than the table read would be if I had actually projectile-vomited in Jack Turner-Jones's stupid face.'

'His face *is* stupid,' Hannah agrees loyally, even though a few weeks earlier she had been munching popcorn in front of *A Tale of Two Cities*, rhapsodizing about his eyes.

I groan, resting my forehead against the steering wheel. I think I'm going to be haunted by that table read for the rest of my life. It was almost an out-of-body experience, watching myself mess up over and over again, having to breathe slowly through the entire script, barely able to force the words out in a coherent order. Actually 'acting' had been very low down my list of priorities, far, far beneath 'not passing out' and 'not stabbing Jack with his stupid fancy pen'.

Thanks to his conversation with Logan and our subsequent argument, I know precisely how little Jack thinks of me and that he's actively trying to get me sacked. (Although as I'm still here, I guess that particular gambit was unsuccessful.) Let's just say that *that* hasn't made for the best working environment. The animosity between the two of us has only grown over the past week.

'So you got a bit of stage fright,' Hannah says now with a shrug. 'It happens. Surely a bunch of actors know all about that.'

'But I've never had it before.' My voice is muffled thanks to the fact I remain wilted over the steering wheel. The injustice of it still burns. 'Why did it have to happen then? Right when I was trying to prove that I wasn't a total waste of space. Maybe Jack was right. All that stuff he said about me ruining the whole movie—'

'Hey!' Hannah cuts in. 'Don't say that. He was totally out of order. Just because he's got famous parents doesn't mean he gets to throw his weight around. Whatever he might think, it's not actually *his* film.'

An image of Jack's face swims into my mind. I can hear, as clearly as the moment it happened, the words he said to Logan ringing in my ears.

What the hell is Cynthie Taylor doing here?

'Ugh, he's just ... insufferable.' I squeeze my eyes closed, trying to banish the memory of a scene that has played on a loop in my head every time I've turned the light off at night. (What a relaxing experience that has been, like whatever the opposite of a white noise machine is: Jack Turner-Jones' voice telling you you're an absolute failure.)

'Excellent use of Regency-speak,' Hannah says approvingly.

'Thank you. But I can't believe how smug he is. He's so full of himself, with his *process*, and his solid-gold fountain pen and his designer clothes. He's clearly never had to actually try for anything in his life,' I rant. 'And then, he couldn't even apologize to me like a normal human being! It was all "you need to toughen up, you need to work harder." As if *he* knows anything about hard work.'

'On the plus side, it sounds like you absolutely demolished him,' Hannah puts in cheerfully. 'I always think of a hundred clever, hurtful things to say hours after an argument, but you just' – she points her finger like a gun, mimes pulling the trigger – '"You're only here because of your parents." Bullseye.'

I feel an unwelcome flicker of guilt at that.

'The annoying thing ...' I admit, slumping back in my seat. 'The worst of it, is that what I said to him isn't even true. He's actually good. *So* good.' I chew on my bottom lip, remembering our last rehearsal when I missed a cue because I'd been so busy watching Jack, so absorbed in his performance that I lost track of what I was even doing there. It was mortifying, and of course Jack had been delighted to rub it in my face. 'And I'm just . . . so not,' I finish, wearily.

Hannah is quiet for a moment. 'Cyn,' she says finally, 'I've known you my whole life. You've always been so sure of yourself when it came to performing, but it's totally normal to get overwhelmed or nervous. You have to accept that this is a whole new world to you, while he's been doing it for years. You're feeling more comfortable every day; you've got an entire film crew on your side; you're going to get your confidence back and you're going to smash this. I know you will, because you're the most passionate, talented person in the whole world, and Logan and Jasmine and all the producers saw that when you auditioned.'

She leans over now, slinging her arm around my shoulders and squeezing. 'They didn't offer you the job as a favour; they did it because they believe you can give the best performance. And I know you're destined for greatness, not only because I've seen you on stage, being absolutely, breathtakingly brilliant—'

'*School* plays,' I interrupt. '*Community* theatre.'

'Cyn,' Hannah tuts, 'you've known what you were going to do with your life since the moment of rude awakening when someone told us we couldn't grow up to be dogs and would have to get actual jobs.'

'I still believe you can be anything you want to be,' I say solemnly. 'Even a Great Dane.'

'I don't know how to explain it to you,' Hannah persists, stubbornly. 'You have a gift. To this day I remain so deeply traumatized by that time when we were seven and you re-enacted the child-catcher scene from *Chitty Chitty Bang Bang* that I should probably raise it with a therapist. You were born to do this. Also, you've practised your Oscar acceptance speech in my bedroom mirror so many times that *I* can recite it. The bit where you thank Ewan McGregor is always especially moving'

'I'd like to thank my husband, Ewan,' I sniffle, 'who loves me beyond all reason and sings "Your Song" to me every single night.'

'You never did get over Moulin Rouge.' Hannah smiles.

'And I never will.'

I turn to hug her back, and even though I haven't undone my seatbelt and it's an awkward angle and my face is pressed into her hair, tickling my nose, I feel so much better.

'Okay,' I say, finally, disentangling from her. 'That was a great pep talk.'

'Did you expect anything less from your newly minted personal assistant?' Hannah buffs her fingernails on her T-shirt. 'Now, let's get inside and check out the new digs. You've got hair and make-up tests all afternoon.'

My best friend picks up the ring binder in her lap, which I know is full of the colour-coded charts and calendars that make her so happy. When Marion mentioned that I'd have a runner on set who would be assigned to me, I begged her to offer Hannah – who had been job-hunting for months – the position.

At their first in-person meeting, Marion and Hannah started ooh-ing and ahh-ing over spreadsheet layouts, and it was clear that I was going to be in good hands. Not that I ever had any doubts – no one can out-organize my girl.

We get out the car and grab our bags – plural – from the boot and the back seat. Four weeks is a long time to be away and we've both panicked and packed pretty much everything we own.

'Are you ever planning on coming back?' my dad grunted while helping us load the car. It's still unclear which answer he would have preferred.

Anyway, better to be over-prepared: the fact that it's the first week of September in England means that literally anything could happen when it comes to the weather – as demonstrated by the fact that the biblical sheets of rain have stopped, and the sun is struggling out from behind the clouds.

'It's very cool that this whole place is being used for cast and crew accommodation,' Hannah huffs, as we stagger towards the front door, laden down with heavy bags. 'It's going to be like summer camp.'

'Hopefully we won't get cabin fever, squeezed in like sardines,' I say, shoving at the door which sticks slightly. 'I don't want to spend any more time than I have to with a certain pompous, arrogant di—' Naturally, at that moment someone pulls the door handle from the inside and I go sailing forward, my balance off thanks to the giant backpack fastened to my shoulders.

'Agh!' I screech.

'Oof!' a horribly familiar voice exhales as I bash straight into Jack's stomach, sending both of us ricocheting backwards.

My arms windmill comically at my sides, but with the weight of my bag, I'm top-heavy and I can't steady myself. I go down like a felled tree, landing hard on my back, and feeling various pairs of shoes digging into my spine. With a wince, I wriggle my legs, trying to roll over or pull myself up, but the heavy backpack keeps me firmly pinned to the ground. Curse my absolute lack of core strength! This is why people do a thousand sit ups a day instead of watching 90's exercise videos while eating scones and commenting on people's leotards, like Hannah and I do.

Speaking of Hannah, she is crumpled helplessly against the doorframe, looking down at me as her shoulders shudder and she gasps for air.

'Cyn,' she chokes out between wheezing bursts of laughter. 'Cyn . . . you look . . . you look like a stranded turtle.'

I only flail more vigorously at that.

'Will you stop thrashing about before you kick me in the face?' Jack appears above me, grumpy and dishevelled.

'Don't tempt me,' I mutter.

He holds out his hand and with a show of reluctance I take it. Warm fingers wrap around mine and he tugs me up as if it's nothing, the muscles in his forearms flexing outrageously.

I'm back on my feet, but for a moment the floor tips below me. I'm shockingly aware of his big hand cradling mine, little electric sparks skittering across my skin where he touches me.

Jack stares down at our clasped hands, a look of bemusement on his face. Then I tug my fingers away, wiping my palm against my jeans, like I can wipe away the feeling.

I am, thankfully, distracted from his terrible, beautiful face by the room we are standing in – it must once have been an entrance hall, but it's large enough to accommodate a couple of sofas in front of the stone fireplace. The walls are panelled with polished wood the warm colour of maple syrup, a large rug – faded in an expensive way – stretching over the flagstone floor.

'You could say thank you,' Jack breaks in, voice cool.

I turn back and glare at him. 'If you hadn't yanked the door open without looking, I wouldn't have fallen.' I try to bend over and gather the items strewn across the floor back into the tote bag that had been slung over my shoulder, but once more I've forgotten my own compromised centre of gravity and I teeter, but manage to right myself. '*You* should be apologizing to me,' I carry on, breathlessly.

'Oh, yes,' Jack mutters, bending down and scooping up the tangled mess of my headphones, a battered Jilly Cooper paperback (*Harriet*, the best one) and a now slightly bruised apple, stuffing them back into the cotton tote bag that I got from our local library. '*I* should apologize,' he says. 'I should apologize for the fact that you're barging around with your whole bloody life strapped to your back, *bulldozing* people . . .'

He reaches out, and before I can compute what he is doing, he tugs one strap of the backpack off my shoulder, spinning me away from him as he does, so that he can lift it off my back entirely. As the second strap slides down my arm, I make a grab for it, but it's too late: he's hefting the whole thing up on his shoulder, as though it were full of nothing but feathers and bubble wrap.

Once again, I am treated to a spectacular view of all his muscles at work and I am furious about it.

'What do you think you're doing?' I hiss. 'And why must you have your . . . your naked arms out on display all the time?'

Jack lifts his brows, looking down at the perfectly normal T-shirt he is wearing. 'My naked arms?' he repeats with a smirk. 'Honestly, Taylor, I had no idea you were so Victorian. Is the sight of all this manly flesh overwhelming you?'

'Cynthie has been getting into character,' Hannah says primly, cutting in over whatever extremely rude words were about to start pouring out of me. I lift my chin and smile like everything is totally normal and I am not distracted by his very ordinary arms. What are arms, anyway? Just a pair of meat sticks. Nothing to get worked up over.

Jack only gives a derisive huff of laughter, but he heads over to a small desk in the corner – on the wall behind it are lots of gold hooks with old-fashioned keys hanging from them.

'Claudia, the housekeeper, is settling Hattie in now,' he says. 'But I know where your rooms are, so I can show you up.' He reaches for a couple of the keys.

'Stalking me?' I ask sweetly.

'Just wanted to make sure that we were staying as far apart as possible,' Jack retorts. 'Here.' He holds out his hand towards Hannah, his voice gentling. 'Let me help you with your bag.'

'Thanks,' Hannah replies, and I can't even blame her for the flush that creeps over her cheeks.

'Who knew you actually had any manners,' I grumble as he slings her backpack over his other shoulder and takes Hannah's little carry-on bag in hand.

'Let's just say I'm getting into character, too.' His smile is a baring of teeth that doesn't reach his eyes. He looks like he wants to take a bite out of me, and something dark leaps in my blood, telling me I wouldn't mind if he did. I swallow, pushing the thought somewhere deep, deep down, and Jack watches the movement of my throat through hooded eyes.

Without any further conversation he stomps towards a wide staircase, guiding us up two flights and along a corridor.

'There are so many rooms.' Hannah looks around her with interest.

'The rector had fourteen children,' Jack and I say at the same time, and I scowl. It seems I'm not the only one who read the building history on the website, although it's hard to believe Jack has been as excited about this trip as I have.

'And then the rectory was extended,' I add as if he hadn't spoken.

'Twice,' Jack puts in quickly, another flash of his teeth as he delights in getting the last word.

Something mean simmers between us again. I battle the urge to stamp on his foot.

We come to a stop.

'It's these two,' he says, pointing to two doors next to one another. Dropping the bags unceremoniously to the floor, he hands us both a key, and I notice he's careful not to touch me at all.

'Don't forget you have hair and make-up tests this afternoon,' he says over his shoulder, already striding away.

This time, I don't have to be outraged, because Hannah, furious that anyone might be questioning her organizational skills, yells after him. 'We *know*! It's in *the binder*!'

She's still grumbling in exasperation as I turn the key and push open the door to my room.

'Oh!' I exclaim.

We're up in the eaves of the house and the ceiling slopes gently. A small, square window frames a view of pure, leafy green. The walls are papered with a wildflower print, and a pretty patchwork quilt stretches over a bed with an old-fashioned metal frame. The whole effect is one of clean, peaceful, coziness.

'This bed has bedknobs!' I yelp. 'It's an actual *Bedknobs and Broomsticks* bed!'

'It's like we're in a Jane Austen novel,' Hannah calls from her own room, and I step back out into the hall to find it is a mirror image of my own.

'I love it,' I say. Suddenly it all feels more real – not only that we're about to begin four weeks of filming, but that I'm stepping into the role of Emilia.

'Okay, five minutes to dump our bags and then we're heading out,' my personal drill-sergeant says, clapping her hands.

I'm happy to fall in line. For the first time since the table read, I feel excited at the thought of performing, and I sail back out of Alveston Hall on a wave of optimism.

Chapter Nine

Cynthie

'Oh my god, what have you done to your hair?' The woman in front of me stands with her mouth open, eyes wide in a mask of horror.

The wave of optimism comes crashing down.

I lift a hand to the back of my neck, brushing the short, unruly strands. 'Er . . . I had it cut.' I wince.

She steps forward, and I'm enveloped in a cloud of her perfume, which smells delicious. She flicks her own, beautiful curtain of flame-red hair away from her shoulders. 'Tell me the truth.' Her voice lowers, her tone hushed. 'This is a safe space. Did you do this yourself?'

'No!' My eyes widen. 'A hairdresser did it.'

The woman sucks in a sharp breath. 'They should be struck off!'

'I wasn't aware that hairdressers could be struck off?' I manage. 'I thought that was a thing that happened to . . . um . . . doctors?'

'Well, we should start doing it. This monster should never be allowed to wield scissors again.'

That seems a little extreme. Hannah, sitting in the corner with her beloved binder in her lap, makes a sound that is suspiciously close to a snigger. The trailer we are in is currently located around the back of Alveston Hall, but tomorrow it will move – along with everything else – to the National Trust property where we're doing the first lot of filming. I thought I was here for a hair and make-up test, but it seems it's just one more stop on Cynthie's tour of humiliation.

'Patty!' The man beside the horrified woman says in a soft, Northern accent. 'You're scaring her!'

He smiles sweetly at me from underneath a crop of bleached blond hair. 'Don't mind my friend.' He gestures at Patty, who is staring at my fringe like it's a war crime. 'She's very passionate about her work. I am too . . . just in a less terrifying way. I'm Liam.' He leans behind him and plucks a make-up brush from the counter. 'I'm doing your make-up, and Patty – as I'm sure you've worked out – does hair.'

Patty and Liam are probably a handful of years older than me and Hannah. Patty is all sharp angles, tattoos, flame-red hair, and perfect eyeliner, wearing black leather trousers and a David Bowie T-shirt. She emits a vibe that is frighteningly cool. Liam looks like a gorgeous cherub, apple-cheeked, blue-eyed, dressed head-to-toe in white and radiating goodwill. I wonder if they have co-ordinated as some sort of double act on purpose: if ever there were to be a devil and an angel on your shoulder, here they are live and in person.

Patty reaches out her hand and takes mine in a firm grip.

'I promise you,' she says, murder in her eyes. 'I will find the person who did this to you. I will make them pay.'

'All right, Mr Neeson,' Liam nudges her in the shoulder. He turns to me, sympathy all over his pretty face. 'I expect it was a bad break-up, was it?'

I would love for this conversation to end.

'No, no break-up,' I say, tucking my much-maligned hair behind my ear. 'Honestly? This is my first real acting job and I'm totally out of my depth. I thought if I got a sophisticated haircut, it would make me feel . . . more together. Only that was a disaster, and actually this whole thing has been a disaster, and I am very, very worried that I'm about to single-handedly bring down an entire movie, probably destroying several careers and bankrupting multiple studios in the process.'

My breath is coming fast now, and I feel perilously close to tears.

'Well, fuck,' Patty says after a moment. 'I guess I'd better fix your hair, then.'

'You poor thing.' Liam nudges me towards the chair between them, the one facing the mirror. 'Why don't you tell us all about it? You wouldn't believe the problems that get fixed in here . . . I swear the UN only needs a hair and make-up department, and the world would be sorted like that.' He clicks his fingers.

I sink into the chair and Patty brandishes her scissors. 'Sophisticated.' She tilts her head, frowns in concentration. 'I can do that. And the good news is you're wearing wigs on-screen, so shorter is actually more manageable.' She gestures to the shelf behind her, which holds half a dozen wigs arranged on mannequin heads. 'Go on then, give us the whole story.'

So I do. I tell them I'm a waitress without so much as an A-level in drama, that acting has been my dream as long as I can remember, that I scrimped and saved for a six-week acting class, signed up for every amateur society I could. I tell them about the casting call and the audition, about the table read and what I heard Jack say. I tell them about the argument we had afterwards, about the week of rehearsals and how anxious I am, and all the time, they fuss over me, playing with my hair, smearing my face with delicious-smelling lotions. Liam takes my hands and massages them.

They make sympathetic noises, and gasp and laugh in all the right places.

'Sounds like Jack is a right monster,' Liam says with a loyalty I'm not sure I've earned.

'Not surprising.' Patty pauses in her snipping and leans forward over my shoulder. 'I worked with his mother once – my god, what a nightmare. I hear his dad's the same.'

'Incredible actors, though,' I murmur.

'Oh, of course,' Patty agrees, turning her attention back to her work. 'But that's part of the problem if you ask me: so much bad behaviour in this business gets put down to artistic temperament.' She scoffs. 'They call it genius; I call it being a dickhead.'

'Was Caroline Turner really awful then?' Hannah asks, obviously delighted by this bit of A-list Hollywood gossip.

Patty rolls her eyes. 'Oh god, yes. *Nothing* was good enough for her. She had a rider that was like a copy of *Ulysses*. A thousand pages long and made about as much sense.'

'A rider?' I ask.

'Oh, sweets!' Liam coos. 'You have to have one! It's the list of demands the talent make . . . you know, like "I must have a thousand rare orchids arranged in the shape of my beloved dead Pekinese, Alfred, or I can't possibly work."'

'Ah,' I nod. 'I think Gayle asked me about that. I said some tap water would be great.'

Patty lets out a bark of laughter.

Liam shakes his head. 'We need to work on that. At least ask for a set of crystals – rose quartz for sure, maybe amethyst. When they're fully charged they'll help with all this anxiety and negative energy.'

'How do you charge a crystal?' Hannah asks, perplexed.

'*You* don't charge them, silly,' Liam replies, dabbing something shimmery along my cheekbones. 'The *moon* does.'

'Forget moon crystals,' Patty advises. 'Go straight for the hard liquor and personal masseuse.'

'You love a Mars bar,' Hannah supplies helpfully. 'Maybe you could ask for some of those. Oh! Or how about crisps and bread so we can have crisp sandwiches like we used to make when we got home from school? You can probably even have branded ones. Oh my god! You can probably ask for Kettle Chips. I bet film stars eat Kettle Chips *all the time*.'

While crisp sandwiches are an elite snack, I don't think her suggestions are striking a very worldly, sophisticated note. I wonder what's on Jack's rider ... Probably a giant pyramid of Ferrero Rocher and gold-plated underpants.

'Anyway,' I say, steering the conversation back on track, and my mind away from Jack Turner-Jones's underwear, 'you were saying about Jack's parents ...' I can't help my curiosity – after all the pair of them did manage to spawn Satan himself.

'Oh, yeah.' Patty shrugs. 'It just sounds like the apple hasn't fallen far from the tree. They're both incredibly rude. You can tell a lot about a person by how they treat the crew on a film set, and Caroline Turner treated everyone like dirt on her Jimmy Choos.'

'Patty,' Liam chides, 'you're not being very discreet.'

'It's not like it's a secret,' Patty exclaims. 'Everyone knows that they're terrible. At this point there are about a hundred books and documentaries and an Emmy-Award-winning mini-series about the two of them behaving outrageously. If you ask me, Caroline enjoyed playing up to the image of the demanding diva.'

'We haven't met Jack yet,' Liam puts in, 'but obviously we're already Team Cyn.'

'We should get T-shirts,' Hannah says. 'And then we should wear them in front of him.'

I feel something loosen in my chest. God, this is nice. To feel safe and comfortable and to remember that I am a normal human who doesn't have any trouble making friends. This weird stand-off with Jack has clearly thrown me off-balance in more ways than one.

'Of course, the real problem is that the man is so gorgeous he can get away with anything,' Patty says now.

'Boooooo!' Hannah jeers.

'Hey, buddy,' Patty gestures to her with her scissors. 'A fact is a fact. He may be a terrible human, but at least it should be no hardship staring at his face all day.'

'You'd think,' I mutter.

'Patty has absolutely awful taste in men,' Liam confides.

'That is true,' Patty agrees easily. 'The worse they are, the better I like them.'

'Then you're going to *love* Jack,' I grumble.

'The guy she just broke up with . . .' Liam shudders dramatically.

'Hey!' Patty interjects. 'Brian wasn't that bad.'

Liam catches my eye in the mirror. 'Brian had an un-ironic goatee and drove a hearse.'

'A hearse?' I repeat blankly. 'As in an actual hearse? Like for funerals?'

'He won it in a bet,' Patty hums, stepping in front of me and leaning in to snip my fringe, 'and you know what, you could park that thing *anywhere* without getting a ticket, and no one ever cut you off in traffic. I've never known drivers in London to be so respectful. Sure . . . he can only drive twenty miles an hour but he said he'd never go back to a normal car now.'

'That is *so* wrong.' Liam shakes his head as the rest of us burst into laughter.

'Anyway,' Patty says once we've recovered. 'The question is, after the way he's behaved . . . how are we going to even the score with Jack Turner-Jones?'

'What do you mean?' I ask, interested despite myself.

Patty puckers her lips. 'Well, I've got four brothers, so if you want to talk pranks then I'm your girl. Prank wars on set are a time-honoured tradition. George Clooney is an absolute menace.'

I groan. 'I would love that,' I say, 'but unfortunately, I think I need to try being super professional and mature. Even if he is despicable.'

'Take the high road, babe.' Liam nods. 'Karma will get him in the end, anyway.'

'All I'm saying is that sometimes karma needs a helping hand' is Patty's reply. 'Now' – she steps back – 'what do you think?'

I look in the mirror, and my mouth falls open. 'How did you do that?' I ask.

'I'm a witch,' she replies, and I'm not sure she's joking.

It certainly seems possible, because my hair is no longer a tragic disaster, but a very cute pixie cut that makes my eyes look enormous and my cheekbones razor-sharp. Although, that could also be down to Liam and his magic potions.

'Not many people have the bone structure to pull this look off.' Patty eyes me critically in the mirror. 'But you have a great face.'

'I'll say,' Liam chimes in. 'The cupid's bow! The eyes! It's going to be a dream on camera. You're definitely giving Audrey Hepburn.'

Once more I'm embarrassed to find myself blinking away tears. 'Sorry!' I say mistily, 'I know it's silly, but I feel so much better. At least I won't be walking around looking like a disaster. One less thing to worry about.'

'It doesn't sound silly at all.' Patty is brisk. 'There's a lot of power in what we do, and from now on Liam and I have your back, okay?' Her hand closes on my shoulder. 'Now, let's have a look at these wigs. We'll get them on and style them and take some polaroids for Jasmine to look over. She and Logan are already running around like headless chickens. You'd think having two directors would mean they'd each have half the workload, but I swear the two of them can't agree on anything.'

'I want to try a deeper colour on the lip,' Liam muses. 'We've obviously got to keep things natural, but I think more of a rose shade could work.'

'Mmm.' Patty tips her head to the side, observing my reflection with a clinical detachment. 'Yes, and don't you think the darker wigs will be better for contrast?'

As Patty and Liam chat details, I catch Hannah's eye in the mirror, and she's beaming.

You look beautiful, she mouths.

So do you, I mouth back. And just like that, it feels like everything is right with the world again.

Chapter Ten

Jack

When I wake on the morning of the first day of filming, the sun is barely struggling up and the weather outside my window is dreary and overcast. I try not to take that as a sign, but I'd be lying if I said I wasn't shaking in my nineteenth century riding boots. So much of my future hinges on the next few weeks, and rehearsals haven't exactly gone smoothly.

I'm ready to admit that some of that might be my fault. After my spectacular argument with Cynthie in the coffee shop, I decided to embrace the time-honoured British tradition of pretending that nothing had actually happened, while letting the animosity simmer.

The trouble is that the simmering is really more of a roiling boil at this point. I'm worried that the stupid feud that has grown between us is going to seriously derail production, and I know that I have to put the good of the film ahead of my own pride.

Honestly, though, it would require the patience of an actual saint to deal with the woman – not only is she still not up to the job, but she seems almost gleeful when presented with any opportunity to unsettle me.

I glance at my phone, and as well as informing me that it's 4.30 a.m., I also have a new message waiting from my dad.

Dad

First day. Don't fuck it up, and try not to go too big. You know what you're like. Remember it's not a bloody pantomime!!!!!

Stirring words of support as usual. My anxiety spikes and I draw in several deep breaths, trying to settle my body. I check the time again. There's absolutely no point in trying to go back to sleep, so I might as well try to do something productive.

Heaving myself out of bed, I move to the bathroom and splash some cold water on my bleary face, brush my teeth, then I pull on a pair of jogging bottoms and a T-shirt and head for the gym.

It's a small space, tucked away in the basement, and this morning I am – as I expected – the only person here.

My parents have had me working with a personal trainer since I was thirteen, but Jasmine and Logan want Edward to have quite a tough physique so I've been doing a lot of lifting, trying to bulk up. I pull up my workout mix and stick my headphones in, letting the music blare as I lose myself in the soothing repetition of the exercises. My mind empties and it's a blissful relief.

I'm standing in front of the mirror, on my second set of bicep curls, when I become aware of a presence in the doorway. I think I knew she was there even before I saw her move in my peripheral vision: somehow I always seem to know when Cynthie's around . . . She's like a thunderstorm, bringing a shift in the atmosphere along with her.

I pause the music.

'Oh, god.' Cynthie closes her eyes, she looks tired and pale in sweatpants and a ratty jumper. 'It's far too early for me to deal with you.'

I was also counting on ingesting an enormous amount of caffeine before having to speak to her, but right now I can only stand there blinking owlishly while my brain tries to catch up.

Clearly her hair and make-up trials have been a success because the awkward haircut is gone, and I feel inexplicably furious about it. She looks ... Well, if she was anyone else, I'd say she was beautiful – all eyes and mouth and soft, glowing skin. But I know all too well that behind that sweet face lies the blackened soul of a banshee, and no haircut is going to make me forget it.

Her gaze travels over me, and when her eyes meet mine in the mirror there's a second when that unsettling, unwelcome heat pulses between us again.

I pull a headphone from my ear. 'Can I help you? Or have you just come to stare at my naked arms some more?'

'It doesn't look like you need an audience – you're clearly more than capable of admiring yourself. What a surprise to find you working out in front of a mirror.' Her eyes brush over me again. 'Like a budgie with its favourite toy. A tiny-brained little narcissist.'

'You're supposed to lift weights in front of a mirror so that you can work on your form,' I reply stiffly. 'Which you would know if you ever lifted anything heavier than a paperback.' I take my time giving her my own once-over in the mirror, and a slow, pink flush creeps into her cheeks.

'God, you really are the worst,' she spits.

'Right back at you.'

There's a heavy pause. 'What *are* you doing here, anyway?' I ask.

'I was just ... wandering about a bit. I didn't know there was a gym down here.'

'Couldn't sleep?'

She shrugs her slender shoulders. 'First day.' She flashes me a careful look. 'We mere mortals are entitled to be a bit nervous. I'm sure you slept like a baby.'

My jaw tightens, but I'm certainly not going to correct her or share my own nerves – you don't show a predator your vulnerable underbelly, do you? I bet she'd just *love* to know about the nightmares I was having all night, the ones that featured me running down endless spiralling staircases, all my teeth falling out, and my parents turning up on set where I was naked and forgot all of my lines. You don't exactly need a degree in Psychology to see what was going on there.

Instead of answering, I put my headphones back in, and turn the volume up, pointedly ignoring her until she leaves, the angry stomp of her feet audible even over the blast of the music. It takes a long time for my pulse to settle, and I know I can't blame it all on the workout.

This is an untenable situation.

Which is why – I remind myself – today, before we actually start filming, I need to suck it up and make peace. It's not going to be a good look if the two leads on the film actually murder each other. One of us needs to be mature, and *clearly* that person is going to have to be me.

Decision made, I finish up another two sets and replace the weights, throwing a towel over my shoulder before leaving in search of coffee and Cynthie. Preferably in that order.

My phone pings with a text message and I pull it out of my pocket.

Lee

Good luck today. Gran and I are thinking of you

Lee

> Gran says she would text you herself but she's lost her phone again.

Lee

> Gran says that makes her sound senile. She hasn't lost her phone. She's left it at the home of one of her many loverrrrs.

Lee

> She rolled all her r's like that. It wasn't great for me.

Despite my mood and lack of coffee, I smile. My sister, Lee, is eighteen, and while we aren't precisely close (a six-year age gap feels pretty insurmountable when you're a kid), like soldiers on the battlefield we have trauma-bonded over having Max Jones and Caroline Turner as parents. Our gran is the one who undertook the practical aspects of raising the pair of us, and I can absolutely hear her voice in Lee's message.

I send Lee back a quick thumbs up emoji and head for the kitchen. Cynthie has clearly had the same idea because she's already there, leaning against the counter, cradling a cup of tea. When she sees me, her face falls, but neither of us says anything.

I move past her around the kitchen island and flick the kettle on. A strained silence falls as I scoop an irresponsible amount of instant coffee granules into a mug and add a splash of water. It looks like mud and tastes like petrol, but does the job. My brain lurches slowly to life.

'I'm glad you're here,' I say, mirroring her stance and leaning back against the counter so that we're facing each other, the kitchen island between us like a safety barrier. 'I wanted to talk to you before we start filming.'

'I'm sure you did,' she says wearily. 'Time for another one of your little pep talks about how I'm going to single-handedly bring down this entire production?'

I take another fortifying sip of coffee. 'I just want the shoot to go well,' I say.

'And I don't?' Cynthie's voice is sharp. 'I'm absolutely sick of this holier-than-thou attitude from you. You're the one who started all this.'

'If you're trying to claim some sort of moral high ground,' I say, 'then I'll direct you to our conversation of . . .' I look at my watch, '*ten minutes ago*, when you called me a tiny-brained little narcissist.'

She has the temerity to snort with laughter. 'I think I was referring to a budgie,' she says, schooling her face into the picture of innocence.

'I think you were comparing the budgie to me, so the point is moot,' I snap. My temper is fraying already. I came here to try and make peace, but it's useless, just useless, trying to have a civil conversation with this woman. 'Anyway,' I continue, drawing in a deep breath and thinking calming thoughts, 'I think you know that acting like I'm the problem and you're just a poor innocent is disingenuous at best.'

'*Disingenuous at best*,' Cynthie drawls. 'No one knows how to pull out those sick burns like a public-school boy.'

'You seem very hung up on my education,' I reply coldly. 'I can't imagine why.'

She stills, but temper leaps in her eyes.

'At least you can draw on all your repressed, uptight bullshit when you're playing Edward,' she says, and she takes a slow, dangerous step towards me. 'It's just a shame you don't have any of his charm. Not sure you're going to be able to pull it off, are you?' she sighs, affecting sympathy. 'I don't blame you. And you seem pretty desperate to have a scapegoat in place if things go badly. But do you know what I think?'

She takes another step towards me, and all I can hear is the sound of my own heartbeat in my ears.

'I think,' she says softly, 'that you're worried that you're about to fail, that you're going to be the one who can't live up to people's expectations. Me?' she shrugs, a sinuous movement. 'They're not watching me ... not yet, anyway. But Jack Turner-Jones?' She exhales a low whistle. 'If his performance isn't up to scratch, that would be quite the ... disappointment.'

Yet again, she's throwing darts at me with an uncanny precision. I wouldn't be surprised to find her words have drawn blood.

There's a moment of loaded silence while we glare at each other.

'Right,' I say finally, concentrating on getting my breathing back under rigid control. I have a lot of practice in this area, so it's going to take more than Cynthie Taylor to break my composure. 'Well, I suppose we'll find out, won't we? Because today the cameras are going to be rolling and there's no getting away from any mistakes then. Trust me when I tell you there's no faking it now. So if my performance isn't up to scratch, everyone will know. But, Cynthie,' I pause here, allowing a wintry smile to curl on my lips as I deliver the killer line, 'the same goes for you.'

I've willed myself to an appearance of calm now, and the words are frigid even though the argument has left my blood running hot. If Cynthie knew how hard I'm having to work to keep my emotions hidden then she certainly wouldn't be questioning my acting skills.

As it is she glares at me, but the colour has left her face and I know that I'm not the only one with weak spots.

For a moment I feel guilty about it, remember that I was supposed to be making peace, but the insults she flung at me last week are back, ringing in my ears: every insecurity I have is blasting at full volume, and that text message from my dad is in my pocket reminding me that I can't fuck this up.

'Oh, sorry,' a soft voice interrupts then, and Claudia, Alveston Hall's housekeeper, comes bustling in, pausing when she sees Cynthie and I locked in a vicious staring contest.

'I didn't think anyone would be up yet. Can I get you some breakfast?' Claudia continues, and she's eying us warily, presumably because we're poised like two snakes about to strike out at each other.

I force my shoulders down, turn and smile. 'No, thanks, Claudia,' I say lifting my now empty coffee cup, 'just needed some fuel to start the day. I'll grab something from craft services when we arrive on-set.' I look at my watch. 'Speaking of which, I'd better go grab my stuff. The cars are coming at six.'

My eyes slide over to Cynthie who is still standing rigid, but she forces her own smile.

'That's right,' she says. 'Hannah will probably be looking for me. Don't want to be late on our first day.'

'Well, good luck,' Claudia beams.

'Thanks,' I say as I duck out the kitchen, leaving the two of them behind.

I'm fairly sure we're going to need it.

Chapter Eleven

Cynthie

When Hannah and I step out of the car we are pummelled by a wave of sound so intense that I flinch.

Today, we're filming exterior scenes outside a huge National Trust property called Darlcot Manor about thirty minutes from Alveston Hall. The sheer *number* of people involved is mind-blowing – there must be well over a hundred crew members here, and the National Trust volunteers in their green fleeces look as shell-shocked as I feel while electricians and camera operators and sound technicians and goodness knows who else charge about, yelling at one another in front of the handsome building.

I take a moment, standing on the gravel driveway, in the middle of this wild storm, just to let it sink in: that I'm really here, that this is really happening.

Today we're planning to shoot a scene where Edward and Emilia talk while walking in the grounds, and I spot Jasmine and Logan in the crowd but currently they're little more than fast-moving blurs of activity in designer waterproofs.

After my argument with Jack this all feels even more surreal. If ever there was any dim hope that his opinion of my skills might have changed during rehearsals, that is long gone. He thinks I'm not good enough. He couldn't have made himself clearer if he'd hired a skywriter to emblazon the words CYNTHIE TAYLOR DOESN'T BELONG HERE over our heads.

'I'm going to be sick,' I murmur, and Hannah steps up and squeezes my hand.

'I've got peppermint tea bags, indigestion tablets, diarrhoea-relief tablets, and I found some of my mum's anxiety medication rolling around in her handbag if things get really bad.' She taps the side of the backpack she's wearing, which is enormous and straining at the seams. 'There's nothing we can't handle,' she insists.

'Okay,' I murmur. 'But you do know there's a paramedic on set at all times. You don't have to carry an entire pharmacy with you.'

Hannah's eyebrows shoot up. 'As if I'm going to trust some Hollywood type to feed you drugs.'

'Says the woman with a sandwich bag full of loose tranquillizers.' I laugh, feeling better.

'Right.' Hannah scans the scene in front of us like a battlefield. 'First step: dropping stuff off at your trailer before rehearsal and blocking, then hair and make-up. I think we're supposed to meet—'

'Hi!' an extremely tall, gangly guy with deep brown eyes and a killer smile pops up in front of us. 'Cynthie and Hannah, right?' We nod. 'I'm Arjun, the third assistant director. We haven't met yet.' He holds out his hand and grins down from his lofty height.

'Nice to meet you.' I wrap my fingers around his and shake.

'Remind me.' Hannah frowns down at the binder that hasn't left her hands all morning. (I'm more than half convinced that she slept with it on the pillow beside her.) 'Third assistant director . . .'

'Ah.' Arjun nods. 'Basically, Jan – that's Janice Howard, the second AD – co-ordinates everything from base.' Here he gestures towards the cluster of trailers and canopies over to one side of the building that looks like the backstage area of a circus. 'She knows exactly where everyone is supposed to be and when, and then I run around herding people while she tells me where to go.' He lifts his walkie-talkie. 'I've got Cynthie,' he says into it. 'We're walking now.'

He turns back to us. 'Let me show you to your trailer, while everyone finishes setting up, then we'll get you into rehearsal.'

'Sounds good,' I manage, my stomach in knots once more.

As if things hadn't been bad enough before my blow up with Jack this morning, now I get to hear his words ringing in my ears, too. For a moment I almost felt guilty when I watched my own insults hit home – the man might be a wet sneeze in human form, but he's undeniably talented. It's interesting that he isn't quite as sure of himself as he likes people to think. The things he said, though . . . well, best not to dwell on that, or I really will throw up.

'So, this is your first movie, right?' Arjun says as he strides along, his long legs eating up the distance, while Hannah and I trot behind.

'Yeah.' I smile weakly. 'I guess it's going to be a steep learning curve.' I glance around as we dart past dozens of busy people.

Arjun laughs. 'Don't be intimidated by the set up. There are a lot of people but that's because everyone has a specific job. Think of us like a well-oiled machine – we keep things running smoothly so that you can concentrate on your part.'

'It's actually my part that has me worried at the moment,' I admit.

'That's totally normal.' Arjun's voice is reassuring. 'I've worked on a bunch of films now and I have yet to meet an actor who doesn't get first-day jitters . . . or fourth day jitters for that matter.' He guides us past a large, tented canopy and a couple of food trucks, waving at people as we pass. 'Craft services are here.' He gestures. 'They've got snacks, hot and cold drinks, and they'll serve lunch and dinner here too.'

We keep walking and he stops in front of a small trailer. There's a piece of paper taped to the door that says CYNTHIE TAYLOR.

I stop in my tracks. 'Wow,' I whisper.

'Oh my godddddd!' Hannah squeals. 'Cynthie! Your name on a TRAILER!'

'We should take a picture,' I say, dazed.

Of course nothing throws Hannah, and she digs a camera out of her massive bag. Arjun is more than happy to snap half a dozen photos of the two of us standing by my name.

'Do you think you're ready to see inside?' he asks finally, clearly entertained.

The inside of the trailer is very ordinary and very beige and I'm obsessed with it, and insist Hannah takes pictures of me sitting on the sofa, turning on the kettle, admiring the empty shelves like I'm starring in a catalogue for extremely bland trailers.

'Okay,' Arjun says finally, 'I've got to jet. Before I forget, Hannah, here's your walkie-talkie. It's already tuned in to the right frequency, but let me know if you have any problems.' He pulls a hand-held radio from his belt and gives it to Hannah, who looks like she's going to burst into tears.

'Wait, wait,' I say. 'Arjun, hand it to Hannah again, I need to get a photo.' And I click the button on the camera as Arjun good-naturedly presents the walkie-talkie like it's a sacred offering. Hannah thrusts it victoriously up into the sky, and I snap away as she and Arjun laugh.

'I'm sorry,' I say in the end. 'I promise we're going to be cool and professional now.'

'Your secret is safe with me,' Arjun replies, already on the move, and I have the feeling that this superhero-style blur of activity is him in his natural state.

'I'm going to make you that peppermint tea,' Hannah says after he closes the door behind him, 'and then I'll get you some breakfast when you're in hair and make-up. Unless you want something now?'

'Tea is good,' I say, perching on the narrow sofa. 'I don't know if I'll be able to eat anything.'

'Of course you will,' Hannah replies. 'You'll get used to all this; we both will. It's not always going to be so overwhelming.'

'It seems impossible.' I glance out the window at the mass of activity.

'Remember when we started secondary school?' Hannah says, dunking tea bags into two cups. 'And it was an enormous labyrinth full of a million giant teenagers and we were so freaked out we hid in Miss Fletcher's supply cupboard during lunch?'

'You shared your KitKat with me,' I say.

'I'll *always* share my KitKat with you, Cyn.' Hannah grins. 'The point is, we got through that, and within a few weeks we were basically running the place. It'll be the same here.'

'I think your memories of school and mine are quite different,' I say, but Hannah makes a dismissive gesture.

'It's all just people,' she says. 'Soon, this will feel normal. You've just got to ride it out.'

'You're so wise.' I take a sip of the tea she hands me. 'Like a beautiful owl.'

Hannah's walkie-talkie crackles and her face lights up. 'Okay,' she says. 'Show time!'

As we leave the trailer, Jack steps out of the one next door. Of course. I link my arm through Hannah's, making sure we stay in front of him as we head to the spot where Logan and Jasmine are setting up for the first shot of the day.

According to the schedule there are eight shots – or set-ups – of this scene to film today, and I know – from the extremely intense amount of research I've been doing on the subject – that each one requires its own lighting and camera positioning. Still, it's quite a different thing to know this fact and to see it in action.

'Greetings, you two gorgeous people.' Logan bounces up, a lab-rador who has just been shown a tennis ball. 'It's here! Day one!'

Jasmine drifts along behind him, frowning and carrying a note-book in one hand and a cigarette in the other, which she waves in the air expressively. 'I think we might have to add in a couple of lines of dialogue here,' she says to the woman beside her, who she introduces as Laurie, the script supervisor.

'Jas!' Logan shakes her arm. 'Just be in the moment, will you? Day one!'

'I know it's day one,' Jasmine says. 'And I also know that some-how we're *already* behind schedule. How have we managed that?'

Logan rolls his eyes. 'Well, on that stirring note, shall we start blocking our first scene?'

He guides us around the various cables and pieces of machinery. 'So it's a fairly light scene to kick off with,' he says. 'Just a bit of jibber jabber as you walk.'

'*Jibber jabber.*' Jasmine closes her eyes, pained.

'We'll start up here,' Logan says, and then he and Jasmine walk us through the shot, and we work out where we'll stop and where we'll turn, where all the cameras will be positioned, and where our eyelines have to be so that we're always looking in the right direc-tion. It's a lot of information, and I'm focussing on it so hard that I don't have time to dwell on Jack's presence or the fact that a couple of hours ago he basically admitted he's rooting for me to fail.

'Ah!' Logan suddenly gasps, delighted. 'My sheep!' He lopes off, as a man appears with a truck carrying a bunch of very noisy, extremely woolly sheep.

'Him and his bloody mutton,' Jasmine says wearily, rubbing her forehead.

'They do look very . . . historical,' I admit, taking in their curly coats and horns as they're unloaded. 'Not like normal, modern sheep at all.'

'Yeah, and we've got the insane bill to prove it,' Jasmine says, clipped. 'Spending all our damn budget on a bunch of fluffy mammals that are going to baa all over everyone's lines. Apparently if they fall over, they can't get themselves back up, so we've got a dedicated runner on sheep-tipping duty which is just ...' she exhales – a sound of noisy exasperation.

Logan looks up from beside the sheep and waves to us, his grin wide like a child on Christmas morning.

'*Look at these fucking sheep!*' he mouths, delighted.

Even Jasmine can't help smiling a little at that, though she quickly covers it with her hand.

'Right, while my brother is busy with his new friends, let's run through that again,' she says, shoving us back up the gentle grass slope.

'It has been quite the social season.' I say my line, trying not to look at my feet as we walk.

'And you and my brother have made a stir,' Jack responds, and he definitely doesn't look like he's thinking about the cameras at all. He's already Edward, even in the middle of all this madness, still dressed in his jeans and a jumper. Somehow he's shrugged the part on, as if it were a perfectly tailored jacket – made just for him.

He's Edward, he's Edward, he's Edward, I tell myself.

'Do you—' I begin, but then I turn a fraction too early, and end up bashing into his side.

'For fuck's sake,' Jack grumbles under his breath, Edward falling away. 'This is really going to be a disaster if you can't even walk in a straight line.'

He's Edward, he's Edward, he's Edward, I tell myself again, gritting my teeth as we head back to our first position. *He's funny and handsome and intriguing, and he's your fiancé's off-limits brother, who you fancy the pants off. He is not a terrible excuse for a human who you'd like to push down this hill.*

We go through the scene and make it to the end this time, without any more disasters.

'Okay, Cynthie,' Logan calls from behind the monitor, having abandoned the sheep for the time being. 'It looks like you're a bit off your mark at the end there, so can we make sure you stop right on that last line, *please*.' There's exasperation in his voice.

'Of course, sorry,' I mumble.

'Jack, that was perfect,' he adds. 'Don't change a thing, not a thing.'

'You've got it,' Jack calls back, and he turns to whisper in my ear. 'Remind me again which of us got here on merit?' His voice is low, his breath curling over the shell of my ear, and I indulge in an elaborate fantasy where I chop him into bite-sized pieces and feed him to the historical sheep.

'I'm sorry,' I say, smiling back with all my teeth. 'I couldn't hear you over the sound of that scenery-chewing you were doing.'

His smile drops and the look he shoots me is poisonous.

'Let's have talent in hair and make-up,' Jasmine's voice breaks in, echoing over several walkie-talkies around us. She moves away to talk to Marion, who stands with her ever-present clipboard, casting her eye over the scene.

Arjun descends – a whirr of long-limbs – guiding Jack away, while Hannah appears at my side, a bottle of water in her hands which she thrusts at me.

'How about those tranquillizers?' I say.

'I've decided they might actually be Tic Tacs,' she replies.

'Sounds about right,' I sigh, as we trudge off towards base once more.

Chapter Twelve

Cynthie

'Okay, I've thought about it, and I've decided I'm totally in,' I tell Patty as she fusses with the wig on my head.

'In what?' Patty asks absently, adjusting one of the curls framing my face.

'In on payback for Jack.'

It came to me as I was walking away from the rehearsal, clinging to the last scraps of my sanity. I need a distraction, and Jack needs to be taught a lesson. Hadn't Patty already offered up a suggestion for both?

I watch my face in the mirror as a villainous smile spreads, like I'm the damn Grinch about to steal Christmas. 'Let's hear what ideas you have to make him suffer.'

'Yes!' Patty hoots. 'This is going to be so much fun.'

'What happened to being professional?' Hannah asks drily.

I scoff. 'According to Jack, that ship has already sailed so we might as well make the most of being rogue agents of chaos.'

'Ooooh, love that for us,' Liam whispers, delighted.

'Besides,' I add, 'it doesn't matter what we do . . . as long as we're sneaky about it and don't get caught.'

'Hmmmm,' Liam tilts his head. 'We're not talking, like, actual murder, right?'

'Tempting' – I widen my eyes in an expression of innocence – 'but no. Only a few harmless little pranks. We just want him ... *squirming* a bit.'

With the added benefit that thinking about pranking Jack will take my mind off the fact I'm going to have to go and film my first actual scene soon ... and it's incredibly likely I'm going to fall flat on my face. (I mean this metaphorically, though given my new-found inability to walk in a straight line I'm not ruling it out as a literal concern.)

'Hmmm,' Patty says thoughtfully. 'Well, obviously you've got your classics – sign him up for a load of weird mailing lists, fill his trailer with balloons, swap all his sugar sachets for salt, fill his tea bags with gravy granules, Vaseline on all his doorknobs, pins on his seats ...'

'Yes, yes.' I nod, already imagining Jack's disgruntled reaction and the way I will drink it up like fine wine. 'All of these are very doable.'

Even Hannah starts nodding. 'Okay, as long as we're not doing *actual crimes*, I'm in too ... It's like vigilante justice.' Her face darkens, and she's obviously remembering what I told her about the argument between Jack and I this morning.

'But the real payoff is going to come when we draft in a couple more crew members,' Patty says. 'I have a few people who could come in handy. And if you change your mind about the murder...' she flips her hair over her shoulder, 'let's just say I know how to clean up a crime scene.'

'Remind me not to get on your bad side,' Hannah says.

'You have no idea—' Liam begins, but he's cut off by a knock at the door.

'Hi.' Jasmine sticks her head in the trailer. She stands and scrutinizes me for a moment, then nods. 'Yes, this is looking good.'

'Cynthie's face makes it easy.' Liam smiles.

'I actually wondered if I could borrow her for a couple of minutes?' Jasmine looks to them. 'Is now a good time?'

'Sure.' Patty hits me with another blast of hairspray. 'I think we're about done here. Let me take a couple of polaroids.'

Patty snaps the pictures, and I glance at them, surprised once more by the transformation offered by the wig and the make-up. I really am becoming Emilia. I'm so close to her, I can feel it, like she's there in my brain, waiting to take over. Although I know that sounds objectively like the premise of a horror movie, I'm actually thrilled by the idea.

'Can we talk in your trailer?' Jasmine asks.

'Of course,' I reply, and I'm hit with a fresh rush of nerves, particularly as I eye the laptop tucked under her arm. I have no idea what this can be about, but given the way things have been going for me lately it's probably safe to assume it's not good.

Oh god, maybe she's going to sack me. Maybe missing my mark was the last straw and they're going to fly in some actress from LA who actually knows what she's doing.

By the time we reach my trailer I've worked myself into such a state of anxiety that I'm practically humming like a tuning fork. I worry that the frantic pitch of my nervous energy is going to start shattering windows like the world's most rubbish superhero: Anxiety Woman.

'Can I make you a cup of tea?' I ask, marvelling at how calm I sound when my body can't decide if it wants to cry, scream or throw up.

Jasmine shakes her head, pats the seat beside her. 'No, thanks. I actually want us to have a quick chat.'

'Oh?' I sit down, bracing myself for the inevitable bad news. 'What about?'

Jasmine opens her laptop and starts clacking at the keyboard. 'I know that you're new to filmmaking, so perhaps you're not familiar with the concept of dailies?'

'Er,' I riffle through all the information I've crammed into my brain over the last few weeks. 'When you send the first unedited copies of the day's filming to the producers, right?'

'That's it,' Jasmine nods. 'And different directors work in different ways, but Logan and I have decided we're not going to be sharing the dailies with the cast. I don't think it's helpful when it comes to informing a performance.'

'Okay,' I say slowly. That's probably for the best – I can see how watching all the raw footage out of context would make a performer get in their own head ... and I certainly don't need help in that department.

'But before we start filming, there *is* something I want to show you.' Jasmine turns the laptop screen to face me, and she has my audition cued up on-screen.

'Oh.' My eyes widen. I haven't seen this before, and even though we filmed it only weeks ago, it feels like a lifetime has passed.

'Just watch.' Jasmine hits play, and the sound of my voice pours from the speakers.

At first, I can hardly get past the fact of my face and my voice on the screen; I wince as I make a mistake with a line, but gradually, I relax and then ... I start to see it.

I watch myself laugh, watch my body language change, watch as I stop being Cynthie and become Emilia. The tone of the scene shifts, and there's sadness in my face. The camera picks up the sheen of tears in my eyes. My voice trembles with emotion. It feels so ... real. I'm absorbed enough that I make a sound of surprise when the video comes to an abrupt stop.

A heavy silence hangs in the air.

'Why are you showing me this?' I ask, finally.

Jasmine closes the laptop with a snap. 'Because I know how anxious you've been since we offered you the part, and I think you need to know exactly *why* I fought hard for you to get this role.' She drums her fingers across the computer in her lap. 'I'm not going to tell you that everyone was on board with casting an untested performer in our lead role. There are a few people who think the idea is ... eccentric at best. But I wrote those words, and when you said them I believed them. I saw them come alive. You have a wonderful natural instinct.'

'I feel so out of my depth,' I admit quietly. 'I don't want to let you down.'

Jasmine huffs, her tone brisk, pure business. 'You haven't made a film before. It's not a surprise or a secret. We all know that. If it takes you a little longer to grasp the technical aspects of your performance, that's understandable. It's going to be worth the delay, the extra work,' – she looks me in the eye here – 'for the sort of performance I believe you are capable of. That you and Jack are capable of together.'

She gets to her feet. 'You can do this, Cynthie. I need you to trust me when I tell you that. It's going to be almost impossibly hard work, but I swear at the end of it, I am going to get a brilliant performance out of you. Not just adequate, not promising for a first role, but *brilliant*.'

'That means a lot,' I reply ardently.

She hesitates, frowning at me. 'Look, I'm not here to be your friend or your mentor,' she says finally, clearly horrified by the very idea.

'No,' I murmur, 'of course not.' Even though my heart sinks and I want to ask her why she can't be those things. 'That would be ... *bad*?' I manage to make it sound like a question and I try not to look as pathetic and desperate as I feel.

'I'm going to be your director,' she continues, the words sharp. 'We're making this piece of work *together*. Bring the joy and energy that you brought into that audition room onto set with you. Turn up, do the work. Be prepared to do it over and over again, until you hate me, until you're dead on your feet, because we're not settling for anything less than perfect. You have it in you to be great at this and we're about to prove it. Do you understand?'

I feel like if the directing thing doesn't work out, Jasmine could have a career as the American football coach to a scrappy team of underdogs, because that ended up being some rousing half-time speech. It's all I can do to stop myself from leaping to my feet and starting to applaud.

'I understand,' I say instead, and I mean it. Because I can feel my heart beating harder, because I hear the truth in what she said. She really believes that I can do this, and after being so ruthlessly pummelled by self-doubt for the last few weeks, it's a lifeline, a hand reaching down and offering to help me to my feet.

I know, somewhere deep inside me, that she's right, that not only can I do this job, but that I can do it *brilliantly*. If she'd been kind and gentle and told me I only needed to do my best, it would have flattened me, but this – this *demand* that I reach my potential – has me practically levitating off the ground. Maybe it's madness, maybe it's ego, maybe it's just what a person has to have to be able to make something like this happen at all – but my outrageous self-belief is what has got me this far, and I feel it settle around me now.

'Good.' Jasmine nods. 'Don't be afraid to ask questions or to make suggestions.' For a moment the stern façade drops away, for just a second her mouth curves and I see a glimmer in her eye that makes her look like Logan. 'Let them underestimate us. We'll have the last laugh.'

'You've got it, boss,' I agree. I think I would lie down in traffic for her if she asked.

She only nods once more, the cool expression falling back into place, as she lets herself out the door, passing Hannah on her way.

'There you are,' Hannah says, bouncing up the steps into the trailer. 'Are you ready to get into costume?'

I stand, grin at her. For the first time I'm not faking it when I pull my shoulders back, lift my chin and say, 'Absolutely.'

By the time I am laced into my corset and buttoned into a gown of creamy silk trimmed with green ribbon and delicately embroidered with trailing green vines, I feel ready. Of course there are still nerves there, but they simmer, a low, gentle heat underneath the roiling thrill of excitement. I look in the mirror and all I see is Emilia.

Hannah must sense my mood because she doesn't try to talk to me as we pick our way over towards the cameras.

'Okay!' Logan says, clapping his hands together when he sees us approaching. 'Here we go!' His smile is wide, but there's a tightness around his eyes. His sister might believe in me, but Logan's definitely not sure I can do this.

Jasmine lurks behind him, swathed in black and looking grimly like she's about to attend a funeral. It is strangely reassuring.

The grey clouds have drifted away, and the sky is mostly clear now, though Marion is staring up at it, deep in conversation with Mark, the head of cinematography. Logan's sheep have been dotted artistically around in the background, and between them and the rolling green landscape intersected by low dry-stone walls, the scene is bucolic.

Waiting up at the top of the gentle slope, under a handsome oak tree, is Jack. Dressed in breeches, dark riding boots, and a navy jacket that appears to have been moulded to the muscular lines of his upper body, he looks every inch the romantic Regency fantasy. As I walk towards him, I notice he has his eyes closed, just as he did that first day at the read-through, and when he opens them, they catch on me and flash, full of an electric blue heat.

In that moment I'm not sure if the zing I experience is between Cynthie and Jack or Emilia and Edward, but I know that it will help with the scene, and instead of tamping the feeling down, I let heat unfurl inside me. I allow my mouth to curve: a smile and an invitation, and Jack's whole body goes utterly still, wariness creeping into his gaze.

'Last looks,' Logan yells, and Liam rushes forward from behind the huddle of the cameras, pulling brushes from his belt as he dabs first at Jack's face and then at mine.

The people around us fall back. Logan and Jasmine are positioned behind their monitor. The camera operators close in, a boom mic hovers in my peripheral vision, and I take a breath, narrowing my focus so that I don't see them, don't hear them. All I see is Jack, and I'm so focussed on him, I'm convinced that I can hear his heartbeat, thrumming in time with my own.

'First positions,' Marion calls, and I move to the agreed upon spot.

'Roll sound,' Logan's voice comes, and then there is the quick patter that I know signals the start of filming.

'Sound speed!'

'Roll camera.'

'Camera rolling.'

A young woman steps forward with a slate. 'Scene seventeen, take one.' She claps the slate shut, and I feel the thrill you get when the rollercoaster is climbing, climbing, climbing.

'Set,' one of the camera operators says.

The moment teeters on a knife's edge – the split second before free fall. My eyes close.

'Action,' Logan shouts, and if I were Cynthie, I might wonder why Jasmine hasn't said anything at all yet, but I'm not Cynthie anymore. My eyes snap open, and I say my first line.

'It has been quite the social season.'

'And you and my brother have made a stir.'

I tilt my head, considering the man beside me. He holds himself stiffly, emotions in check.

'Do you think so?' I ask, lightly. 'I wonder how such information reached you, when it seems you've been avoiding society altogether.'

Edward's jaw tightens, and my heart leaps. He thinks he's hiding his feelings, but they're easy enough to find if you choose to look for them.

'I have been busy,' he says, stiffly.

I stop walking, and his good manners force him to stop beside me. I take a step closer.

'Busy avoiding me, I think,' I say, the words gentle, a little sad. 'When I was under the impression that you and I were friends.'

Our eyes meet for a long moment, and there's such heat in his gaze I almost falter.

'Friends,' he bites out finally with a hard laugh.

I lift my eyebrows in challenge, take another step closer, playing with fire. 'What would you call it?' I ask the question softly, reach out, my hand hovering for an instant of indecision before I place my fingertips on his arm. It's a light touch, but I can feel the heat of his body, even through the sleeve of his coat, through my gloves. He hesitates and looks down with a frown. Then, just as I'm about to pull away, embarrassed, he covers my fingers with his for a second of desperate contact, before he moves away. My own hand drops to my side, and I continue walking, my heartbeat erratic.

'*Friends*,' he says again with an ironic curl of his lips, while struggling to hide how affected he is. 'I suppose so.'

'In that case,' I reply with an easiness I don't feel, as we continue to walk, 'you won't mind when I beat you at cards later.'

This time his laugh is real, drawn out of him by surprise. 'You mean I won't mind when you try to cheat me at cards later.'

His smile transforms his face. I blink – dazzled.

'I have no idea what you are talking about,' I manage finally, schooling my expression into one of innocence.

The two of us continue to walk and to tease one another, and I try to pretend that the pleasure I take in this simple exchange is ordinary, that it doesn't feel like snatching something precious.

When a voice finally shouts, 'Cut!' I flinch.

The world rushes in, and I find to my surprise that I'm shaking. Jack looks at me like I've just sprouted an extra head.

'That was—' he starts, but he's cut off by Jasmine and Logan bustling over.

'Great, Jack. *Great!*' Logan enthuses, clapping Jack on the arm.

My eyes go to Jasmine, whose face gives nothing away. 'A good start,' she purses her lips. 'I think we need to pick up the pace on those last few lines. We might need to tweak something there ... The end of the scene felt flat.'

I nod. 'I think ...' I hesitate, but Jasmine inclines her head, and I remember her saying I should speak up. 'I think maybe we need to keep walking a bit further. It felt like the momentum in the movement was off.' I sound tentative.

'Mmmm,' Jasmine murmurs thoughtfully.

I'm on the brink of telling her to ignore me, that I don't know what I'm talking about, when Logan turns to Jack. 'What do you think about that, Jack?'

Jack glances over at me and frowns. 'I was going to say the same thing,' he says finally, and it sounds like he's confessing to a crime.

'Okay, good,' Logan nods. 'Let me just have a chat with Mark.' He looks up at the sky. 'I think the cloud cover is steady for now, so we'll go again asap.'

'Oh, and Cynthie,' Jasmine says, 'I know it wasn't scripted, but the arm touch was good. Keep that in.'

She walks away to talk to Marion and I laugh, delighted. Adrenaline is thrashing so wildly through my body, I feel like there are fireworks going off inside me.

Jack looks like he's just found half a worm in his apple.

'Right, everyone,' Marion shouts, clapping her hands together. 'Back to firsts.'

'Did you have anything you wanted to say to me?' I ask Jack sweetly, as we climb back up the hill.

'I have to admit I'm impressed,' he replies, his tone matching mine. 'I had no idea you could say your lines *and* walk in a straight line at the same time. Better get ready for that Oscar nomination.'

I only have time to growl before Liam is there, powdering my face again.

Never mind.

First I'll prove Jack Turner-Jones wrong about me, and then I'll enact some vigilante justice. He won't know what's hit him.

Chapter Thirteen

Jack

'What. The. Fuck?' I stand, stunned, staring through the open door of my trailer. Instead of the soothingly uninteresting beige interior that usually greets me, the entire space is so stuffed with balloons that I can't get inside.

This is only the latest indignity in what I now recognize is full-out prank warfare. It started small, last week: a few misplaced pins from the wardrobe department on my chair; salt in my coffee instead of sugar (I drank a worrying amount before that registered, but in my defence it was very early); an influx of spam emails from companies promising to increase the size of my genitals.

At first, I thought the sporadic incidents were a coincidence, but now . . . now, as a muscle begins twitching under my eye, I see the truth.

I take a deep breath. The first thing I'm going to do is to start popping all these stupid balloons, then, when I can actually get inside my trailer and make myself a cup of coffee, I will begin to plot my revenge. She may not have signed her name, but I'm confident I know who's behind this . . . After all, the woman has swiftly become the bane of my existence . . . even if she's not a *total* disaster in front of the camera anymore.

'Whoa.' My assistant, Scott, arrives behind me, with Arjun alongside him. 'What happened here?'

'Well,' I say slowly, 'if I had to guess, I'd say someone filled my trailer with balloons.'

Arjun stifles a laugh. 'Why would anyone do that?'

My eyes narrow. 'Because they're a vindictive shrew with the sense of humour of a three-year-old?' I suggest.

Scott blinks, his brow furrowed like he's trying to work out this particular head-scratcher. He's a few years younger than me, a relative of Logan and Jasmine's who smiles a lot and always carries the light, earthy scent of weed with him. Despite these unpromising details, he's surprisingly good at his job, and he makes an excellent cup of coffee (when he's not being sabotaged by insane pranksters).

'I guess we should . . . burst them?' he says, finally.

'Yeah,' I agree with a sigh. 'I need to get a pin or something. I was just going to head back to wardrobe.'

'We could stamp on them?' Scott suggests.

'We can use the prongs on our belt buckles,' Arjun advises, with the air of a man who's had to burst a lot of balloons, and I have no idea why this would be the case . . . Maybe I'm just convinced by his quiet air of competence.

My eyes narrow. It's actually possible he knows something about this – Arjun's gentle, easy-going nature means he makes friends easily, and he and Cynthie seem to get on pretty well. Of course that could be because he finds any opportunity to haunt the hair and make-up trailer where Cynthie seems to have established a little gang: his crush on Patty is astronomical. I swear I saw him doodling their names surrounded by hearts yesterday.

Either way, what he suggests makes sense, and so without further conversation the three of us unbuckle our belts. As we stand on the threshold of the door, brandishing them, I can't help laughing. Obviously it's an annoying practical joke, and I'm tired after a long day of filming, but still, there's something about three grown men about to go on a balloon-bursting frenzy that feels ... *fun*.

Not that I'd ever admit that to the architect of this particular piece of nonsense.

'On your marks,' Arjun says, clutching his buckle.

'Get set,' Scott adds.

'Go!' I yell, and the three of us charge forward into the trailer, stamping our feet and jabbing into the balloons, which pop easily enough once the sharp prongs dig in.

Immediately, it becomes clear we've made a huge mistake.

'SHIT!' I yell.

'Ack!' Arjun sputters.

'Is this ... glitter?' Scott asks ponderously.

As the cloud of multi-coloured sparkles settles over the three of us, I decide this question is rhetorical. Unfortunately, Scott elects to pop a couple more balloons, just to make sure.

'Stop, stop!' I am literally spitting purple glitter as I grab his arm. 'She's filled all of them!'

There's a choke of laughter from behind us, and I swing round to find Cynthie, Hannah, Liam and Patty cracking up outside.

There's a flash as Patty takes a polaroid of the three of us, shell-shocked and sparkling like a trio of fucking magical unicorns in the doorway.

'Oh no,' Cynthie says, solemn and wide-eyed. 'What happened here?'

'*You*,' I growl, starting towards her, and she dances back.

'Uh uh,' she waves her finger at me. 'Don't come too close. I don't know if you're aware of this, but it's very hard to clean up glitter. That stuff gets *everywhere*.' She smirks, her gaze running slowly from my face to my feet, and then – pointedly – over my shoulder towards my trailer, which looks like a Jackson Pollock/My Little Pony collaboration.

I close my eyes as I realize she's right. I'm going to be finding glitter in my things for the rest of filming. At least I'd changed out of my costume and I'm wearing my own clothes ... although that was probably part of her plan. I don't think she'd do anything to actively sabotage the film, but then again, I hadn't seen this coming, so I suppose anything is possible.

I glare at the little she-devil in front of me. 'Cynthie Taylor,' I say dangerously, though I'll admit the glitter all over my face is probably ruining the menacing picture I'm trying to present. 'You're going to regret this.'

She doesn't even flinch, only laughs and turns to walk away. 'Ooh,' she calls over her shoulder, 'I'm quaking in my boots.'

Patty takes another picture, and hands the still-developing polaroid to me, careful not to touch my glitter-covered hands. 'A little memento,' she says, then she glances over at Arjun, and winks. 'Looking good, boys.'

Arjun's big, lovelorn eyes are glued to her as she shimmies away.

'You're not being subtle,' I tell him.

'I'm not trying to be. She says I'm too nice for her,' Arjun replies sadly, still watching Patty go. 'But, man, every time I see her ... my heart ...' He lays a hand over his chest.

'So what do we do now?' Scott asks, eying the remaining balloons with trepidation.

I look down at the photo in my hand – three startled, sparkly faces stare back at me. 'First,' I say, 'we dispose of these' – I gesture at the balloons – ' ... *very carefully*. And then, we plan how to get even.'

It takes us ages to transport the balloons to a safe spot for bursting. We handle each one like it's a tiny explosive device about to detonate and we're the bomb squad. Scott digs us out some paint-spattered hooded coveralls from the props department so we even look the part. I spend the time focussing on how sweet my revenge will taste.

By the time I'm back at Alveston Hall, it's late and I'm exhausted. I've taken three showers but am still finding bits of glitter not only on my body and my clothes, but somehow all over my room here as well. I glare down at the smear of pink glitter on my favourite T-shirt, and when my phone rings the name on the screen makes my heart sink.

'Hi, Mum,' I say, reluctantly picking up the call.

'Hello, darling,' Mum's voice rings out. 'Your father is here, too.'

'Oh, good.' I sink down onto the side of the bed, picking at the glittery T-shirt with my free hand. 'I thought he was still filming in France.'

'Got back yesterday,' my dad booms. He likes to project when he's on the phone, like he's in a thousand-seat theatre and you're sitting at the back. 'Rained the whole bloody time. And that director didn't know his arse from his elbow. I don't care how many Academy Awards the man owns, he doesn't have the first clue about Voltaire. No fucking subtlety!' This last part is bellowed without a hint of irony.

'I'm sure you were great,' I mutter.

He scoffs. 'It wasn't *my* performance that was the problem. Speaking of which . . .'

'Jack, your father and I were watching the dailies and we have some notes.' My mum's voice is echoing as if she's stepped away from the phone. There's the distinctive sound of ice hitting a glass.

'Dailies?' I repeat, confused. 'What do you . . . Wait . . . Do you mean the dailies from *A Lady of Quality*?' I laugh, a sound of pure disbelief.

'Of course,' Mum replies tranquilly.

'I—' I start, and then stop, my brain unable to take in what she's saying.

'You've got to work on your diction,' my dad cuts in. 'It's like all those years with the vocal coach were for nothing. Enunciate! Are you doing your warm-ups? You should know better than to skip them.'

'How did you even get hold of the dailies?' I ask, rubbing my forehead. 'Jasmine and Logan aren't sharing them with us.'

'But darling, you know Peter's one of the producers!' Mum's voice is closer to the phone again. 'You must have expected he'd share them with us.'

'No,' I manage. 'It hadn't occurred to me at all.'

'The girl's not as bad as I thought she'd be,' Dad says. 'Bit green.'

'She's got a very common face,' Mum sniffs.

'But I do feel there needs to be more dynamism in your move-ment,' Dad carries on as if she hasn't spoken. 'Your performance is lacking a certain ...'

'Spark?' Mum suggests.

'Spark!' he agrees happily, and I'm glad the two of them are having a nice time, because I feel like I'm about to be sick.

'More dynamic movement,' I echo hollowly. 'Got it.'

'Now,' Dad continues, and there's the sound of paper shuffling. 'Let's talk about the scene in the ballroom ...'

It's another forty minutes before I manage to get off the call, and by that point I'm limp with exhaustion. My head is pounding, but inside I just feel ... numb. I want to lie down and sleep for a week. My parents' copious notes on my apparently lacklustre performance circle round and round in my head. It will be a miracle if I can get through a single line tomorrow. Crushing bands of tension wrap themselves around my chest.

I know I should be *grateful*. It's just hard when sometimes I feel like the disappointing product of an experiment, as if they were hoping that between them they'd create some sort of super-actor. But instead they ended up with me.

I look down at the phone in my hand and notice in a detached sort of way that my fingers are shaking. A fleck of glitter on my phone case catches the light, and I stare at it for a moment then close my eyes, drawing in a shaky breath. Cynthie's face swims into focus behind my eyelids. She's wearing the smirk that stretched across her lips earlier. Something breaks through the numbness then, something hot and bright.

Cynthie.

I push my parents' voices aside, focus my attention instead on the chaotic little demon who is turning my life upside down. Tomorrow, I'll get her back for what she pulled today. I lie down, my head hitting the pillow. It's Cynthie I'm thinking of when I fall asleep.

The next morning, Scott and I stand, poised outside the hair and make-up trailer. The muffled sound of conversation and laughter indicates that the group inside have no idea what's about to happen.

I can almost visualize Arjun reaching carefully through the open window we have scoped out.

'What was that?' Liam's voice rings with alarm, as the first domino falls.

There's a crashing sound, a stifled expletive.

And then the screaming starts.

When the door to the trailer bursts open, and the four of them come tumbling out, I'm ready with my own camera. There's even more shrieking than I had expected, and the sound is music to my ears. I let the laugh that's been building up in my chest loose, and press the shutter.

When the flash bursts, Cynthie comes to a screeching halt in front of me, her mouth hanging open. I watch the realization dawn in her eyes.

'Is it on me? Is it on me?' Liam's voice is shrill, and he and Patty dance around on the spot while Hannah bats ineffectually at their clothing.

'Stop,' Cynthie wheezes, cutting through their panic. 'It wasn't real. It wasn't . . . It was . . . *him*.' She points at me, venom in her words.

I don't care; I'm too busy laughing. When I went to Pete in the prop department and explained the situation, he was only too happy to let us dig into their supplies. One extremely realistic, remote-controlled tarantula later, I knew we were in business.

'Wait . . . what?' Patty stares at me, wide-eyed.

'How?' Liam asks.

I look past them, and Arjun wanders nonchalantly round the side of the trailer, a grin on his face. He pulls a remote from his pocket and drops something to the floor. The spider skitters towards them, and even though they know it's fake now, Liam and Patty jump back, cursing like sailors.

'You shouldn't leave your windows open,' I say with a shrug. Arjun sends the spider running back towards him and scoops it up off the ground, waggling it in the air. In fairness, the thing is absolutely, horrifyingly realistic, all hair and legs.

I look down at the polaroid of the four of them jumping around in a chaotic blur. 'I think I'm going to frame this one.' I smirk. 'Although, maybe Pete will want to pin it up in the props trailer? Just goes to show what good work those guys are doing.'

Cynthie takes a step towards me but I don't budge, and suddenly she's right there in my space. God, it feels good to get back at her. The fury is pumping off her body and it's doing something intoxicating to my bloodstream. I think I'm drunk on sweet, sweet revenge, and I like it. The bad taste that last night's phone call from my parents left behind is gone now. I feel invincible.

Then, just when I think she's about to start yelling, Cynthie does something totally unexpected: she lifts her hand and runs her fingertip lightly over the curve of my cheekbone.

And everything stops.

I exhale in surprise. She's so close that the toes of her scuffed trainers kiss my own. My gaze drops to her mouth, and the moment stretches between us. Time thickens and slows and her perfect pink lips part, drawing in a ragged breath. I lift my gaze up to meet hers, and something flares in her eyes.

Cynthie takes a sharp step back, but then she steadies herself. 'Sorry,' she says, her expression composed, her voice full of nothing but triumph as she holds up her finger, 'just thought you'd want to know you missed a spot.' A fleck of gold glitter shimmers in the early morning light.

I can't do anything but stare at her, while I still feel the ghost of her touch, hot on my cheek.

'I can't believe you did that, Arjun,' Patty's voice is a welcome distraction, interrupting us, as she glares daggers at the man in question.

Arjun's smile only widens. He shrugs. 'Maybe I'm not such a nice guy after all.'

There's a beat of silence.

Liam lets out a little hoot, and I choke on a laugh. Even Cynthie looks amused.

Patty blinks, dazed, and I'm pretty sure my friend's chances just increased exponentially.

I return my attention to Cynthie, my galloping heart mostly back under control. It's just the rush of the prank, that's all. The thrill of victory obviously feels a lot like being painfully turned on.

'I told you that you'd regret messing with us.'

'To be fair, we didn't know Scott and Arjun would get involved,' Cynthie crosses her arms. 'We were only gunning for you.'

'I quite liked it,' Scott says now. 'The glitter was a good touch. Clever.'

I shake my head, but Cynthie's smile grows. 'Thanks, Scott,' she says, pleased. 'At first I thought water balloons, but then I realized glitter was so much more . . .'

'Evil?' I supply.

'But now we're even, right?' Scott asks innocently. That sweet, summer child.

Cynthie and I both laugh like a pair of maniacs.

'Even?' I say, glaring at her. 'You must be joking. She's been pranking me since filming began.'

'We haven't even started,' Cynthie hisses. 'I won't be satisfied until he's face down in the dirt, weeping for his mother.'

I don't even want to think about why the weird feelings of arousal intensify at this – that's going to require the intervention of a qualified psychoanalyst.

'Bloody hell, Cyn,' Liam's eyes widen.

'Very cool,' Patty whispers with a look of respect.

Hannah only chuckles fondly, as if her friend is being adorable.

My lip curls. 'And I won't be satisfied until you're on your knees, *begging* me to stop.' The words come out in a low rumble.

I watch as Cynthie's pupils are blown wide, two pools of black swallowing her green–gold irises, her breath catches, her teeth sink into her full bottom lip.

'*Good Lord,*' Liam murmurs. I tear my gaze away from the thorn in my side, and see Liam fanning his hand in front of his face, while the others try (and fail) to stifle their laughter.

'That's enough,' I snap, annoyed that my skin feels too tight for my body, and I have to resist the urge to run my finger around the edge of my collar.

'Yes, *sir,*' Patty purrs.

'Whatever this is,' Liam stage-whispers, 'I think it's my kink.'

I let out a huff of annoyance.

'Did he just . . . growl?' Hannah asks, and her cheeks are pink, too.

I choke on a reluctant laugh, clearing my throat. 'All right, you perverts,' I say. 'We'll let you get back to your trailer. Don't want to delay filming.' I glance over at Cynthie, just long enough to meet her eyes so she'll know how unaffected I am. 'See you on set.'

'Oh, yes. See you there,' Cynthie replies.

Somehow, she makes it sound like a threat.

Chapter Fourteen

Cynthie

The pranks continue over the next week, with each side drawing in new recruits. My personal favourite effort is when Hilary in the costume department agrees to let out the seams on Jack's sleeves by an almost imperceptible amount, and then makes a (carefully scripted) innocuous comment about his arms getting skinnier. That evening I catch him doing hundreds of press-ups and I cannot contain my glee.

In retaliation, Jack manages to get the team at craft services on board, and Hannah and I show up one morning to find my entire trailer has been wrapped in clingfilm. This act of disloyalty really stings – betrayed by the same people who have been lovingly feeding me bacon sandwiches every morning.

I feel like Michael from the second *Godfather* movie.

'I know it was you, Pam,' I say sadly to the guilty-looking woman inside the food truck. 'You broke my heart. *You broke my heart.*'

Jack snorts from his seat at a nearby table, where he is busy wrapping his mouth around a sausage sandwich with what looks suspiciously like *extra* sausages inside.

I turn to glare at him, but he only shrugs. 'Just wondering if Pam should be worried about finding a horse's head in her bed.'

'Eh?!' Pam looks startled.

'That was the *first* film,' I say, my tone withering. 'You're confusing your *Godfathers*.' I turn to Pam. 'And I would never do anything to hurt you. I know you were taken advantage of by a heartless charmer.'

'I made her an offer she couldn't refuse,' Jack says, doing an irritatingly good impression of Marlon Brando, and I have to swallow my answering gurgle of laughter.

'He's just such a nice boy,' Pam says, clearly the victim of a vicious delusion. She smiles fondly at Jack, before turning back to me. 'And he did say that you'd propped a bucket of ice water over his trailer door the day before . . .'

'Mmm.' I take a moment to relive that particular incident while Jack observes me sourly. His shrieks of outrage were so delicious.

For the rest of the cast and crew, the practical jokes are a fun way of blowing off some steam. Everyone has joined in with cheerful enthusiasm, and Jasmine and Logan seem to have adopted a benevolent 'don't ask, don't tell' policy. For Jack and I, however, this isn't a game – it's war.

Despite the fact that my co-star and I are still at each other's throats on a regular basis, I have to say that the filming has been going well. Every day I feel more comfortable, more confident, I make mistakes, of course I do, but they no longer feel like they're going to bring the whole film crashing down around me. It's like Hannah said: as time slips by, the whole process starts to feel less overwhelming, more manageable. I'm learning an insane amount, and the work leaves me buzzing. I feel, for the first time, like I'm exactly where I'm meant to be.

Or, at least, I did . . . until they put me on a horse.

'It's really quite high up, isn't it?' I say breathlessly to Hattie, later that morning, while she looks utterly at ease. She's resplendent in a blue riding habit with a lot of gold frogging, and smiles at me from under her bonnet.

'You get used to it.'

'Okay,' I murmur doubtfully, as my horse – Domino – tosses her head about in a way that indicates she knows precisely how incompetent I am, and she is doing me a tremendous favour by not simply shaking me off her back.

'A filly needs to know who's in charge,' Rufus says with a leary wink. 'Horses are like women: they need a firm hand and a good hard ride every so often.' He laughs loudly at his own joke while I smile wanly and Hattie rolls her eyes.

Rufus might look like a gentleman right now, but I've been warned by several female members of the crew to make sure I'm not left on my own with him. I believe *handsy* is the euphemism.

We're currently waiting for the crew to finish setting up for the shot, and thankfully, Domino seems content to stand still. I'm not sure what I would do if she decided she wanted to go off exploring because I don't think she's buying the idea that I'm in charge.

'Honestly,' Hattie continues in the mellow, musical voice that has made her a star in the world of audiobooks, 'I've been making period dramas since long before you were born, and you spend an awful lot of time up on these lovely animals. The trainers are wonderful, and they only use very well-behaved horses. Plus, they're shooting all your galloping bits using a stunt double, so it's going to be very sedate. Just sit back and try to think of her as an armchair with a tail.'

'This chair has a mind of its own,' I say. 'Literally.'

Domino makes a huffing noise that sounds like agreement.

'See,' I exhale, tentatively patting her neck. 'Clever girl.'

'I'll admit it's tricky getting the hang of side saddle.' Hattie looks amused. 'But in some ways it's better that you haven't ridden before; this way you don't have to get used to the difference.'

'I suppose,' I reply, still nervous. 'But it would be nice to have a bit more of an idea of what I'm doing.' The couple of training sessions I squeezed in between working with the choreographer and the movement coach passed in a blur. Also, then I was wearing jeans and – crucially – a helmet. I doubt my fetching little bonnet is going to do much to protect my fragile skull if I fall off. *Oh god, don't think about falling off.*

'Nothing to it,' Rufus reassures me heartily.

We're interrupted then by the appearance of two other riders who are clearly not having the same crisis of confidence. Simon, the actor playing my fiancé, looks as at ease as Hattie – he sits, tall and lean, an elegant figure on a dappled grey horse, but I barely glance at him.

Jack.

Jack is a full sentence.

It's deeply, deeply unfair that there is obviously some thousands-year-old instinct, some biological hangover in my DNA, that means the sight of him, strong and in control on the back of a magnificent, midnight-black horse, makes all my bones feel like they're dissolving.

My eyes linger on his muscular thighs, clad in light breeches, before moving up to take in the rigid torso, the broad shoulders in the perfectly tailored jacket, the strong hands negligently wrapped around the reins, the rakish tilt of his hat casting his face in interesting, angular shadows.

There's a flash of white teeth.

'Careful, Taylor. You're drooling.' His amused voice does a fantastic job of breaking the spell.

'I was admiring the horse,' I say coldly.

'Sure you were.'

I grind my teeth together. Surprise, surprise, Jack Turner-Jones is a very experienced rider who looks incredible on a horse. Apparently it's one of many skills his parents deemed necessary from a young age. These, I have discovered in the last couple of weeks, also include fencing, speaking fluent French and playing the violin.

This is quite a contrast to the special skills that Hannah and I mastered in our early years – performing a flawless Macarena; being able to play Britney Spears' 'Toxic' on a recorder (self-taught); knowing all the words to 'The Real Slim Shady'.

'You know we've got a late start tomorrow,' Simon says, as we watch one of the unfortunate runners try to herd Logan's sheep into position with middling success.

'I *know*.' I sigh, deeply, happily. 'A lie-in!' The days have been punishingly long, more often than not starting at six a.m. and then lasting into the early hours of the evening.

'So we're all headed to the pub tonight,' Simon continues. 'You in?' He smiles hopefully at me.

'A night out actually does sound great,' I agree. I have to admit: I thought that there'd be a lot more partying on a film set, but by the time we limp back to Alveston Hall in the evenings we're all exhausted. 'I'll ask Hannah, Patty and Liam.'

'Cool,' Simon nods.

'I already asked them,' Jack butts in, his mouth curling up in satisfaction.

'What?'

'I already asked Hannah. And Patty and Liam,' he repeats slowly, as if I'm having trouble keeping up.

'Why would *you* invite them?' I straighten, my voice laced with suspicion, and I feel Domino's muscles ripple underneath me, a reminder that she's not – in fact – an armchair. I go as still as possible, and Domino doesn't move any further. When I'm sure it's safe, I glance over to the side, where Hannah usually sits, behind the wall of camera equipment, but she's not there.

'I don't know where you get the idea that I don't get on with people,' Jack muses. 'I happened to run into them a few minutes ago, and I invited them out. It's not a big deal.'

'But you must have known they'd invite *me*,' I say slowly.

Jack only shrugs, but I leap on this like a cat on one of those little laser pointers.

'Why, Jack,' I bat my lashes, beaming wide. 'If you wanted me to come along, you could have just asked.'

Hattie smothers a laugh.

'It's not their fault if they have terrible taste in friends,' Jack says, bored.

'Anyway,' Simon puts in, clearly trying to smooth out the tension. 'It'll be great. And I'm glad you're coming.' He smiles at me, and I smile back.

When I glance over at Jack, he is glaring darkly at the pair of us.

'Okay, gang,' Logan shouts then. 'Sorry for the delay, but we're ready to run through now.'

He and Jasmine come and stand in front of the five horses.

'So, as we practised, we start off with Jack, Hattie and Rufus at the back with Simon and Cynthie in front. After Rufus's last line, we should be approaching the curve in the path, which is where Simon and Jack change places, so that Jack and Cynthie can finish out the scene,' Jasmine says, gesturing with her hands as she talks. 'We're going to be doing multiple shots, so don't worry too much about the choreography running smoothly, just make sure you're on the mark for your lines. Got it?'

We all nod in agreement, and I try to ignore the flutter of nerves in my belly. Having to stay in character while another part of my brain is trying to make a horse do choreographed moves, sounds like a nightmare, but I try to remember what Hattie told me.

'Just an armchair with a tail,' I murmur.

Domino makes a huffing sound, deeply offended, and Hattie gives me a thumbs up.

It takes us a while to get into position, and then – as expected – the first couple of takes are a write-off. All five of us are so busy wrangling the horses and remembering where we're supposed to be, that I'm not the only one who falls out of character. Eventually, though, I start to feel more comfortable with the rhythm of it, and Domino is reassuringly chilled out.

'When we finish this, you're getting all the apples you can eat,' I murmur to her, and her ears twitch. I pat her neck and think maybe all this time I've been a secret horse-person. Maybe horses and I just get each other and I've missed my true calling as an Olympic equestrian. Plus, I bet I'd look amazing in the boots.

On the next take, I'm actually able to get into it, and I've reached the part of the scene where I'm riding beside Jack, when I notice that his hands are shaking, all the muscles in his arms held tight.

His horse – Reckless Ed – takes a couple of skittering sideways steps, and Jack is clearly trying to stop him from pulling away in the wrong direction.

'Cut!' Logan calls, and he and Lucy, the horse trainer, hustle over.

'What's the problem?' Logan asks, as Lucy holds Reckless Ed's head in her hands and murmurs to him.

'I don't know,' Jack grits out. 'He's fighting me on every step. I think something must have spooked him.'

Logan looks to Lucy, who shrugs. 'He seems fine now,' she says, after checking the horse over.

'Okay, let's go again.' Logan nods. 'Reset.'

Unfortunately, the same thing only happens once more, and Jack isn't able to get through his lines, too busy focussing on keeping the horse under control, as Reckless Ed repeatedly tries to charge down towards the cameras.

'I'm so sorry.' Lucy looks flustered, having checked him over again. 'I have no idea what's wrong. He's never done this before.'

'That name seems a little on the nose at the moment, Reckless,' I say to the horse, trying not to look smug from atop my own perfectly behaved animal. I'm definitely planning on hand feeding Domino an entire packet of Extra Strong Mints as soon as we're done.

'Are you doing this?' Jack hisses at me, as we take our places to try again.

'What?' I ask, startled.

'Is this some stupid prank?'

I blink. 'I mean I'm glad you're acknowledging my pranking prowess, but no, I haven't yet mastered the trick of getting giant horses to do my bidding. I'm not Doctor Dolittle.'

'Don't fuck about, Taylor,' Jack says through gritted teeth. His cheeks are pink. 'We're filming; this is serious.'

I inhale sharply. 'I'm not doing anything. How *could* I be doing this?'

Jack only makes a rumbling sound of frustration.

'Maybe if there's something bothering him, we should give him his head for a minute, and see what he does,' Lucy suggests after another aborted effort at the scene.

It certainly seems that Reckless Ed has his own agenda, because the second Jack relaxes his hands on the reins, the horse heads straight for the cameras ... no, not the cameras, but the folding seats next to them, where my best friend sits, having returned with a travel mug of tea.

Reckless Ed trots over to Hannah, letting out a happy whinny, while Jack sits on his back, looking totally bemused.

'Errrr, what . . .' Hannah manages to squeak, her eyes enormous, before the horse butts his huge face up against hers.

She shrinks back in the seat, but he huffs a breath that ruffles her hair and then begins gently nuzzling her shoulder.

'Um. Good horse,' Hannah whispers. 'Good, giant horse with giant horse teeth.' She looks desperately in my direction, but I have no idea how to help her. 'Horses are vegetarian, right?' she asks, quaveringly.

'Huh,' Lucy frowns. 'That's weird. He only usually behaves like this with his favourite groom. Have you been spending time at the stables?'

'The closest I've ever been to a horse is seeing one out the car window,' Hannah says, and now that it seems unlikely Reckless Ed is about to take a bite out of her, she reaches tentatively up to pat his neck. The horse makes another happy, huffing sound, and I can't bite back my laughter.

'He's in love with you, Han,' I giggle.

'Can't blame a lad for trying!' Rufus guffaws.

'Here,' Lucy says, grabbing hold of Reckless Ed's harness and leading him away. 'I'm sorry but I think if maybe you could remove yourself from the set, we should be fine.'

'Absolutely,' Hannah gathers her things and practically sprints back towards base. 'Just let me know if you need anything on the walkie-talkie, Cyn!'

I'm too busy laughing to reply. Rufus, Hattie, Simon and half the crew are also in hysterics. Jack looks deeply pissed off, and that only makes me happier.

As predicted, now that Hannah is gone, Reckless Ed seems more than happy to co-operate, and the rest of filming goes smoothly, although it takes longer than expected as the sun keeps going in and out and we have to make sure we cover the scene, getting every shot in sunshine and under cloud, while head electrician, Sam, stares up at the sky shouting things like 'Sun in about three minutes' like a very shit Nostradamus.

'So, are you going to apologize for accusing me of sabotage?' I ask Jack when we finish the final take. My feet are back on solid ground and my legs are shaky. My non-existent core is also suffering – muscles that I didn't even know I had are aching.

He scoffs. 'I wouldn't put it past you to stuff your friend's pockets full of sugar lumps, just to make me look like a fool.'

'If only I'd thought of it,' I say smiling sweetly. 'But then, it doesn't look like you need any help from me. Don't worry.' I pat him on the arm. 'You can apologize tonight . . . The drinks are on you, posh boy.'

Then I walk off, a definite spring in my step. It seems the universe is firmly on my side in the prank war. Maybe Liam was right and karma is going to catch up with Jack in the end. Still, it's always fun to give karma a bit of a nudge.

Chapter Fifteen

Jack

There are about thirty of us who have decided to make the most of our morning off tomorrow by heading out for a drink tonight. A bunch of taxis arrive at Alveston at eight p.m. to pick us up, and we pile in while Hattie waves us off at the front door like an indulgent parent.

The prospect of a night out has everyone in high spirits, and those spirits only climb higher when we tumble out in front of a quaint-looking pub in the nearest village. In large, wonky letters, a blackboard outside the door proclaims, KARAOKE TONIGHT!!!!!!!

'Oh, yes.' Arjun rubs his hands together. 'I am about to absolutely murder some 80's power ballads. You aren't even ready.'

When I follow him through the door, the bartender looks up from behind the beer taps, her face brightening as we all filter inside. Apart from a few locals, the place is pretty dead, and I can almost see the pound signs in her eyes at the sight of us. The noise level increases dramatically, an instant buzz in the air.

Several people head straight for tables surrounding the small stage that has been set up at the back, the karaoke machine, forlorn and ignored in the middle. A bored-looking younger guy sits to the side on a bar stool, a clipboard covered in band stickers in his hand, and he, too, perks up at our rowdy entrance.

'Do you have any ABBA?' Simon's excited voice cuts over the crowd . . . It's possible that he might have already had a drink or two; he finished earlier on set than I did today, leaving once we finally had the riding scene in the bag.

What a shit show that was . . . Although once Reckless Ed's one true love was removed from the scene, it went well enough. If I hadn't been stuck on the horse's back like a useless barnacle, I'm sure I would have found it funny. As it is, let's just say I'm looking forward to a night off.

'Drinks first,' I say, and Arjun nods in agreement.

'What can I get you?' the bartender asks, after serving a couple of other customers with brisk efficiency. She's a pretty blonde with a Cornish accent and I smile as I lean against the bar.

'What do you recommend?' I pitch my voice low.

Her answering grin stretches wider. 'We have a couple of beers from local breweries that are good. I'm a tequila girl myself.'

'Nice.' I run my hand across my jaw, considering. 'I'll take two pints of the IPA and two shots of tequila.' I catch sight of Scott making his way through the crowd, and lift my hand in greeting, gesturing for him to grab a table. 'Actually make that three of each.'

'Good choice,' the bartender says with a wink.

She sets about making the drinks, and I'm half-thinking it might be nice to strike up a bit of a flirtation when I'm distracted by a familiar sweet citrus scent. One that makes all the hairs stand up on my arms.

As casually as I can manage, I turn to the side, and Cynthie is standing next to me, her forearms resting on the bar.

She's wearing tight jeans and a top made of slinky, silver fabric that leaves most of her back bare. When she turns to look up at me, her lips are painted the red of stop lights, warning signals, imminent danger, and I swear my vision goes hazy.

'You made it,' I say, blandly.

She shrugs. 'I like the company . . . with one notable exception, of course.'

'Of course.'

The bartender finishes delivering the drinks I've ordered.

'Could you add four more tequila shots to his tab?' Cynthie asks, shooting her the sort of charming smile I'm never treated to. 'And a bottle of pinot grigio?' She places her hand on my arm, and I look down at her fingers. 'Drinks are on you, right?'

'Right,' I mutter, too discombobulated to come back with a response as I hand over my card. I can't even concentrate on chatting up the pretty bartender, because Cynthie Taylor is a walking threat to my sanity, and my traitorous heart leaps about like an Olympic gymnast doing a full floor routine whenever she's near.

How is it possible to be so consistently annoyed by a person, and yet also painfully turned on by their presence? I swear, even in my dreams she won't leave me alone, and I've been waking up every morning hot, hard and increasingly frustrated. This level of obsession is troubling: I'm about five minutes away from turning into one of those stalkerish *Twilight* vampires my sister is obsessed with. I'm already alarmingly aware of Cynthie's scent; next it'll be drinking her blood under a full moon with my wolf friends (full disclosure, I may have drifted off during the film Lee dragged me to). It has to stop.

Most importantly of all there is this: all my focus needs to be on work. If there's one thing my dad has drummed into me, it's that you don't fuck around on set. The film comes first. Always. Is this totally rich coming from him, considering he met my mother on a film set and they had a raging affair when they were both married to other people? Absolutely. But it doesn't mean he's wrong . . . In fact, if anything, it's further proof that he's right. This is my chance to prove myself, and getting distracted by Cynthie Taylor and her sexy mouth is not an option.

Balancing her drinks and glasses on a tray, Cynthie only grins and cuts away through the crowd, while I stop myself from turning to watch her go.

'Three of your finest ales, please, barkeep!' Rufus suddenly booms from beside me, and I'd say he's already more than half cut as he tries to get a good look down the barmaid's top. She gives him a thin smile, and starts pouring his drinks. 'Good place, this,' Rufus says to me with a wink. 'Always nice to get a look at some of the local talent.'

When Arjun and I gather ourselves and finally make our way towards Scott, we find him grinning happily in the company of Cynthie and her little coven, all crowded around a small table in front of the stage. Arjun is, naturally, delighted. I place Scott's pint down in front of him with a little more force than necessary.

'Thanks for the drinks.' Patty smirks, as Arjun pulls out the seat beside her.

'We brought lemons and salt if anyone wants them,' Arjun says. 'Cynthie left before the bartender gave them to us.'

'She was probably distracted by Jack's shit attempts at flirting.' Cynthie snorts into her wine glass.

'No lemons for Cynthie,' I say, twitching the plate away from her. 'She's bitter enough.'

'As fun as this is,' Hannah pipes up, 'I think you two should declare a ceasefire for tonight.'

'I agree,' Liam nods. 'It *is* our night off.'

'Can't we all just be friends?' Scott asks, spreading his hands expansively, and looking at his enormous pupils, I'd say he's higher than usual tonight. '*Love* . . . right?' he finishes, profoundly.

Cynthie shrugs. 'I'm not the one you need to worry about.'

I give a short bark of laughter. 'I can be perfectly civil. It's *you*—'

I'm interrupted by Hannah's gusty sigh. 'Off to a great start, guys.'

'How about this?' I lift my shot glass, my eyes meeting Cynthie's in a challenge. 'Temporary truce. One night only.'

Her gaze narrows. 'Sure. I can pretend I don't despise you for a few hours. Probably.'

'I mean, I guess it's something,' Liam says doubtfully.

'To peace in our time!' Patty lifts her tequila shot.

'Peace in our time.' We all echo her toast, tipping back the shots, and biting into lemon slices with grimaces and groans.

The alcohol slips pleasantly into my bloodstream, just as the microphone lets out a screech of feedback, and Jan, the second AD, launches into an enthusiastic rendition of 'Bat Out of Hell'. Just like that, the energy in the room spikes, and the air fills with whoops and cheers.

'Oh, hell yes.' Liam beams. 'I'll get us more shots. This is going to be a great night.'

'I need to sign up.' Arjun leaps to his feet. 'You haven't lived until you've heard me sing "Total Eclipse of the Heart".' He grins at Patty, who does her best not to smile back.

'You're such a dork,' she mutters, but Arjun looks far from discouraged.

In the end, everyone signs up for something, and the next hour is spent getting increasingly tipsy, and egging on whoever is on stage performing.

When it's my turn, I can't help the swagger in my step. I had sing-ing lessons with one of the best vocal coaches in the country from the age of nine until I was sixteen, so I approach the microphone with confidence. My go-to karaoke track is 'I'm on Fire' by Bruce Springsteen, and I'd love to say that I manage to avoid looking at Cynthie while I sing, but that would be a lie, especially because all the lyrics about burning up for someone feel uncomfortably relevant.

For a split-second, I catch a look on her face, an answering flash of heat. Then, deliberately, she looks away and buries her face in her wine glass.

I leave the stage to enthusiastic applause.

'Wow, man,' Scott says. 'That was better than Springsteen.'

'Let's not get ahead of ourselves,' Cynthie mutters, but when Hannah sends her a warning look, she plasters on a smile. 'But it wasn't bad.'

'Can't wait to see what you've got, Taylor,' I smirk.

Something dangerous creeps into Cynthie's expression then, but she doesn't respond, only turns to the stage where Arjun is about to deliver on his promise.

This he does with more energy than skill. I wouldn't have expected 'Total Eclipse of the Heart' to inspire quite so many hip thrusts, but everyone laughs and cheers as he thoroughly enjoys himself.

Patty watches through her fingers, but she can't help the delighted chuckle that escapes her.

'Is it just me, or is this kind of hot?' she asks Liam.

'It's really something,' Liam agrees diplomatically.

After Arjun finishes, Mark and Marion go all in on 'Summer Nights' and the entire pub is on their feet, joining in, yelling the lyrics back and forth. Simon's version of 'The Lion Sleeps Tonight' is another hit – his falsetto taking everyone by surprise. It's a good night. Cynthie and I even manage to remain reasonably civil, barely glaring at each other at all.

I'm surprised when my name is called again, but Arjun has signed the pair of us up for a duet, and apparently I'm taking Kiki Dee's part on 'Don't Go Breaking My Heart'. I do my best, but when Arjun's enthusiasm leads to him singing both parts and attempting some interesting harmonies, I'm laughing too hard to concentrate on hitting the notes. I wonder why it feels better that way.

Eventually, the guy with the clipboard shouts Cynthie's name. Hannah's head snaps up.

'Cyn ...' she says as her friend gets to her feet. 'What are you singing?'

That wild look is back, and Cynthie says nothing.

Apparently this means something to Hannah, because her eyes widen in alarm. 'No,' she shakes her head vehemently. 'Cyn, you promised after last time ...'

'Don't worry about it,' Cynthie murmurs, sliding around the table and heading for the stage to raucous applause from the crowd.

'Oh, shit.' Hannah's head sinks into her hands.

'What's going on?' Patty asks, frowning in confusion.

'It's a Code Black Velvet,' Hannah whispers, as if that means anything. 'Just ... brace yourselves.'

I'm as baffled by this as the others around the table, but we all turn to watch as Cynthie moves to the centre of the stage and picks up the microphone.

A moment later the air fills with the sultry twang of a guitar, a pulse of bass, the soft crash of a snare, and Cynthie sends Hannah a wink, before she starts moving in time to the beat, her hips swaying in a hypnotic, sinuous motion.

Something electric moves through the room. There's a collective intake of breath, even before she opens her mouth and starts to sing about Mississippi in the middle of a heat wave.

Her voice.

I was so unprepared for her voice. It's dark, husky magic. It sounds like the title of the song she sings – soft, seductive, just a little rough. The entire room is spellbound, and something alarming is happening inside me. I wonder, dimly, what total organ failure feels like.

A whoop from the crowd breaks the spell, and the temperature spikes, the room suddenly ten degrees hotter.

'Whoa,' Scott murmurs, his eyes like saucers, but this time I don't think it's drugs; this time it's all Cynthie.

'Oh my God,' Patty croaks. 'This is the hottest thing I've ever seen.'

'I am having some very confusing feelings.' Liam is breathless.

I can't say anything. Nothing at all.

'She promised she wouldn't do this song anymore.' Hannah's voice is muffled, her head still in her hands. 'Last time she caused an actual riot.'

The news doesn't surprise me. As the music continues, it's like someone is pumping waves of pheromones straight into the air. Arjun and Patty have shifted closer together, their gazes locked, and they're not the only ones – one of the camera operators is enthusiastically making out with one of the runners in a dark corner. Someone actually howls like a wolf. I know I've heard this song before, but has it always been so . . . fucking *hot*?

Cynthie's eyes meet mine, and I'm glad we've called a truce because I can't summon the energy to sneer. I just look and look, as her voice wraps around me. I watch her red lips move and imagine them leaving their mark all over my body. Whatever she sees in my face makes her voice just that tiny bit huskier, and I have to put my beer glass down so that it doesn't shatter between my fingers.

She finishes singing and the backing track ends. There's a second of pure, crystal silence before the whole room is on its feet, stamping and whistling and calling for an encore.

Cynthie doesn't break eye contact with me. For an endless, hungry beat we stare at each other, and it's like everything else falls away. The sound of the crowd is a dull roar under the pulsing of my own blood in my ears.

Eventually, Cynthie seems to snap out of it, shaking her head and grinning at her audience. She murmurs her thanks into the microphone and steps down from the stage, chatting for a moment with the young guy who is visibly enthusing over her performance.

I turn back to the table and find five pairs of eyes trained on me.

'Well. That was . . . interesting,' Arjun says.

I want to take a swig of my drink but I can't be sure that my hand is steady, so I clench it in my lap instead.

'What?' I try to sound nonchalant, but I'm not pulling it off. I sound whatever the opposite of nonchalant is: really-fucking-chalant.

'How we all just watched you and Cynthie eye-bang each other across the room?' Patty says like it's a question. 'You don't think that's interesting?'

I can't cope with this. I already feel like my brain has been put through a blender. I am painfully aroused in the middle of a room full of my co-workers. I'm not up to fielding questions about what just happened when *I* don't know what just happened.

Fortunately, Cynthie arrives back at the table then, and the attention shifts to her.

'What?' she asks looking puzzled. Her eyes flick to mine.

I clear my throat. 'Arjun was just saying he's getting the next round in.' I look at my friend, who takes pity on me, leaping to his feet.

'Yup,' he says quickly. 'What are we all having?'

As everyone shouts out their drinks orders, I avoid looking at Cynthie and wait for the conversation to settle back into its normal rhythm.

I tell myself I'm fine.

I tell myself nothing happened.

I tell myself I'm in control.

I lie. I lie. I lie.

Chapter Sixteen

Cynthie

We arrive back at Alveston Hall just after midnight. Last orders were called and consumed before we were kicked out: rowdy, cheerful and in excellent spirits. I am happily buzzed, relaxed for the first time in weeks.

Well, almost. There was that small incident with Jack earlier. But as we've both been carefully ignoring each other since the moment he stared at me like he wanted to rip all my clothes off and fuck me on a stage in front of all our friends and co-workers and I stared back like I'd be totally okay with that, I'm sure it's all fine.

Totally fine.

Rather than call it a night, someone has lit the big fire pit in the back garden, and we cluster around it on a variety of blankets and cushions that we've gathered from the house. Thankfully, Rufus and the lairy group of crew members (all older men) he'd been knocking back pints with have peeled off elsewhere to drink themselves into a stupor.

The evening is mild, one of those perfect early-autumn nights where you can still feel the edge of summer in the air. Scott passes a joint around, and I inhale a few drags, appreciating the slow, warm feeling that gradually softens my limbs.

This is a bit like how I imagined going to university would feel – being part of a big, happy group, staying up late talking and drinking and laughing together. It was something that I worried I'd missed out on, and it's just another part of this whole adventure that feels like a gift.

Someone has a guitar, and usually I'd roll my eyes over that kumbaya-summer-camp round the bonfire nonsense, but the tequila and the weed have left me feeling generous. Maybe it's actually kind of lovely hearing someone strum a guitar under a velvet night sky full of stars.

'I don't think that joint was very strong,' Hannah murmurs from beside me where she is sprawled over the little nest of cushions we built together. 'I don't feel anything.'

'Just give it a minute,' I reply, watching the flames in the fire pit dance and twine together in a curiously erotic display. I frown. Am I getting turned on by . . . fire?

'You know what I'd love right now?' Hannah pipes up thoughtfully. 'A bag of . . . like . . .' – she casts about as if searching for the right word – 'overskirts.'

'Overskirts?'

'Yeah,' she nods seriously. 'M&M's overskirts. The overskirts they wear. Not the chocolate. The skirts.'

I wrinkle my brow. That doesn't seem right. 'The shells,' I say. 'You mean the shells.'

Hannah laughs. 'Shells? Like from the beach? I don't think so. I don't want to eat shells, Cyn.'

I laugh, too, because words are funny.

'Do you think they have any in the kitchen?' she asks after a moment, her tone hopeful.

'Any what? M&M's shells?'

'Yeah.'

'I don't think so.'

'I'm going to go check.' She gets to her feet. 'I'll be right back.'

'If you find any with their skirts on, bring them out,' I call after her. I think I could eat an entire family-sized bag without blinking right now.

Hannah lifts her hand in acknowledgement and I watch her make her way back towards the house, calling out to people as she passes, including Patty and Arjun, who ignore her because they're currently engaged in a very heavy make-out session. Patty is sitting in Arjun's lap and his fingers are buried in her hair.

'Do you mind if I sit down?' a voice asks, and I turn and peer up to find Jack looking down at me. I reach automatically for the animosity I feel around him, but I can't find it.

'Sure,' I say. 'Pull up a cushion. The fire is being . . . hot.'

'Fire will do that,' Jack agrees sitting down beside me, not so close that we actually touch, but close enough that I can feel the warmth from his body wrapping itself around me along with the heat from the flames. It's . . . a lot.

He's misunderstood what I was trying to say about the fire, but I don't correct him, only smile.

'Let me guess,' he says, examining my face like it's a piece of art up on the wall. 'You're stoned.'

I only smile wider. 'You're not?'

He shakes his head, picks at the grass by his feet. 'I don't. No judgement,' he's quick to add. 'It's just . . . My family have a bit of a history when it comes to drugs and alcohol, so I avoid the first and keep a pretty tight lid on the drinking.'

I frown, considering this. There's something deeply sad and heavy at the centre of what he just said, but I can't focus on it right now. 'You were drinking though,' I say finally. 'In the pub.'

'Yeah, a bit more than usual. I was driven to it by my awful co-worker.'

I know those words would usually make me angry, but now

I only hear a teasing note in them, and I laugh. Jack laughs too, sounding surprised.

'So,' he says after a moment, 'where did you learn to sing like that?'

'My mum,' I reply, leaning back, away from the fire so that the cool air caresses my cheeks. 'She was always singing. She wanted to be a performer, but she had to give up all that when she had me.'

'I'm sorry,' Jack murmurs.

'Why?'

'You just talked about her in the past tense, so I thought ...' he trails off, and I think if I stay quiet, he'll just change the subject. Normally, that's what I'd do.

'Oh, she's not dead,' I say instead. 'She left us. When I was eight. Poof.' I make a gesture with my hands, splaying my fingers to indicate that she disappeared like a puff of smoke. My hands are tingling, and I make the gesture again, enjoying it. 'She has a new family now.' I stare into the fire, dimly aware that saying all this would usually hurt, a needle of pain, sharp under my skin, but the weed has acted as an anaesthetic and it's surprisingly easy to open up to Jack. He's watching me, careful and steady.

'Not that *she* knows that I know that,' I continue. 'I tracked her down last year. It's funny; I thought she left so she could go and chase her dream of stardom, but all she did was move to Norwich and have a bunch of other kids. Ones that she actually wanted, I guess.' I shrug. 'I don't think they even know about me and my dad. It's like we never existed at all.'

'Shit,' Jack exhales. 'That's ... I'm sorry, Cynthie. That's ... really wrong.'

I turn to get a good look at him, and I'd forgotten that he was so close, close enough for me to see the concern softening those sharp blue eyes, the way his mouth pulls down, the small crease between his brows as if he was sad and angry. It's dangerous being this close to his face. It makes me want to run my fingers along his jaw. I can already imagine exactly how his skin would feel under my fingertips. I bet he'd taste even better than a bag of M&M's.

Warning sirens are wailing somewhere in the back of my mind, but I want to ignore them a while longer. I watch as his irises are overtaken by his rapidly dilating pupils, like drops of ink spreading in blue water, and I wonder if he lied, because from where I'm sitting, he looks pretty stoned to me.

'What about you?' I ask, and the words are rusty, like I haven't spoken for hours or days or weeks. Maybe I haven't . . . Time is doing something wavy right now.

His face snaps back, further away from me, and I pout. I liked it close.

He looks at my mouth, presses his lips together in a firm line. He shakes his head, as if to clear it, puts a bit more careful distance between us.

'What about me?' Jack repeats, confused.

I've almost lost the thread of conversation, but I grab at it before it slips through my fingers. 'Where did you learn to sing like that?'

'Ah.' He raises a hand to rub the back of his neck, a gesture I've noticed he makes when he's uncomfortable or embarrassed. 'I had singing lessons as a kid. All part of my stage training.'

I mull this over. 'Is it strange?' I ask. The question is one I've been wanting to pose for weeks now. 'Being born into it like you were?'

He exhales. He's quiet for a long time, long enough that I think maybe he won't answer, but his posture softens; he leans back, bracing himself on his elbows and looking into the bonfire. 'I don't know how to answer that,' he says in the end. 'It's all I've ever known. But . . . yeah . . . yeah, I think it's probably pretty strange. It feels like a lot of pressure, a lot of the time.' He laughs, but it's a sad sound. 'All the time, actually.'

I frown. 'That doesn't sound very fun.'

'Fun?'

'Yeah.' I gesture expansively at the scene around us. 'This is just . . . so much fun, right? Making this film. Being here with these people. Getting to perform and play and make something beautiful. It's the most fun I've had in ages. Maybe ever.'

He falls back into silence, but I don't mind. I think I could sit here like this for ever, somewhere between the cool ground and the wheeling stars overhead, with Jack beside me. It's strange to feel peaceful around him; it's never been like that with us before. Normally, I feel like there's some sort of caged animal inside me, throwing itself against the bars.

'I don't remember a time when I wasn't working towards this,' Jack says, breaking the quiet between us.

'Me neither,' I reply, and we're talking more softly now, sharing secrets. 'I decided I wanted to be an actor when I was a kid, but it was like . . . like telling people I wanted to be an astronaut. They just rolled their eyes. No one believed I could do it. Only me. And Hannah.'

'I don't remember deciding at all,' Jack murmurs. 'It just always was.'

'What about your sister? Is she an actor?'

'Lee?' Jack's brow furrows. 'No. She hates all that stuff.'

'Then you must have chosen it,' I point out. 'Or at least, she chose not to.'

He hums thoughtfully. 'I guess so. My parents certainly put a lot of money and energy into getting me here.' He says this neutrally, although there's something off about it.

'My dad doesn't get it at all,' I say. 'I mean, we never talk about it, but his silence feels pretty heavy. I always thought he resented it because it was my mum's thing . . . singing, performing.'

'You and your dad aren't close?' Jack asks.

I snort. 'No.' When it seems like he's waiting for more, I carry on, but it's like pushing open a rusty door. 'He isn't really a natural at the whole parenting thing. And then when my mum left, he was sort of . . . stuck with me, I guess.' I try to shrug like it doesn't matter, but maybe the drugs are leaving my system because I can't quite pull it off. 'Our relationship is a bit like . . . if your mum asked your next-door neighbour to keep an eye on you, and then she disappeared for twelve years.'

'That sounds . . . not ideal.' Jack says softly.

'Well, I have Hannah.' I smile. 'And her parents. They live a few houses down from us, and she and I have been best friends ever since we were in nursery.'

'Yeah, it's pretty obvious you guys are close,' Jack chuckles drily. 'She's been giving me some good death stares these last few weeks.'

I laugh. 'It's nice to have someone who's always on your side.'

'Mmm,' Jack makes a sound of agreement, but his face is sad, and I find that I don't like that. I reach out, and wrap my fingers around his wrist. It's a sudden gesture, unexpected, and both of us jolt.

I look down at my fingertips, resting either side of his pulse. Even though I want to touch him, my subconscious must have instinctively stopped me from grabbing his hand. Holding hands would feel like something . . . tender. This, this is something else. His shirt sleeves are rolled up, baring his forearms, and I watch a trail of goosebumps break out across his flesh.

Neither of us speaks, and I squeeze a little tighter, my nails leaving tiny pink crescent moons against his golden skin. It feels obscene, seeing those marks on him, knowing that I put them there, and my heart hammers relentlessly in my chest. It's barely anything. I'm touching his wrist, for god's sake . . . It's hardly a particularly erotic body part, and yet something – that something that is always just frustratingly *there* between us – flickers.

I look up and find his head bowed, his whole-body tense, like a spring coiled tight. When he lifts his gaze to meet mine, his eyes have changed again. There's nothing cool about them now. Now, they're full of storms.

I tilt my face, bringing it closer to his, close enough that for a moment we share the same air, his exhalation coasting across my lips.

I'm about to close the final painful millimetres of distance between us, when he yanks back, the movement so violent that I almost fall over. My hands spring away from him, and I feel my eyes widen.

'No,' he snaps, already getting to his feet. 'I shouldn't have ... I'm sorry. It's not appropriate to ...'

It's a jumble of half-sentences, but their meaning is painfully clear. So is the angry edge to his voice. He's rejecting me, and the swift stab of pain in my chest that accompanies this leaves me gasping for air.

He stands over me, and my brain is still too slow, still trying to catch up, so I can do nothing but gape at him as he glares down at me.

'I would *never* ...' he begins, but again he stops himself.

He would *never*? The words slash my defences to ribbons. What was I thinking? Jack Turner-Jones has made it clear over and over and over again that he doesn't consider me up to his weight.

Not good enough, my brain sings. *And you never will be.*

Had I really been about to kiss him? *Him*? The man who has been tormenting me for weeks?

'It's fine,' I say stiffly. 'I guess the truce is officially over.' But I'm talking to thin air, because Jack's already striding back towards the house.

I sit for a moment, watching as the fire dies down. All the heat is gone, the cold night air beginning to leach into my bones. I feel so small, so stupid. With a sinking heart, I realize how vulnerable I just made myself to a man who has made no secret of the fact he dislikes me. I can't believe I said all those things to him, told him so many personal, private details that I never share with *anyone*.

Eventually, Hannah appears again. She's clutching an entire block of cheese and is gnawing on it like some sort of wide-eyed woodland creature.

'Fucking hell, Cyn,' she says, collapsing unceremoniously next to me on the ground. 'You've got to try this cheese. It's the best thing I've ever tasted. I think it's, like, made by unicorns.'

She holds out the cheese to me. The label says MEDIUM CHEDDAR.

'I'm good, thanks.' I shake my head.

She looks at me, narrows her eyes. 'Hey . . . are you okay?'

I tuck my hand through her arm, lean against her. 'Yeah.' I force a smile. 'I'm fine.'

I sound so convincing, even I almost believe it.

NOW

THIRTEEN YEARS LATER

Chapter Seventeen

Jack

For our first public outing, Cynthie has suggested brunch with friends in LA. This actually makes a lot of sense: it takes some of the pressure off the two of us, but I know it also means that she'll have moral support. It will be the first time she's been seen in public for weeks so every detail has to be carefully managed. There's going to be plenty of scrutiny.

I tell myself that's why I'm feeling nervous again when I pull up to the restaurant, which is a low-key little spot in Venice, not far from the beach. There are already a couple of photographers across the street, so they must know Cynthie is in there.

'Jack!' One of them has recognized me and is calling my name. 'Over here!' There's a ripple of surprise and the cameras flash. I lift a hand in casual greeting, smile, and make my way inside. I guess that means part one of the day's plan is complete – the paparazzi know we're in the same place. Chances are there'll be more of them out here by the time we leave.

The hostess greets me with a professional smile and shows me to Cynthie's table.

'No way!' I can't help but exclaim, when I catch sight of the familiar faces. This, I hadn't been expecting.

'Hey man!' Arjun leaps to his feet and comes around the table to pull me into a hug. We pat each other on the back with plenty of manly vigour. 'It's so good to see you.'

'You too,' I reply, meaning it. Arjun and I had pretty much lost touch after we finished filming *A Lady of Quality*, which isn't unusual, but I've always felt a bit sad about it. A few years ago we started following each other on social media and have exchanged the occasional message, which is how I know he's now married to Patty.

The woman herself approaches me next, and while Arjun looks almost exactly the same, her bright red hair is dark now, shoulder-length with a wide grey streak at the front. She's added a few more tattoos to her arms, but despite the LA heat she's still wearing black leather trousers. It's nice to see some things don't change.

'Hi, gorgeous,' she says, pecking me on the cheek. 'You've only improved with age.'

I laugh. 'I was going to say the same about you, but I don't want to flirt too hard in front of your husband.' I gesture to Arjun who wraps his arm around Patty's waist. 'I can't believe you pulled it off . . . Wasn't this basically what you had written down in your dream journal?'

Patty laughs, and Arjun's own smile widens. 'I wore her down.'

'And you guys have a daughter, right?' I ask.

Arjun nods. 'Priya. She's seven and already plotting world domination.'

'And Arjun will be happy to show you a million pictures plus the fifteen physical photographs of her he carries at all times,' Patty puts in, 'just in case – and I quote – his phone explodes and the cloud turns out to be the work of our robot overlords.'

'AI, man,' Arjun shakes his head. 'It's coming for us all.'

'And Liam.' I turn to the table, where Liam sits, affectionately rolling his eyes at Arjun. 'I can't believe it; the gang is really all here.'

Liam dimples at me. 'Like any of us were going to miss this.' He gets up to give me a hug.

Hannah remains in her seat. 'Nice to see you again, Jack,' she says, a touch cool, and I have the distinct impression she's going to wait and see how this plays out before she decides if she's actually happy I'm here. Which I guess is fair enough.

That just leaves Cynthie, who has been hovering to the side while I greeted everyone else.

The smile she gives me is rueful, as I take a step towards her and bend down to give her the agreed-upon kiss on the cheek – times have changed since we last did this, now anyone with a phone can be a reporter, and it's important that we start selling ourselves as a couple.

'No awkward greetings,' Cynthie warned me when we spoke on the phone late last night, her voice curling softly through the darkness of my bedroom. 'It'd be just my luck if the first photo of us that leaked was of us banging our foreheads together or doing some awkward high-five.'

'Ruling out my go-to moves, I see,' I replied.

'Let's say you'll lean in and kiss my right cheek. Just one kiss on one cheek.'

'Have I not mentioned that I go for the traditional Normandy greeting these days? I'm a minimum of four cheek kisses kind of guy now.'

I heard the quiver of laughter she tried to repress when she said sternly, 'One kiss, right cheek.'

Now, my lips skim her right cheekbone, a light touch, the first time I've touched her in thirteen years. My heart stutters and I can't resist the temptation to lean into her. Her perfume surrounds me, and it's different now. No longer the sweet citrus scent she used to wear, but something more grown up, more sultry, like dark, ripe berries. She smells like incredibly sexy jam and I fight the urge to bury my face in her neck and inhale.

Good to know that my body is going to continue its tremendous freak-out every time we're in the same room, and that our last meeting in the hotel was not the fluke caused by residual weird feelings that I'd hoped it was.

I step back from her, and there's a flush to her skin that wasn't there a second ago.

'Hey,' she says softly.

'Hey,' I reply.

She's dressed casually in jeans, trainers, and a cropped white T-shirt that shows off a tiny sliver of her stomach. A delicate gold chain glints around her neck, and my eyes linger on her clavicle. I don't know if being turned on by a woman's bones is a low point but it certainly feels like it. Her hair is pulled up in a high ponytail, and she has sunglasses perched on top of her head. I'd be willing to bet that despite how effortless she appears there was an entire council of war about her outfit.

As I slip into the seat next to hers at the table, it's impossible not to notice the interest from other diners at the restaurant. Even in LA, spotting a celebrity like Cynthie Taylor is a big enough deal for most people to shrug off their jaded indifference. There are plenty of eyes turned in our direction, plenty of low conversations being had that are less subtle than their participants might imagine. I even spy a couple of phones being held at weird angles, so it looks like photographs are already being snapped. I wonder how long it will be before we pop up on DeuxMoi.

'So, Jack, how have you been?' Patty asks.

'Not too bad, thanks,' I reply. 'Although I guess thirteen years gives us a lot of ground to cover.'

'I can't believe it's been thirteen years.' Arjun sounds dazed.

'Surely impossible,' Liam agrees. 'When we are fresh-faced little babies.'

The waitress appears, and – establishing that everyone is starving – we order a good percentage of the menu. In no time at all she places an enormous cup of coffee in front of me, and I sigh, content.

Cynthie laughs and the sound is silvery and lovely. 'Still a caffeine fiend, then?'

I grin. 'It's only got worse actually. Scott tries to limit me to five cups a day with middling success.'

'Scott?' Arjun perks up. 'As in our Scott?'

'Yeah.' I nod. 'I don't know exactly how it happened, but after we finished filming, he just ... never left.'

'That is the most Scott way possible to get a job,' Patty chuckles.

'You'll have to bring him along next time,' Liam says. 'It would be so nice to see him.'

'I'm sure he'd love that,' I reply. 'He's away at the moment – always takes a couple of weeks off to visit his family, when I wrap up filming on the series.'

'We're big fans of *Blood/Lust*,' Arjun says then, throwing his arm around the back of Patty's chair.

'Oh?' I smile, pleased. 'That's really nice. It's a lot of fun to make.'

'Not exactly the sort of thing I thought you'd end up doing,' Hannah puts in here.

I feel Cynthie stiffen beside me, but I shrug easily. 'No. It's not the sort of thing I thought I'd end up doing either, but then a lot can change in thirteen years. I really love it, and it seems to bring people a lot of joy.'

'That's for sure,' Liam agrees. 'My god, that whole arc last season with the cursed rings? The theories we were coming up with were *wild*. I still think Bas is going to turn out to be Constantine's son, though I can't quite work out how.'

'You watch it, too?' I ask.

'We all watch it together every week,' Liam replies easily, and then – along with everyone else – he freezes.

They're all looking wide-eyed at the woman next to me, and I turn slowly to face Cynthie. She is glaring at Liam, but when she catches me looking, her expression quickly smooths out.

'You *all* watch it?' I ask.

It's her turn to shrug. 'I might have seen an episode or two.'

Arjun chokes on a laugh, and even Hannah is trying to hide her smile.

'Oh, really?' I say, delighted. 'So you get together and watch it every week?'

'*They* watch it every week,' Cynthie says sweetly. 'I find it's a good time to catch up on my puzzles.'

'Big puzzler are you?'

She inclines her head seriously. 'I mean, I don't want to blow my own horn or anything, but I have got Wordle in one go . . . twice.'

'I'm more of a crossword guy.'

She scoffs. 'You would be. I bet you even prefer the cryptic ones.'

'Of course, I'm not an animal.'

She laughs, and I do too, and then when I look back at the rest of the table it's to find everyone staring at us in bewilderment.

'Well, this is certainly *different*,' Patty says archly.

I glance over to Cynthie again, sorry to see that carefully blank expression has crept over her face. For a moment she looked the way I remember her – sparkling.

'I'm just going to use the restroom,' Cynthie says, abruptly getting to her feet. 'I'll be right back.'

There's a moment of silence, and I shift in my seat.

'So—' I start, but Hannah cuts me off.

'We need to talk,' she says.

'Okay,' I agree, and then I wait as the four of them exchange lots of significant eye contact. Finally, Patty huffs an impatient sigh.

'We need to know your intentions,' she says.

'My intentions?' I assumed that Cynthie's best friends would all be in on the plan, but maybe I was wrong. Maybe they also think we're a couple? This could get complicated . . . fast.

'Obviously we know about the arrangement,' Hannah says

briskly, and I exhale a sigh of relief, but then no one says anything more.

'In that case, I'm not totally sure I understand the question,' I reply, finally.

'Look.' Hannah crosses her arms, leaning over the table towards me. 'I was the one who told Cynthie this could be a good idea, and I still think that on balance it was the best option, but . . .' she trails off here, and bites her lip. She looks uncertain. 'Cyn has been through a really awful time,' she says quietly after a beat, and her face is suddenly bleak. 'I mean really fucking awful. And despite what you might have read, she did absolutely nothing to deserve it.'

'I never thought for a second that she did,' I interject, which earns me a slight softening of her expression.

'I'd like to get five minutes alone with that shithead,' Patty growls under her breath, and Arjun takes her hand, rubbing his thumb back and forth across her knuckles.

'Get in line.' Even gentle-hearted Liam looks like he's ready to start cracking skulls.

'So maybe you can understand our concern,' Hannah presses on. 'This might be the best plan we have right now, but you're a wild card. And you and Cyn . . . didn't exactly leave things on good terms.'

I wince. That's the understatement of the century. 'I do get it,' I say, leaning back in my chair. I want to choose my words carefully. I've been so worried about how this was going to work, about Cynthie's animosity towards me and the complication of our history, but it's clear that she's hurting, perhaps more deeply than I realized. This intervention makes me think I've only seen the tip of the iceberg.

'The last thing I'm interested in doing is upsetting Cynthie or making her life harder,' I say, finally. 'We both have our own reasons for going along with this plan, and for what it's worth I'm not the same person I was thirteen years ago. I doubt she is either. It's been a long time and . . . I want us to do better this time around.'

That is definitely the truth. Looking back on everything that happened between us, I can see now that I made a lot of mistakes, the sort of mistakes a hot-headed twenty-four-year-old is bound to make, but that justification doesn't necessarily make things easier. Those mistakes sit between the two of us, dark and heavy, and now Cynthie and I have to find a way to deal with them.

'I know she's been going through a lot,' I add. 'My guess is she could use someone else who's on her side. I'd like to be that for her, if she'll let me.'

It's a big *if*.

I clear my throat and take a sip of my coffee, trying not to flinch as the four of them stare at me like we're in an extremely intense job interview.

Eventually, Hannah blinks. 'Okay,' she says. 'We'll take you at your word. But I should warn you, if you hurt her—'

'We know ways to make you suffer,' Liam says sweetly.

'And how to get rid of the evidence.' Patty's smile is like a knife.

'Welcome to the family!' Arjun beams.

Chapter Eighteen

Cynthie

When I get back to the table after giving myself a stern talking to in the bathroom mirror, it's obvious that my friends have been grilling Jack. He has this slightly glazed look in his eyes, and I notice that his coffee cup has been refilled again.

He summons a smile when he sees me, and that smile does something to my knees. I really thought that thirteen years would have been enough time for the relentless sexual tension between us to dissipate, but if anything it's even worse. He's so gorgeous it's *dazzling*. Ever since he walked into the restaurant, I've been trying not to look directly at him, like trying to safely observe a solar eclipse.

He's also not being a dick, and that's just as confusing as his outrageous good looks. He's being funny, and charming, and he's getting on so well with my friends, while I'm here struggling with the heat and the wanting and feeling pretty bewildered by it all – especially considering that a week ago I swore off all men for ever and committed myself to a life of celibacy and self-improvement, a claim which Hannah had found insultingly funny.

'Oh, no,' Jack says, looking down at the photo Arjun has thrust under his nose. 'You guys made the actual cutest kid on the planet.'

'Right?' I agree. 'Embarrassing for all other children. The pinnacle has been reached.'

Jack glances back up at Arjun and grins. 'She's got to be, like, 99% Patty's DNA, right?'

'She got her mum's looks,' Arjun agrees, 'but her dance moves are all me.'

He pulls up a video of him and Priya singing and dancing to *Moana* while Patty cackles in the background. Arjun is shirtless and wearing a Maui wig and a grass skirt made of green streamers. It's a video that I've watched approximately one million times, and Jack chuckles, delighted.

'That's nothing,' Hannah huffs. 'You need to see me and Cyn teaching her the Macarena. Passing on our rich cultural history to the youth.'

'The children are our future,' Liam intones solemnly. 'Priya and I are having a Britney debrief next week. She has a lot of questions about the eye shadow in the "Oops! . . . I Did it Again" video.'

'That is definitely going to end with me in a red PVC catsuit,' Arjun groans.

'Excellent.' Patty smirks.

'Hey,' Jack leans in close to me, his voice a warm touch against my ear. 'There are a couple of people with a pretty good view of us, who are taking photos. Is it okay if I put my arm around the back of your chair?'

I'm surprised but pleased that he asked first, mostly because I think I would have jumped out of my skin the second he touched me if I hadn't had any warning. Now, at least, there's time to prepare myself.

'Sure,' I whisper, and when I turn to look at him, his face is still close enough for me to see every silver fleck in those blue, wolf eyes of his.

His arm slips around my back, and when his fingers toy casually with the end of my ponytail, I realize how laughable it is that I thought I could prepare myself. I am instantly enveloped in the scent of him, clean linen, and the sort of aftershave they make mad TV adverts about — men who smell like the desert and also pine trees and the moon, then suddenly they're walking through the stars and for some reason there's a panther ... I'm getting distracted. I can't concentrate on anything when his big body is right next to me, and his white T-shirt strains around his biceps.

We sit like this for a while, and I keep half my mind on the conversation, and half on the exact position of Jack's fingers at all times. Okay ... maybe it's more like forty per cent on the conversation sixty per cent on him. Thirty/seventy at the worst. At one point he leans forward to pass Patty a dish: the hand behind me slides up, brushing the bare skin of my arm, and I drop my fork with a clatter.

I definitely need to get a grip. On more than my cutlery.

Eventually, Jack leans into me again and asks, 'Do you like ice cream?'

I lift my brows. 'Is that some sort of trick question?'

'Not at all.' His mouth pulls up. 'There's a really good ice cream shop down the block. I wondered if you wanted to go get one ... It'll give us a chance to see if the photographers have taken the bait.'

'Right,' I say, butterflies suddenly alive in my stomach. 'Good idea.'

I must not look very happy because he removes his arm from around me and says, carefully, 'But we don't have to do that. I know what we planned, but you can change your mind about any of it at any time. We're in charge here, so we can absolutely call it a day.'

I feel the blood rush to my cheeks, because the vague plan that we made for today involved us getting 'caught' kissing by the photographers, though we hadn't yet gone into the details of how we were going to make that happen. It would depend on if the paparazzi turned up.

When I first suggested this plan, I told myself that it was absolutely no different from kissing someone on camera; it was only acting a part. Unfortunately, what I had conveniently put out of my mind was that kissing Jack on camera had been a disaster of epic proportions. Now that he's actually here in front of me, that particular memory comes sharply back into focus, and I would rather it didn't.

'No,' I say after a moment. 'It's fine. It would be good to know what we're dealing with either way. Ice cream is a good idea.'

'Well, ice cream is *always* a good idea,' Jack says. 'But as for the rest of it, let's go out there and then play it by ear.'

'Improv.' I smile weakly. 'I like it.' I turn to face my friends. 'Okay, guys, we're going to love you and leave you.'

Everyone gets to their feet, and there's a round of hugging and kissing before Jack and I slip away.

'I wonder—' I begin as we make our way outside, but I don't have time to finish that thought because there are about twenty photographers camped outside and they all start going wild as soon as we walk out the door.

'Okay,' Jack says, curving his body protectively to shield me from the barrage of flashes. 'I guess they really did take the bait.' For the first time he sounds nervous.

'Are you all right?' I ask, glancing up at him.

I have a terrific view of the way his jaw tightens. 'Yeah, it's just a bit more than I was expecting.'

I shrug. 'Maybe you didn't hear, but I'm a pretty big scandal right now. Everyone wants a picture of me looking sad and repentant. Or – even better – out of control and on a bender.'

He looks down at me, and his eyes narrow. 'Well, fuck that. How about a photo of you looking happy and eating ice cream instead?'

I manage a smile. 'That sounds good.'

We head down the block, and the photographers follow or try to run in front of us, taking pictures and shouting our names.

'Cynthie! Jack!' one of them calls. 'Does this mean you guys are back together?'

We ignore them as best we can, and Jack continues to walk on the outside, blocking me from the worst of the rabble. He doesn't hold my hand – we haven't discussed hand holding, and I'm starting to realize he's really not going to touch me unless I ask him to. So he doesn't hold my hand, but he stays close to me, closer than a casual acquaintance would. The photographers are loving it.

We reach the ice cream shop, which is charming with its stripy red awning, and provides a sweetly innocent backdrop for our 'date'. I wonder if that's why Jack thought of it. When we duck inside, the shouts of the photographers cut off dramatically. The shop is relatively empty, so there aren't too many curious faces in here.

Jack exhales a sigh of relief. 'That was a bit more intense than I'd anticipated. People aren't usually so bothered about getting a photo of me buying ice cream.'

'Half those guys were parked outside my house twenty-four/seven for the first couple of weeks after the story broke,' I say. 'I guess I shouldn't be surprised they've turned up. Gayle did say there'd be a lot of interest.'

Jack's mouth thins. 'It looks like she was right. I hadn't really thought about this whole thing except in a sort of abstract way ... The reason you have to do it ... It's not right. I'm sorry.'

'Don't be sorry. You're helping me. This is much better than doing it by myself.'

He still looks annoyed. 'I didn't exactly volunteer because of my chivalrous nature,' he says. 'And that pisses me off.'

'It pisses you off?'

His eyes meet mine. 'Yes, it does. I'm pissed off with myself.'

'Would ice cream help?' I ask after a moment.

There's another beat and then he sighs. 'It wouldn't hurt. Come on, my treat.'

We move to the counter and eye all the flavours. There are loads, and each one sounds better than the last. 'I'll get a scoop of lavender honey in a waffle cone,' I decide.

Jack wrinkles his nose. 'Aren't those ingredients they make soap with?'

'All right, Mr Sophisticated Palate. What are you having?'

'Bubblegum,' he says decisively. 'With rainbow sprinkles.'

I laugh. 'What are you? Six years old?'

His mouth tips up, his eyes crinkle. 'It's called nurturing your inner child, Taylor.'

'Wow,' I say as he accepts his lurid blue ice cream. 'I had no idea bubblegum ice cream was therapy.'

'Lots of things can be therapy,' Jack says, licking his ice cream as I try really, really hard to look away. 'But actual therapy is usually the best therapy.' He cocks his head, levels his gaze at me. 'Have you got someone you can talk to at the moment?'

'I have Hannah.' I take my own ice cream from the woman behind the counter, while Jack hands over some cash and tells her to keep the change.

It's not like it's the first time anyone has suggested therapy to me, but I can't bring myself to do it. Opening up like that to a stranger? Especially when so much of me is already up for public consumption? Let's just say I don't find the idea appealing.

Jack seems to accept the answer, or at least he doesn't pry further. He only lifts his brows and says, 'So do you want to eat these in here, or do you want to face the screaming hordes?'

I lick my ice cream thoughtfully, and it's so delicious, I moan in appreciation. Beside me, Jack flinches like he's just received an electric shock.

'What?' I ask, startled.

'Nothing.' He clears his throat. 'Brain freeze.'

I wince sympathetically. 'The worst.' The photographers hover outside the window. 'I think if you can bear it, we should go and walk a bit. After all, the more pictures they get now, the better.'

'Sounds good,' Jack replies easily.

'And then we can ... you know ... what we talked about,' I manage, and I want to kick myself, because instead of sounding cool and nonchalant, I sound like a twelve-year-old girl, and I just *know* that I'm blushing, too.

To his credit, Jack tries to hide his amusement when he says. 'Kiss, you mean?'

I blush harder. 'Er ... yeah,' I mumble.

Jack makes a thoughtful noise. 'Have you ever seen *While You Were Sleeping*?'

'What?' I ask, thrown by the seemingly random segue.

'*While You Were Sleeping*,' he continues. 'It's a film—'

I cut him off. 'Um, yes, I have seen the seminal 1995 classic *While You Were Sleeping*,' I huff. 'And it's not just a *film*; it is a work of cinematic perfection. Hannah and I watch it every Christmas. Why?'

Jack's smile is back, the really good, charming one, the one that makes it feel like we're in cahoots. 'Because I was thinking instead of kissing, I could just ... lean.'

My breath catches. 'You mean like Bill Pullman does in the movie?'

'Yeah.'

My brain goes fuzzy, because while what Jack is suggesting might *sound* like it's a step down from kissing, *everyone* knows that the Bill-Pullman-Leaning scene in *While You Were Sleeping* is the hottest thing to ever happen.

'"*Leaning*",' Jack says, directly quoting the film, his voice going soft and gravelly like Bill's does, '"*involves wanting and accepting ...*"'

Dead. I am dead.

'Yes, I know the line,' I say breathlessly, aiming for brisk. 'I know the scene, and I guess it could work. It could be better, I mean. I don't know. Ha. Hahahaha.' Now I am laughing, and I sound like I've been sucking down a load of helium.

Get it together, Cyn!

'Cool,' Jack agrees, politely ignoring whatever is happening to me. 'And what if we hold hands? Holding hands isn't really a big "friend" thing once you're over the age of seven.'

'I don't know,' I point out. 'You are eating a bright blue ice cream cone.'

'With rainbow sprinkles,' Jack adds. He puts on his sunglasses and holds out his free hand to me. I look at it for a second, and then, carefully, tentatively slide my fingers through his.

'Ice cream cones and hand-holding,' I say. 'This is a very wholesome date. Is that for their benefit? It's a clever idea,' I add quickly, so he won't think I mind.

'Honestly, I wish I could say I'm that Machiavellian,' Jack replies after a moment. 'I just wanted to get you an ice cream.'

That makes me smile.

'Right.' I draw back my shoulders. 'You ready?'

'Let's do it.'

When we go back outside, it seems like the paparazzi have been spawning, and we make a truly ridiculous picture as we walk down the pavement, eating our ice creams, holding hands and pretending we don't notice the horde of screaming people dogging our steps.

Thankfully, we're both exceptional actors.

We wander aimlessly, under a brilliant blue sky. The road is full of little shops and occasionally we stop and pretend to look in the windows. There are palm trees lining the street, and a gentle breeze takes the worst of the bite out of the blazing sun. All in all, it's a perfect day, and I suppose that we look perfect, too.

We didn't co-ordinate on purpose but even our outfits match: Jack's white T-shirt and worn Levis fit him like a dream; he's left his face unshaven again, and with the tousled hair and sunglasses he looks alarmingly handsome.

He tugs my hand, pulling me into the doorway of another shop, and holds his ice cream out towards me. I've already demolished mine, but he's taken his time, there's a little left at the bottom of the cone. 'Before I finish this off, I think you should try it, given all the stick you've given me over my flavour choices.'

I roll my eyes, but take a bite. Sugar explodes over my tongue, and I experience a little thrill about putting my mouth where his mouth has been, which might be a new low.

'Well?' he asks, polishing off the last bit.

'I think I need to book a visit to my dentist.'

He reaches out, and his thumb brushes the corner of my lips. 'You have a little, just here,' he says, his voice rough, and then, slowly, he lifts his thumb to his mouth and sucks it clean.

'Thank you,' I manage. I'm glad that my eyes are hidden behind my own sunglasses, because I can only imagine how wildly horny they are. Suddenly ice cream and hand-holding don't seem wholesome at all. Suddenly this seems like the most startlingly erotic date imaginable.

He presses me further back into the doorway, crowding me in a way that leaves me breathless.

'Oh!' I murmur. 'This is it, right? It's happening? The lean, I mean.'

For a moment – somehow – I'd forgotten the photographers clustered a few feet away, but Jack obviously hadn't. The ice cream sharing thing probably looked very effective. It's a good job at least one of us is focussed on the task in hand rather than just melting into a useless puddle of hormones.

'It's happening,' Jack confirms, and his hand goes up to rest on the wall next to my head.

He *leans*.

I wonder if Gayle will be upset if I faint in front of the cameras. Jack hasn't kissed me . . . He's actually not touching me at all. His chest is separated from mine by a few precious millimetres, though even that distance is almost closed every time I inhale.

His sunglasses slip down his nose, just a touch, and I glimpse amusement in his eyes before they move to my mouth and his face grows serious.

We stand like that for a while – I don't know how long – looking at each other, and I can't seem to steady myself.

I need to catch my breath, need to be able to think straight. This whole thing is supposed to be a business arrangement, but it's day one and I already feel wildly out of control.

It's this realization that helps me to recover my grip on what remains of my sanity.

'I think that's probably enough leaning, now,' I say, keeping my voice under rigid control.

He freezes. The hand near my head peels slowly away from the wall, and he pushes his glasses back up, shielding his expression.

'Yes, they should have what they need, don't you think?' he asks mildly, like he's commenting on the weather.

He pulls away, and the distance he puts between us isn't just physical; it's something else, too, like the barriers have gone back up. It's a firm reminder that what we're doing is only acting. We're playing pretend for an audience. Jack Turner-Jones isn't my lover; he's not even my friend.

'Yes. That's plenty for today,' I agree. 'I'm going to head home.'

When Jack sees me to my car, I get in and drive away.

And I don't look back.

THEN

THIRTEEN YEARS EARLIER

Chapter Nineteen

Jack

The day after karaoke brings a fresh supply of disasters.

I'm woken at six a.m. by the shrill ringing of my phone. I blink, my eyes gritty with lack of sleep, and the ceiling wavers above me, taking a moment to steady. I didn't go to bed until two, and I spent another hour or so after that lying awake and viciously torturing myself with the memory of what had happened – or almost happened – with Cynthie.

That whole scene by the fire has completely messed with my head, and honestly, I was barely clinging to my sanity long before that. She'd been so open with me, had let her guard down for the first time, and – miraculously – I had too. I said things to her, this woman who an hour before I would have called my worst enemy, that I've never said to anyone else.

And then we nearly kissed. So nearly, that I can still taste the breathy little sigh she made against my mouth. I had to physically run away to keep myself from leaping on her – had practically left a trail of smoke behind me as I tore out of there.

Hours later I'm still vibrating with want, a need that threatens to choke me, but I know I did the right thing, that I pulled back just in time. She was drunk and stoned and vulnerable, *and* she's my co-star.

There are rules, rules I have for good reason. My brain knows that I can't even entertain the idea of kissing her.

But try telling that to the rest of me.

Shit.

The phone is still ringing, and I grab for it.

''Lo?' I manage, voice husky. As someone who doesn't usually drink much, the mix of tequila and beer has left me feeling rough.

'Jack?' Marion's voice is a direct contrast to mine, crisp and efficient – even though the last time I saw her she'd been playing beer pong on the pub's pool table with the entire sound department. 'We've got a bit of a problem with the property schedule, and we've had to shift things around. I need you on set as soon as possible. We're going to film scene forty-five today instead of later in the week.'

'Scene forty-five,' I repeat, trying to pull the schedule up from the dark, dusty recesses of my brain.

'Yes,' Marion agrees. 'So get caffeinated and get moving. Your car's on the way.' She hangs up without any further ado.

I sit up, scrubbing my hands over my face. It's far from unheard of for the schedule to change suddenly due to weather conditions or the availability of cast members or locations. In fact, it's only Marion's iron will – which I'm convinced extends to controlling the weather – that has kept us perfectly on track for almost three weeks. Staggering over to the desk where my filming schedule is laid out, I try to get the letters to stop jumping around in front of my tired eyes.

When I finally make sense of what I'm looking at and get to scene forty-five, I stand very still, staring for a long moment before I let out a string of impressive curses. Someone out there is seriously fucking with me.

Because it looks like I'm going to spend today kissing Cynthie Taylor, after all.

*

When I reach set an hour later, it's to find that I'm not the only one having a tough morning.

'Please,' Patty whimpers, face down on the sofa in my trailer. 'Close the door. The light! My god, the light!'

I pull the door closed, shutting out the weak morning sunshine. 'Patty,' I say evenly. 'What are you doing in my trailer?'

'Whaaa?' comes the muffled response, her head still buried in the cushions.

'My trailer,' I try again. 'Did you need me for something?'

Finally, and with visible effort, Patty lifts her head, twists her neck to look blearily up at me. 'Your trailer?' she says, then she seems to finally take in her surroundings. Her eyes widen. 'I thought I was in hair and make-up.'

'Right.' I glance around. Pause for a moment. 'But hair and make-up doesn't have a sofa.'

Patty frowns. 'I'm on a sofa?'

I'm not sure what to say to that, but she staggers to her feet. Her red hair is pulled up in a ponytail and her face is pale. She's still wearing the same clothes she had on last night, although her T-shirt does seem to be on inside out. And back to front. Finally, she grins at me. 'Good night, eh?' she says, wobbling a bit and then righting herself.

As the last time I'd seen her she was trying to detach her jaw and swallow Arjun whole, I smile back.

'You certainly looked like you were having fun. Where's Arjun this morning?'

We're interrupted by a knock on the door, and then the man himself strides in. 'Oh, hey, Jack,' he greets me, before turning to Patty, and holding out a brown paper bag. 'I got you a bacon sandwich.'

Apparently such a romantic overture cannot possibly be ignored, because Patty launches herself at him, wrapping her legs around his waist and kissing him hungrily.

I stand frozen, but when neither of them looks like they have any intention of stopping, I clear my throat noisily. 'Er . . . still in my trailer, guys.'

They break apart, and Arjun regards me with stars in his eyes. 'Oh, hey, Jack,' he says again, blankly.

'There you are, you horny trolls,' Cynthie's voice interrupts from the open doorway. She's already in her costume, but the historical effect is slightly ruined by the enormous pair of sunglasses she's sporting.

'Patty, Liam says they need you now.' She turns to Arjun, a smirk pulling at the corner of her mouth. 'And I think your walkie-talkie must be off.'

'What?' Arjun's eyes widen and he removes his hands from Patty's ass. 'Oh shit,' he mutters, pulling the radio from the back of his belt and fiddling with the buttons. 'Sorry, babe, got to go.' He presses another hard kiss to Patty's mouth and then sprints outside.

Patty just blinks.

'So.' Cynthie's tone is teasing. 'You two had a good night then.'

Patty licks her lips, her expression one of deep satisfaction. 'Let's just say, I was wrong . . . That is definitely not a *nice* boy.'

Cynthie laughs, pushes the sunglasses up onto the top of her head revealing tired eyes. 'Well then, come and give us all the gossip. Liam's practically climbing the walls.'

'Cynthie,' I say. 'Can we have a quick word?'

She impales me on a glare, but nods, jerkily. 'I'll catch up,' she says to Patty. 'Just don't spill any of the good stuff until I get there.'

After Patty leaves, I hesitate for a moment, not exactly sure where to start. 'About last night,' I say finally. 'I'm sorry if I gave you the wrong impression . . .'

I know her well enough now to see the flare of temper in her face. 'You don't need to apologize,' she grinds out. 'We'd been drinking. I was stoned. I didn't know what I was doing.'

'But that's exactly why I owe you an apology,' I try again. 'I shouldn't have let it get so far.'

'Let what get so far?' Her laugh is brittle. 'Nothing happened.'

Even though that is technically true, it doesn't *feel* true.

'Look,' Cynthie carries on impatiently. 'We called a truce, right, and obviously that was a mistake, but it's over now. Everything can go back to normal. We don't need to talk about it.'

'I don't think the truce was a mistake.' I frown.

'Yeah, I bet you don't,' she finally snaps, and for a horrible second I think tears glitter in her eyes, 'I'm sure you just loved it that I was spilling all my secrets and giving you more ammunition for this stupid fight we're trapped in. Can't wait to see how you're going to use all the tragic little details of my sad life against me.'

'Wait.' I hold up my hand. 'Where has that come from? I wouldn't—'

'Of course you would!' Cynthie exclaims. 'I'm just the fool who forgot who you were for five minutes, but don't worry, it won't happen again.'

I rake my hands through my hair and a rumble of frustration escapes me. My head is pounding. I need someone to inject espresso directly into my bloodstream at this point.

'You are *impossible*,' I sigh, finally. 'I don't know why you're so determined to turn me into some sort of Disney villain, but fine. *Fine.* Let's not talk about it anymore. That's probably for the best, given we've got scene forty-fucking-five to get through.'

'Right,' Cynthie agrees, her face carefully neutral. 'So, I'll see you on set.'

'Sure,' I mumble, but she's already out of here.

'Hey, boss!' Scott shouts as he passes Cynthie on the steps. He's reaching towards me with a bucket-sized cup of coffee, and I fight the urge to fall, weeping on his neck.

'Some night, last night,' Scott says cheerfully, looking absolutely none the worse for wear.

'Yeah,' I mutter, burying my face in my coffee. 'Some night.'

The scene we're filming today is a big one, and it's set up on the long lawn out the front of Darlcot Manor, with the building looming in the background. There's already a mist machine on set, a big cylindrical thing strapped to the back of a truck, kicking out huge clouds of soft, grey mist, which roll across the lawn looking atmospheric. An enormous, collapsible tank of water is positioned nearby to supply the stands of the rain machine, which loom high overhead.

Everyone is running about, looking damp and harried in waterproof gear. Cynthie is deep in conversation with Jasmine. She's wearing the sunglasses again, as well as an enormous puffy anorak. As Reckless Ed is involved in the shot, Hannah is nowhere to be seen.

The horse stands looking mildly interested in the mist machine but largely unbothered by the chaos around him. Today, it seems, he's chosen professionalism.

'Jack!' Logan rushes up to greet me. 'Sorry to call you in on short notice like this.'

'It's fine,' I say.

'So,' Logan pulls me to one side. 'I want to have a quick word before we get started.' His gaze slides towards his sister, and I brace myself. Jasmine and Logan often disagree on how a scene should be handled, and it's a weird balancing act trying to juggle their conflicting expectations. 'This is a big scene, and I know Jasmine is going to have some notes for you, but I want you to take them with a grain of salt.'

'What do you mean?' The ache in my head pulses harder.

He grimaces. 'Well, much as my sister might not care to admit it, we're making a film for an actual audience, and – frankly – sex sells.'

I'm totally thrown by this. 'Sex sells?' I repeat slowly.

Logan laughs. Loudly. 'Don't worry, we haven't changed things up on you – it's still a kissing scene ... but while Jasmine's instinct is always to make things subtle, shrink them down, we don't really want that here. All that repressed Regency bullshit is fine up to a point, but we need some heat. Less Austen, more lusty wenches making out in the rain, right?'

'*Lusty wenches.*' I repeat his words again, unable to do anything else. There's a tremor of laughter in my words, but Logan nods seriously. 'Right, so ... you know, you're the pro here, and Cynthie is doing fine, but I don't want to overwhelm her with notes. I mean at the end of the day she just has to stand there and take it, right?'

I blink. This is a horrifying insight into Logan's romantic life, and I have no idea how to respond except with commiserations for whichever poor girl he's currently seeing. Also maybe the number of a good therapist.

'I think it'd best for Cynthie to be an ... active participant,' I say finally.

'Sure, sure.' Logan nods again, wisely. 'Active in a sexy way.'

Thankfully, Jasmine chooses that moment to interrupt, with Cynthie trailing behind her.

'Are you feeling good about the scene, Jack?' Jasmine asks, shooting her brother a death stare.

'Er ... yes?' I reply. Cynthie has lost the sunglasses, and now when I meet her eye she looks similarly shell-shocked. I wonder what Jasmine has been saying to her.

'Okay.' Jasmine starts walking us through the scene. 'So Edward rides into shot, and then ideally we want a smoothe transition from the dismount into a purposeful stride towards Emilia.' She looks over at the horse. 'Lucy has assured me that if you drop the reins, Reckless Ed will stand still, out of shot. Then, Emilia steps towards him and says her line,' Jasmine continues.

'"I thought you had left,"' Cynthie murmurs.

'And then, Jack, you take Cynthie in your arms,' Logan says. 'Passionately. Think hot thoughts.' He winks.

Jasmine sniffs. 'Try not to make it look like you're mauling the poor girl. She's an innocent, and Edward is a gentleman after all.'

'People don't want the gentleman to *be a gentleman* about things all the time, Jas.' Logan rolls his eyes. 'You're such a prude.'

'I'm not a prude!' Jasmine snaps. 'I appreciate a bit of tasteful erotica as much as the next person.'

I wince, and catch Cynthie doing the same.

'I'm extremely sex-positive,' Jasmine continues on a huff. 'But we can't suddenly stick a rampant sex scene at the end of what is an elegant, thoughtful—'

'But tongues, yeah?' Logan interjects here with a wave of his hand. 'As long as that's cool with you guys.' He looks at me and Cynthie, wide eyed, and I have no idea how to respond to this. '*Plenty of tongues*,' Logan adds, and this time I do laugh, because he sounds like a mad pervert. This man is a decade older than me, but sometimes I feel like I'm talking to a horny teenager.

Cynthie also makes a funny, choking sound.

'Fucking hell, Lo!' Jasmine explodes. 'I swear, if you had your way there would be a high-speed car chase ending with Edward shagging Emilia on the hood of a monster truck!'

'Not all of us can get excited over ten minutes of a leaf falling in slow-motion, Jas!' is the response. 'Even if it *does* symbolize the inevitable decay of human existence.'

'Okay,' I interject, torn between anxiety and amusement. 'So I take Cynthie in my arms, then say my line, "How could I leave my soul behind me?" and then we . . . kiss.'

This time when my eyes meet Cynthie's she swallows.

'The rain machine is ready,' Marion calls, and thankfully, after a little more back and forth and several specific but contradictory instructions about hand positions and angles, this meeting concludes and we start getting in to place.

'Can Jack lose the jacket?' Logan asks.

'Why would he be riding without his jacket?' Jasmine's tone is venomous.

'Um, because he's rushing to her in a fit of passion?' Logan replies. 'Look, I know you don't like it, but *please* give me the wet shirt moment. The audience will love it.' His eyes get big, his hands clasp, pleading.

Jasmine eyes me speculatively, and eventually she must decide that the sight of me in a wet shirt falls into the category of tasteful erotica. 'All right,' she says finally, grudgingly. 'I can see it; we'll give it a go.'

Mandy from wardrobe rushes over and takes my jacket and the tie at my throat, and opens my collar just one restrained, Jasmine-approved, button. (Logan, I'm convinced, would have it undone to my waist given half a chance.)

Cynthie is hustled into position, her waterproof removed, and I can already see that the shot is going to be beautiful. She looks ethereal, standing in her white dress with the mist swirling around her skirts. Her head is uncovered for once, dark hair curling damply against the pearlescent glow of her skin.

Something twinges in my chest.

'Sorry, I just have to . . .' A blushing runner approaches me with a glorified supersoaker and proceeds to spray me down so that I'm not entering the scene in totally dry clothes.

Patty rushes over afterwards to tousle my damp hair. 'God, this is really working for you,' she says with a wink.

'First positions!' Marion calls, and I make my way to Reckless Ed, hoisting myself up in the saddle. He gives a happy whicker, which I hope means that he's planning on co-operating. I turn him around a couple of times, just to make sure, and he follows my lead flawlessly.

'Cue rain!' someone shouts, and the rain machine is switched on, water pouring at high enough speed from the tall stands to create a light shower.

As agreed, I stay where I am, outside the circle of the rain, but Cynthie is getting wet pretty quickly – not that she so much as flinches. She stands perfectly still, waiting for action to be called. I take a breath to centre myself, to let go of everything that isn't Edward and this moment. As always before we begin, I feel my adrenaline spike.

'Scene forty-five, take one.' The slate is clapped.

'Set!' Comes from the camera operators.

'Action,' Logan shouts.

I urge Reckless Ed into a canter, and we move into shot, the sweet sting of the water cold against my skin.

When we reach our spot, I pull at the reins, and as he responds, I swing my leg over the saddle, dismounting before the horse comes to a complete stop. I don't break stride as I move towards Cynthie. As the camera passes Reckless Ed to follow me, I'm barely aware of it – barely aware of anything but the woman standing in front of me.

I move towards her, eating up the distance between us with a desperation that feels utterly real.

Trembling in the rain, Cynthie looks up, her eyes enormous. Her lips – stained the colour of ripe raspberries – part, and raindrops kiss her delicately flushed cheeks. My hand goes to her waist, and I pull her against me, hard. Her head tips back and she exhales in surprise. My other hand moves to the side of her face, and my thumb brushes under her jaw, presses over her pulse which jumps desperately beneath my touch. All the time the rain falls and falls, our bodies separated only by the thin, damp fabric of our costumes.

She opens her mouth to say her line, and I don't know what happens – I don't even know who I am in that moment – but I don't wait, can't wait, and my mouth comes crashing down on hers.

The world drops away.

Her lips part under mine with a whimper that sounds like relief, and she presses into me, deepening the kiss. I can't get enough of the taste of her, the feel of her under my hands, under my mouth. For a handful of aching seconds, I forget the cameras, forget the audience. I'm Edward kissing Emilia, but I'm Jack kissing Cynthie, too, and I know it. I tip her back in my arms, sweeping her up and off her feet, cradling her soft curves against my body and never breaking the kiss. I feel like I'm burning up from the inside out; I half expect the water around us to spit and sizzle. Every soft, desperate touch of her lips, her tongue, has me craving more, and I take and I take for as long as I can.

Finally, reluctantly, I pull back. Cynthie blinks up, raindrops clinging to her long lashes, and for a moment I see the same panic that I feel, reflected in her eyes. We stare at each other, and I know we're not in character as my chest heaves, as she trembles in my arms.

'Cut!' Logan yells.

The sound of applause and whoops fill the air, and I slowly lower Cynthie to the ground. It's like I'm seeing and hearing it all from a great distance. I don't understand what just happened – all I really know is that it was the most unprofessional thing I've ever done.

Logan and Jasmine move towards us. I force myself to look at Cynthie again. I want to check in with her, but she's avoiding my eye. She's so pale. Underneath the spots of pink blush Liam applied she's bleached of all colour.

'Oh my god!' Logan is giddy, practically skipping. 'That was so fucking hot!'

'You cut the lines,' Jasmine says, sternly.

'I'm sorry.' I shift on my feet. 'I don't … It just … It felt right in the moment.' It sounds weak to my ears.

Jasmine treats me to a long look, but finally, reluctantly she nods. 'It was better,' she says. 'And you won't often hear a writer agree that cutting dialogue is the way to go. It felt' – she purses her lips here – 'honest.'

I clear my throat. I guess honest is one word for it. I'd maybe go with disastrous.

'What do you think, Cynthie?' Jasmine asks.

When I look back at Cynthie, she's still shaking – harder now – and although the rain machine has been turned off, I realize she's standing, soaked in her thin dress. She must be freezing.

'Hey!' I snap, 'Can we get a blanket or something over here?' I touch her arm, and her skin is painfully cold, covered in goosebumps.

'It's okay,' Cynthie says distantly. 'I'm fine.'

And then she passes out in my arms.

Chapter Twenty

Cynthie

I can't sleep.

It's hardly a surprise, given the events of the day, but it's still deeply frustrating. I don't *want* to be lying awake, tossing and turning while I relive the passionate, scorching hot kiss that I shared with a man I hate. It's bad enough that I'm going to be teased relentlessly for the rest of my life because I *swooned away* afterwards. Maybe they should all be applauding my dedication to the role of Regency ingenue, because according to Patty, the sight of Jack catching me in his strong arms and yelling furiously at everyone was like something out of a novel.

It wasn't the kiss. Not really. It was the hangover and the lack of sleep. It was dehydration, and the fact I hadn't eaten, before being drenched in freezing cold water while wearing a glorified nightie. But that isn't going to stop the rest of the cast and crew from mocking me about it. For ever.

I'd have thought Jack would be loving this, that there'd be plenty of smirks and dry comments about his prowess, but he looked utterly traumatized by the whole ordeal. I half thought the paramedics should have been checking him over instead of me.

I don't know if it's a good thing or a bad thing that Jasmine and

Logan agreed we didn't need to do another take of the actual kiss after my spectacularly embarrassing display. Probably for the best, because I wasn't sure I could go through that again. I just hope that their confidence that they have a single, perfect take is not misplaced.

I have no idea how it will look on-screen. It feels utterly mad that it's going to be on-screen at all, because the moment Jack's mouth touched mine, I knew I wasn't acting, and worst of all ... I think he did too.

With a growl, I push my duvet away and swing my legs out of bed. The clock beside me says 1.25 a.m. in big red numbers. If I don't get to sleep soon, I'm going to be totally useless tomorrow, and I cannot possibly have a repeat performance of today. My best bet is to go and hunt out some chamomile tea, and hope that it quiets my noisy brain.

Unsurprisingly, the whole, giant house is shrouded in darkness, and I stumble along the corridor and down the stairs as carefully as possible. When I reach the kitchen door, however, there's already a narrow strip of light underneath it.

My fingers hesitate on the handle. With a curious sense of certainty, I know exactly who I will find in there. I could turn around, go back to bed, but I don't. Instead I push the door open.

Jack is leaning back against the long kitchen counter, a glass of water at his side. He's wearing a pair of soft plaid pyjama bottoms and a worn grey T-shirt. His hair is mussed, like he's been running his hands through it, like he couldn't sleep either.

At the sight of me, his head snaps up, and there's a look in his eyes that I can't quite decipher. He stands up straight, every line of his body radiating tension.

'What are you doing here?' he asks, and his voice is hoarse.

I push the door gently closed behind me. 'I couldn't sleep,' I say, warily. 'I came to get a cup of tea.'

I don't understand the mood between us: it's dark and snarled, a tangled web of unspoken things.

'Are you feeling better?' he asks stiffly.

'I'm fine.'

I take a step towards the kettle. Towards him. He doesn't move.

'I *hate* this,' he says, his voice low, vicious.

I don't need to ask what he means; I understand all too well. I take another step.

God, I want him. I want him so badly it's painful, and I don't *want* to want him.

'I hate this, too,' I whisper.

Time stops. We stand, frozen, for half a heartbeat, then Jack comes violently away from the counter, and I leap at him. We crash into each other, his mouth coming down on mine, hot and relentless, and I curl my hands in his hair, pulling it hard enough that he gives a low moan against my lips.

I want to bite and scratch and claw at him. I want to tear him apart. I'm so feverish and so angry and his fingers on my skin feel so good. His hands move to my ass, and he lifts me, my legs wrapping around his waist as he pushes me back against the fridge door, a shock of cold metal pressed against my back. Jack rocks his hips and the sensation has more helpless noises escaping my mouth. He kisses my jaw, my neck, clamps his teeth lightly around my earlobe, and I wriggle against him, the friction right there where I want it.

Jack groans. 'Just once,' he rasps. 'Just one time to get it out of our systems.'

'Yes,' I pant, almost beyond thought. 'Once. Now.'

My mouth finds his again, and I bite down on his bottom lip. His hand cups my breast over my thin pyjama top, and when his thumb brushes across my nipple, I whimper. I've never felt like this before. I didn't know I *could* feel like this.

He relaxes his hold on me for a moment, so that I slide down until my feet are back on solid ground. Our bodies are pasted together. He holds me there, caged against the fridge, and when he looks at me, I see my own wildness reflected back in his eyes. Before he can kiss me again, I grasp the bottom of his T-shirt, tugging it up in silent demand, and he's happy to follow my lead, leaning back so that we can dispose of it, and his T-shirt is quickly followed by my own top. I run my fingers over the lean muscles of his chest, down his stomach, which ripples under my touch.

He bites out a curse, bends down and flicks his tongue over my nipple.

The world goes fuzzy. I swear I can taste colours.

As his lips travel over my chest and throat, the sandpaper feeling of his jaw a delicious roughness against my skin, his fingers drop to my waist, dipping below the band of my pyjama shorts. When he touches me, I think I'm going to come apart there and then.

'Oh my god, Cynthie,' he says, the words strangled. 'You're so wet.'

He slides one finger inside me. Two. I ride his hand, delirious. He crooks his fingers and I see stars. His mouth punishes mine in a hard, frantic kiss while he swallows all the needy little moans that slip from my lips, drinking them down like they taste delicious.

Past reason, I reach for his trousers, tugging them off. When I take him in my hand, he hisses. His eyes are pure, feral animal. There's more kissing, more touching and it's not gentle or tender; it's increasingly desperate. We clash like we're fighting, like we can't get enough of each other.

Then, we're on the floor, and he's underneath me, gloriously naked, and my fingers wrap around his wrists, *hard*, pinning him to the ground as I straddle him, leaning down to sink my teeth into his shoulder.

Jack makes a sound like a snarl and rolls us so that I'm underneath him. He yanks my shorts off with such violence that I wonder if he's ripped them clean in half. Not that I'd care either way, because now he's here against me and there's nothing between us, nothing at all.

Suddenly he stills, looks down at me, pupils blown wide with lust. 'Are you sure?'

I think any other time, with any other person, I'd be able to appreciate this careful consideration. Even in the grip of this moment of madness, I recognize that it is something good and right, but I can't help it when I snap, practically sobbing. 'Yes, for fuck's sake. Yes. *Now.*'

And then he pushes into me, and his hand comes over my mouth to muffle the scream that flies out of it, and he's so big and I'm so full, and my body is on fire, everywhere he touches me.

He leans down to kiss me again, and his tongue thrusts against mine in time with his hips, and I'm vicious, my fingernails digging into his back. When his hand reaches down between my legs and he circles my clit as he rocks into me, a warm, building sensation starts in my toes and spreads through me until suddenly, I detonate, fracturing around him in a million sharp-edged pieces, and sobbing his name, totally stunned by the force of my own orgasm.

'Fuck, Cynthie, fuck,' Jack groans. 'So good.' And then, pressing his face into the side of my neck to stifle his own exclamation, he follows me over the edge. The two of us lie, shuddering for air, suspended from reality, while there is only this: his mouth on me, my hands on him.

Eventually, I come back to myself. Floating back from wherever I went, to settle in my body, and I'm aware that the floor is hard and cold underneath my back, and that Jack is hard and warm on top of me. I touch a shaking hand to my mouth, tasting blood.

Jack lifts his head and looks down at me. His cheeks are pink, his hair stands on end, and I realize the blood in my mouth is his, that I've bitten his lip that hard. His expression is one of absolute shock.

'I . . .' he starts, but clearly doesn't know what to say next.

I push my palm against his chest. 'Maybe you could get off me,' I suggest. My voice is uneven.

'Oh, yeah, sorry.' Jack looks down at where our naked bodies are still joined, and his eyes widen, darting up to meet mine. 'Oh, shit,' he whispers, and I come to the same realization at the same time. 'I'm so sorry, Cyn . . . I didn't . . . We didn't . . .'

'I'm on the pill,' I croak. 'And I get tested.'

'Okay.' He nods, his eyes drifting closed. 'Me too. Get tested I mean. And I've never . . . I mean not without protection before.'

'Me neither,' I manage.

'But I should have checked, *before*,' he says, and he sounds angry. This time, fortunately, I realize it's with himself. 'I can't believe I just . . .' He looks down at me again, sighs, his expression troubled, and then he eases off of me.

I feel alarmingly naked. Like a whole new level of nakedness exists without the warmth of Jack's body on mine. He grabs his pyjamas, and pulls them on, before handing me some kitchen towel so that I can clean myself up.

This is the moment when it fully sinks in that I just had sex with Jack Turner-Jones on the kitchen floor where absolutely anyone could have walked in on us, and the insanity of it is *dazzling*.

What the hell is wrong with me? And why, why, why did the first orgasm I have ever had with another person have to be courtesy of someone I can't even stand? God, my ears are still ringing.

Fortunately, it turns out my own pyjamas are indeed still in one piece, and I waste no time in putting them back on. Then Jack and I stand across from each other once more.

'So . . . that happened,' I say.

Jack's mouth pulls up on one side. I try not to think about kissing it, about how the desire I feel for him hasn't been tempered at all — that it's worse than ever. Because of course it is. I want to scream at myself. It's like I've never read a romance novel before — *just once to get it out our systems?* That shit notoriously *never works*. I want to hurl myself at him and wrap my body around his like a vine.

I am so fucked.

I think Jack might be reaching a similar conclusion because his expression grows wary.

'We shouldn't have done that,' I say before he can. I can't face another rejection like last night, but the words suck all the air out the room.

His eyes shutter, and he takes a step back. He rubs a hand absently over his chest. 'No,' he says after a moment. 'Probably not.'

Perversely, I realize it's not the answer I wanted. I don't know how to handle this. Do we still hate each other? I thought I hated him, but maybe ... maybe I don't. Maybe – and this feels like the scariest thought of all – maybe I could have very different feelings for him. If I let myself. It's hard to concentrate when my entire being is still singing with the intensity of what we just did.

'It was a mistake. We don't even like each other,' I say, and a pathetic part of me, one that I wish didn't exist, hopes that he'll disagree.

'I don't think what we just did had much to do with liking each other,' he says instead, and he runs a hand through his hair, smoothing it back into place and undoing the work of my busy fingers. Removing the evidence.

It's the wake-up call I needed. He's made no secret of how unwelcome he finds the attraction between us, his words shouldn't come as a surprise ... and still, there's a pain in my chest, still my stomach drops.

'Right,' I say hollowly. 'So now we can just ... pretend this didn't happen.'

After a beat, Jack shrugs. 'Sure,' he says. 'Like you say, it was a mistake. It's not as if it's going to happen again.'

I keep my face as neutral as his, even though the fact that he really does consider what we just did a mistake makes me want to throw up. There's no way I'm giving him the upper-hand. There's no way I'm going to let this . . . *madness* derail me when everything I've ever wanted is within my grasp. I can't believe I was so reckless.

'No one can know,' I add quickly.

'I'm not in the habit of sharing details of my sex life with people.' Jack's voice is cold, remote. 'Especially when it's going to make me . . . make *both of us* look unprofessional.'

He's right. He's right and I'm so pissed about it. I feel the unwelcome sting of tears at the back of my eyes.

'Cynthie . . .' he says then, his tone uncertain.

I paste on my most glittering smile. 'Good. Now that we've got that out of our systems, we can go back to hating each other,' I say. 'It should be easy enough.'

And with that I hurry from the room, leaving the door open behind me. I move away from the cold light that spills out into the hallway.

Away from Jack.

Never again, I swear to myself. *I'll never forget myself like that again.*

NOW

THIRTEEN YEARS LATER

Chapter Twenty-One

Cynthie

The week after our brunch date, Jack and I have arranged for him to come to my place. Things have changed since the last time we did this. *Then* it may have been enough for us to hold hands on a red carpet, but now, well, now we're a lot more well known, I'm absolutely mired in scandal, and there's a constant stream of celebrity gossip being beamed into everyone's hands twenty-four/seven.

People care just as much about a blurry picture of Jack arriving at my house as they do about one of us perfectly groomed and holding hands at a film premiere – maybe even more – and since our outing, the photographers have been back, haunting the gates to my property.

'This is . . . a lot,' Hannah says, looking up from her tablet where she's watching the slideshow of images that Gayle's assistant sent through. I'm not totally sure if she misunderstood the assignment or it's an error, or maybe just Gayle's idea of a joke (I'm leaning towards the latter), but the slideshow contains dozens of images of Jack and I eating ice cream, and then him leaning over me, all dissolving into each other to a soundtrack of Celine Dion's 'My Heart Will Go On', which feels like . . . a choice.

'I knew there'd be interest, but I had no idea it was going to be *this* big a deal,' I confess, leaning against the kitchen counter. The response since the photos hit the gossip sites has been intense to say the least. They've been picked up by all the tabloids, and they spawned such a huge quantity of memes that you cannot engage with social media without running into them.

('Me looking at the new Emily Henry novel', one Instagram account I follow had written over a picture of Jack gazing down adoringly at my face.)

'Are people honestly that invested in the idea of Jack and me as a couple?'

'Are you kidding?' Hannah puts the tablet aside and looks at me. 'A real-life second chance romance? It's like catnip for millennials. Actually, scratch that, because all the youths are into it, too . . . even if they do consider it a vintage throwback.'

'*Youths*,' I huff. 'All right, thanks Grandma.'

'Anyway,' Hannah continues, with a wave of her hand, 'the point is that the entire internet is rabid over the pair of you, and even though you might not love it, you have to admit it's done the trick. No one is talking about you and the shithead anymore. All anyone sees is you living your best life. You two made quite the scene.'

'Gayle is practically turning cartwheels,' I murmur, my eyes drifting to the tablet which is still playing the pictures on a loop. There's Jack feeding me ice cream as I gaze up, lovestruck, into his face; there's Jack leaning over me in a doorway, and it actually looks even hotter than I imagined it would – insanely intimate, like I'm about to drag him off and do wicked things to him.

'I think he out-leaned Bill,' Hannah says, her eyes following mine.

'You wash your mouth out,' I reply, but there's less heat in the words than I'd like, because yeah . . . maybe he did.

'It was a good idea,' Hannah muses. 'The pictures look so convincing, but he made sure you didn't actually have to do anything you weren't comfortable with.' She's watching me carefully now. 'That was thoughtful of him.'

I make a vague noise of agreement, but offer up nothing else.

'So he's really going to stay over tonight . . .' Hannah says, and though she sounds innocent, the look she gives me is sly.

'In the spare room,' I reply, defensively. 'We'll probably barely even see each other. It's just so they can get a picture of him arriving and then leaving again in the morning. Gayle said it would be a good idea to fan the flames.' I don't want to admit that I only put up the most token resistance against the idea, that after our last meeting I've been thinking about Jack more than I'm comfortable with.

'And you're sure you don't want me to stay?' Hannah asks.

'Don't be silly,' I scoff, busying myself with getting a glass of water from the fridge so that I don't have to look at her. 'You have things to do, an *actual* date, not a pretend one for the benefit of strangers on the internet. I think I can handle one evening alone with Jack Turner-Jones.'

Hannah barely manages to keep a straight face. 'Sure,' she says. 'You just let me know if you need any help cleaning up the crime scene. We can use a code word on the phone so that law enforcement is kept in the dark.'

'Interesting. What will our code word be?'

Hannah purses her lips. 'Coffee beans. You call and ask me for coffee beans and I'll know that you've murdered Jack and you need me to roll up with a body bag.'

'But what if I actually want coffee?'

'You make a good point. Perhaps we're not cut out for a life of crime.'

'Don't say that, we're extremely capable. We could be in our Thelma and Louise era.'

'Thelma and Louise both die at the end.'

'Right, I always forget that part,' I sigh. 'I guess I'll just have to refrain from murdering Jack tonight.'

'You know, he doesn't seem so bad,' Hannah says, grabbing her handbag off the side. 'A lot more evolved than he was thirteen years ago. Maybe if you gave him a chance the two of you could . . . bury the hatchet.'

I look at her suspiciously. 'Why did that sound dirty?'

She laughs. 'Because I meant it to. He's also got even hotter in the last thirteen years. I'm just saying!' She waggles her fingers at me. 'Anyway, I'm off, have fun.'

'Thanks.'

I manage to keep a smile on my face until I hear her close the front door behind her and then I lean my head against the cool marble countertop. *Please, please, please let this not be a disaster.*

I potter aimlessly around the house for another hour, one eye on the clock, until I'm alerted by a buzz from the gate that Jack has arrived. Taking a deep, calming breath I go to meet him outside the front door. The paparazzi are forced to remain on the other side of the gate, but I know that's not going to stop them from getting pictures up the driveway.

Sure enough, as Jack's car pulls up, several long lenses appear over the top of the closed gate, flashes still popping like mad.

Jack parks and gets out the car. He grins and I try not to dwell on the little jolt of pleasure I feel at the sight of him.

'Hey,' he says. 'I think half the photographers in LA are camped outside.'

'Better give them something to talk about then.' I sigh like it is a hardship.

With a laugh, he pulls me into a hug. His body is hard and warm under his T-shirt.

'There, that's not so bad, is it?' Jack's voice rumbles under my ear.

I pull back from him, look up into his face. He's wearing a baseball cap and sunglasses that hide his eyes, but I can still feel the amusement coming off him. Hannah was right when she said he's changed, I realize. He seems so much easier in himself than I remember.

I tuck a strand of hair behind my ear, suddenly nervous. 'Um, why don't you come in?' I say. 'That should have given them enough to keep them happy.'

'Sure,' he replies, and he reaches into the back seat of his car to grab a holdall and a grocery bag. 'Lead the way.'

When we get inside, he looks around with appreciation. 'Your place is lovely.'

'Thanks,' I say, leading him through to the kitchen. 'I'll give you the tour later if you like. Just dump your bag in here for now. Can I get you a drink?'

'I'm good at the moment,' he replies, although he eyes my fancy coffee machine with obvious interest. 'But you should put this in the freezer.' He places the grocery bag he brought with him on the kitchen counter and I peep inside. It's full of tubs of ice cream from the place we visited at the weekend, all with neatly handwritten labels attached, including one that says *Lavender and Honey* in swirling cursive.

'Oh!' I exclaim. 'That's so nice. Thank you.' Inexplicably, I feel my eyes fill with tears, which I try desperately to blink back. Has it really come to this? A small act of kindness and I'm coming apart.

Jack only shrugs. 'I didn't want to turn up empty-handed, and I already know you like ice cream.'

'Still,' I say, shifting on my feet and clearing my throat. 'It was thoughtful.' I start to put the ice cream away into my giant freezer and find there's a nice bottle of white wine in the bag as well so I grab a couple of glasses.

There's an awkward silence.

'I thought I could cook dinner,' I say finally. 'If that's okay with you? If not, we can get takeout.'

'I'm not going to complain about a home-cooked meal,' Jack replies gently. 'Mind if I stay in here and keep you company?'

He's looking at me the way you might look at a nervy animal, and I realize I'm not doing a great job of covering up my anxiety.

'No,' I reply more firmly. 'Of course not. You can stay if you want. Is vegetable curry okay?'

'Sounds great.' Jack slips onto one of the stools at the breakfast bar and takes off his sunglasses and hat, running a hand through his hair. 'Can I do anything to help?'

'No, no.' I move to the fridge and start gathering ingredients. 'I like to cook when I get the chance.' I don't say that I also thought it would give me something to do with my hands, something to concentrate on other than the fact Jack Turner-Jones is in my house.

'Do you have a corkscrew?' Jack asks. 'I could open this wine? The ice cream kept it cold.'

'Good idea.' I pull one from the drawer and hand it to him.

While he pours the wine and I chop vegetables, I can't help but notice this scene feels incredibly domestic. And weirdly not-weird. Especially because Jack keeps up a stream of idle conversation as I work, almost like he's deliberately trying to put me at my ease.

'It was good to see everyone at the weekend,' he says, pushing my glass towards me. 'I didn't realize you guys were all still so close.'

I nod. 'It took a couple of years, but I was able to hire Patty and Liam as my hair and make-up team and they moved out here full time. Obviously Arjun came too, which ended up being great for his career. Then he and Patty had Priya, and Liam married David. We all live within a couple of miles of each other.'

'So Patty and Liam work for you?' he asks.

I laugh. 'No. As they'd be the first to tell you, they work for themselves. They have other clients too, but they're with me whenever I need to be presentable for something, and I usually have them written into my contracts, so we've done almost all my films together. It's perfect, like having family around. We have a lot of fun together.'

'And Liam's husband wasn't at the brunch, but you all get on?'

'David.' I shake my head fondly. 'Yes, he's great. He's actually Theo's assistant and he travels a lot. He's very uptight, super fastidious, secretly big-hearted, and he adores Liam. The two of them balance each other out.' I take a sip of my wine, thinking about it. 'Liam needs someone with a little bite, you know?'

Jack makes a sound of agreement and then very casually says, 'Theo is Theo Eliott, right? You guys used to date?'

'Years ago,' I agree. 'Now he's one of my closest friends. Our real legacy as a couple is that we set up Liam and David. They're much better suited than Theo and I ever were.' I laugh. 'A lot of the time now it seems wild that we were together for so long.'

'How long was it?'

'About five years.' I move to the hob, heating the ghee in a pan. 'But honestly, given our respective schedules I'd be surprised if we spent as much as a single year in each other's company, all told. It wasn't the right time for either of us ... or the right person.'

'Yeah, I know what that's like,' Jack says, his expression rueful.

'I heard something about you and one of your co-stars on the show ...' I say, adding ingredients to the pan so I don't have to look at him. No need for him to know that I googled his love life, or that I had weirdly hostile feelings towards the series of perfectly nice, attractive women he'd dated over the years.

Jack groans, tops up the wine glasses. 'No, that was total fabrication. Not even a publicity thing, just wishful thinking on the part of the fans. Em's just a friend. It's a pretty hard line for me, actually. I don't date people I work with. It's always a bad idea.'

He adds this last part absently, but as the words settle in the air, both of us tense.

'Sorry, I shouldn't have said that,' Jack manages after several seconds tick by where it's not just my disastrous relationship with Shawn that fills the space between us, but a whole lot of unspoken history. 'I only meant—'

I wave my hand airily to cut him off, which would probably be more convincingly casual if I wasn't holding a glass and sloshing wine down my front. 'Don't worry about it,' I say, rubbing at the stain. 'I can't exactly disagree with you given my current situation. It's a good thing you and I are only pretending to date.' I'm very careful not to make any reference to anything that might have happened between us in the past. What we did could hardly be called dating, anyway.

Jack slides from his stool and moves around to the sink. After a moment he hands me a warm, damp washcloth for my wine-stained jumper. While this is perfectly nice of him, it does bring him into my personal space, which I could live without. I don't trust myself around him. The urge to rub myself against him like a cat is alarmingly strong.

He leans back against the kitchen counter, and I can't stop my brain from leaping to another kitchen, to another time when Jack and I were alone together. My gaze moves to his mouth and my fingers tighten around my wine glass. I set it down and turn my attention to dabbing at my clothes.

'It's actually a rule I learned from my dad,' Jack says, and despite his conversational tone, my eyes fly back up to meet his. I thought we would be shutting down this line of conversation, but it seems not. 'He kind of drummed it into me when I was starting out.'

'Oh?' I give up on my jumper, turn back to the curry which is simmering now on a gentle heat, filling the air with the warm scent of spices. 'Didn't he and your mum meet when they were starring in a film together?'

Jack chuckles wryly. 'They did, but I'm not sure he sees the irony.

He's not the most self-aware person you'll ever meet. Their relation-ship is one of the reasons I've stuck to that particular rule, though.'

I wince. 'That doesn't sound great.'

'Nothing about the pair of them is great. Let's just say that Lee and I didn't exactly grow up in a household that modelled healthy relationships. I was always very certain I didn't want to end up like the two of them.' Jack has his arms crossed now, one hand still cradling his wine glass. I'm surprised that he's opening up like this, but even more surprised that he doesn't seem self-conscious about it. He looks and sounds relaxed, an open book.

It's not at all what I expected of him. Again, the line between past and present wobbles precariously.

He takes a step towards me, and I stiffen, but Jack only peers over my shoulder with interest, looking at the food on the hob.

'This smells incredible. Where did you learn to cook?'

I smile, feeling my shoulders relax. 'Hannah's parents. Her mum's side of the family are Bangladeshi, so I make a mean chorchori, and her dad is Italian so I know my way around a plate of pasta, too. Food was always a big deal in their house, and they taught us both to cook when we were kids.'

'I remember you saying you were close with Hannah's family,' he says, and he steps back, returning to his stool and allowing me to unscramble my brain a bit.

'Yes, Nadiya and Enzo, they're like my surrogate parents. Actually, they were over a couple of months ago for a visit. It was really good to see them.' It was also right before the metaphorical shit hit the fan and my life imploded, but best not to dwell on that.

Jack only nods, and he doesn't ask any follow-up questions, but he looks pleased, and maybe he knows I offered up that tiny nugget of personal information as a peace offering.

While I finish cooking, he makes small talk about some of the people we both know in the business.

'Okay, this is done,' I say, dishing the food onto two plates. 'Where do you want to eat?'

'It's nice out,' he says. 'Is there somewhere to sit in the garden?'

'Sure.' I lead him out the sliding French doors to the deck. He brings the rest of the wine with him and we sit at the dining table under the enormous rustic pergola. I light a citronella candle held inside a misshapen, paint-splattered clay holder that Priya made at school.

We dig in and Jack murmurs in appreciation. 'Holy shit,' he says. 'This is delicious.'

'I'll pass on your compliments to Nadiya. She'll be delighted. She's a big *Blood/Lust* fan.'

'Well, let's raise a glass to the chef *and* her teacher,' he replies, raising his wine glass, and I tap mine against it.

We sit in a companionable silence for a bit, and I relax in a way I wasn't expecting. It really is a beautiful evening, warm with a slight breeze, and the little white stars of the jasmine that creep over the pergola smell deliciously heady.

'This is nice,' Jack says, finally breaking the quiet.

'Yeah,' I agree. 'Weird.'

He laughs. 'Who would have thought you and I could get along peacefully for a whole evening?'

'Not Hannah. She wanted a contingency plan in case I murdered you.'

'Ah well, the night is still young.'

'What do you think about ice cream and a movie?' I ask. 'In the spirit of peaceful interaction, I'll even let you choose the film as long as I have veto power.'

'Sounds good to me.' Jack gets to his feet. 'But as you cooked, I'll clean up.'

'You won't hear me argue.'

He scoffs. 'Well, I suppose there's a first time for everything.'

I only laugh and head inside.

'I know what we should watch,' Jack says, carrying a pan to the sink. 'I've been thinking about it all week.'

Jack chooses *While You Were Sleeping*.

Chapter Twenty-Two

Jack

I lie on the bed in Cynthie's spare room trying to concentrate on the book in my hand. Despite the fact that it's late and I've had half a bottle of wine, my body is buzzing like I've done nothing but down energy drinks all night. It probably has something to do with the fact that Cynthie sat next to me on the sofa while we watched a film and I could barely focus on a single frame because she looked so gorgeous, her chin propped on her hand as she drank in a movie that I know she's seen a million times before, with a rapt expression.

I kept having to distract myself by focussing on the bizarrely phallic lamp sitting on the table beside her.

The evening has gone better than expected, and hopefully I've made some tentative inroads in helping Cynthie to see I'm not the same scared, unhappy kid she once knew. All of that good work would definitely be undone if she knew how much I wanted to press her down on the sofa and ease her out of that soft, oversized jumper that she wore.

I shift on the bed. Whatever this feeling is, I need to get a handle on it. Not only are Cynthie and I in precisely the same precarious situation we were in before – co-starring in a film and being forced to pantomime a relationship for the press – but it's increasingly obvious that she's had a tough time lately. There's something fragile and sad about her that makes me want to plough my fist into Shawn Hardy's face, even without knowing all the details. The spitfire I knew is there, but she's taken a battering, that much is obvious. She practically burst into tears over a couple of tubs of ice cream, and in that moment I realized that for weeks she's had nothing but vitriol and abuse directed at her. I can't even imagine what that must have been like. Thousands of strangers on the internet baying for blood.

What she needs right now is a friend, not a man with a giant, thirteen-year-long crush on her.

I turn my attention back to my book with renewed determination. A couple of pages in, there's a soft knock at the door.

'Jack?' Cynthie's voice calls softly. 'Are you still up?'

I scramble from the bed with a speed that is frankly embarrassing, and pull the door open.

'Hey,' I say as casually as I can manage. 'What's going on?'

Cynthie blinks. An adorable line appears between her brows and she stares at me. 'What?' she asks, finally.

I can't help smiling. 'I don't know. You knocked on my door.'

'Oh!' she starts. 'Yes, sorry, I was thrown by the . . .' She gestures in front of her face, and it takes me a moment to work out what she's talking about.

'My glasses?' I ask, suddenly self-conscious. 'I need them for reading.'

'Mmm,' she says, her eyes – still wide on mine – look a bit glazed. 'They . . . They suit you.'

An inconvenient punch of desire jabs me in my gut. 'Thanks,' I reply, clearing my throat.

Her gaze finally moves from my face to the room behind me. The bed sheets are rumpled, and my book is open face down on them.

I watch the movement of her throat as she swallows. 'Are you reading *Persuasion*?' she asks, and she sounds even more flustered.

'It seemed like a good idea,' I reply, still feeling edgy. 'With the film. You know, thwarted lovers, second chances.' Our eyes meet for a beat too long, and I hurry on, ' . . . er, Regency England setting. I figured it would put me in the mood. Have you read it?'

She nods. 'It's one of my favourites.' The line is back between her eyes, and we stand in silence for a moment while she seems to be having some sort of internal conversation.

Like me, she's changed into her pyjamas, and despite the fact that they cover as much of her as her regular clothes, it feels intimate. Her hair is pulled up in a knot on top of her head and her bare toes peep out from under her plaid pyjama bottoms.

I've never previously understood people with foot fetishes, but the sight is enough to have me shifting uneasily, wanting to scoop her up, throw her on the bed and kiss those pretty little toes before turning my attention elsewhere . . .

'So,' I say finally, my voice rough. 'Was there something you needed?' *ME PERHAPS???* my brain yells, while I try to ignore it.

Cynthie snaps back to focus. 'Yes! Right, sorry. Gayle just sent me this, and I thought you'd want to see it . . .' She holds out her phone, swiping at the screen.

It shows a slightly grainy photo of the two of us hugging outside her house. *Spotted!* the caption below it reads, surrounded by red flashing light emojis. **Jack Turner-Jones visits Cynthie Taylor at her home in LA. Looks like things are heating up for these former lovebirds**.

'Jesus,' I murmur. 'They really didn't waste any time, did they?'

Cynthie turns the phone around and examines it for a moment. 'Gayle said it might be a good idea for you to pop out for coffee or something in the morning . . . just to, you know, really sell it that you . . .'

'Spent the night?' I finish.

A hint of colour hits her cheeks and she nods. 'Sorry, I know it's awkward.'

I shrug, lean against the doorway. 'Not really. As long as I can get doughnuts too.'

Her smile is a surprise to both of us, I think. It's sweet and genuine, scrunching her nose. 'I'm going to insist on it.'

'No problem.' I smile back, wanting to keep that look on her face for ever.

And then it's just the two of us smiling at each other, and I don't know how to break us out of this moment, don't think I even want to.

'Well, I'll let you get back to your book,' she says eventually, taking a step back. 'Sleep well.'

'I'll see you in the morning.'

'With doughnuts?'

'With doughnuts,' I promise. ''Night, Cynthie.'

'Goodnight, Jack,' she replies softly, and as she turns away, I close the door before I do something reckless like drag her over the threshold.

It takes me a long, long time to get to sleep.

The next morning I'm up early, and I head straight out on my promised coffee run. Despite the hour there are still a handful of photographers camped outside who are beyond delighted to see me and to catch me in the act of obtaining some post-coital sustenance.

If only, I think.

When I get back there are more paparazzi waiting – clearly the bat signal has gone out – and I make sure they get photos of the tray with the two to-go cups in, and the box full of doughnuts, making it as clear as possible that I'm bringing back breakfast for my girlfriend.

There's no sign of Cynthie yet, so I set myself up in the kitchen, enjoying the light, cheerful space. I wasn't just being polite about Cynthie's house the night before: it really is spectacular, but not in a showy way. It's warm and it feels like a real home. The shiny designer fridge is covered in children's drawings (presumably Priya's handiwork); the long kitchen table is scattered with books, pens, a script with Cynthie's name on, and a large vase of sunny daisies sits in the middle. I pull up a seat at the table with my coffee and my book, eating a Boston cream doughnut and enjoying the morning sunlight, the dappled green of the garden through the wide French windows.

In the end it's only ten minutes before Cynthie appears, still in her pyjamas and looking half-asleep. She rubs her eyes.

'Good morning,' I say.

'Hey,' she croaks. 'I thought I'd be up before you. I was going to make coffee.' She runs a hand over the slightly wild mess of her hair and grimaces.

'I think I'm still on New York time at the moment,' I say, mesmerized as she smoothes her fingers through her hair and twists it up on top of her head, securing it with a hair tie. 'I brought you a coffee instead. Should still be hot.' I gesture to the kitchen counter.

'You've already been out?' She takes the coffee cup, looks at the writing on the side and her eyes widen. 'And this is my coffee order. What are you, magic?' She flips the lid on the doughnut box and selects a glazed ring, sinking her teeth into it with a murmur of appreciation, which I try manfully to ignore.

'I texted Hannah. Predictably, she's an early riser.' I shrug, secretly delighted by how pleased she looks, even gladder that I had taken the time to get Hannah's number at brunch.

Cynthie groans. 'I know. She's always been a chipper morning person. I cannot count the number of times I've wanted to smother her with a pillow when it's six a.m. and she's acting like a Disney princess who gets dressed by tiny birds.'

'The worst,' I agree, watching her mouth as she polishes off her doughnut in a few neat bites. 'Usually I'm all about a lie in, and don't even try to talk to me before I've had my coffee.'

'I remember.' Cynthie laughs, and then she cuts herself off, her face a picture of dismay.

'You don't have to do that, you know,' I say softly.

'Do what?'

I sigh, leaning back in my chair. 'Pretend like we don't have history. Mentioning the past isn't going to be the end of the world for either of us.'

'Isn't it?' Cynthie asks cautiously.

I hesitate, unsure whether we should just have it all out right now, but I don't want to spook her. 'No,' I say instead, making my tone easy. 'It was a long time ago. I think both of us could use a fresh start.'

Cynthie brings her coffee over to the table and sits across from me. She narrows her eyes, observing me with careful consideration. 'Possibly.'

I lean forward. 'How about this?' I say. 'A truce. A real one this time, with no time limit.'

'An indefinite truce with my mortal enemy?' She lifts her brows.

'I don't think I've been your mortal enemy for a long time, Cynthie.'

She lifts her shoulders in a graceful shrug. 'Maybe not. I guess we'll see.'

'We could try something new,' I suggest softly. 'We could try being friends.'

She treats me to another long look, and I can't tell what she's thinking. 'Fine, a truce.' She says in the end.

'And friends?'

'Let's take it one step at a time.'

'I think I'll win you over. I can be very charming, you know.'

'So you're always telling me.'

When I offer my hand to shake on it, she goes to take it, but in doing so she accidentally knocks her coffee cup, sending the remains of her lukewarm drink spreading across the table.

'Shit!' she exclaims, jumping up. 'Let's hope that's not an omen for our truce.'

She hurries to grab a tea towel and I start picking stuff up off the table top to move it out the path of the spill. When Cynthie returns, I'm holding a book in my hand, staring down at it. My heart is beating very fast.

'Um, Cyn,' I say and my voice is a bit high. 'Is there anything you want to tell me?'

'What?' she asks, looking up from the mess she's busy mopping up. The book that I am holding is *What to Expect When You're Expecting*, with a woman cradling her very pregnant belly on the front cover.

Her eyes widen as they dart from the book to me and back again. 'Oh god, Jack,' she manages. 'I didn't want to break it to you like this, but it's . . . it's true . . .'

'What's true?' I ask slowly.

Her hand flies to her flat stomach. 'I'm pregnant,' she whispers. 'And we want to pretend you're the father.'

I feel all the blood drain from my face. My hand goes to the back of my chair, to stop me from falling straight over. 'Cynthie,' I manage. 'Shit, that's . . .'

There's a long, terrible beat as I wrestle with all the emotions that are flying through me. Then, Cynthie's shoulders start shaking and for a second I think she's crying, her head bowed, before she lifts her face and there's nothing but glee in her expression. She's laughing.

No, she's *cackling*.

'Oh my god,' I say, my heart starting up again. I drop into the chair. '*Oh my god*, you little monster!'

Cynthie is still laughing too hard to talk, and I reach for my coffee with a shaking hand.

'I'm sorry,' she says finally, wiping tears from her eyes. 'It was just too easy.'

'So, to be clear . . . you're not pregnant?' I ask.

'No.' Cynthie tries to look solemn but mostly fails. 'It was research for a part I was considering.'

'Right, that makes sense,' I say, and my voice is under control as I treat Cynthie to a stern look. 'But that was not a promising start to our friendship. You almost gave me a heart attack.'

'I only wish I'd had a camera. Your face was priceless.' Cynthie's own face is lit up, and it's impossible not to grin back at her. All the tension falls away from her, all that caution gone as she laughs, and I wish I could bottle the sound.

'How about—' she starts to say, but she's interrupted by the rattle of the front door opening.

A woman's voice calls. 'Hello! I am here!'

It's Cynthie's turn to pale. 'Oh no,' she whispers. 'I forgot she was coming.'

'Who?' I ask, pushing back up to my feet. 'How did anyone get past the gate?'

Cynthie is busy shoving the box of doughnuts into a cupboard. 'She has a code.' Cynthie runs her eyes over me in obvious distress. 'Listen, I'm sorry, okay? I'm so sorry . . .'

Before I can ask her what she's sorry for, a tiny blond woman dressed in hot-pink Lycra comes barrelling through the kitchen door. She's slurping on a disgustingly green smoothie, and when she sees me, she stops in her tracks.

Her eyes run over me in a very slow inventory and then she asks in a heavy accent. 'Who are you?'

'Um, hi,' I say moving towards her and holding my hand out. 'I'm Jack.'

The woman looks at my hand for a moment, and then instead of shaking it she places her smoothie down, takes my forearm in both of her tiny paws and turns it, folding it up so that my bicep flexes.

'Wha—' I manage, casting a look at Cynthie, who is no help because her face is buried in her hands. I have a horrible suspicion she might be laughing again.

'Hmmm,' the tiny woman says clinically, 'not bad, but how is your core?' She blinks up at me with enormous blue eyes.

'It's . . . fine, thanks.'

She huffs. 'We will see. Who is your trainer?'

'My trainer?'

'You do have a personal trainer?'

'Yes, it's Gunther Meyer in New York.'

Cynthie lets out a little squeak of distress and the blonde hisses like an alley cat. 'Gunther,' she spits, her voice laced with poison. 'I should have known. All these muscles. Your cardio will be all to shit. Probably you cannot even row a boat.'

I am bewildered by this requirement, by this entire conversation actually.

'Jack, this is Petra.' Cynthie finally decides to join in. 'She's my trainer. And I should probably tell you that Gunther is her nemesis.'

Petra nods, and then releases a string of words that I think may be Serbian and that I'm certain are not complimentary.

'What does that mean?' I ask, dazed.

'Believe me, you don't want to know,' Cynthie cuts in before Petra can enlighten me.

'Jack is just . . . visiting,' Cynthie says to Petra whose eyes gleam appreciatively.

'Ah yes, a new sex partner for you!' she sounds delighted. 'This is a good idea. It has been too long.'

There's an awkward pause. 'Well, at least it's good cardio,' I say finally.

Cynthie looks aghast, but Petra's smile widens. 'This is funny. You are funny and you have big muscles. That is good for Cynthie. She deserves a nice time.' She narrows her eyes. 'I know you from somewhere?'

'Jack's an actor. He's in *Blood/Lust*,' Cynthie says quickly.

'Ah,' Petra nods. 'That is right. The sexy vampires.'

I choke on a laugh.

'Well, come on, sexy vampire. Today you join our workout,' she continues airily.

'I don't actually play a vamp—' I begin and then the rest of what she said registers. 'I don't want to crash your session,' I say uneasily. 'And I don't have my workout gear with me . . .'

Behind Petra's back Cynthie makes a frantic *shut up* gesture, swiping her hand across her throat.

Petra scoffs. 'What do you need, princess? Special tights? You forgot your Lulu Lemons?' She giggles at her own joke. 'You have sneakers?'

'Well, yes . . .'

She eyes the grey jogging bottoms I pulled on before my trip to the coffee shop. 'Then you are fine. You wear those and you just lose the shirt. It is not so complicated.'

Cynthie's eyes close, and I think she mutters something under her breath.

'I'll just go and get changed,' she says.

'Excellent. I will wait in the gym,' Petra agrees. 'Don't forget the electrolytes,' she barks over her shoulder on the way out.

'What just happened?' I ask, dazed.

'You just got roped into a sweaty, shirtless workout session,' Cynthie says, and she sounds even less happy about it than me.

'But . . . why?' I ask. 'I really didn't mean to intrude on your morning, obviously you have plans. I'll just tell her I need to get going.'

Cynthie's laughter holds an edge of hysteria. 'Sure. You do that.'

And then she leaves me standing, bemused, in the middle of the kitchen.

'Please, just make it end,' I moan almost ninety minutes later, lying in the foetal position on the floor of Cynthie's home gym.

As promised, I am shirtless and sweaty. Very, very sweaty.

For some reason the *Thoroughly Modern Millie* soundtrack is blasting through the speakers.

Cynthie has flopped next to me on the floor, splayed out like a star fish. She is also sweaty. In other circumstances I would sincerely appreciate this – she's wearing tight black leggings, and a matching sports bra; her cheeks are pink and her hair curls damply around her face – but as it stands my brain and possibly all of the rest of my organs are melting, so I'm in no position to admire her excellent physique.

Petra looms over us, making vague sounds of disapproval. 'Gunther', she sniffs, 'is a very foolish man.'

'What is happening?' I choke, increasingly convinced I am stuck in some strange fever dream. I only came down here to say goodbye. But that was a lifetime ago. I was different then. 'And why is Julie Andrews involved?' I wonder aloud.

'You have something to say about Julie Andrews?' Petra sounds like she's about to commit several violent crimes.

'Hey, nothing but respect for her majesty, Clarice Renaldi, Queen of Genovia,' I pant, holding my hands up in surrender.

Cynthie gurgles with something that might be laughter, or might be the shuddering sound of her own death rattle. I try to check on her but can barely lift my head, and I let out a groan of pain.

'You need more stamina,' Psychopath Barbie says, leaning down to poke me in the stomach. 'It will make things much better for Cynthie.' She raises a knowing brow.

'I think …' Cynthie says, dazed beside me, 'that I might be having an endorphin.'

I wheeze out my own laugh. 'Listen, if you're doing it right, you don't *think* you're having one, you *know*.'

Cynthie snickers.

'This is enough with the dirty talk, you sex perverts,' Petra says primly.

'Hey, you started it,' I protest.

'Do you want to do some more burpees?' she asks sweetly. 'I think maybe you have fifty more in you.'

I tap my hand twice against the floor. 'You win. You win,' I agree. 'I give up. I'm a sex pervert with no stamina. Gunther is fired. Anything you want.'

'Cynthie, I like this one,' Petra says approvingly.

'Yeah,' Cynthie mutters, almost under her breath, sounding resigned. 'I might, too.'

I think I might be having an endorphin.

THEN

THIRTEEN YEARS EARLIER

Chapter Twenty-Three

Cynthie

As the credits roll across the screen I realize that my face is wet. I don't know how long I've been crying, but it could have been since the opening shot and I wouldn't have noticed.

I can't believe this exists. I can't believe there's a film, a real, beautiful film with me in it. My name is there. My name is *right there*. And I was . . . good. I think. I mean, obviously it's impossible to watch yourself on-screen in an objective way, but I didn't actively embarrass myself, and that in itself feels like a win.

'Oh my god, Cyn . . .' Hannah whispers from beside me, her own voice thick with tears. On the armrest of the chair in the screening room, our hands are clasped tightly together. 'You were wonderful,' she finishes on a watery gasp.

Somewhere in the darkness, in this tiny, fancy cinema, I know Jack is watching the screen as well. I haven't seen him for months, and I wonder what he's thinking, what he feels right now, watching the two of us fall in love so convincingly. And it *was* convincing – there's no denying it: the chemistry between Jack and I on camera is ridiculous. The scene where we kissed in the rain is beautiful – and extremely sexy – and elicited actual gasps and cheers from our small audience. Despite their differences, somehow Jasmine and

Logan have found a delicate balance between Jasmine's thoughtful introspection and Logan's dynamic sense of action.

It's so surreal, so uncanny to watch the work we'd done be transformed into something that really looks like a proper film. The first time I heard the score kick in behind the action I almost lost my mind. There was music playing while I spoke, and it was beautiful and it had been written for this exact moment! There were scenes where it looked like I actually knew how to ride a horse! There were rooms that looked like they were from the 1800s, but that I know were actually filmed in a studio in Shepperton!

Every frame was like a surprise, even though – as I had to keep reminding myself – it was me on-screen; I had actually been there.

'Well, that was a fucking triumph,' Gayle says loudly now from where she sits on the other side of me, as excited chatter breaks out in the room. I still can't believe she's made the effort to come in person. It's the first time I haven't dealt with one of her associates.

'Darling, you're going to be so big, it's embarrassing.' She sounds genuinely delighted.

'Um, thanks,' I reply.

'Jasmine was right to make sure I came today. We're going to need to be very savvy about how we handle this,' she says, sitting back in her seat and steepling her fingers like a Bond villain, eyelids heavy, her expression one of calculation. 'I think it's going to be best for you to come out to LA sooner rather than later. We have a few meetings to take anyway, and I know you've been raring to go, but as I suspected, the buzz around this is going to make it worth being picky about what you do next.'

My wide eyes move to meet Hannah's. We've been talking about going out to California in a vague way, but it has felt very abstract, like talking about how nice it would be to visit Paris one day, or travel in a hot-air balloon.

Yes, we had spent four weeks shooting on location, and three more in a studio in London, working painfully long days and living and breathing the script, but this was followed by six long months twiddling my thumbs at home, so it was easy to feel like the idea of a career in acting was a bizarre delusion. In fact, if it wasn't for Gayle's assistant sending me a couple of scripts to look at for my 'next project', I would be fully convinced that I was lying in a coma somewhere, experiencing extremely lucid dreams caused by a traumatic brain injury.

Hannah and I had waded deep into the philosophical weeds one day, when I asked if she could prove that she was a real person and not simply part of my dream world. She solved this problem by sitting on me and pinching the skin on my arms sharply between her fingernails in a method of torture she described as 'Smurf bites'. Between the pain and the bizarre nature of this interaction, I was convinced, forced to admit, that my brain didn't have the necessary creativity to come up with whatever it was she was doing.

'Okay, everyone.' My thoughts are interrupted by Logan's voice, as he and Jasmine move to stand in front of the screen and the lights come up. Immediately, my attention is focussed on the back of Jack's head. He's sitting on his own several rows in front of me and he doesn't turn around. My pulse goes into overdrive. If I really was in a coma then the machines would all be beeping like mad. I can practically hear the handsome but overworked doctor shouting, 'She's crashing! She's crashing!'

'We hope you all enjoyed this screening of *A Lady of Quality*,' Logan continues, but he's interrupted by a raucous commotion of clapping and cheering. Gayle sticks her fingers in her mouth and lets out a shrill whistle.

Logan looks dazed but pleased, and beside him Jasmine is so close to actually smiling that I think it might be hurting her facial muscles.

'We're really proud of this thing we all made together,' he says, after we calm down. 'And none of it would have been possible without the incredible team I see in front of me. Jas and I just want to say thank you to every single one of you, and in that spirit, if everyone would like to head out to the room next door, we have champagne and refreshments waiting, because I think we can all agree that we should be celebrating.' There are more cheers at this, then Logan's eyes scan the room before landing on me. 'But can I ask Cynthie and Jack to stay behind for a moment? Thanks all!'

'Ooooh, someone is in trouble!' Rufus's voice calls jovially as the others start filing out the room. I look to Gayle, experiencing a flutter of panic.

'I'm sure it's just a pep talk before you begin promotion,' she says, 'but I can stay if you need me?'

'No, no.' I shake my head. 'You go and grab a glass of champagne. I'll join you as soon as they're finished with me.'

While everyone else leaves, I try to take a few deep, soothing breaths. Jack and I haven't interacted at all for months, though as I told Hannah, this is hardly surprising: we didn't exactly exchange contact details and promise to become pen pals when shooting ended. After 'the incident in the kitchen' (this is how I refer to it in my own mind, refusing to give it any other name), Jack and I resumed our attitude of animosity towards each other, albeit with less high jinks. The prank war was officially over and in its place was an icy professionalism that had everyone scratching their heads.

I haven't even talked to Hannah about what happened, and I'm sure Jack hasn't told anyone either. I hate sharing this secret with him; it feels like one more intimate way that we are tangled up together. Like the fact that I know how his skin tastes, or the sounds he makes when he's turned on. Like the fact that even though I hate him, I still want him. I thought six months apart would be enough to put everything behind us, but clearly that was wishful thinking.

Now, when his eyes finally meet mine, it's like being struck by lightning. Neither of us says a word but I drink in the sight of him, my blood buzzing as I take in every tiny change in his appearance. His hair is a little shorter. He looks tired. His mouth is pressed in a hard, firm line. He's still gorgeous.

Logan and Jasmine hover near the front of the screening room with a polished-looking woman in dangerously high heels who they introduce as Lorna, the head of publicity for the film.

Lorna gestures to two seats in the front row, and Jack and I sit down, carefully leaning away from one another.

'Thanks for staying behind.' Lorna smiles, wide and winning. Her accent is American, her teeth so white that they hurt my eyes. 'The studio sent me to have a somewhat ... delicate conversation with the two of you about the next few weeks.'

'Delicate?' Jack says with a lift of his eyebrows. It's the first time I've heard him speak in months and I wish I didn't like it so much.

Lorna's enormous Cheshire Cat grin seems to stretch even wider. 'So, naturally, everyone's very excited about *A Lady of Quality*, and we really want to make sure that we make the most of our stars, positioning the two of you as fresh, young, new talent. You're both gorgeous; you're crazy good in this film; you're extremely marketable ...'

So far, so good, I think.

'Jack has the acting family royalty thing going on ...' Lorna continues, and if I wasn't so utterly attuned to every particle of his body, I might have missed his tiny flinch at this. I try to be pleased about it, but my heart's not really in it. I can't help remembering what he said that night by the bonfire. Something tells me life as a Turner-Jones child is complicated.

'And Cynthie.' Her enthusiasm ratchets up even higher. 'You're a real Hollywood fairytale. Plucked from obscurity to land a starring role in your first movie ... It's gold.'

I don't love being reduced to playing Cinderella, but I can hardly argue.

'Everyone who has seen the film has said the same thing.' Lorna's tone is earnest. 'That the two of you together are absolute dynamite. The reaction at our test screenings has all of us paying attention. Your chemistry is incredible, and we'd love to capitalize on that in our promotion.'

'Capitalize on it how?' I ask with a frown.

Lorna's smile becomes a little more fixed. 'What we were thinking was that we would *suggest* to some of the press outlets that your on-screen romance has . . . progressed.'

'Wait,' Jack says at the same time as I murmur, 'What?'

'We'd like to sell the idea that the two of you are a real-life couple,' Lorna finally spits out, her smile never faltering. The teeth are starting to look a bit menacing now.

'Ha!' I exclaim, the sound reverberating around the near-empty room.

Lorna grimaces. 'Now, I know how that sounds,' she adds hastily, 'but it's actually incredibly common practice. There's nothing untowards about it. We simply plant a couple of stories; you do a handful of photo-ops and with a tiny bit of suggestion we let the narrative spin itself. This kind of thing goes down great with the sort of fans who are our target demographic here. The movie is testing insanely well with young women aged sixteen to twenty-four, and we think they'd be very likely to invest in an off-screen romance between the two of you.'

'There is absolutely no way,' Jack says, flatly, and even though I was going to say the same thing, I am enraged by his casual dismissal.

'Oh, of course not,' I snort. 'The great Jack Turner-Jones wouldn't be caught dead with a girl like me.'

He turns to me, wide-eyed. 'Are you saying you want to take part in this insanity?'

'No!' I exclaim, noticing he doesn't deny my accusation. 'Obviously not. I'm just saying that Lorna is the expert here, and we shouldn't be so quick to dismiss her ideas.'

'That's such a great attitude, Cynthie,' Lorna praises me, and I feel a bit guilty because I only said it to piss Jack off.

He obviously knows that because he treats me to one of his classic sneers. 'Oh yes, Cynthie. Great attitude. Never mind that the two of us can barely be in the same room without wanting to murder each other.' He freezes, like he suddenly realizes we're not alone.

My eyes shift to Jasmine and Logan. We've never talked about our dislike of each other openly before. I guess now that filming is over the gloves are off.

'Hey.' Logan holds his hands up in mock surrender. 'Don't look at us.'

'But if that was supposed to be a secret,' Jasmine puts in, drily, 'then I have to tell you, you're not quite the actors you think you are.'

I absorb this for a moment. It's just another crime to lay at Jack's feet as far as I'm concerned: he's made me look unprofessional in front of a woman I deeply respect. And also her brother who is sort of okay.

'Fine,' I grind out. 'If that's the case, then it should be clear to everyone involved why this is such a terrible idea.'

'Not at all,' Jasmine pipes up, surprising me. 'I have every faith that you and Jack can hold it together for the duration of a press junket. The film comes out in four weeks, so we're not talking a long-term commitment, just the odd appearance together over the next few months.'

'I told you from the beginning,' Logan interjects. 'Sex sells, guys. You should be flattered . . . You really did manage to make Regency England feel hot. People are picking up what you're putting down.'

I look from Logan to Jasmine. '*Really?*' I ask her, brows raised.

'He's not wrong,' Jasmine says firmly. 'Even if he sounds like he should be. And, look . . .' Here she blows out a slow breath. 'The film is good. Better than it has any right to be on the budget and schedule we had to work with. It could be a big break for all four of us, so if this is what the studio thinks will help, then I say, do it. It's not like they're asking you to sell an organ on the black market. This is just doing what you spent seven weeks doing on set . . . pretending that you're in love with each other in front of the cameras.'

Jack and I eye each other warily.

'The organ thing sounds preferable,' he mutters, but there's less heat in it now.

'No one wants your organ, Jack,' I snap back and then, realizing how that sounds, I have to force myself to sit very still rather than squirm with embarrassment.

Jack sends me a withering look.

'So,' Lorna says breezily. 'Feel free to pull agents and managers into the conversation too if you want, but please keep the circle tight . . . We want this to seem as real as possible. I think you'll find everyone will agree this is a small price to pay for the sort of exposure we might pick up.' She clasps her hands together. 'And if you *are* on board, we'll start work straightaway to lay the groundwork ahead of the press tour and premiere. Okay?'

'Okay,' Jack and I both mumble, careful not to make eye contact.

'Why don't we . . .' Logan gestures to the door, and looks at Lorna and Jasmine.

'Right, right.' Lorna nods. 'You guys talk it over.'

Apparently Lorna and her giant smile have decided to ignore the news that Jack and I can't stand each other. I suppose from her perspective, it doesn't really matter . . . as long as we agree to her plan.

I don't want to be left alone with Jack, but given what has just happened, it's only going to make me look bad if I run screaming from his presence. Time to locate some poise.

After the others have gone, we sit in silence for so long that it becomes clear we're locked in some sort of stand-off.

'Well,' I say, finally, giving in because it's getting so ridiculous. 'Just when we thought we were done with each other.'

Jack groans and leans forward in his chair, elbows braced on his knees, head in his hands.

'Is all *this* really necessary?' I make sure I sound bored, as I wave my hand in front of him. 'Like Jasmine says, it's no different from what they've already asked us to do. It's only for a few weeks.' I get to my feet and stand in front of him, arms crossed. 'I know it's a terrible hardship for you to be forced to pretend you like me – and the feeling is mutual – but after everything Jasmine's done for me, I'll basically do anything she asks.'

This is true. Despite Jasmine's insistence that she's my director and not my friend or mentor, I crave her approval like a drug. I don't need the intervention of a professional to understand this probably has something to do with my mother, but whatever. Wanting to impress Jasmine made me work harder and better, so I'm leaning in to the dysfunction.

I force myself to look at Jack now. I still can't work out if I want to murder him, or straddle him and smash our mouths together. I don't understand how these two instincts can feel so close to one another.

Jack lifts his head at this, and daggers me with a glare that I think means the feeling is mutual. Getting stiffly to his feet, he looms over me.

'Six months,' he mutters almost under his breath. 'It's been six months. Why does it still feel like this?' For a moment he sounds bemused.

'I don't know,' I admit, angrily. I reach up and place the palms of my hands against his chest. I can *feel* his heart hammering, the beat of it ricocheting through my whole body. I don't know if I'm going to push him away or pull him closer.

Jack makes the decision for me when he steps back. My hands fall back to my sides.

'Fine,' he snaps. 'If you want to carry on pretending nothing happened and put us through this, then so be it.'

'*Me* pretend nothing happened?' I choke. 'Hi, pot, have you met kettle?'

Something flares in his gaze, but whatever it is, he shuts it down almost instantly. 'What the fuck else am I supposed to do?' he says the words quietly, stepping even closer into my space. 'Weeks of silence on set, months of silence afterwards, and now you think it's a great idea for the two of us to pretend to other people that we're in love? I don't understand you. What do you *want*, Cynthie? Because I haven't got a fucking clue.'

Neither do I, I want to scream. I'm supposed to be concentrating on my career. This is the biggest moment of my life. Everything is about to change. Apparently I'm about to uproot my whole life and move to another country. And when I'm around Jack I'm unable to *think*. It's dangerous; it makes me feel vulnerable and out of control. I'm so confused.

Why is he even asking what I want? Like it matters, like he cares. Nothing he's said or done has made me think that he finds the attraction between us anything other than a huge inconvenience. Surely ignoring it is the only solution, when acting on it only made things worse.

He looks at me like he's waiting for something. There's an emotion in his eyes that I tell myself I can't read, but it makes me feel even more unsteady.

'I want the film to be a success,' I say, finally, because it's the only truth I can hold on to with both hands. 'I want to do whatever it takes to make that happen.'

He lets out a huff that is part laugh, part something else. I think I'm waiting for him to touch me, but he doesn't, only clenches his fists at his side.

'And *you're* the one . . .' I manage, defiant. 'You're the one who said we needed to be professional. You're the one who said what happened was a mistake.'

'No,' he snaps. '*You* are. *You* said that.'

'And you agreed!' I feel on the edge of tears again.

His eyes bore into mine, and it feels like the ground tilts beneath me.

'We need to shut it all down. Whatever this is.' He gestures between the two of us with his hand. 'It's obviously not headed anywhere good.' Without another word he turns and leaves the room.

I stand frozen in front of the now-blank cinema screen and wonder why it feels like I've just lost something I never had.

Chapter Twenty-Four

Jack

I think sitting in a hotel room being interviewed by an endless stream of journalists while pretending to be coy about my romantic relationship with Cynthie Taylor might be the death of me. Particularly when the woman in question cannot stop acting like a splinter burrowed under my skin.

'I'd love a sparkling water, thank you,' I say when Lorna's assistant, Suzy, offers to grab me a drink. It's hot in here, under the lights, being forced to spend hours sitting inches away from Cynthie and her bad temper.

'No one actually *likes* sparkling water,' Cynthie grumbles, the second Suzy leaves the room. 'It's just normal water full of tiny knives.'

'What are you babbling about now?' I ask, shifting in my seat in front of the enormous *A Lady of Quality* poster. The photograph they've used is a still from the film, Cynthie looking up at me, with her hand on my sleeve. Her expression is melting. It's very different from the look she is currently giving me.

'I'm just saying, who would think, *you know what the experience of drinking water is missing? An element of pain.*' She crosses her legs, pulling the skirt she's wearing down to cover several more centimetres of thigh. The short, designer leather skirt that they put her in, paired with knee-high suede boots, is giving me heart palpitations every time she fidgets.

'What can I say, Taylor?' I say, offhand. 'I guess I'm just a masochist with a thing for bubbles.'

'More like you're a pretentious twat who always orders the fanciest thing available. Why didn't you ask Suzy if she could bring you up a plate of caviar, too?'

'Because the caviar is a garnish,' I say, almost automatically, slipping into an American accent.

Cynthie looks like her head is about to explode. 'Don't you quote *You've Got Mail* to me!' she hisses, quivering with indignation. 'Don't you *dare*. You leave Meg Ryan out of this.'

I can't help the choked laugh that escapes me. 'Sorry, I didn't realize I was bringing Meg Ryan *into* it.'

Cynthie just glares at me, and moves in her seat again. It doesn't take a genius to work out that she's nervous. She's been needling me in increasingly bizarre ways in between every interview, presumably to let off some steam. It's been a delightful way to keep my blood pressure elevated to a dangerous level.

The hotel where the press junket is taking place is a smart location in central London, and – not that I'd ever admit it to Cynthie – the frantic pace of the thing has my head spinning, too. Each reporter has had about ten minutes to fire rapid questions at us. The majority of the questions have been the same thing over and over, so it's been difficult to maintain an appearance of interest and make our answers sound warm and spontaneous.

I will grudgingly admit that Cynthie has actually been doing a good job, though I suppose I shouldn't be surprised – she's perfectly capable of being charming with anyone who isn't me. I don't want to think about why that hurts my feelings.

Hurts my feelings.

This woman is reducing me to the emotional state of a thirteen-year-old girl doodling in her diary. I hate that I'm still into her ... more into her than ever, but I've given her plenty of openings to show me anything but vicious animosity, and she's turned away from me every time.

I thought after what happened at Alveston things might be different, but after we slept together, she just ... shut down. I don't know what the hell there is between us beside animosity, but at this point, I'd love for it to disappear because it's making everything much more difficult than it needs to be.

Suzy sticks her head round the door. 'You guys ready for the last one?'

Cynthie and I both make noises of agreement, and Suzy comes in with two bottles of cold water (still for Cynthie, sparkling for me, and I can practically feel the woman beside me roll her eyes). A young guy follows behind her, looking cheerful and enthusiastic, which must be easy when you haven't been at this for five long, long hours.

'I'm VJ from the *Observer*,' he says shaking our hands.

We all exchange pleasantries while VJ gets comfortable in the chair across from us and sets up to record our answers.

'So,' he says brightly, diving in. '*A Lady of Quality*. Tell me a bit about the film.'

We go into our usual spiel about the pair of star-struck lovers we play, passing the conversational baton between us with ease.

'But if you want to know what happens, you'll have to watch the film,' Cynthie finishes with a cheeky grin.

VJ chuckles. 'Fair enough.' He looks down at his notes. 'Jack, this is your first film, but you're no stranger to the world of movie-making. Did your parents have any helpful tips or guidance for you stepping into the role?'

'I'm lucky that my parents are so supportive,' I say, and I've repeated the words so many times I almost believe them myself. 'Actually,' I hear myself saying, 'the person who gave me the best guidance was Cynthie.'

'Oh, really?' VJ perks up.

Cynthie flashes me a look of suspicion. I can't blame her; I'm deviating from our script.

'Yes,' I carry on, not sure why I've brought this up. 'Cynthie reminded me that making a film is about the joy of creating, that this job we do is supposed to be fun. I think maybe that's something I'd lost sight of.'

Cynthie's eyes narrow, and it takes me a moment to realize why: that particular conversation took place the night of the bonfire, and she thinks I'm bringing it up to mess with her. She assumes I'm making fun of her, when the truth is that the words just spilled out of me, and what she said that night has been ringing in my ears for all these months.

Not that I'm going to tell her that. She's spent every interview so far hiding clever little barbs towards me in all her answers.

'I don't think I'd take my advice over Caroline Turner and Max Jones,' Cynthie says lightly, 'but it's kind of Jack to say so.'

'I mean don't get me wrong, I love picking Mum and Dad's brains when it comes to work. They're the best.'

VJ smiles approvingly. 'It's great that you're such a close family.' I can see that he means it. People love the idea that despite the passionate turmoil of their relationship, Caroline Turner and Max Jones have built a happy family. My parents are acting royalty and that makes me a part of their larger-than-life image. It's something Mum and Dad have always made very clear: that my choices are a reflection on them.

'We are,' I agree. 'In fact, we're grabbing dinner together tonight.'

I don't tell VJ that the thought fills me with dread, that I'm bracing myself for a healthy dose of criticism and interference in whatever the next part of my career looks like.

VJ makes a sound of appreciation, before casting his eye over his notes.

'And the way this all played out has been a real *Cinderella* story for you, Cynthie. Is it true that you got the part through an open audition?'

Cynthie nods, laughs self-deprecatingly. 'Yes, I'm incredibly lucky that Jasmine and Logan and the producers decided to take a chance on me. I hope they feel it's paid off.'

'What about you, Jack,' VJ asks. 'Were you apprehensive about starring opposite someone without any experience?'

Cynthie looks at me with big, soft eyes. Only I can see the cynical spark of laughter lurking in her gaze.

'I told Cynthie exactly how I felt about her involvement from the very first day,' I say, smoothly. 'That opinion hasn't changed.'

It's a lie of course, but I know it will drive Cynthie crazy.

'You're so sweet,' Cynthie coos. *I want to strangle you*, her eyes add.

'I heard that it was the chemistry read between the two of you that really cemented the casting decision,' VJ says.

'Apparently,' Cynthie agrees. 'I've never watched the footage so I can't tell you exactly what they saw, but with me and Jack, it's always been . . .' she trails off, looking at me.

Catastrophic. Calamitous. ' . . . dynamic,' I finish, diplomatically.

'Yes,' Cynthie agrees with a curl of her lip. 'Very *dynamic*.'

'And early reviews of the film are all quick to mention the chemistry between your characters as a highlight. Did you find it easy to work together?'

Cynthie tilts her head to one side. 'I can honestly say that working with Jack has been like something from a dream,' she says sweetly, and I hear – as if she'd whispered the words in my ear – the clarification of *a total fucking nightmare*.

'Wow,' VJ enthuses, 'so it really has been a match made in heaven.' He leans forward, and I know exactly what's coming next.

'It seems like a good time to address the rumours that sparks may have been flying between the two of you off-screen as well as on. Would you care to comment on that at all?'

We fall back into our well-rehearsed answers, the ones the publicity team prepared for us.

'We're trying to keep our private lives private,' I say ruefully, even as my hand reaches out to touch Cynthie's leg in a casual gesture. Thanks to her ridiculous excuse for a skirt, however, the gesture is anything but casual – the smooth skin of her thigh is warm under my palm, and my whole arm tingles.

'I think it's safe to say we're both very happy with the way things have worked out,' Cynthie giggles, looking up at me adoringly. She shifts in her chair, and my hand slides further up her leg. It's the tiniest movement, certainly nothing indecent, but both of us freeze. Our eyes meet, and I hear her breath catch.

Slowly, I pull myself away and find VJ observing us with a very knowing look.

'Interesting,' VJ says, and the two of us try to appear flustered, like we've accidentally said too much. This is easy enough for me because even though I've removed my hand, I can still feel the heat of her naked flesh like it's branded into my skin. And now I'm thinking about Cynthie and her naked flesh and I absolutely cannot sit here in an interview trapped in a fantasy about the co-star who hates me. This nightmare is going from bad to worse.

VJ continues asking his questions for another couple of minutes, while I try to relax into the now-familiar patter with middling success.

After the interview wraps up and VJ leaves the room, I exhale, rolling my shoulders. Thank fuck that's over.

'You were both so great!' Lorna bustles forward from the corner where she's been lurking on her BlackBerry. 'Terrific stuff!'

'Thank you,' I say.

'Just a thought,' Lorna puts in brightly, 'but is there any way Cynthie could crash this family dinner of yours tonight? I'm just thinking it would be a great photo opportunity for us.'

I can literally feel all the blood draining from my face. I cannot think of anything worse. Seriously, this is some ninth circle of hell shit. My parents would rip Cynthie to pieces, and smile the whole time they were at it. I could never put her through that.

'I'm busy,' Cynthie says shortly, and I exhale in relief.

'Oh well, it was only an idea.' Lorna shrugs. 'Maybe some other time.'

'Maybe,' I murmur unconvincingly.

'Do you need anything else from me, Lorna?' Cynthie asks, slinging her handbag over her shoulder.

'No, no.' Lorna shakes her head. 'But let me see you out so we can discuss tomorrow's schedule.'

The two of them leave, and only Lorna bothers saying goodbye to me. I want to bash my head against the nearest wall. I wish I could go home, order a pizza, watch a movie, but the icing on the cake of this awful fucking day is that I have to head to some stuffy restaurant for a stilted dinner with my parents instead.

My phone rings, and seeing Nico's name on the screen, I pick up the call with a sigh. 'Talk about perfect timing.'

'I had a feeling,' Nico's voice drifts down the line, full of his usual laughter. 'Didn't you say you had all those interviews today?'

I sigh. 'Yeah, and it went pretty much as you'd expect.'

'Well, guess who happens to be in town for one night only ... Fancy a drink?'

'You're in London?' I ask. Nico has been on a 'gap year' that is currently well into year three. He travels all over the world falling in and out of trouble, making friends, and taking incredible photographs.

'I've got a connecting flight and I'm off again in the morning, thought I could buy you a beer and let you pour out all your troubles.'

'I'd love that,' I say. 'Unfortunately I have dinner with my parents.'

Nico inhales sharply through his teeth. 'Oof. Not a fun evening. Is Lee going?'

'No, she and Gran are starting the BBC *Pride and Prejudice* box set again.'

'Nice!' Nico says thoughtfully. 'I wonder if I can crash. Do you think Gran's made her ginger biscuits? I dream about those things when I'm away.'

'If she hasn't, she'll probably start whipping up a batch the second she lays eyes on you,' I say. 'You *are* her favourite grandchild.' It's barely an exaggeration, Nico is so much a part of our family.

Nico hums happily. 'Maybe I'll pop by her place then. We could meet for a drink when you're done with dinner?'

'Sounds good,' I agree. 'I'll text you.'

I head out of the hotel feeling lighter. Nico is my best friend, and even though he doesn't know the *whole* story about me and Cynthie (I did promise her I wouldn't tell anyone we'd slept together), he knows enough for me to be able to vent. Maybe he'll even have some advice on how I can make things less tense. Nico is great with people. All I have to do is get through dinner first.

Unfortunately, when I arrive at the restaurant it's to find my parents have invited a director friend of theirs along. Apparently wanting quality time at 'family dinner' was a half-hearted ruse, and instead I've found myself thrust into an impromptu audition over plates of tiny, fussy French food. I wish I could say this was the first time something like this has happened.

'So, Jack.' Guy, the director, beams while my dad tops up his wine glass again. 'You trained at RADA, just like your old man?'

'That's right.' I try to sound easy while anxiety simmers in my veins. I need to make a good impression and I've had no time to prepare.

Guy turns to Mum, 'Remind me, Caroline, were you at RADA too?'

She takes a sip from her own wine glass. 'Certainly not, I was a Central girl. I thought Jack would have been better off there, but you know Max, he likes to get his own way.'

'Central is fine.' Dad waves a hand through the air, his words softer at the edges, and I'd guess this isn't the first bottle the three of them have put away while waiting for me. 'But RADA is the *best*.'

'I'm sure Olivier would have disagreed,' Mum says wryly, flashing Guy a conspiratorial smile. 'I worked with him, you know, in the '80s. Such a charismatic man.'

'Some pretty big shoes to fill, Jack,' Guy laughs.

'You have no idea.' I manage a wan smile.

When Guy excuses himself to use the bathroom, I turn to my parents, who look extremely pleased with themselves. I hate it when they pull shit like this. My palms are sweating, my heart hammering. I'm scrambling, trying to remember Guy's past work, to think of something insightful to say about it.

'Why wouldn't you warn me Guy was coming?' I keep my voice low. 'I could have prepared. I don't even know if I'm interested in whatever part this is.'

Dad rolls his eyes. 'What an entitled brat we've raised, Caro. Of course you're interested! Guy is an eminent director, exactly the sort of person you *should* be working with.'

'And darling you know this is how it's done,' Mum puts in. 'You'll get more from an informal meeting like this than you will attending an audition with dozens of others. Let him see your natural charm, make sure your face is at the front of his mind during the next conversation he has about casting.'

'Nepotism is alive and well,' I mutter, and I'm even more grateful

Cynthie's not here. She'd fucking love this: my mum and dad about to wine and dine me into a role.

I clear my throat. 'Anyway, I was thinking I might take a break. Really think about what I want to do next. Find something that makes me feel *excited*.'

'For fuck's sake, Jack,' my dad roars, not caring that his sonorous voice basically echoes off the walls. 'Now is not the time to be taking a bloody holiday! When I was your age, I was doing nine performances a week at the Old Vic!'

'I thought we'd instilled a better work ethic in you than this.' Mum sounds disappointed.

'You have,' I protest.

'Then act like it,' Dad advises. 'And when that man comes back to this table, you make sure you charm him.'

So that's what I do.

And I try to ignore the fact that I'm miserable about it.

NOW

THIRTEEN YEARS LATER

Chapter Twenty-Five

Cynthie

It's been a couple of weeks since he stayed over at my place, and tonight is the night Jack and I are making our official debut as a couple at a black-tie charity gala in Beverly Hills.

I'm trying not to feel nervous about it, but as we sit in my dressing room at home, Patty and Liam demand all the gossip they've missed while being out of town on a shoot. Let's just say reliving all the details has me jittery.

'And then,' I say, as Liam dusts powder over my nose, 'he opens the door, and he's just standing there in his pyjamas, and his hair is all messy, you know . . .'

'Mmmm,' Liam makes an appreciative sound of agreement.

'And he was wearing . . .' I trail off, helpless.

'What?' Patty's eyes widen in the mirror as she stands looking over my shoulder.

'He was wearing reading glasses,' I finish with a whisper.

'Nooooooooo!' they both screech in unison.

'Yup,' I sigh. 'Those round tortoiseshell ones. Like a hot librarian.'

'Oh my god,' Liam murmurs. 'Your kryptonite.'

I nod glumly, because he's right. Hot librarians are my thing. (Formative crushes on Giles in *Buffy* and Rachel Weisz in *The*

Mummy made this inevitable). Jack's character on *Blood/Lust* is a buff, clever, waistcoat-wearing librarian/demon hunter, and my friends have teased me mercilessly for years over the fact that my nemesis is on TV playing my teenage fantasy. Now I just happen to be trapped in a fake relationship with him while he insists on being sweet and charming all the time.

It's a nightmare.

Over the last couple of weeks, Jack and I have hung out a handful of times. One of those times we didn't have anything planned, but he dropped me a text.

Jack

Hey, friend. Want to go see a movie?

So we went to a midday screening of a big action film. We were the only people in the theatre. No one saw us or took pictures of us, and we bickered over superior cinema snacks and made fun of the clunky dialogue, spending the afternoon talking to each other like action heroes. There were lots of references to choppers.

It was light and fun, and we weren't performing for an audience so I'm not exactly sure why it happened, or what it meant.

Maybe Jack and I really are becoming friends. And maybe hell is freezing over.

'Tell them about the book!' Hannah sings now from her seat on the couch, her feet tucked up under her.

'He was reading *Persuasion*.' If it weren't for Liam and Patty's ministrations, I would put my head in my hands.

'That's hot,' Patty says wisely. 'Men reading Austen is always hot, but *Persuasion*? That's the hottest one.'

I don't know why this is right, but it absolutely is.

'But nothing's happened?' Liam asks, his tone sceptical.

'Nope.' I pop the p sound. 'He did offer me a truce. He said we should be . . . friends.'

'Huh.' Patty frowns.

'Well, that's nice, right?' Liam asks.

'I guess,' I reply. 'I never really thought there was any possibility of Jack Turner-Jones being my friend, but . . . maybe?' I can't keep the doubt from my voice. 'He does seem different.'

'Yes!' Patty agrees, fussing with her curling tongs. 'I was saying to Arjun that he seems so much happier.'

Liam nods wisely. 'His aura has totally changed. I could see it right away. He's let go of a lot of darkness.'

I nibble on my lip. 'Whatever it is, at least we might be on the same team this time. I guess it takes some of the pressure off filming.'

I watch Liam and Patty exchange a look in the mirror.

'How are you feeling about starting work on the film?' Patty asks carefully.

My eyes drop to my lap where my fingers twist a ring on my index finger. 'You know . . . a bit nervous. I'm sure it will be fine.'

There's an unspoken tension in the room and I know exactly why. The last film I made was with Shawn and it left me raw and anxious – the part was demanding and so was he, even without factoring in our fraught relationship. I wasn't in a good place by the end. Honestly, the idea of being on a film set again makes my stomach clench.

My friends are the ones who had to pick up the pieces after everything that happened, so it's no surprise they're worried too.

'It will be great,' Patty says staunchly. 'Just think, all the gang together back at Darlcot. It's been ages since me and Arjun got to work together, and we're bringing Priya to see where Mummy and Daddy fell in love.' She bats her lashes.

'You mean where Mummy and Daddy got drunk and made out in every shadowy corner?' I laugh, pleased to be distracted.

'Potato, po-tah-to.' Patty grins.

'What about the documentary?' Hannah asks. 'Did you say you're meeting the crew tonight?'

'Mmmm,' I agree. 'The director, Brooke, wants to get some B-roll of me and Jack being a couple, I suppose.'

'Speaking of which,' Hannah says gleefully, 'tell them about the shirtless workout.'

'Excuse me, *what?*' Patty looks like she's about to burst.

'Please.' Liam's eyes are wide. 'Spare no detail.'

I groan.

'It was all Petra's fault,' I say after I fill them in. 'I could have killed her.'

'Shirtless Jack.' Patty has a distant look in her eyes. 'Is it as good in real life as it is on TV?'

'Better,' I admit, remembering how distracted I'd been trying hard not stare at the sweaty, rippling muscles, the six-pack, the broad shoulders.

There's a moment of reverential silence.

'And we're sure . . .' Liam hesitates, clearly still reeling from the shirtless reveal. 'Just friends?'

'Do you mean with the man I used to hate who I'm now pretending to be in a relationship with to fix my image thanks to a massive scandal, oh, *and* with whom I'm about to spend the next three months making a film in front of a documentary crew?' I say.

'Right,' Liam nods. 'Good point.'

'I think I know better than anyone that getting involved with a co-worker is a mistake.'

'I notice there wasn't anything in there about how you don't *want* something more with him,' Hannah says innocently.

'I don't want anything more with him,' I reply, serene.

All three of my friends start laughing and, frankly, it's insulting. It was barely a lie and I'm a very good actor.

'Anyway, it's not like he's made any kind of move,' I say, and I know I sound petulant, but it's true. Jack hasn't so much as touched my hand without it being agreed in advance. He's been the perfect gentleman. 'He's been extremely careful about it. I don't think he wants me to get the wrong impression.'

Now the three of them are exchanging loads of significant eye contact.

'Maybe *he* thinks *you're* not interested,' Liam says, finally.

'Which I'm not,' I remind them. And I'm not sure I'm fooling anyone at this point, not even myself. I did not have 'confusing feelings for Jack Turner-Jones' on my bingo card for this year, but here we are. Again.

'Well,' Patty says, giving my hair one final brush and shaking all the bouncy curls out down my back. 'The good news is the entire world is buying the fake romance thing, and the story's doing exactly what it was meant to.'

She attacks me with hairspray, and Liam carefully blots my lips, while Hannah retrieves the garment bag with my gown in.

Stripping out of my robe, I step into the custom Dior gown, which is a dramatic rustle of emerald satin with a boned bodice. Thin straps sit wide on my shoulders, creating a low, dipping neckline. The cut is simple but the dress is a knock-out.

'Oof, that is gorgeous,' Liam says, his fingers stroking the fabric.

'Lola sent over a load of jewellery options,' Hannah says, bustling over to the table which is covered in black velvet boxes, courtesy of my stylist. 'She said any of these will work.'

I start flipping the boxes open and we all ooh and ahh over the jewellery inside. I choose a pair of diamond earrings, and hesitate over a delicate gold charm necklace. An idea forms in my mind and I feel my lips curve up.

'Uh oh,' Hannah says. 'That look means trouble.'

'No, no.' I grin. 'I was just thinking . . . why don't we give people something to talk about?'

Jack and I have arranged to rendezvous at the hotel where the gala is being held. In fact, he's already there waiting for me when my car pulls in to the wide, semi-circular driveway. The place is full of people in their finest evening wear, and no one takes much notice when I step out, taking Jack's offered hand.

I don't know how, or why they'd be looking anywhere else when Jack is wearing a perfectly tailored tuxedo.

I linger over his appearance, taking it all in. When I finally look up, I realize he's doing his own slow inventory, and when his eyes drag up to meet mine, I lift my brows.

'Well?' I ask.

'You'll do,' he says, and his voice is a gravelly shiver that belies the lightness of the words.

It's not in the least *friendly*, and my interest sharpens. 'You, too.'

'Shall we?' he asks, holding out an arm to me.

'Sure.' I take his arm and we join the throng, moving down the drive towards the entrance. The hotel is lit up like a gorgeous birth-day cake under the night sky. The atmosphere is happy, celebratory, the crowd a mixture of celebrities, wealthy donors, and families who have benefitted from the work the charity does helping young cancer patients. I'm far from the centre of attention, and for once I don't feel like a bug under a microscope.

It's a wonderful cause, and the annual gala is a glitzy event in a big ballroom lit with fairy lights. There's live music and dancing and genuinely good canapés, and most importantly of all it raises a huge amount of money. I've always enjoyed it.

'Cynthie!' At the door, we're greeted by Sasha, one of the organizers, and her assistant. Sasha kisses me on both cheeks. I've been involved with the charity and this particular event for years, so we've got to know each other quite well, but initially I found her pretty intimidating. She treats Jack to a cool look that just might be tinged with approval.

'Who do we have here?'

'Sasha, this is my date, Jack Turner-Jones.' I make the introductions, and Jack is charming enough that Sasha is soon smiling and making small talk – a feat which took me years to achieve.

'Let me show you through,' Sasha says finally, after her assistant whispers something in her ear. 'Are you both happy to have your picture taken?'

'Of course.' I try not to laugh because that's basically the whole reason we're here. I realize that if it wasn't for Jack coming back into my life, I would probably still be hiding out at home, having sent Sasha a cheque along with my regrets. Now, I'm here and the anxiety and tension that has been dogging me is finally loosening its grip.

I can't deny that I owe a lot of that to the man beside me, and I squeeze his arm. When he looks down, I smile at him and his expression is quizzical.

'I'm glad you're here,' I whisper.

His face softens. 'Me too.'

Sasha guides us through the large reception area to a space where backdrops have been set up with the charity's logo on them. Instead of the wall of photographers we often face, this time there are only two, a young man and an even younger woman, hired by the event, and they greet us, slightly wide-eyed.

I shake out my skirts and look up at Jack. 'Do I look okay?' I ask, 'Anything in my teeth?'

I bare them at him, and he shakes his head. 'You're perfect,' he says with feeling.

The girl who's about to photograph us melts just a little. 'Great, if I could just get you guys to stand over here ...'

She gets us into position and Jack's hand slips easily around my waist, as if it belongs there.

'Okay, excellent,' the photographer says, snapping away. 'And if you could look at each other?'

I lift my chin so that I can look up into Jack's face, and his eyes crinkle when he smiles. His gaze drops to my lips, and then to my throat, lingering there. His breath hitches; his fingers tighten around my waist and heat flares in his expression.

I feel that look all the way down to my toes, and bite my lip.

'That's wonderful, thanks,' the male photographer says.

The young woman clears her throat, nervous. 'I know I shouldn't say anything,' she says in a low voice, 'but I think you make such a great couple.'

'That's very sweet, thank you,' I say.

The woman beams and turns back to greet the next guests to be photographed.

'Shall we get a drink?' I ask Jack.

'One second,' he says, tugging me over to the side of the room. When we're in a shadowy corner, largely hidden from view by a leafy palm, he crowds me back against the wall. He pinches my chin between his thumb and forefinger, tipping my face up, and I let out a huff of surprise. Slowly, slowly, he draws his fingers down the side of my bared throat. I can't help the shiver that passes through me as his thumb brushes across my clavicle, gently hooking under the delicate gold chain around my neck.

'What is this?' His voice is little more than a growl.

'I thought it would give them something to talk about,' I say, breathless, 'when the photos get sent out to the press. They like to dissect every picture of us so much.'

The gold chain holds a single charm, a tiny letter J, currently resting in Jack's large hand.

'I like it,' he says, and something in his voice has me swallowing back a whimper.

'You do?'

'Mmmm.' He lets the necklace drop and turns his hand, palm down, fingers splayed so that he's loosely gripping the base of my throat. His thumb strokes up and presses gently against the pulse in my neck; I feel it thrashing under his touch. It's the first time he's really put his hands on me, and the relief of it is almost painful. My back is pressed more firmly against the wall, and all I can see is him. 'Maybe a little too much.' His voice is deep and dark now, the gentleman falling away. I fidget, rubbing my thighs together, so painfully turned on I can hardly breathe.

All I can feel is his hand on me, the warm, rough caress of his fingertips on my sensitive skin, the light pressure on my throat.

We stay where we are for a beat, then two.

I wanted this, I realize. When I chose the necklace, it wasn't just for our audience, it was for him: a challenge, a dare. Something to upset his perfect manners, something to prove I'm not the only one affected. Only I hadn't thought it all the way through, hadn't thought about what would happen if I *did* provoke him, how that would feel, how I would find myself drowning in lust in the middle of a party.

Somewhere nearby a glass shatters, a clumsy guest knocking it to the ground, and the sound is a sharp, sudden shock causing both of us to freeze.

Our eyes meet for an instant before Jack carefully eases himself back.

'Sorry,' he says, fingers going to the knot of his bow tie. 'Got a bit carried away there.'

'I think we both did,' I agree, my heart pounding in my ears. 'We should get back to the party.'

I press my hands to his chest. He catches my wrist in his fingers and brings my palm to his lips, placing a soft kiss against my skin before bringing it down, twining his fingers through mine so that he holds my hand at his side. It's a surprisingly tender gesture.

'Sure,' he agrees easily, already back in control. 'Let's go and find those drinks you mentioned.'

We step out from our hiding spot while I try to keep my knees from shaking, and find that the crowd has grown. I'm about to tug Jack in the direction of the bar when I hear a familiar voice.

'Oi! Cyn!'

I turn, and I'm met with the sight of the man standing near the entrance, his smile so wide that his dimple is out on full display.

'Oh my God! Theo!'

Chapter Twenty-Six

Jack

I'm still trying to get myself back under control after pinning Cynthie to a wall in the middle of an enormous party, and now it looks like her ex-boyfriend has turned up. Fucking perfect.

'Be with you in a second,' Theo mouths at Cynthie, who holds her hand up in acknowledgement.

She turns to me, and there's no hiding how pleased she is to see him; it's written all over her face.

'I can't believe he made it!' she says.

I watch as Theo Eliott makes his way over to the photographers, his arm wrapped tightly around his date's waist. The two of them stand in front of the photo backdrop, and I take a minute to look him over. No one can deny that he's a good-looking man, and he certainly has that rock star magnetism, drawing the attention of everyone in the room. Both photographers look flustered as he smiles and jokes with them.

The woman by his side is gorgeous in a sequinned black dress. Small and curvy with fiery red hair tumbling down her back, she's what the Regency writers I've been reading would refer to as a 'pocket Venus'. I can practically see her emerging from a seashell. The expression on her heart-shaped face, however, is one of deep discomfort, her smile frozen as the cameras flash. Theo leans down, carefully tucks her hair behind her ear and whispers something. The woman laughs, her cheeks turning pink, and she relaxes into his side. Her smile is genuine and – for a moment – dazzling.

The moment passes, and with a quick goodbye to the couple taking the pictures, Theo makes his way towards us, pulling the redhead along behind him.

'Hey, trouble,' Theo says when he reaches us, and Cynthie launches herself at him. He laughs, scooping her into his arms for a bear hug that lifts her off her feet. 'I've missed you,' he murmurs against her hair.

'I didn't think you could come,' Cynthie says when she pulls away from him.

'Thought you might need some moral support,' Theo replies, his hand squeezing her shoulder, and even though he's still touching her and she's looking at him like he hung the damn moon, I feel myself soften towards him at that. 'I'm sorry I couldn't get away sooner.'

'I'm just glad you're here now,' Cynthie says, and there's a vulnerability in her voice that has me stepping forward, ranging myself behind her.

'Oh!' she exclaims. 'I need to introduce you. Jack, this is Theo, and My-Wife-Clementine.' At this Cynthie wraps her arm around the redhead's shoulders pulling her forward and hugging her at the same time.

'Your wife Clementine?' I repeat, confused.

The woman laughs. 'Don't pay any attention,' she says in a sweet, husky voice. 'Cyn's just making fun of Theo. Please, call me Clemmie.'

'It's how he introduces her to everyone,' Cynthie explains. 'They got married six months ago and it's still, "My-Wife-Clementine this" and "My-Wife-Clementine that" at literally every opportunity.'

'What can I say?' Theo shrugs. 'I'm enjoying married life. With my wife, Clementine.' The dimple in his cheek pops out, and Clemmie rolls her eyes fondly.

'So,' Theo's attention turns to me, and his expression sharpens. 'Jack Turner-Jones . . .' I brace myself, ready for the sort of inquisition that I faced from Cynthie's other friends. Instead, he says, very intensely, 'What the fuck is going on with Caleb? Is he really dead? He can't be, right?'

Caleb is the character I play in *Blood/Lust* and I blink. 'How do you . . . Those episodes haven't even been released yet.'

Theo grins. 'Yeah, but I sweet-talked the studio into sending me them early.' He leans in closer, confiding, 'Honestly, I think it's half the reason Clemmie agreed to marry me.'

'Sixty per cent at least,' Clemmie says earnestly. 'But, seriously, Caleb can't be dead, can he? Not after everything he's been through . . .' She looks up at me, and her eyes have gone all big and pleading.

Theo makes a dismissive sound. 'Of course they won't kill off Caleb. It's obvious he'll turn vampire.'

'Caleb would *never*,' Clemmie returns hotly. 'Have you forgotten about the blood feud? What about Constantine's involvement in his sister's death?'

'I've forgotten nothing,' Theo says firmly. 'But I think *you're* forgetting the flashback in season two where Caleb's ancestor was the one who came upon the prophecy . . .'

'Oh, it's always about the prophecy with you,' Clemmie grumbles.

'Okay so you guys are like, *real* fans,' I say on a laugh.

'I'm not saying Theo has actually written Bas and Lucy fan fiction . . .' Clemmie tilts her head. 'But I'm also *not* not saying it.'

Theo only shrugs. 'Hey, I'm not ashamed. Bas and Lucy are endgame.'

'You two are such a pair of nerds,' Cynthie says.

Theo scoffs. 'You're one to talk. Who was FaceTiming me in floods of tears after the season four finale?'

'Oh *really*?' I purr, pleased.

Cynthie reaches out and pinches the top of Theo's arm. 'Shut up,' she hisses. 'Jack's head is big enough already.'

'I think he has a very nice head,' Clemmie says, and then her cheeks flush when everyone turns to her. 'I mean . . .' she flounders. 'Your head is normal sized, and your face is pleasing.' She's only turning redder as Cynthie watches, clearly entertained.

'That's kind of you to say,' I reply, gravely. 'My sister used to make fun of my oversized head, but I like to think I grew into it.'

Clemmie smiles shyly at me, and when I look over at Theo, his eyes have narrowed.

'Yes, well.' He places his arm firmly back around Clemmie's waist. 'Shall we go through to the ballroom? I heard there are tiny cheeseburgers doing the rounds so I'd like to eat a dozen or so.'

The four of us make our way, winding through the crowd, though Cynthie and Theo stop often to greet people.

'Have you met my wife, Clementine?' I hear Theo say over and over, and I exchange a look with Cynthie, who is barely concealing her amusement.

'It would make a good drinking game,' she whispers, her breath coasting across my ear in a way that makes all the hairs on my arms stand up. 'A shot every time he says it.'

'We'd be absolutely wasted in five minutes.'

'This is my wife, Clementine,' Theo says on cue, and Cynthie giggles at my side. I'm becoming addicted to her laugh. Whenever I see her relax, drop some of the anxiety that she's been carrying, it's like feeling sunshine after a long winter.

I've been trying hard to be a friend to her, and I was doing a reasonable job of keeping my infatuation to myself, until I saw her wearing my initial around her neck and turned into some sort of lust-fuelled caveman.

Not that she seemed to mind, a voice in my head insists.

When we finally reach it, the ballroom is atmospheric, the walls swathed in navy silk, a gorgeous canopy of fairy lights suspended from the ceiling. A famous DJ is positioned behind a sound deck and the dance floor is already well populated. Round tables are covered in crisp white linens, and a long bar stretches down one side of the room.

Theo rubs his hands together. 'I'll go get the drinks in, shall I?'

'I'll give you a hand,' Cynthie says, shooting me a quick look to check I don't mind being left.

'Sounds good,' I agree. 'Clemmie and I can talk vampire lore.'

'Hey!' Theo exclaims. 'No lore discussion without me, please.'

'We'll save you a couple of seats.' Clemmie beams, and once again Theo shoots me a suspicious look before Cynthie asks what we want to drink and drags him away.

My eyes follow them, as they walk. They look good together, and Cynthie is obviously happy to see him.

'They really are just great friends, you know.' Clemmie's voice draws my attention and I realize she's watching me with amusement.

'Oh,' I flounder. 'I'm not ... I wasn't ...' I don't know what to say, and not only because I have no idea how much Clemmie knows about the reality of my arrangement with Cyn.

'I know it's weird that they used to date.' Clemmie leads the way to an empty table, and I pull out a seat for her before taking one myself. 'I was definitely freaked out about it at the start. *Imagine* being in a relationship with someone when their ex-girlfriend is actual Cynthie Taylor.'

I exhale. 'Yeah. I mean, on the other hand her ex is the most famous rock star on the planet so ...' I trail off with a helpless shrug.

Clemmie shakes her head. 'I really wanted her to be a tremendous bitch, you know? When she turned out to be an amazing person it was very disappointing.' She grins. 'I did worry for about five min-utes that I was the person standing in the way of their aesthetically pleasing love story, but then I realized that there's really nothing romantic about their feelings for each other.'

'I hate to break it to you, but it's pretty obvious your husband is obsessed with you,' I say. 'Every time you smile at me, he looks like he wants to kick me in the shins.'

She laughs. 'Don't mind him. He's not usually like that, but he's obviously remembering one or two throwaway comments I might have made during our *Blood/Lust* viewings.'

'Ah, let me guess. The shirtless fight scenes?'

Laughter gurgles in her throat and her cheeks redden again. 'Maybe.'

'What did we miss?' Theo arrives, placing a glass of champagne in front of his wife.

Cynthie is behind him holding her own glass, and a whisky on the rocks for me.

Clemmie and I exchange a look. Probably best not to say *shirtless fight scenes*. 'Clementine was just commenting on the architecture of the building,' I say airily.

'Yes,' she agrees. 'The architrave has a really baroque influence, don't you think?'

Theo looks baffled. 'What the fuck is an architrave?'

'It's ... um ... a decorative feature.' She buries her face in her champagne.

Cynthie is very obviously not buying any of this, so I decide to change the subject.

'Didn't the studio say that Brooke was going to be here?' I ask, looking around. 'She's the director of the documentary they're making about the movie,' I clarify for Theo and Clemmie.

'Yeah.' Theo takes a swig of his drink. 'Cynthie mentioned that. Is it going to be weird having them follow you around when you're trying to work? Not sure I'd like it.'

I shrug. 'Honestly? Yes, but that was the studio's condition, and I think it will be worth it if we get the film right.'

'You start rehearsals soon?' Clemmie asks.

I nod. 'I actually fly back to the UK in a few days.' I glance over at Cynthie and she's staring down into her glass, her expression hard to read. Her other hand is in her lap, and I take it in mine and squeeze. Her fingers are cold. She gives me the ghost of a smile. 'Cynthie's coming out the week after.'

'Funny to be going back,' she says, and I'm not sure if she means to England, or to the film, or to thirteen years ago. Maybe it's all of the above.

I look over to the dance floor, where the pulsating beat of the music has dropped to something slower.

'How about a dance?' I ask.

'Good idea,' Theo agrees instantly, holding his hand out to his wife. 'Let's slow dance and then find a dark corner to make out in, like we're back at school.'

'I think you and I had different teenage experiences,' Clemmie says, but he's already tugging her to the dance floor and pulling her close, gazing down at her like she's the loveliest thing he's ever seen.

'No school dance chaperone would allow it,' Cynthie shakes her head. 'There's not a millimetre of space between them.'

'They're a great couple.'

'I know. Being around them is enough to restore a person's faith in love stories. Which is lucky when we're about to film an epic one, and I feel a bit shaky about pulling it off.'

'Don't tell me you're nervous?' I ask, idly. 'I've seen everything you've ever made, and you could do this in your sleep. You're an incredible actor. The script reads like it was written for you ... which – I should remind you – it actually was.'

A shadow passes over her face, but she straightens her shoulders, shakes her golden-brown hair so that it spills down her back. 'I suppose so,' she says.

I'm about to push a bit further when we're interrupted by a chipper voice.

'Cynthie? Jack?'

I turn and find myself facing a young Asian woman dressed all in black.

'Hi!' She grins, her eyes wide underneath the blunt cut of her fringe. 'I'm Brooke. I'm so excited to meet you.'

She smiles sunnily, and I'm surprised by how young she looks – she can't be much over twenty.

'Hi.' Cynthie recovers first, holding out her hand to shake Brooke's. 'We were just talking about you. We knew you were supposed to be about somewhere, but it's a big place.'

'Oh, yeah, we've been shooting around a bit. It's a great venue.' She gestures over her shoulder, and a lanky guy around her age moves forward with a video camera in his hands. 'This is Declan, our videographer. We're a pretty small operation. You'll meet the rest of the team when we're in the UK, but it's just us tonight.'

There's another round of introductions, and my brain latches on to something she said.

'Sorry, Brooke,' I cut in, 'did you say you've already been doing some filming?'

'Absolutely.' Brooke beams. 'You knew we were covering the event, right?'

Cynthie and I exchange a quick look as I remember the moment we shared after being photographed. I'm fairly sure Cynthie is thinking the same thing.

'Yes, of course,' I say. 'We just hadn't realized—'

'I was hoping you could do me a solid and ask Theo Eliott and his wife if they'd be willing to sign waivers for us?' Brooke interrupts, and her face is the picture of innocence.

'I'm sure I can ask,' Cynthie says faintly.

'Cool,' Brooke nods. 'Well, now that we've introduced ourselves, we'll get out of your faces. Really excited to be working with you both, and looking forward to sitting down with you on set, soon!' With that, Brooke gives us a jaunty wave and hares off into the crowd. Declan treats us to a nod before loping along after her.

'Oh god,' Cynthie sighs. 'Do you think they saw . . . ?'

'No,' I reply firmly.

'Really?' she looks up at me.

'Actually I have no idea, but they didn't say anything . . . and I guess nothing really happened, did it? What would they have seen? Us standing behind a plant.'

'Right.' Cynthie nods, but her hand lifts to the base of her throat, her thumb rubbing across her collarbone, and I swallow.

'So,' I say finally. 'Shall we dance? I mean . . . do you still want to?'

I can't help the feeling of relief that I experience when Cynthie smiles.

'Sure.'

Chapter Twenty-Seven

Cynthie

As we move across the dance floor, I try not to think about the fact that Brooke and her cameraman might be filming us. I mean, she didn't actually say that they were leaving, did she?

'You're still worried about Brooke?' Jack asks, reading my mind. He's holding me close, one hand round my waist, the other cradling my own.

I grimace, pulling back to gauge his expression. 'I know it shouldn't make any difference. This whole thing has been about getting cameras on us ... It just feels different.'

'Yeah,' Jack sighs. 'I know what you mean. She seemed sweet though, right? Harmless.'

He guides me around the floor, and I try to put Brooke out of my mind. Instead I concentrate on Jack like he's a meditation exercise. Rather than focussing on the different parts of my body that I want to relax, I dwell on all the places we touch: his fingertips splayed across my back, each one a separate point of heat against my skin; my hand curved over his shoulder, the muscle there under the fabric of his tuxedo; my chest pressed to his, our hearts beating in sync; my temple so close to the side of his jaw that he stirs my hair with his breath when he sighs.

'Hey.' My words come dreamily. 'You're a very good dancer.'

I've only danced with Jack once before, and it was on-screen in *A Lady of Quality* – a carefully choreographed Regency number that involved very little touching. Now, I realize that while I've been worrying over the documentary, he's been leading me with the graceful ease of a man who knows what he's about.

In answer to my comment, he twirls me away, reeling me back in and catching me in his arms, almost before I know it's happening. When I look up, his white teeth flash.

'You've had lessons.' It's not a question, just an observation.

'For years,' he agrees. 'All part of my theatrical training. When I was a kid, I wanted to be a song and dance man.'

'You can tap dance?' I ask carefully, because we're straying into more of my childhood fantasies here. Gene Kelly in *Singin' in the Rain*? HOT.

I feel him shrug under my hand, and it looks like that's all the answer I'm getting.

'You're a good singer, too,' I say, remembering his karaoke performance. 'So what happened? You went off the idea of being Gene Kelly and decided you wanted to be Olivier instead?'

Jack huffs a laugh. 'Not exactly. When I told my parents I wanted to go into musical theatre, they told me in no uncertain terms that it was not a dignified job for an actor, and that the singing and dancing had to come to an end.'

'What?' I pull back to look at him, but he doesn't look hurt or unhappy; if anything I'd say his expression is one of resignation. 'That's some elitist bullshit,' I fume. 'And you listened to them?'

'It was kind of my thing for a long time. Listening to them.'

I let that sit between us for a moment, while he pulls me back in close, while we dance. What I've heard about Max Jones and Caroline Turner leads me to believe they are not ideal parents. 'I'm sorry that they had that sort of hold over you,' I say, finally. 'It must have been difficult.'

The song comes to an end, and Jack spins me one more time. When I end up back in his arms he smiles down at me, a soft smile. 'Thanks for the dance,' he says.

I'm about to suggest we track down Theo and Clemmie when I hear a familiar voice, and my entire body descends into chaos so fast I barely have time to register what's happening.

'Cynthie?' Jack's voice sounds urgent, but also far away as I turn. My limbs move slow and heavy, like I've suddenly found myself underwater.

It's easy enough to find him. In a cruel twist, the lights from the dance floor spotlight him perfectly, as if he's been placed there, centre stage.

Shawn Hardy is here. And he's not alone. He stands next to his pregnant wife, laughing at something someone else is saying. He shifts, and his gaze meets mine. It's like an electric shock, and not the same way it is with Jack – not the sparky, tingling, thrill – no, this is more like my organs are shutting down and I'm about to collapse. A call-911 kind of shock.

Something flares for a moment in his eyes, but otherwise there's no sign that he's even recognized me. He lifts his hand but it's not to acknowledge me, instead he places it on his wife's waist, and then – very deliberately – he turns away.

'Cynthie.' Jack's voice is louder now, closer to my ear. His hand is on my shoulder and he tugs gently, so that I spin around, so that I'm facing him.

'I can't . . . I can't breathe,' I manage to whisper over the frantic clattering of my heart. My fingers are full of pins and needles.

Jack wraps his arm around my shoulders and pulls me against him. 'Okay, we're getting out of here.' The words are soft, and he's already guiding me towards the back of the room, away from the crowd. I don't know if people are watching me melt down. I can't bring myself to care about it right now. Every bit of my focus is on the air sawing in and out of my lungs.

'Just take it slow,' he says, and I cling to his voice as dark spots start to dance in the corners of my vision.

'Hey, is there a back door out of here?' I hear him ask. He pulls something out of his pocket with a rustle, and dimly, I understand that it's cash changing hands. There's the murmur of more conversation, and then we're slipping behind one of the swags of navy silk that line the walls and through a door into a narrow corridor.

'Just down here,' Jack says, and then at the end of the corridor there's another door, and this one – blessedly – leads outside.

We're in a dingy courtyard, the home to a couple of large recycling bins, but the air is cool and sweet, and I try to pull in more of it.

'Cynthie.' Jack comes to stand in front of me and takes my hand in his. Carefully, he places my palm over my heart. 'Do you feel your hand against your chest? Do you feel your heart beating?' His voice is low, hypnotic, and I nod. 'Okay. Now, picture yourself sending warmth through your hand into your chest,' he says.

I try to concentrate on what he's saying, and something is working; I feel more connected to my body, my fingers on my skin, my heart thumping under my palm. The tight bands wrapped around my chest start to loosen.

'Concentrate on the pressure of your hand,' he says again, 'And take a deep breath with me.'

I do as he says, and this time the breath comes easier, the buzzing in my ears starting to recede.

'That's good, now take another one. In and out, just like that.'

I keep my hand on my chest, and close my eyes, focussed only on the sound of his voice curling towards me like a golden thread in the dark. I don't know how long we stand there, but eventually I settle, feel my body come back under control, and my eyes flutter open.

He's standing in front of me, his hands cupping my elbows. His expression is serious, his sharp, wolf eyes soft and worried.

'There you are,' he murmurs.

'What just happened?'

'You had a panic attack, but you're good now.' His matter-of-fact tone is helpful. 'Come here and sit down for a minute.' He ushers me over to a low wall. I perch tentatively on it, and he sits beside me, his thigh pressed against mine.

I look around, and we're at the back of the hotel, somewhere the staff sneak off to for breaks, if the cigarette butts on the ground are any indication.

'Sorry. I've never had a panic attack before,' I say, dazed.

'You don't have to apologize.'

'Did you see—' I start, but he cuts me off.

'Yes.' The word is hard.

I sigh, feeling wrung out. 'I didn't know he'd be here. I wasn't ready . . .' I drift off, because I'm not sure I could have been ready. I close my eyes. 'Did everyone see me make a scene? Oh god.' The thought occurs to me, 'Brooke?'

He's already shaking his head. 'No one saw anything. You went white as a sheet and I realized right away what was going on. I had you out of there really fast. Everyone was too busy dancing and having fun to pick up on it. Just a waiter who thinks you had a bit of a dizzy spell and was happy to show us this picturesque spot.'

My shoulders slump. I lean into him, resting my head against his shoulder, and I don't worry about it, don't question if we should be this close because I'm just so glad he's here, because he feels broad and strong and safe beside me.

He wraps an arm around me, presses a kiss to the top of my head. We sit for a minute in silence, and I feel the muscles in my body start to unwind.

'I suppose we'd better go back in,' I say reluctantly.

'Fuck that.' Jack is succinct. 'I've already asked them to bring my car around to the back. We can leave anytime you want.'

'But the benefit . . . Theo . . . What about Brooke? She's still in there.'

'You've had your picture taken and spoken to a lot of people,' Jack says. 'They've got the publicity they want, and if I know you, you've already made a sizeable donation. You've done your bit. You can text Theo and explain, though I don't think you'll need to. And as for Brooke . . . well, she'll just think we've snuck off early together, which is perfect.'

'You seem to have it all figured out.' I can't help the thrill that goes through me at this take-charge attitude. 'What do you mean I don't need to explain to Theo?'

'I mean he saw that prick was there too, and it looked like Clemmie was talking him down from punching his lights out.'

I sigh. 'Oh, that's not great.'

'My money is on his wife,' Jack sighs, 'unfortunately.'

'Can we just sit here for a little while longer?' I ask.

'As long as you want,' he says, and then he moves away from me. I'm about to protest when I realize he's shrugging his jacket off and pulling it around my shoulders. I slip my arms through his sleeves, which fall far past my fingertips. It smells like him, and it's still warm with the heat of his body.

I snuggle in. 'Thanks.' I hesitate. 'That thing that you had me do when we came out here . . . the thing with my hand.'

'Hand on heart.' Jack nods. 'It's a technique for coping with anxiety and panic attacks.'

'You seem to know a lot about it.'

'I used to have panic attacks,' he shrugs. 'Quite regularly, actually.'

'Really?'

'Mmmm.' He's quiet, and I don't ask anything else, just wait to see if he wants to share anything more.

'Do you remember,' he says after a moment, his tone thoughtful, 'the night we all went out and did karaoke? Then we came back for the bonfire?'

'Yes,' I say. 'I remember.'

'You were pretty stoned. I wasn't sure.' His eyes slide to mine. 'Anyway,' he exhales. 'We talked and you asked me if it was strange, being born into the business like I was.'

'You said it was a lot of pressure,' I say, nodding. 'You said you didn't know if you'd ever really chosen it.'

'You really do remember.' His mouth tugs up. 'You also told me it didn't sound like much fun. That conversation was a pretty big turning point for me. I started asking myself whether I was doing things I enjoyed, what work made me happy.'

'Apparently I get insightful when I'm stoned.'

'I'm serious,' he says. 'It took a long time to unpick it all, but it started then, with you. For years I'd been plagued by anxiety, trying to live up to my parents' expectations. I regularly had panic attacks. Before I went on stage, before I went on camera.'

'I had no idea,' I murmur, shocked. 'This was going on when we were filming?'

His smile is rueful. 'Yeah. I used to think I needed to keep it a secret, hide it from people in case they thought less of me.' He runs a hand over his jaw. 'Obviously now I know that only made things worse. There's no shame in having a brain that works a little differently, but at the time . . .' He sighs and there's a dull ache in my chest as I think of the Jack I knew then, as I rearrange the facts I thought I understood.

'It's one of the reasons you and I clashed, I think,' he continues. 'I was a scared, anxious kid, and I tried to cover it all up with a layer of arrogance. I was blind to how right you were for the film . . . All I saw was a threat to me, to my career. I panicked. It was selfish and I acted like an asshole. It's thirteen years too late, but I'm sorry.'

'You don't need to apologize,' I say, and I mean it. I give him a watery smile. 'You weren't the only one who made mistakes. I'm sorry you were going through that alone. Why don't we just say we were both young and foolish.'

'Okay,' he says softly. 'That sounds good.'

'So.' I get to my feet, shake out my skirts. 'Can we really go now?'

'Absolutely.' Jack gestures towards an alley down the side of the bins. 'I'm told this leads down to the delivery area where my car should be waiting.'

'And you're okay to drive?' I ask, as we pick our way through the shadows.

'I was always planning to drive so I only had one drink,' he replies. 'But I can call you a cab if you'd rather?'

'No.' I shake my head. 'I want to go with you.'

When we emerge, we find one of the kids from the valet stand waiting with Jack's car. His face clears when he catches sight of us. I wonder just how much money Jack thrust at the server.

'Thanks for waiting,' Jack says, already fishing out another tip for the boy, who is staring at me. I smile.

'Oh!' he squeaks, his cheeks going pink. 'It's no problem, sir.' He hands Jack his car keys.

'Don't tell anyone we're sneaking out early,' I tease, making my way round to the passenger seat.

'I won't,' he says earnestly.

We get in the car, and when Jack pulls away, he shakes his head. 'Thought the poor guy was going to swallow his tongue. The Cynthie Taylor effect.'

I scoff, and as we drive out under the streetlights, I check my phone and find a bunch of missed calls from Theo. I text him and Clemmie back in our group chat to let them know what happened and they reply instantly.

Theo

Don't worry, Clemmie just about stopped me from committing GBH with a dessert fork.

Theo

But she also managed to sneak over and empty a saltshaker in his drink.

Theo

He spat it down the front of some politician.

Clemmie

Vigilante justice. He deserves a lot worse.

Clemmie

LMK if you want to perform some sort of hex on him. My sisters are on standby.

Theo

YES! Clemmie's curses are serious shit.

Theo

We've got your back.

Clemmie

And we love you.

Clemmie

Also. JACK. So dreamy. We will discuss later. IN DETAIL.

Theo

Don't love my wife finding another man dreamy.

Theo

But he kind of is, Cyn.

It makes me smile, and I settle back into the comfortable leather seat. Jack has the radio on low, playing something soothing. We drive home in silence and when we finally pull up outside my house, I ask him if he's coming in, without blushing too much.

He shakes his head. 'I already texted Hannah,' he says. 'She's waiting for you.'

I swallow, touched again by his thoughtfulness. 'Thanks.' I carefully slip his jacket from my shoulders and try not to feel too bereft about it.

'I'll see you in London,' Jack says, and his fingers tap the steering wheel. His face is in shadow, so I can't read his expression. 'But you've got my number. Let me know if you need anything.'

'I will.' I find that I want to tell him I'll miss him, which is ridiculous when we'll be seeing each other in a little over a week. I've gone thirteen years without his company, so why does a week apart suddenly feel impossible?

'Goodnight, Cynthie,' he murmurs.

''Night.'

I cross my arms, and watch as he begins to turn the car around. Before I can think too much about it, I step forward, and tap on his window.

He rolls it down. 'Did you forget something?'

'Yes,' I say, bending down so that we're level.

I place a hand on his jaw, my fingers scraping lightly across his stubble as I turn his face, then I press my lips softly to the razor-edge of his cheekbone.

He holds himself utterly still for an instant, and then his palm comes up, cupping the back of my neck, the touch warm and steadying. He turns. Our noses brush, his forehead resting against mine, and I close my eyes. For a moment we breathe the same air. For a moment, there's nothing else in the whole world, just this.

'Thank you again,' I whisper, almost against his mouth. 'For tonight.' I open my eyes and let my hand fall, stepping back from the car.

'Any time, Cynthie.' Jack's voice is low.

I watch him drive away then, and my head is swimming. A lot has happened tonight, but one thing is certain . . . Jack Turner-Jones isn't who I thought he was. In fact, I have a horrible feeling he's much, much more.

THEN

THIRTEEN YEARS EARLIER

Chapter Twenty-Eight

Jack

By the time the film's official premiere in London rolls around, the world is fully convinced that Cynthie and I are a couple. Lorna was right: all we've had to do is not directly comment on the matter and everyone was happy to draw their own conclusions – the narrative really did spin itself.

'I can't believe this is real,' Cynthie says now from her seat beside me in the back of the limo.

We're making our way through London towards the cinema where the premiere is taking place, and it was decided that we should arrive together – like a real couple would. Cynthie is wearing a long, strapless blue dress, made out of a fabric that shimmers like iridescent scales when the light hits her. She spent the afternoon closeted with Liam and Patty, and the result is that she looks more beautiful than ever. Not that I could tell her that. Being forced to be with her all the time is the sort of torture that could only be thought up by a bunch of sadists. Or Hollywood producers, I guess.

It's not only Cynthie's presence that has my heart racing, though. All day I've felt the familiar keen edge of a panic attack in my chest. I guess it's because the premiere makes it real. The film will finally be out there, and everyone will have their say. My future rests on this moment, and my anxiety has – unsurprisingly – shot through the roof. The collar of my shirt is too tight; my breath comes choppily. To distract myself, I look at Cynthie.

She's leaning against the soft leather seat, her eyes shut as we continue to crawl through the central London traffic towards Mayfair. She looks pale. I watch her the way you might watch a spider in the corner of your bedroom: we'll all be fine as long as there are no sudden moves and everyone stays exactly where they are.

'Stop staring at me, you creep,' she says without opening her eyes.

'I'm not staring,' I say, keeping my voice level. 'You've gone all pasty. I'm making sure you don't pass out.'

'I'm not going to faint.'

'You've got form,' I remind her.

She scowls. 'Well, as I'm not hungover, dehydrated, and being forced to stand under a glorified garden hose pumping out ice water, I think we'll be fine.'

'Just didn't want the sight of me in a tuxedo to have you swooning away,' I say lightly, adjusting my cuffs. Bickering with her has a weirdly calming effect, the tension easing from my shoulders.

She forces one eye open and glares at me, though when she first saw me earlier I had the satisfying experience of seeing her rendered briefly speechless. I can't blame her . . . I know I look good.

'Can we just . . .' She sighs, eyes fluttering closed again. 'Can we just call a truce for one minute? We're in a limousine on the way to the premiere of our film,' she continues, and her voice is small. 'I just want to be able to . . . take it all in. I want to be in this moment. I can't . . . focus when we're like this.'

It's an unexpected admission. 'Okay,' I say. 'Truce. Just for a minute.'

Her body relaxes, and she opens her eyes. For the first time in months the look she gives me is unguarded. Tears shimmer, threatening to spill over, and I flinch as though she's struck me.

'Whoa, whoa,' I say quickly. 'Truces don't include crying. Liam spent about four hours doing your make-up so you need to get it together, okay?'

She blinks, sniffles. 'You're right.'

In the spirit of our truce, I bite down on my tongue to stop myself from making a smart comment at that. I think she must realize, because an almost-smile tugs at her mouth.

'So . . .' I say after a moment. 'I guess we pulled it off. It's really happening.' I hope she doesn't hear the nerves in my voice.

'Yeah,' she breathes out. 'I still can't believe it. I wonder what will happen next.'

I shake my head. 'I have absolutely no idea.'

'That's scary, right?' she turns to me.

'It's fucking terrifying.'

She looks surprised by my honesty. Our eyes meet and there's a moment where something like understanding passes between us. It's different from the looks we usually share – it's not hot and angry or hot and horny, but something softer, sweeter. I glance at her hand, resting on the seat between us, and I edge my own fingers closer.

The buzzing sound of the divider between us and the driver coming down breaks the silence. 'Here we are,' he says, cheerfully announcing our arrival.

I move my hand back into my lap.

'I guess the truce is over,' Cynthie murmurs, already reeling herself back in. It's like I can see her taking all her feelings and stuffing them down, locking them up somewhere tight, somewhere I can't get to. She sits up straight, brushes down her skirts, and her chin takes on the determined angle that I recognize. She's ready to face whatever waits outside the car.

'Truce over,' I agree, my hand on the door handle. I take one final deep breath and then open the door, willing my hand to stay steady.

The Curzon in Mayfair is one of my favourite places. I used to come here as a kid to watch films every weekend. It feels very full circle to be here now at my own premiere. I try to let myself enjoy it for a second, to let myself just be here, like Cynthie said, but again I taste the fear in my mouth, tangy and metallic. My ears are full of the sound of my own heartbeat, and my vision wavers. *Not now.* I think. *Please, not now.*

I take a breath, try to force my body back under control, then I lean back into the car and hold my hand out.

'Come on then,' I say, my voice clipped as Lorna and Suzy approach the car in a flutter of excitement. 'Let's do this.'

Cynthie shuffles forward, and when my fingers wrap around hers, her hands are cold. She's nervous, but no one else would ever know. The second she emerges from the car, she's all smiles.

There's a small crowd of young fans standing behind a barrier, and they start shouting when they see us. As agreed, I keep Cynthie's hand in mine.

'Hi, guys,' Lorna greets us breathlessly. 'You both look wonderful!'

'Thank you,' Cynthie says, and I wonder if anyone else notices the way she toys with the delicate chain around her neck, the way her hands are trembling, just a touch.

'You have some time to sign autographs before we hit the carpet ... if that's okay with you?' Lorna says, more than half her attention on the phone in her hand.

'Sure,' I agree. 'Sounds good.'

'Yep.' Cynthie's voice is pitched higher than usual. 'That sounds great.'

We move over to the crowd and their excitement climbs to a frenzy, as do the squealing noises they're making. Grasping hands reach towards us, and there are people shouting my name, shouting both our names. We approach the barrier and Suzy hands us a couple of markers.

Notebooks, scraps of paper, and even a few copies of the poster for the film are thrust in front of me, and I scrawl my autograph over and over again, smiling and greeting people as I go. The crowd is mostly made up of teenage girls and they look at me with hearts in their eyes. When I watch Cynthie with them, I notice they wear the same look with her.

'She's so pretty,' I hear one girl sigh.

'They look amazing together,' her friend replies. 'They're, like, the perfect couple.'

The whole time, I can feel the attack pressing in on me. I try to fight it, to ignore it, but I know it's inevitable. I can't get enough air into my lungs, and my chest is rising and falling too rapidly. Someone's going to notice. My fingers wrapped around the pen are tingling. I have to get out of here. Fast.

I take an abrupt step back. Put my hand in my pocket.

Cynthie looks up at me, startled.

'What are you—' she starts, but I cut her off.

'There's a call I have to take,' I snap, already moving away. I clutch my phone in my hand like the prop and the lifeline it is.

'You can't be serious,' I hear Cynthie murmur, but then she's laughing, bright, making jokes and excuses for me to the crowd.

I stride away back towards the car, which is still idling, waiting in the queue to turn around.

'I just need somewhere private to take this call for a second,' I say to the driver, amazed that I've kept the words steady, when my lungs feel like they're full of broken glass. Then again, I've had plenty of practice hiding my panic attacks from people.

When I get into the back seat, I tug at my bow tie, pulling it away and unbuttoning my collar. Sweat beads on my forehead. I place my shaking hand on my chest and focus on the feeling of my thumping heart under my fingers, on breathing slow and smoothe. It feels like it always does: it feels like I'm dying.

Even if they stretch endlessly it's really only a few minutes before I'm back under control. I know how to manage things, but it doesn't make this any easier. I hate that it happened here, today, that I couldn't just enjoy myself and be happy like a normal person. It feels like something has been taken from me, and I won't be able to get it back. I grab a water from the mini-bar in the console in front of me and swig at it, press the cool bottle to my forehead. I do up my shirt and retie my tie with steady fingers. I push my hair back from my face and straighten my jacket. When I leave the car, I'm sure no one would ever guess what just happened, but I feel hollow, exhausted.

'Oh, there he is.' Lorna looks relieved as I reappear. She turns to the crowd. 'Sorry, we need to get these two down to the red carpet now.'

There's a collective groan of disappointment, and Cynthie disentangles herself. After a second's hesitation, I take her hand in mine and the group behind us shriek their approval as we walk away.

'Perfect,' Lorna murmurs, clearly pleased. 'You're doing great. So, just remember what we talked about for the carpet . . . it's all about body language. We want the two of you to look like you're together.'

'I cannot believe you did that,' Cynthie hisses through gritted teeth, her expression pleasant. 'Those people waited hours to see you and you just fobbed them off for a phone call?'

'I needed to take it,' I say, abruptly.

'You really are the most entitled, selfish . . .' Cynthie begins, but she doesn't get to finish that lovely thought, because Lorna hustles us through a barrier into the holding area.

I wish it didn't sting so much to know that's how Cynthie sees me. Part of me wants to tell her the truth. So much of my life is a lie, a performance, and with Cynthie there have been moments where all of that has fallen away. I wish I could tell her how I feel. I wish we could cut through all the bullshit between us, but I don't know where to start.

Outside the cinema, there's a wide strip of red carpet in front of the backdrop printed with the name of the film in the stylized calligraphy that appears on all the promotional materials. I watch as Simon makes his way slowly down with his date, stopping every so often in front of the gaggle of photographers, lined up behind another barrier.

'Wow, there's more of them than I expected,' Cynthie manages.

'I know.' Lorna gives her big, alligator grin. 'All the press you two did really paid off.'

When Simon finally reaches the other end of the carpet and disappears inside the cinema, Suzy scuttles down after him, holding up a card with our names printed on it.

The interest from the photographers kicks up a gear, and Lorna practically shoves us out there, with a whispered hiss of 'Remember, you're *in love*.'

Cynthie's hand tenses in mine, but we walk out, smiling wide. When we reach the first place where we're supposed to stop, Cynthie steps into me, and my arm slips around her waist, pulling her tightly into my side. I don't feel panicked now, but I do feel sick and empty, sort of grey. I smile like it's the best day of my life.

'Jack! Jack! Cynthie!' The photographers shout, flashes bursting in front of my eyes, leaving behind stars at the edges of my vision.

My hand splays on Cynthie's stomach, and the slip of her silk dress is cool under my fingers.

'Give us a kiss!' one of the photographers yells, and the shout is picked up by some of the others. 'Kiss! Kiss!' they chant.

I watch Cynthie's eyes widen a fraction and my hand tightens on her waist. I dip my head towards hers and something flares in her gaze. I don't have time to decide if it's lust or panic, before I drop a kiss on the end of her nose.

When I pull back, Cynthie looks up at me, delightfully befuddled, and then she laughs that great, husky laugh of hers that's like a shot of top shelf whisky, and the cameras flash like mad. Everyone loves it; they can't get enough of us.

We look adorable, I know. Lorna is going to be thrilled. We look like we're totally in love.

We're such good actors.

NOW

THIRTEEN YEARS LATER

Chapter Twenty-Nine

Cynthie

A week after the gala, it's the first day of rehearsals and I can't believe I'm here: back in England, back at Shepperton Studios, and stepping back into a world I left behind thirteen years ago.

As I enter the rehearsal room, the atmosphere is edgy. Most of the cast are already here, and there's a swirling mix of nerves and excitement in the air.

'Cynthie!' Simon greets me with a kiss on each cheek. 'Who'd have thought we'd be here again.' Still handsome in an aristocratic way, with his straight teeth, slightly receding hairline and bluff cheeriness, Simon looks like a lost member of the royal family. Small wonder I heard a rumour he was in consideration for *The Crown* spin-off.

'Hi, Simon,' I reply with a smile. At least I know I'm more than capable of covering up the nerves I feel. There's a lot of weighing and measuring going on right now, and I'm not stupid – I'm the focus of a lot of attention.

I knew Jack was here the second I entered the room, even before I saw him. Somehow I knew. He's currently hugging an incredibly well-preserved Hattie Prince and laughing at something she says, and the sound of his laugh, rich and deep, hits my bloodstream like an illegal substance. He hasn't spotted me yet so I can let my eyes linger on him the way they want to.

I haven't seen Jack since the night of the gala, and I'm overwhelmed by an inappropriate desire to go and throw my arms around him. I've spent a lot more time than I'm comfortable admitting thinking about seeing him again, *wanting* to see him again. Then I remember that everyone thinks we're together and I don't have to pretend I'm not happy he's here.

'Excuse me for a sec,' I say to Simon.

I make my way over to Jack and tap him on the shoulder. When he turns, his eyes light up and he reaches for me as if it's the most natural thing in the world, pulling me up into his arms and hugging me tight so that I'm laughing as the toes of my trainers skim the floor, and he presses a kiss to my temple.

'I didn't see you arrive,' he says.

'Just got here,' I reply. 'Hi, Hattie.' I try not to look ruffled as I emerge from Jack's embrace and move to greet her.

'Hello, darling girl.' She looks from me to Jack and her smile grows. 'I always hoped the two of you would work things out. You make such a lovely couple.'

I feel myself stiffen at that. I thought Jack was just happy to see me, but maybe he's been putting on a show for an old family friend. After all, we agreed that no one outside our immediate circles would be in on the truth.

His face doesn't offer any clues – all I see when I look at him is a relaxed sort of pleasure, but then I know better than anyone what a good actor he is.

God, this is confusing. I'm fully aware that our relationship is pretend, but there's a lot of stuff going on that feels frighteningly, exhilaratingly real.

There's another man standing with Hattie and Jack, and in my flustered state it takes me a moment to recognize him,

'*Scott*?' I gape, finally.

'Hi, Cynthie.' He gives me the same sweet smile that I remember. It's about the only familiar thing about him. Gone is the scruffy stoner, and in his place is a man with a sharp haircut and an even sharper suit.

'I can't believe it's you!' I laugh, hugging him.

'I guess I have changed a bit,' he says solemnly, and over his shoulder Jack is grinning.

'I suppose we all have,' I say faintly. 'Hannah will be gutted she missed you. She's not with me today because there's so much to do before we leave for location.'

'Tell me about it,' Scott says, tapping the fancy leather portfolio he holds in his hand. 'I was just going over some details with Jack, but I can't wait to catch up with everyone next week.'

With another smile he finishes up his business with Jack and leaves in a flurry of goodbyes.

'I can't believe it,' I say again after he's gone.

Jack chuckles. 'He drinks protein shakes and colour codes his wardrobe,' he says fondly.

I shake my head. 'Bizarre. Speaking of which . . .' I glance around the room where we're standing. 'We're really here again.'

Shepperton is the studio we used for the first film, and we're working out of Littleton House, or 'the Old House' as everyone calls it, which is a beautiful red brick manor house located smack in the middle of an industrial mess of buildings that include fourteen enormous sound stages, as well as workshops, backlots, and every other facility you can think of when it comes to filmmaking. I haven't been in these particular rooms since we were here for the first movie. The sense of déjà vu is overwhelming, particularly with all the same faces popping up.

Well, most of them. Rufus Tait is noticeably absent, his character having been killed off – a wise move given that he was recently exposed in the press as a massive sex-pest, news which seemed to come as a shock to the man himself, but surprised precisely no one who had ever met him.

I wonder how much of the anxiety I'm feeling now is down to nerves about today and how much is a strange, ghostly echo of what I felt when I rolled up here the first time around and I was barely able to string my lines together.

'Hi, guys!' We're interrupted then by Brooke bouncing over, looking as bright-eyed and sunny as she did when we met her at the gala.

Jack introduces Brooke to Hattie, and Brooke glances around the room. 'This place is unreal,' she hums with appreciation. 'Did you know they filmed *The Mummy Returns* here?'

'I *love* that film,' I exclaim. 'I went to see it four times at the cinema.'

'Wow,' Brooke says, solemnly. 'I wish I could have seen it on the big screen, but it came out the year before I was born.'

'Oh,' I manage, feeling as though I'm about to start desiccating in front of her. I am the living embodiment of that Titanic meme . . . *It's been 84 years*.

'If you think that makes you feel old, you should try being me.' Hattie twinkles, clearly reading my expression.

The gentle murmur of conversation in the large, wood-panelled room is interrupted by the arrival of Logan and Jasmine. A small, spontaneous cheer goes up, and Logan hurries in, delighted, his sister behind him.

Jasmine hasn't changed a bit – it's almost uncanny. Perhaps a steady diet of cigarettes and existential dread preserves a person, somehow . . . I suppose it *is* very French. She's swathed in an angular, oversized black tunic, her pale face impassive as ever, but I think I see a touch of warmth when her gaze lands on me. Of course, that could be wishful thinking.

Logan, however *does* look different. He's aged significantly and lost a fair amount of weight. I heard on the grapevine that there was a recent, successful trip to rehab, which is the reason he's actually available to make the film. I'm glad that the big enthusiastic energy he always carried still sails into the room with him. Hopefully now it is no longer powered by cocaine.

'Cynthie!' he exclaims, and I'm surprised that he's so excited to see me when, in the past, he only tolerated my presence. He begins to reach for a hug, but then stops himself. 'Do I have your permission to touch you?' he asks earnestly.

'Um, sure,' I say before I'm pulled in and given two smacking kisses. I'm not sure what happened to the guy who once told wardrobe that my Regency costumes 'weren't showing enough in the boob area', but maybe he's evolved.

'So happy that we're working together again,' Logan enthuses. 'I always knew you had it in you! People are forever asking me how it happened, and I tell them that it was obvious from the start, that you had that star quality.' Again, he fixes me with a sudden, serious look. 'And I make it very clear that your success is all you, right? It's nothing to do with the people who gave you your first break. You made this happen, not us. We're just a small part of the story. I would never want to diminish your power.'

'Thank you?' I say faintly, so unsure how to respond to this that the words come out like a question.

'Don't mind Logan,' Jasmine mutters as she comes to stand beside me while her brother sets off around the room, pumping hands and doling out consensual embraces. 'He's terrified of being cancelled, so now he's a born-again feminist. It's very hit and miss, but at least he means well.' She shoots him a look of fond exasperation which sets off another flood of déjà vu.

Turning her steady gaze on me, she lifts her brows. 'Didn't think we'd ever get you here.'

'I'm excited to work with you again,' I say, honestly. 'I learned a lot last time.'

'Mmmm.' Jasmine's mouth twitches, and I think this means she's amused. 'Well, you certainly put it to good use.'

It feels like getting a gold star off your favourite teacher, and I practically levitate. Apparently I'm still desperate for Jasmine Gallow's approval. Given the soft cough of laughter I hear Jack make, I'd guess my feelings are obvious.

'Good to see you, Jack,' Jasmine says, and his amusement vanishes, his spine straightening like a soldier snapping to attention as he offers a polite, 'You, too.'

'God, she's still terrifying,' he whispers to me as she moves on to talk to Hattie and Brooke.

I laugh. 'I didn't know you were ever scared of her.'

'Are you kidding?' Jack lifts his hand to rub the back of his neck. 'I always felt like she could see right through me.'

I think about the conversation we had after my panic attack. While I was oblivious to everything going on with Jack under the surface, I'd be willing to bet that Jasmine wasn't.

'Okay, gang,' Logan says, clapping his hands together. 'Before we get down to business, I want to take this opportunity to introduce Brooke and her team, who are filming for the documentary you've all signed on to so please . . . everyone on your best behaviour!' His smile is strained.

'Please *don't* be on your best behaviour.' Brooke grins, and a flutter of nervous laughter runs around the room. 'Seriously though,' Brooke continues, 'we're not here to make your lives harder. We're going to be very fly-on-the-wall. Most of the time you should hardly notice we're here, though we will be taking you aside for interviews when it's convenient.'

She gestures to three other people standing in the corner of the room. 'Our team is small but perfectly formed. There's Dec, our videographer with his trusty camera.' Dec, who I recognize, is already filming but he lifts his hand in greeting. 'Then we have Kara, our sound technician.' She gestures to a small blond woman with blue streaks in her hair. 'And Cooper who is our runner and general dogsbody.' The boy next to Kara looks about thirteen, though I assume he *is* actually older, his face set in sullen lines.

'We're really excited to be working on this project,' Brooke finishes up. 'All of us love the original movie, and I know the fans are going to be thrilled to get such an extensive look behind the scenes of the sequel.'

'Thank you, Brooke,' Jasmine says. 'I think we're all intrigued to see what you come up with.'

Brooke beams at her, and I can tell that she's a fellow acolyte, a certified member of the Jasmine Gallow fan club.

Logan steps forward. 'You're probably wondering why we've gathered you in this room ahead of the read-through, but it's because I'd like us to start the day right, to enter into our practice with our hearts open, so with that in mind we'll begin with a brief meditation and sound bath.'

While more than one confused set of eyes looks on, Logan moves to the door and opens it with a flourish.

'I'd like you to welcome my friend, Acorn. We'll give her a moment to set up her Tibetan singing bowls . . .'

At this, a petite woman in a cream tunic comes staggering in with a stack of hammered metal bowls of various sizes.

'My goodness,' Hattie murmurs. 'A sound bath? That seems rather . . . intimate.'

'It's not an actual bath,' I reassure her. 'They sort of bathe you in sound waves. I've done one before and they're quite nice.' I don't share that this was part of an ill-advised yoga trip that Hannah and I took together. I got food poisoning from a horrific wheatgrass concoction and vomited a stream of bright green puke during the sound bath. The instructor did not take that as a compliment. Hopefully this one will go better.

Hattie isn't the only one having doubts. 'I'm off for a smoke,' Jasmine says. 'I hate this sort of thing.'

'Negative emotions can be very ageing,' Acorn murmurs, over-hearing. She is seemingly unmoved by the ice in Jasmine's glare.

'Unless that face of yours conceals the fact you're actually a one-hundred-and-fifty-year-old sea hag, I'm not interested in your opinion on ageing,' Jasmine announces, before clamping an unlit cigarette between her lips and stalking off.

God, I love her so much.

Acorn only laughs, the sound like a peal of sweet, chiming bells. 'It's not for everyone,' she says serenely, and actually, maybe I could use a sound bath if it's going to give me that sort of sangfroid.

We're encouraged to sit on the floor and Acorn guides us through a thirty-minute meditation. It's not her fault that I'm absolutely not in the headspace to be able to focus. I keep getting distracted. First by Jack who is sitting beside me. He doesn't have to actually *do* anything to upset my concentration; he just has to sit there, breathing handsomely. He looks so still and serene, and I wonder what he's thinking. I wonder if it's normal to fancy some-one so much that you want to crack their heads open and climb inside. Probably not.

Then I am distracted by Logan who smiles beatifically like a happy toddler throughout the session, and keeps humming as if the bowls are playing a familiar tune.

Finally, when Simon starts lightly snoring, I know that it's hope-less. There's to be no relaxation for me, and I have to question if I'm the only person to leave a meditation more stressed out than when I started.

I tune Acorn's soft voice out, and instead I start to hear a different one: one that tells me I'm not a good actor, that I've lost my edge, that I'm soft and that I lack subtlety. My heart starts beating harder, and as soon as I notice that, my breath starts coming faster, too.

The room feels hot and stuffy, and there are too many people sitting too close to me. They're going to hear me, going to notice that I'm breathing too hard.

I get abruptly to my feet and head for the door.

Chapter Thirty

Cynthie

'Not to worry,' I hear Acorn's voice floating after me. 'Meditation can bring up a lot of emotions.'

This room connects to another one with a long table running down the centre, scripts laid out behind name cards, ready for our read-through. My breath is still coming in short, sharp drags. I head for the French doors which open up onto a small green space. There's a covered patio with a tiled floor and a collection of utilitarian metal garden furniture, and a square of lawn with a couple of benches. It's quiet and the air is cool and I suck it down eagerly.

I sit on one of the cold, metal chairs, and place my hand on my chest like Jack showed me. I close my eyes and try to remember what he said, try to breathe just as he told me, and slowly, as I focus my awareness on the pressure of my fingers, the panic eases.

When my eyes open, I find Jasmine standing in front of me. She holds a lit cigarette, and eyes me with mild interest.

'Are you all right now?' she asks.

I nod, embarrassed. 'Yes, I just had a bit of a funny turn.'

Jasmine rolls her eyes. 'There's no need to be so Victorian about it. Don't bother with euphemisms on my behalf, just call it what it was – a panic attack. It's not like you're the first person in the entertainment industry to have one. You're not even the first person in this garden to have one.'

Somehow this brusque response is extremely soothing. I manage a smile. 'Give me a chance,' I say. 'It's only my second one. I'm still getting used to the idea.'

Jasmine takes a thoughtful drag on her cigarette. 'Interesting,' she says finally. 'I don't suppose this would have anything to do with a certain dickhead named Shawn Hardy?'

I flinch at the name, but then I suppose Jasmine isn't one to mince her words. 'I don't know,' I say, and I rub my fingers against my forehead. 'Probably.'

I don't hear whatever Jasmine starts to say, because the door behind her opens and Jack appears with a glass of water in his hand. He hesitates on the threshold.

'Sorry.' He looks from me to Jasmine and back. 'I wasn't sure what to do, if you wanted company or not . . .'

'Don't mind me,' Jasmine says, tossing her cigarette to the ground and grinding it under her clompy black boot. 'I'm going to go and extract everyone from my brother's wellness retreat and see if we can get some work done.' She shoots me a sharp look. 'You take a few minutes, whatever you need.'

'Thanks,' I murmur, but she's already stomping back inside.

'Hey,' Jack steps towards me, a tentative smile on his face. 'You rushed out of there. You okay?' He hands me the glass of water, and I sip it gratefully.

'I had another panic attack,' I admit, and his expression softens with concern. 'It wasn't as bad as before,' I add quickly, placing the glass down on the table beside me. 'And I got it under control.'

'That's good,' he says, and he pulls out the chair across from me, sitting in it and leaning forward. 'Was there something specific that triggered it?'

'You mean you don't find Tibetan singing bowls and women called Acorn to be panic inducing?'

He laughs. 'I mean, it isn't how I'd choose to spend my morning, but I thought it was okay.'

'Yes, I know. You looked totally zen. Top student.'

His mouth pulls up. 'I was reciting my lines in my head,' he admits. 'I didn't take in anything poor Acorn was saying.'

It's my turn to laugh. 'You phoney.'

'So,' he says, reaching out and tugging one of my hands into his. He brushes his thumb across the top of my knuckles and I watch the movement avidly. 'What's going on?'

I shrug. 'Just first day nerves I guess.'

'Is that usual for you?'

His thumb still moves gently back and forth over my skin. 'I suppose not,' I say reluctantly.

I can feel him waiting, patiently. I have a horrible feeling he'd sit and wait all day.

'The last film I made wasn't a great experience,' I say, finally.

'The one you did with Shawn?' I can hear the distaste in his voice as he says the name.

I nod.

'I saw it,' Jack admits. 'You were wonderful.'

'I suppose.' I pull my hand away from him, too agitated to keep still. I get to my feet and wrap my arms around my stomach. 'There's Oscar buzz, you know,' I say flatly. 'Which is actually a nightmare because it means more press, more headlines. Being in a room with him for the campaign.'

'I get that,' Jack says. 'I'm sorry that his behaviour would taint a huge achievement. You should be proud of the work.'

The bark of laughter I give is devoid of humour. 'Proud of the work?' I exhale shakily. 'I barely remember doing it. The whole experience was awful, even before Shawn and I . . .' I trail off.

'I've heard he's difficult to work with,' Jack says carefully.

'Yeah. Difficult is one word for it. Nothing I did was good enough,' I say. 'The subject matter was so harrowing, you know – a young mother losing her child in mysterious circumstances, trying to uncover the truth but questioning her own sanity . . .' I shiver. 'It was hard to live with, and Shawn was determined to wring an authentic performance out of me. I guess he did.'

'What do you mean?'

I sigh. 'I don't . . .' I start to tell Jack that I can't talk about it, but something makes me stop. Maybe I can talk about it. With him. 'It's hard to explain,' I say instead.

'I'll listen. If you want to tell me.'

I'm still not looking at him, but I nod.

I hesitate, weighing my words. 'So much of it I only saw afterwards. That's what's so strange . . . At the time it didn't feel wrong.' I make a sound of exasperation. 'And it's so slippery that there's little to tell. He didn't really *do* anything; he just made me feel small. All the time. He chipped away at my performance first, and then my appearance, the way I moved, the way I talked. I wasn't connecting with the material emotionally or intellectually; I wasn't bright enough to understand what he wanted; I hadn't got the training; I wasn't taking it seriously. I got more and more nervous and edgy, and then I'd break and cry which was humiliating, but he'd be *pleased*, and he'd tell me he was only pushing me so hard because he knew how talented I was, what I was capable of. I started clinging to any bit of praise; I was desperate to make him happy.' I chew on my thumbnail. 'I admired him, and I was determined to deliver. The work was important, you know? We were doing something important.'

I chance a look at Jack and his face is very still, but after a moment he moves his head in a jerky nod.

I huff out another breath. 'But it was hard, I suppose. Harder than anything I'd done before, and I started feeling anxious. I couldn't eat and I lost weight. I looked ill, and he liked that. For the part, he said. It was as if it all started to creep in, the character and her mental state ... I don't know,' I say, rubbing a hand over my eyes. 'He was doing his job, I guess. As you say ... he got the performance he wanted. And a relationship with me, too, such as it was. I don't think he planned for that. God!' I feel for a second like I want to strike out, to hit something. 'It was like I was in a fucking cult by the end. I worshipped him. It makes me feel sick now. I don't know how it got so far.'

I turn to Jack again. 'But he really did tell me he was separated from his wife,' I say a little desperately. 'He told me they were divorcing. I wouldn't have ... I really don't think I would have ... otherwise.' There are tears, and they come suddenly, hard, taking me by surprise.

Jack is on his feet in an instant, wrapping me up, holding me against him so that I can cry, properly cry, against his chest. He holds me for a long time, stroking my hair until my sobs quieten.

'I'm scared I've lost it,' I confess, the words muffled against the fabric of his shirt damp from my tears. 'What if I can't do the work anymore?'

Jack eases back from me, his hands holding my forearms.

'Cynthie,' he says and his face is serious, 'you haven't lost anything. What that man did ... it wasn't directing. It wasn't art, honey. It was abuse, plain and simple.'

The words are like a shock, and I jerk back instinctively. 'No,' I say, a shaky laugh on my lips. 'No, Jack, it wasn't that bad. It was just ...'

'Okay,' he says quietly. 'We don't have to say any more about that now, but you just let it sit with you.'

I rub a hand over my face.

'It's a good thing there isn't an entire room full of actors in there, along with an actual documentary team, or I'd be worried that I look like I've been crying my eyes out,' I say with a tremulous smile.

Picking up on the change in my tone, Jack's body language shifts completely, ready to put me at ease. He grins. 'Yes, at least you can reassure yourself that they're not at all nosy and excited to jump in everyone else's business.'

He reaches into the pocket of his jeans and pulls out a clean white handkerchief.

I lift my eyebrows. 'You carry a handkerchief?'

'I do.' He folds the fabric into a strip and carefully pours some of the water out of my glass over it. 'Here,' he says, 'sit down and put this on your eyes. You'll be good as new in a few minutes.'

'Oh my god,' I whisper, delighted as I turn it over in my hands. 'It's *monogrammed*!'

Colour touches his cheeks. 'My gran gave them to me.'

'Well, that's adorable.' I sit and the damp fabric is cool and soothing against my eyes. We fall into silence, and I try not to think about why sitting quietly with Jack is so comforting.

'Everyone will be wondering where we are,' I say after a couple of minutes.

'Nah.' I feel Jack stretch out in the chair beside me. 'They'll think I'm out here ravishing you.'

'Hey,' I protest, 'I could be the one ravishing you, you know.'

'Good idea. I'm all for equal opportunity ravishment.'

I laugh, something in my chest easing. I pull the handkerchief from my eyes. 'What's the verdict?' I ask. He examines my face carefully.

'Almost back to normal. Think happy thoughts.'

'Distract me with something cheerful, then.'

'Okay.' He gets up, pulling the other metal furniture to the side until he's cleared a large space in front of me.

'What are you doing?'

'You asked me if I could tap dance,' is the only answer I get.

'Nooooo!' I squeal, actually wriggling in my seat. 'You're really going to tap dance for me?'

'I'll do my best.' He pulls his phone from his pocket and swipes at the screen until music emerges tinnily from the speaker. I recognize it at once as Fred Astaire singing 'No Strings' from *Top Hat*.

'An Astaire man,' I observe.

'I bet you were a Gene Kelly girl.'

'I can neither confirm nor deny.' As it happens, I love both of them. When we were kids, Hannah and I devoured all their films leading to our own 'tap dancing' performances which – without the benefit of any actual lessons – consisted of the two of us flailing about and making as much noise as possible with our shoes on her mum and dad's linoleum. 'I just wanted to be Rita Hayworth.'

Jack positions himself in the middle of the space, one hand in his pocket, and he sends me a grin. I have a funny feeling in my stomach, that might be affection, but then he starts dancing and the feeling rapidly shifts into something else.

He's tentative at first, but then the muscle memory clearly kicks in and he's moving effortlessly, the gentle sound of his shoes against the tiles echoing the sharp recorded tapping at the back of the music. I've seen the film enough times to know that he's doing the same dance Astaire does. I know with a strange sense of certainty that he taught himself, practising for hours and hours in front of the footage. I'd bet money on it.

And he looks *good*. He moves with a kind of louche elegance that's all Astaire, but his body is big and powerful. He makes it look *easy*. He's so in control. It is almost unbearably hot, and now I find myself squirming in my seat for a different reason. The look of concentration on his face falls away to be replaced with exhilaration. He's enjoying himself.

Finally, he stops. Pink-cheeked and breathless, he laughs. 'That's all I remember. I haven't done that for ages. Well?' he says in the face of my silence. 'Was it all you hoped it would be?'

'And more,' I manage, and I wish my voice didn't sound so hopelessly needy.

'Are you cheered up enough to head back inside?'

I pull myself to my feet trying to hide the fact my limbs are trembling like I'm a nervous faun. 'I am. That was amazing. You know, I'd pay to watch you up on stage.'

'Yeah?' He sounds pleased.

'Yes. But I appreciate the private performance.'

Our gazes catch, tangle. His chest rises and falls, and maybe it's the dancing that has him breathing hard, but what the hell is my excuse?

I turn and make my way towards the door before I actually *do* decide to ravish him.

'Any time, Cynthie.' The soft words follow me inside, the second time he's said them, and I shiver.

I almost believe him.

Chapter Thirty-One

Jack

The first day of filming dawns bright and sunny, which is quite a contrast to my memory of doing this last time – as is my feeling of cautious optimism.

Rehearsals went well, and despite her nerves, Cynthie handled everything perfectly – if I didn't know for a fact that she was having a hard time, then I certainly wouldn't have guessed it. From the second we returned to the table read after her panic attack, she was a total professional.

Despite the countless hours I've spent fantasizing about grinding Shawn Hardy's bones into dust, Cynthie and I haven't broached the topic of him again. One thing is very clear: Cynthie Taylor has had a rough go of it lately.

And it's this thought that has had me trying to keep a certain amount of distance between us over the last week. Not too much – I don't want her to think I'm avoiding her – but I know I need to be careful because the more time we spend together, the more time I *want* to spend with her. I'm ready to admit that Cynthie is firmly under my skin. I'm even ready to admit that she's been there for thirteen years, but it doesn't change our absolutely shocking timing.

Between the work we have to do, maintaining a fake relationship, the documentary, and her recent trauma, there are more than enough reasons for me to keep those feelings in check. Or at least to make a decent attempt.

So why am I here on set, outside her trailer when I'm not on the call sheet this morning? Let's call it professional courtesy, because I'm trying very hard to pretend that's what it is.

I knock on the door, smiling at the sight of her trailer next door to mine once more. We're back at Darlcot Manor, and aside from the fact that the equipment looks a bit brighter and shinier, it could almost be thirteen years ago. Jasmine and Logan managed to get about eighty per cent of the original cast and crew back which is no small feat, and that means that I recognize almost everyone – from camera operators to caterers.

'Come in!' Cynthie's voice calls, and I climb the steps, pulling the door open.

'Hey, I—' I start before I realize we're not alone. Cynthie is curled up in the corner of the sofa and Brooke and Declan are perched across from her. Declan's camera swings in my direction.

'Oh,' I murmur. 'Sorry, I didn't realize you were in the middle of something.'

'No, no, don't mind us.' Brooke is already leaping to her feet. 'We were just doing some preliminary interviews, but it's great that you're here. Do you mind if I get Kara to come and mic you?'

I glance at Cynthie, who only looks mildly entertained. Her hair is pulled back ready for her wig, and her make-up is done, but she's wearing leggings and an oversized Shania Twain T-shirt.

'Sure,' I say. I guess this documentary business all has to start some time.

'We'll just step out for a second,' Brooke says, pulling her phone from her pocket, fingers flying over the screen. 'Let you get settled.'

I wait for them to do just that, before I turn back to Cyn, raising my eyebrows. 'Is the trailer full of hidden cameras?'

She laughs, but carefully switches off the microphone she's wearing. 'Not as far as I know, but I wouldn't put it past Declan to be peeking through the skylight.'

I huff out a breath. 'I haven't really thought this whole thing through. It's going to be more complicated than I imagined.'

'We'll have to be careful,' she agrees, glancing at the mic again as if wanting to double check it's off. 'With us.'

With pretending we're a couple, she means. Not for the first time I feel my heart sink at the thought. Faking a relationship with her when we hated each other – or at least convinced ourselves we did – was torturous enough, but doing it when I can acknowledge I have very real feelings for her is a whole different kind of nightmare.

'What are you doing here anyway?' She tilts her head at me. 'I thought you weren't on the call sheet until this afternoon. I imagined you'd be enjoying a lie in.'

'I brought you coffee,' I say, holding up a pair of travel cups.

'That's very sweet of you,' she says accepting the cup with a smile, 'but you do know that there are lots of people here who are happy to get me coffee? Or that I could walk over and get one myself.'

'But this is my very own stash,' I confide. 'Scott has my trailer set up like a Starbucks.'

She takes a sip, and chokes. 'Oh god, Jack, this is like rocket fuel. How many of these have you had this morning?' She gives me a stern look, and in return I try to appear innocent.

'This is my first one.'

'Lie.' She points at me. 'You wouldn't be this upright at six thirty if you hadn't already had coffee.'

'Fine, it's my third,' I admit, leaning back against the counter of the thin galley kitchen that faces her seating area, and draining the cup.

Cynthie closes her eyes. 'Your heart is going to explode,' she shakes her head. 'I'm going to start making you drink chamomile tea.'

'You and what army, Taylor?'

She huffs in amusement. 'So aside from bringing me this very strong but very delicious coffee, what are you doing here, really?'

I shrug. 'I didn't want to miss your first scene. And I guess I wanted to check in, make sure you were feeling good.'

Her eyes soften. 'I'm doing okay.' Her gaze moves to the window beside her which looks out over the chaos of the base set up. 'A bit edgy. But no panic attacks or anything. Now that we're here it's like muscle memory.' She manages to smile. 'It's funny the way things work out, isn't it? I felt safe here the first time around, happy.'

'So it's a good place for you to be now when you're feeling vulnerable?' I suggest.

'Exactly that.' She nods. 'Working for the first time after . . .' She trails off for a moment. 'Well, I don't know what would have happened if I'd been on the film I was supposed to be working on now. I have a feeling it wouldn't have been great. Being here, surrounded by people I know. It helps. I guess we'll see when I'm on set.'

'Do you want to run lines?' I ask.

Cynthie's face lights up. 'Really?'

'Scoot over,' I drop onto the sofa beside her and she shuffles down to make room for me. Unfortunately for me (or fortunately depending on how you look at it) the couch is small enough that when I reach for the script on the table our arms brush against each other, and my heart bumps.

'Okaaaaaay,' Brooke comes bouncing in, followed by the whole motley crew, and Kara efficiently mics me up. 'So, if you're happy just to keep doing what you were doing, then we'll grab some footage. It won't always feel this intrusive, I promise,' she says earnestly. 'We'll mostly be melting into the background, but that's a bit harder to do in the trailers, and I really think glimpses into these spaces will make viewers feel involved.'

'Sure,' I reply. Kara leaves and Brooke retreats to a corner where she seems to be engrossed in whatever is happening on her phone.

There's not really any missing Declan, who basically has a camera shoved in our faces, but he tries to be as discreet as possible, and I go through the motions of running lines with Cynthie for her scene this morning.

The problem, of course, is that this is supposed to be behind-the-scenes footage of a loved-up couple and I don't know how to convincingly portray that, especially without making Cynthie feel uncomfortable. Fuck, this is such a minefield.

Clearly sensing my discomfort, Cynthie takes charge of the situation. Twisting herself back into the corner of the L-shaped couch, she stretches out her legs so that they rest in my lap. She gives me a quick look, and I incline my head ever so slightly. Then I put my hand on her leg and she smiles.

We can do this. It's just about checking in with each other.

I get what she was thinking: we look comfortable together, relaxed. She leans back into the cushions, and I hold the script in one hand, the other absently running up and down her leggings-clad calf. She's wearing fluffy socks, and we laugh and mess around with the lines as we throw them back and forth between us.

Only, the movement of my hand isn't absent at all. I'm reading the lines but all my focus is on the feel of her. And Cynthie Taylor might be the best actress in the whole damn world, but she's not fooling me. Every so often I hear her breath catch. When I trace my fingers lazily over her knee and then higher – only slightly higher – there's colour in her face that wasn't there before.

At one point she squirms, the slightest friction in my lap, and I clench my teeth. She huffs a tiny chuckle and I get it: I'm not the only one enjoying this. I just wish we didn't have a fucking audience. Then again, if it wasn't for their presence we wouldn't be sitting like this in the first place.

Complicated.

Finally, Hannah appears, clutching a clipboard and wearing an earpiece. Her eyes move from the two of us to the camera crew and back, and her smile is on the frozen side.

'Hi!' she says, more chipper than I've ever heard her. Panic flickers in her gaze. Hannah is not an actor. I half expect her to start yelling. 'YES, THIS IS TOTALLY NORMAL BEHAVIOUR FOR THEM. BECAUSE THEY ARE A COUPLE. DEFINITELY A COUPLE.'

Instead, she clears her throat. 'We need to get you into costume, Cyn,' she manages and I shoot her an encouraging smile. 'They're almost finished setting up, and Arjun says we're pretty tight for time to make sure we turnaround for this afternoon.'

Marion has retired since we made the first film, so Arjun has been promoted to first AD and I know he feels he has big shoes to fill.

Cynthie untangles herself from me and gets to her feet. 'Great,' she says, the picture of confidence. 'I'll see you on set?'

'You will,' I nod. Then, she leans down and kisses me on the cheek. It's a careless little moment, one that seems like something we've done hundreds of times, and as her perfume lingers around me like a ghost, I find myself wishing that were true.

Brooke and co. traipse off after Cynthie as she goes to be laced into her costume, and I make my way towards the big house where they're filming this morning. Along the way, I come across a lot of busy people who are all happy to wave and call out a greeting as I pass. It's a good atmosphere, warm, like a homecoming.

Inside Darlcot Manor, Logan and Jasmine have set up ready for the first shot of the day in the room that is supposed to be Emilia's bedroom. It's a relatively straightforward scene: there's a conversation between Emilia and her maid, and then she pulls out the box where she's locked away all of Edward's letters and reads through them. It might be simple, but it's always difficult to be in the very first scene of a shoot. It feels like added pressure that Cynthie doesn't need. My nerves jump on her behalf.

'Jack, what are you doing here?' Logan asks.

'Hoped you wouldn't mind me sitting in.'

'All part of your process?' Jasmine asks blandly, which makes me certain she knows more about Cynthie's emotional state than she's letting on.

'Something like that,' I agree.

'Well, it's fine with me,' Logan says. 'We're a bit tight on space, but I'm sure you can find a corner to tuck yourself into.'

In the end, that's literally the case, and I wedge myself into a folding chair at the back of the room behind the monitors with Arjun. Fortunately, the rooms in this grand house are enormous, because there are three cameras, lighting rigs, and a huge number of people in here. I catch the odd, panicked-looking National Trust volunteer paying serious attention to the squeaking floorboards, and hope that we're not going to bring the building down.

After a few more minutes, Cynthie arrives with Patty, Liam, Hannah, and Brooke's crew in tow. The room gets even more crowded. I watch as Cynthie scans the crowd, and my heart lifts when I realize who she's looking for. When her eyes find me, I lift my hand and she smiles with a look that might be relief.

Then everything moves very quickly. Cynthie, Logan and Jasmine block the scene, and any trace of nerves has been ruthlessly suppressed, because Cynthie appears in her element. She's changed a lot, I realize. She's sure of herself in a way she wasn't all those years ago, and it's clear she has her own creative vision because she stops at several points to make suggestions or tweaks.

Jasmine absorbs these suggestions quietly, but Logan leaps on everything she says like an enthusiastic hound on a biscuit.

'Right,' Jasmine says finally. 'I think we're ready to go.'

'First positions,' Arjun pipes up.

'Roll sound.' Jasmine points.

'Sound speed!'

'Roll camera.'

'Camera rolling.'

A young guy steps into shot with a slate. 'Scene four, take one.' He claps the slate shut.

'Set,' the camera operator near me says.

'Action,' Jasmine calls.

And we're off.

It takes about five minutes for me to forget how worried I am. Then, all I can do is watch as Cynthie delivers a perfect take. Seeing her on the monitors is a pleasure. The scene is framed beautifully, and Cynthie is luminous. It's impossible to drag your eyes away from her. When she traces Edward's handwriting with her fingers and a single tear slides down her face, she tilts her chin and the lighting catches it, crystalline and lovely. Every line of her body speaks of an impossible heartbreak, when only moments before she'd looked utterly at ease. I'm not the only one holding my breath.

'Cut!' Jasmine shouts, and there's a spontaneous burst of applause. Cynthie wipes the tear away, and as Liam swoops in to fix her make-up, she glances over in Jasmine's direction.

'I'd like to try it again, but changing up the pace in that middle section,' Cynthie says briskly.

Even Jasmine can barely suppress a smile. 'Sounds good,' she agrees.

'Fuck, she's incredible,' I murmur.

'I know, right.' Brooke's voice comes from close beside me.

I practically jump out of my skin. Where did she even come from?

'I wondered if we could steal you for a quick interview? I know you have a busy afternoon.' Her tone is apologetic.

I glance at Cynthie, but she seems fine now, absorbed in the work.

'Sure,' I say, reluctantly.

'Great. We have everything set up next door.' Brooke is all smiles.

I catch Cynthie's eye and gesture towards Brooke, discreetly rolling my eyes, and she smiles, shoos me off with her hand.

The room next door is empty except for a chair and a small lighting rig. I refrain from mentioning that it looks as though I'm about to be tortured for information, and I try to be as charming as possible as I settle in to answering Brooke's questions.

'So, is it strange being back here at Darlcot Manor after all these years?'

'Definitely,' I agree. 'I thought it'd been a long time since we were here, but suddenly the past feels very close. It's a good feeling though, like coming back to somewhere that was important to you when you were younger. You know, like where you spent that one perfect summer as a kid.'

'*A Lady of Quality* was your first film,' Brooke says. 'Did you think of yourself as a kid when you were making it?'

'God no,' I laugh. 'I was twenty-four and I thought I knew it all. Thirteen years can give you a generous dose of perspective.'

'Do you know it all, now?'

'Nope.' I grin.

'We've just watched Cynthie filming a scene, and I wondered if that felt different from how it was last time around?' Brooke's question takes me by surprise, mostly because it's exactly what had been on my mind.

'Yeah, it's different. *Lady* was Cynthie's first film, too and she was untrained. It's miraculous really, that she was capable of the performance she gave – that she had so much raw talent. She had a lot less control then. It was all instinct and that was . . .' – I exhale – 'exhilarating, actually, to act against. Although it scared the shit out of me at the time.'

Brooke chuckles.

'I've seen the stuff she's made since, but I haven't actually watched her work, and what I just witnessed was, well, a masterclass. And that's all Cynthie.' I shake my head. 'She made that for herself, took all her talent and honed it. The control, the composure ... it's different ...' I trail off here, and I can't help thinking how hard today must have been for her, and how she still managed to turn up and do her job, to do it impeccably. I'd be willing to bet she doesn't give herself credit for that. Perversely, I also think maybe it's a shame that some of that wild, reckless spirit seems to have left her.

'She was pure joy whenever she was performing back then,' I say distractedly. 'It was like looking at the sun come up.'

I catch myself, clear my throat.

'Um, is that all you need?' I ask. 'I should really be going.'

'Yes,' Brooke says, with a small, secretive smile that makes me nervous. 'That was perfect.'

Chapter Thirty-Two

Cynthie

'Listen,' I say as I watch Patrick Swayze on the screen, 'I could write a thesis on this scene. I could have a PhD in *Dirty Dancing*.'

'Swayze is on fire in this movie,' Patty puts in, taking a swig from her bottle of beer.

'No arguments here,' Arjun agrees, his arm around her.

'*So* hot,' Hannah adds emphatically.

'Is there more pizza?' Liam emerges from under a pile of blankets.

'Only the vegan one.' Hannah says, checking the boxes that sit on the coffee table.

'Oh,' Liam sighs. 'Nah.'

'I knew this would happen,' Hannah scolds. 'We ordered the vegan one for you because you said you watched that documentary and you were never touching another animal product again. You said you were vegan now; you gave us all quite a lengthy sermon on the subject.'

Liam blinks. 'I *am* vegan . . .' he says.

'Tell that to my double pepperoni pizza,' Patty snorts.

' . . . most of the time,' Liam finishes. 'It's just the pizza smelled so good . . .' He drops his head. 'I fell at the first hurdle, didn't I? I'm the worst vegan in the world.'

'I don't think you can really call yourself any kind of vegan if you eat cheese and meat,' Hannah points out.

'But I always use almond milk,' Liam says earnestly.

'I heard almond milk is terrible for the environment,' Arjun puts in, and Patty jabs him in the stomach, while Liam looks crestfallen.

We're all sitting in my hotel suite, snuggled in front of the big television after a long day of filming. In the last thirteen years Alveston Hall has become a private residence, so we couldn't stay there again. I don't suppose Gayle would have let them put me in my snug little attic room where I shared a bathroom with Hannah anyway, but I still feel a bit sad about it.

On the other hand, it would probably only have further complicated matters with Jack. Imagine trying to make myself a cup of tea in the kitchen where we once had sex on the floor. My head goes a bit light at the memory – a memory I've been replaying more and more lately if I'm honest.

The first week of filming has gone well enough. My anxiety comes and goes, but for the most part I've managed to keep it together ... even if some of the work feels like it's been done on autopilot, which I hate. I imagine Shawn's voice in my head chastising me about it, telling me that I'm phoning it in, that I'm losing the audience. Somehow Jack always seems to know, and he'll appear like my personal emotional support film star, handsome and kind, and just quietly, stubbornly *there*.

We've spent the week pretending to be a couple whenever Brooke is around, which is – and I cannot stress this enough – *all the time*. We have to keep touching each other and looking at each other and holding hands, and it is fucking with my head in a big way, because I know what acting feels like, and that's not what this is. It's not real, but it's not exactly pretend either.

As if I have summoned him, there's a knock on the door and he comes in, looking tired and rumpled.

'Jack!' Liam greets him.

'Shhhhhh!' Patty hisses, her eyes sliding to the door to the adjoining room where Priya is safely tucked in bed, and we all freeze. If she hears Jack's name, she'll be straight in here. 'Uncle Jack' earned her immediate, undying devotion the very first time they met when he produced a Barbie dream house, seemingly out of thin air. By helping her set it all up and then playing Barbies with her for an hour while totally committing to doing all the different voices, Jack Turner-Jones claimed another heart, and Priya has been hopelessly obsessed with him ever since.

She's not the only one. That particular scene did something unforgivable to my body's biological clock. My ovaries have yet to recover.

'How did it go?' I ask him now. He was filming much later than the rest of us so it's been an incredibly long day for him.

He collapses on the sofa beside me. 'Good, I think. Hattie was unbelievable, had half the crew in tears.'

'I hid some pepperoni pizza for you,' I say, producing a box from under the sofa.

'Betrayed!' Liam howls, chewing on his vegan pizza crust. 'Although actually,' he adds thoughtfully, 'this is pretty good. Really, Jack, you should think about going vegan.'

Jack doesn't answer, already tucking into the pizza as if he's suddenly realized he's famished. It can hit you like that after a long day's shoot. Unthinkingly, I reach up and gently push his hair back from his face, my fingers rubbing over his scalp. He leans into my hand and sighs.

Then we both freeze, realizing at the same time that Brooke isn't here, that we don't have to pretend right now.

Fortunately, my friends are distracted, busy bickering over pizza once more, and I pull my hand away, neither of us acknowledging that anything happened. The story of our lives right now.

'So,' Jack says, leaning back after demolishing another slice of pizza, 'what have you guys been up to?'

'Epic dance party with Priya,' Arjun says, handing Jack a beer.

'Sorry I missed that,' Jack smirks. 'As I recall your moves were always . . . enthusiastic.'

'Let's just say I haven't lost my touch.' Arjun buffs his fingernails on his T-shirt.

'Then we watched *Dirty Dancing*.' Hannah gestures to the screen.

'And now we're on our third re-watch of the last scene,' Patty says.

'A classic,' Jack agrees, swigging his beer. He looks happy and relaxed, slipping so easily into the group.

'I was just saying that I have a lot of thoughts about this scene,' I say. 'I know it's a dance scene but the acting is perfect. So many little touches.'

'Oh, yeah,' Jack nods.

I hit play, and Patrick Swayze stands at the side of the stage, taking off his leather jacket. 'Crooking the finger at her?' I say.

'The way she smiles when he dips her,' Jack gestures at the screen with his bottle.

'The nose kiss!' Liam and Patty squeal at the same time.

On-screen, Swayze and Jennifer Grey continue to dance. So young and in love.

'When she laughs,' Jack says softly, his eyes on the screen. 'Such a great laugh.'

'When he kisses her hand,' Hannah sighs, sinking back against the nest of cushions she and Priya built on the floor.

'The lift,' Liam says reverently, and then we *all* sigh.

'I can do that, you know?' Jack says, offhand, and five pairs of eyes instantly lock on him.

'What . . . What do you mean?' Hannah asks, and it's unlike her to sound so breathless.

Jack looks a bit startled by our intensity. 'Just that I used to do a lot of dance classes and I learned this one. I haven't done it since I was about nineteen, but yeah . . .' He trails off and actually looks slightly embarrassed but that might be because we're all staring at him with wide, unblinking owl-eyes.

'You can do the lift?' Patty's voice is unsteady. She gestures at the screen. 'This lift?'

He looks over to me, but I'm no help. I still haven't recovered from the tap dancing; this new piece of information is a whole other level. 'I mean I'd guess so,' Jack says with a shrug. 'I don't see why not. I'm actually a fair bit stronger than I was then.'

'Yeah, you are,' I murmur, and I sound so thirsty it's a joke.

Jack's gaze snags on mine, and whatever he sees there has his eyes widening. He reaches out and his fingers toy with the end of my ponytail. 'What do you think, Taylor? You want to try?'

My lips part, but I don't say anything, which doesn't really matter, because my friends are losing their shit, clambering to their feet and pushing furniture aside already.

'Shhhh, shhhhh!' Patty cautions, suddenly remembering Priya. After that, they continue to squeal at a lower pitch.

'Are you sure about this?' I ask.

'Don't worry.' Jack stands up and holds out his hand. 'I won't drop you, I promise.'

I let him pull me to my feet, and the others have formed a sort of narrow runway. Patty and Arjun stand on one side, Liam and Hannah on the other.

'What do I do?' I ask, suddenly nervous.

'Just run at me and jump into my arms as high as you can,' Jack says. 'You need to brace your core. Sometimes it helps if you hold your breath. I'll do the rest.'

'Um, okay.' I send silent thanks to Petra for the fact I can at least locate my core these days.

Liam has rewound the film so that the scene plays out on the TV behind Jack. The music starts, and when Baby begins to run, so do I. I don't know what I'm doing, but when I reach Jack, I basically throw myself at him. His hands are around my waist, and he lifts me up a little and puts me back down.

'Okay, you jumped a bit too early that time,' he says, patiently. 'You have to wait a second longer. You need to trust me. I'll catch you.'

'Right,' I say, going back to the start. Liam puts the film back again, and I roll my neck in a few circles, windmill my arms by my side, taking a deep breath like an Olympian limbering up for the big event.

'We've got this,' Jack says, and I nod.

Then he crooks his finger.

Fuck me.

On this go, I time it right and leap into his arms, feeling him grip my hips hard through the fabric of my jeans, his fingers biting into my flesh with a delicious pressure. I fly up and up, and the world tips and I squeak and brace myself, wobbling for a split second, but Jack's arms lock underneath me, and then it's just . . . happening. He's holding me over his head like it's no big deal and I stretch my arms out and laugh like a maniac. He holds me like that for a long moment while the others whoop and cheer, Priya and her light sleeping forgotten in our fever pitch of excitement, and then – *slowly* – he pulls his arms down, reeling me in, his hands slipping down, cupping the tops of my thighs. My arms wrap around his neck and he slides me down the rest of his body, until my feet touch the floor.

I look up at him, and it feels like part of me is still flying. My heart beats hard and fast at our bodies being pressed so tightly together, and the way he looks at me . . . it's as if there's nothing pretend about what's between us at all.

'My turn, my turn!' Liam sings, and Jack lets out a startled huff of laughter.

I step back, out of the circle of his arms.

'Why not?' Jack asks, and Arjun punches the air.

'And then me, Uncle Jack!' Priya stands in the doorway, rumpled and adorable in her pyjamas, her entire being lit with excitement.

Jack crouches down, opens his arms to her. 'Then you, little P,' he promises as she hurls her small body into his.

Hannah appears beside me. 'Oh, shit, Cyn,' she whispers, resigned.

'I know,' I say, because I do, I know what she sees, what she probably saw before I even saw it myself.

I'm totally falling for my fake boyfriend.

And the last time we did this, everything ended in disaster.

THEN

THIRTEEN YEARS EARLIER

Chapter Thirty-Three

Cynthie

Today is the last day I have to see Jack. Those words run over and over in my head.

It's been six months since *A Lady of Quality* came out, and apart from a few publicity events, we haven't had much to do with each other, but today it's the MTV Movie Awards in Los Angeles and the film has been nominated. Unfortunately, the category in which it has been nominated is Best Kiss, and the winners always re-enact said kiss on stage. I never thought I'd find myself hoping with every fibre of my being to lose an acting award, but here we are.

A Lady of Quality outperformed everyone's (admittedly fairly low) expectations by making a modest profit at the box office, and finding a devoted audience, predominantly of young women. There are posters of Jack Turner-Jones in a wet shirt gracing bedroom walls all over the world, and – as Lorna predicted – the rumours of our perfect love affair have captured people's imaginations, giving both the film, and the two of us, a nice publicity boost. To her credit, Lorna hasn't been smug about it, though her smile has only grown wider, and I fear she's sprouted several new teeth.

Next week I start work on a new movie, a fantasy with a big

budget based here in LA. Jack is flying straight back to the UK to start production on a gritty British drama with a big director, and he's already in post-production on another project. Unlike me, he didn't wait around.

It's been agreed by everyone involved that we can let our fake relationship die away, blaming the distance if anyone asks about it. So tonight is our last hoorah, the death rattle of Jack Turner-Jones and Cynthie Taylor as a couple. Finally.

'Where do we want to put this lamp?' Hannah asks, trailing through from her room in the two-bedroom apartment we've rented in Los Feliz. I say we, but Hannah organized everything with Gayle's assistant, and now – unbelievably – we have a six-month lease on our new home and all the visas and paperwork that mean we can stay.

We flew out three days ago, and the combination of excitement, jet lag, and having to see Jack has me feeling extremely edgy.

I eye the lamp that Hannah is holding. 'Why do we have a lamp that looks like a penis?'

Hannah blinks. Looks at the lamp. 'It doesn't look like a . . .' she trails off then tilts her head. 'Huh,' she murmurs finally. 'I guess it is quite phallic . . . because of the decorative orbs.'

'Decorative orbs?' I choke.

Hannah grins. 'We accidentally bought a penis lamp!'

'*You* accidentally bought a penis lamp,' I say. 'And obviously it should go here in the living room for everyone to admire.'

'Obviously,' Hannah echoes, placing the lamp on a side table and flopping down beside me on the sofa. 'How's the prep going?'

I glance at the script in my lap. 'Okay, I think. There are a lot of special effects . . . It's going to be totally different from filming *A Lady of Quality*.'

'And that's . . . bad?' Hannah asks.

I bite my lip. 'No. I'm excited to learn more, to try new things . . .

I suppose I just felt safe on that set in the end. Apart from the presence of you-know-who.'

'Satan's minion.' Hannah nods wisely.

'Precisely. Apart from him, I think I was lucky that it was such a good experience. I hadn't really thought about this part of it, you know . . . that you spend months living so tightly with a small group of people, before you all go your separate ways.' I sigh. 'At least you'll always be there.'

'Always,' Hannah agrees. 'I've got your back, and all your lighting needs covered, too.'

'You are no longer in charge of interior design decisions.'

'Shouldn't you be getting ready?' Hannah asks then, glancing at her watch.

'Gayle said they're sending over hair and make-up people, right?' I stretch, trying to cover the flutter of nerves that I feel.

'Yes, they should be here in the next few minutes.' Hannah gets back to her feet. 'And the car is picking you up in three hours.'

'Three hours to make me look like a human woman.' I shudder. 'Do you think they'll manage it?'

'They can only do their best.'

When the car arrives I'm relieved to find it empty. I half expected to be travelling with Jack.

'He's coming straight from the airport,' Hannah informs me. 'So he'll meet you there, and then you'll do the carpet together.'

She's going to watch the awards from our sofa while eating a giant pizza. When she waves me off from the doorway, she already has a spoon stuck into a tub of chocolate ice cream, and I let out an envious sigh.

I take the opportunity that the drive to the awards ceremony offers to press myself up against the windows and admire the view. I can't believe I *live* here. It seems absolutely impossible that Hannah and I could just pack our lives into a couple of suitcases, bid a tearful goodbye to her parents at Heathrow and then move to *Los Angeles*. I don't know who we think we are.

We drive down roads lined with palm trees, and I keep waiting for someone to tap me on the shoulder and laugh pityingly at my delusions – everything I've wanted for as long as I can remember is laid out in front of me. It feels like I'm on the edge of something huge.

Tonight's ceremony is being held at the Nokia Theatre, which is just over a thirty-minute drive from my place. The time passes quickly, and I twist my fingers in my lap as I think about seeing Jack again.

For the last time.

The jittery anticipation builds, but when I reach the venue and the door is opened, it's Lorna who's waiting, and today her smile seems off. There are far fewer teeth on display than usual.

'Jack's flight has been delayed,' she says, and my heart sinks. 'You need to do the carpet by yourself, and we'll bring him through to his seat during the ceremony.' She glances down to the phone in her hand. 'Your category isn't until near the end anyway.'

'And we might not win,' I say, trying not to sound too hopeful.

Lorna chuckles. 'I'm not so sure about that. And just remember what we discussed if you *do* win—'

'Yes, I know,' I cut in, desperately hoping that it will all be irrelevant. 'We'll do the kiss.' Or a version of it anyway. A quick, chaste version of it. That's what Jack and I agreed via various assistants.

The red carpet passes in a blur. This is a low-key ceremony, with a younger crowd, and I've been dressed to fit, in tight jeans and a pretty, pale pink corset-style top, which I think is supposed to be a nod to the Regency period of the film, but with the hard work it is putting in I'd say it's less Anne Elliot and more Ann

Summers. The cameras flash and the photographers call my name, and I try not to panic about Jack's precise whereabouts.

Before I know it, I'm shown to my seat in the giant amphitheatre, which is worryingly near the stage. (Is that a sign of some sort? Does that mean we're going to win? *Please* don't let us win.) There's an empty chair beside me with Jack's name taped to it. Perhaps with him turning up late, I won't even have to talk to him. We can just sit through the event, smile, and then go our separate ways. I try not to dwell on why that feels like a horrible anticlimax.

After a lot of fussing about with the cameras, the signal is given that we're going live, and the theatre hums with excitement. The charismatic actress who's hosting is doing a great job, but I can't help fidgeting, glancing over my shoulder and looking for any sign of Lorna or Jack. A new fear takes root – what if we *do* win, and Jack's not here? It's going to look like I've been abandoned by my fake boyfriend. I'm going to have to accept the award for best kiss *between two people*, alone. And then the news is going to come out that our relationship is over and people will think he basically dumped me live on camera. Oh, shit.

Time passes with no sign of Jack and as the awards are handed out and I clap with a polite, if frozen, smile on my face, panic sets in. Where the fuck is he? Oh my god, has he left me here alone as some final act of humiliation? No, surely not. Even Jack Turner-Jones is not that evil.

During an advert break where they're setting up the next shot, Lorna comes hustling over. She looks harassed and her mobile is clamped to her ear.

'What the hell is going on?' I hiss quietly. 'Where's Jack?'

'He's on his way,' Lorna promises me before she starts barking directions into the phone. From what I can gather she is micro-managing Jack's driver's route from the airport. I guess that means he's somewhere in LA at least.

'Isn't it almost time for our part?' I ask desperately. 'Do they know he's not here? They're not going to make me go up on my own, are they?'

'Everything is under control,' Lorna tells me soothingly before she clatters off on her high heels, still yelling into her phone and making increasingly dramatic hand gestures. It's not reassuring.

'Everything is under control,' I whisper to myself.

Finally, it happens. Exactly as I was afraid it would.

In an increasingly bizarre series of events, Steve Carell is there, up on stage, announcing the nominees for Best Kiss. The giant screens at either side of the stage play the clips from the nominated films, and when Steve says, 'Cynthie Taylor and Jack Turner-Jones for *A Lady of Quality*,' there we are, a million feet tall.

A passionate trembling of string music fills the air, as the camera follows Jack riding through the rain on the back of a majestic black stallion. His dark hair is wet and tumbled, his jaw tight, his blue eyes burning with intensity. The white linen shirt he wears is almost transparent, and when he pulls the horse to a stop, I swear a collective sigh runs around the room. Throwing one leg over the saddle, he lands lightly on his feet and without hesitation strides towards me, through the long grass and the swirling mist.

The music intensifies, and the camera catches me wide-eyed, as I stand pale and frozen, raindrops running down my face like tears, my lips parting as I drink him in. Without slowing, Jack hauls me into his arms, and it's very forceful and manly, and even I feel my breath catch, watching it. He kisses me, lifting me into his arms while his hand cradles my face, and I kiss him back, burying my hands in his hair and holding him close. It goes on for some time, hungry and desperate, and I feel like I always do when I watch this scene: naked. Because I don't see Emilia up there. All I see is Cynthie and how much she wants that kiss. The crowd are cheering and Steve fans himself with the envelope he's holding.

The camera pushes in on me and I force myself to smile like everything is fine and I'm having the time of my life.

'And the winner is . . .' – Steve opens the envelope – 'Cynthie Taylor and Jack Turner-Jones, for *A Lady of Quality*!'

Chapter Thirty-Four

Cynthie

A wave of applause crashes over me, and I get to my feet, my knees shaking. Oh god, oh god, this is like a nightmare. What's happening right now is the stuff of a very serious anxiety dream, and I don't know what to do except pinch myself because hopefully I am *actually* asleep. All I can think is that I am going to kill Jack Turner-Jones when I see him. I'm going to straight up murder him.

An assistant is gesturing me towards the aisle so I can walk up to the stage. I climb the steps, my heart beating furiously as I scramble to think of something charming to say that isn't going to make me look like a complete fool who got stood up by her boyfriend on international television.

I reach the podium and Steve is standing there, smiling at me, holding out a gold trophy shaped like a bucket of popcorn, and I take it, blinking at him in a way that I hope says, 'Please save me, Steve Carell!'

Sadly, Steve doesn't react to my mute pleas and it looks like it's all on me.

'Um, hi!' I say, hopelessly into the microphone, 'Thank you so much for this. Unfortunately, Jack couldn't—'

I'm interrupted by some sort of commotion at the back of the

theatre, and I squint into the lights trying to see what's going on.
There's a thud and a brief shout and several raised voices.

'Unfortunately . . .' I start again, uneasy. My eyes drift to Steve
Carell who makes a *keep going* gesture with his hand. 'Jack—' but I'm
cut off by a wave of hysterical screaming and cheering, and finally,
I see what the fuss is about and I stop dead.

Because striding down the aisle towards me is Jack.

He looks tired, angry and gorgeous. And wet. He's wet.

He climbs the stairs, two at a time.

It must have been raining outside, because there's water in his
hair. His T-shirt clings damply to the muscles in his arms, the planes
of his chest, as he comes for me, approaching like a thunderstorm,
lightning in his eyes.

I take a sharp step back away from the podium, and then he's
right there, reaching for me. His hand goes to my waist, pulling me
against him, hard, our chests pressed firmly together, and I exhale in
shock, automatically tipping my head back as his other hand comes
up to my cheek. For a second our eyes meet, and the crowd, the
cameras, Steve-freaking-Carell . . . they all melt away.

When his mouth comes down on mine, it's like a bomb goes
off inside me. There's a moment, suspended in bright, white
light, before sensation rushes in. It's all heat and fire and the
taste of him, his tongue against mine, the faintest scrape of his
canines over my bottom lip. I shiver as his arm goes underneath
me, scooping me off my feet while my own arms twine around
the back of his neck, pulling him closer. *Demanding* him closer.
I can feel his heart beating under his damp T-shirt. I run my
fingers through his wet hair, kissing him like I mean it, kissing
him because I can.

Then something happens. The angle changes. His mouth gen-
tles over mine and he presses a final, soft kiss against my lips. The
feel of it is different; the taste of it is different. It's sweet and slow, a

warm-honey kiss that spreads through my whole body. And, slowly, slowly, the world creeps back in.

Our mouths break apart, and Jack looks at me. We're both struggling to catch our breath. The audience are feral; they sound like they're about to tear the theatre apart. The floor is shaking.

He continues to stare at me, his fingers lingering against my cheek, then his hand falls away and he's still carrying me with one arm when he turns and faces the crowd. He leans towards the microphone, getting in really close. The side of his mouth pulls up in an irresistible smirk. 'Sorry I'm late.'

Then, as laughter fills the room, he lowers me to the floor and I slide against his body, pretending to laugh too while he slings a casual arm around my shoulders and picks up the award in his other hand. With a wave to the audience, we make our way off stage.

I can't believe that just happened.

I can't believe he just did that. Of course it was nothing like the brief, low-key kiss we had planned. Of course it couldn't be. No, it had to be *that* – it had to be a kiss that tore me apart and put me back together again, that left me shaking and wanting more, *needing* him in front of a live TV audience.

I am *incandescent*. A tornado made of lust and fury. I want to rip all Jack's clothes off here and now, but I also want to punch him right in the nose.

We're ushered away from the side of the stage and into a small holding area surrounded by black drapes.

'Someone will come and take you along to the green room in a moment,' the production assistant says, already on the move.

'Wow,' Steve Carell says brightly. 'You guys really put on a show there.'

'Not now Steve Carell!' I snap before I swing around to face Jack. 'What the actual fuck?'

And then Jack laughs. *He laughs.*

Nose punching it is. My sweaty little paw is already clenching itself into a fist.

But Jack clearly has no sense of self-preservation, because he only shrugs and runs a hand through his damp hair, and I am forced to watch his bicep flex and ... just ... *how dare he?*

'My flight was delayed,' he says. 'I hate to break it to you, Taylor, but I don't have control of weather patterns over the Atlantic. I made it, didn't I?'

'That is not what I meant,' I reply through clenched teeth. 'Although it would have been nice if you'd made a bit more time in your busy schedule to allow for this sort of problem. Nice to know how little you give a shit.'

His smile fades, and I feel an inconvenient jab of guilt, because there are dark circles smudged under his eyes. He actually looks pretty exhausted.

'I am literally in the middle of filming,' he says, 'and I flew half-way across the world to be here. I haven't slept since ...' He squints. 'Actually, I haven't got a fucking clue because I think today might be my yesterday or something. But anyway, it's been a long time, Cynthie. I am tired; I'm hungry; I'm at an awards ceremony in a wet T-shirt that I've been wearing since ... *tomorrow*, and now you're giving me shit about my commitment?'

'You know that's not why I'm upset,' I hiss, refusing to be talked down. 'That kiss was not what we agreed on.'

He groans, a clear sound of frustration. 'That's it? You're pissed about the kiss?'

Jack looks at me, and I cross my arms, my expression mutinous.

'Of course you are,' he rumbles, and his blue eyes sharpen danger-ously. 'And shall I tell you why? You're pissed because that kiss was the most honest thing to come from your mouth in months. You're pissed because you want me, and you have no idea what to do about it.'

'Ha!' I stride towards him, drilling my finger into his chest. 'You'd love to think so, wouldn't you? You really are the most egotistical, narcissistic—'

'So ... this really seems like a private conversation,' Steve Carell pipes up, edging away. 'I think I should just—' he starts clutching hopelessly at the long black fabric that surrounds us, desperately searching for a way out.

'And I can't believe you're making me fight with you in front of Steve Carell!' I yell.

Jack ignores this completely, stepping into my touch, crowding my space, wrapping me up in the feel and sight and scent of him so that I can't think. It's a low-down, dirty tactic, and I want to claw at him like a cat.

'Just admit it,' he says, like it's a dare. 'Just admit that you have feelings for me.'

'Oh, I have feelings for you,' I snap. 'Loads of them. Animosity, anger, frustration ... the list goes on and on.'

'Cynthie,' his voice softens. He doesn't say anything else, just my name, and my stomach does a vicious loop-the-loop.

The moment stretches out between us, time slowing.

'I'm so sick of this, Jack. You want me to tell you that I have feelings for you? What if I did? What then? You and I are so different. Sometimes I feel like you're from another planet.'

'Just because our backgrounds are different—' Jack starts.

'It's not just that!' I exclaim, 'And the fact you don't get it only proves my point. You have everything you've ever wanted. You were literally born with it all. I moved to LA *three days ago*. My first film just won an MTV Movie Award! And I couldn't even be excited about it. Everything I've worked my whole life for ... the impossible dream, the one no one – and I mean *no one* – believed could come true, the one I've had to fight and claw for ... is happening. It's happening to me right now. You're the one who's always banging on about professionalism, and taking the work seriously, and that's what I'm trying to do.'

'I don't see what that has to do with this situation.'

'Don't you? I'm saying we don't need the distraction, either of us. Especially when I know perfectly well that you're just using me to avoid dealing with the things you're unhappy about.'

'Don't say that,' he grits out.

'It's true,' I insist, feeling reckless, feeling like I'm holding a stick of dynamite in one hand and a match in the other. 'You couldn't even bear the thought of introducing me to your parents when Lorna asked you to. You don't want me in your world. You know I don't belong there ... You just want to get out of it for a while.'

'That's not what happened.' Jack finally looks troubled. 'You misunderstood.'

'It doesn't matter,' I mutter, trying to shrug off the hurt. I'm used to people thinking I'm not good enough. I thrive on it, on proving them wrong. Why should it sting that Jack feels like that, too?

'Is that really what you think of me?' Jack demands. 'That I'm some entitled prick who has everything he wants? And you're just, what? A convenient distraction?'

'You haven't given me a single reason to think anything else.'

'I see,' he says hollowly, after a moment. 'Maybe you're right about one thing. God knows I'm not *happy*,' he says the word on a derisive laugh. 'But at least I'm not so scared of letting my guard down that I push people away.'

My temper leaps. 'You don't know me. You don't know anything about me.'

'I know you better than you want me to. I *see* you and you hate that.'

'Yeah?' I glare at him, my heart beating so hard that my whole body is shaking with it, tiny tremors like something seismic is happening inside me. 'Well, I see you, too. And what I see is an arrogant, over-privileged boy who's not used to hearing the word no.' The pain that flashes in his face then strikes me like a blow, but I don't flinch. 'Fairytales and happily-ever-afters are for fools, Jack. That's not real. Trust me,' I say as coldly as I can manage, 'this isn't that kind of movie.'

We're interrupted then by a young woman who ducks through one of the curtains.

'Hi!' she says, cheerfully.

'Oh, thank god,' Steve Carell whispers.

'Sorry to keep you so long, I'm here to take you to the green room.'

'No need,' Jack replies, not even looking at me. 'Could you just point me towards the exit? I have a flight to catch.'

And that's the last I see of Jack for a long, long time.

NOW

THIRTEEN YEARS LATER

Chapter Thirty-Five

Jack

We've been filming for two weeks, and things have settled into a surprisingly comfortable rhythm. There's a buzz about what we're doing, what we're making here. Everyone can tell they're part of something special. But today is different. Today is ... potentially a problem. One Cynthie and I have avoided talking about.

Steeling myself, I knock on the door of her trailer.

When she opens it, she looks nervous, but she shuts that down quickly enough, her face smoothing out into a mild expression of interest. She doesn't realize that's her tell – that there's nothing mild about the real Cynthie Taylor. Now I'm more convinced than ever that she's feeling as twitchy as I am.

'Hey,' she says. 'I thought I'd be the only one here this early.'

'Big day today.'

She opens the door, gesturing me inside, and closes it behind me. 'Yeah,' she laughs, but doesn't quite hit the breezy note she's aiming for. 'It's not like it's the first time I've filmed a sex scene.'

'It's the first time we've filmed one together.'

We face one another, and the trailer feels so small all of a sudden, like the walls are closing in around us. There's no space, no room to breathe. I should have done this somewhere else, somewhere wide and open where we could stand ten feet apart, and I'd be less distracted by her, although, who am I kidding? All Cynthie Taylor has to do to distract me is exist.

'There's nothing personal about this kind of scene,' she says now. 'It's going to be very professional.'

'I know that.' Somehow I manage to keep my tone even. 'But don't you think we need to talk about things, first?'

'Sure.' Cynthie shrugs, back in control of herself. 'Communication is important.'

'Right,' I agree. 'Right,' I say again as she looks at me expectantly. Now that I'm here, I have no idea how to actually have this conversation with her.

'Are you uncomfortable about filming the scene?' Cynthie asks, a crease appearing between her eyes, and her voice softens. 'Because Nisha, the intimacy co-ordinator, is going to be there, but if there's anything you want to discuss . . .'

'It's not that I'm uncomfortable with the scene,' I say, trying to sort through how I'm feeling. 'I think it's that I'm concerned about what this means for us.'

'For us?'

'There are a lot of . . . layers at work. We're playing Edward and Emilia, but we're also playing the two of us who are supposed to be in a relationship. Brooke's going to be there. I can't work out if filming the scene would be easier or more difficult if we actually were together. Everything feels . . . messy.'

I half expect her to shut me down.

'I know what you mean,' she says softly.

I'm insanely relieved to hear her say it. 'So filming an intimate scene in front of people who think we're a couple might bring up some issues that we should discuss ahead of time,' I point out.

'Okay,' Cynthie agrees. 'Let's tackle it like we would any other part. What's our motivation? If we *were* a couple, how would you feel about today?'

I clear my throat. 'I like to think I'd be able to keep it professional,' I say, 'to separate us from our characters, but I don't know. If we were familiar with each other's bodies ... there would be more intimacy wouldn't there? Between people who really were lovers. An ... ease.'

'Hmmm.' Cynthie tilts her head, thinking this over. Unfortunately, when she thinks things over, she tends to bite down on her bottom lip, and then my brain fills with white noise.

'But it's not like we haven't *actually* had sex before,' she points out, and that cuts through the white noise nicely. 'We did, you know.'

'Yes. I was there,' I reply, dry as the desert, because she says it like it's a detail I could have forgotten, rather than something that's branded into my brain. If your life really does flash before your eyes before you die like a highlight reel, let's just say that particular scene is going to get some serious air time.

'Right,' she swallows. 'So, it's not as if we're not ... what did you say? ... *familiar with each other's bodies.*'

'It was a long time ago,' I say, a little hoarse.

'But we *were* lovers,' Cynthie carries on relentlessly, and her own voice is low. 'Once.'

'I know,' I grind out, shifting on my feet.

'So' – she nibbles on her lip again, and my blood spits and crackles in my veins – 'we should be able to act the part. After all, it's not like we've never seen each other naked ...'

She steps towards me. Without even meaning to, I step towards her. We're drifting closer to each other, that damned magnetic pull at work, and I'm struggling to remember what we're even talking about.

'It's not like we haven't touched each other,' she continues, taking another step.

She's so close now that I watch, fascinated, as a pretty spill of pink stains her cheeks.

'Or kissed each other,' she breathes, and the words themselves coast over my own lips.

'I'm not sure I remember,' I murmur.

'We could . . . remind ourselves,' she whispers. 'For the film.'

'Yes,' I agree. 'For the film.'

And then I lower my mouth to hers.

She sighs against my lips, her arms coming up around my neck, her whole body softening against mine, every delicious curve pressed to me, and I deepen the kiss, dragging that maddening bottom lip into my mouth, tasting her the way I've wanted to for weeks, for months, for years.

There's no hesitation, as we fall into the moment together. Our bodies know each other, her hand coasting over my chest, her tongue brushing against mine. It's tender, something delicate and sweet, until it's not. Then there's a spark that leaps and catches, and suddenly she's shoving me back against the sofa, straddling my lap.

My arm bands around her waist, pulling her more firmly against me, driving my hips up as she grinds against me, right where I want her. We never break the kiss, hungrily demanding more and more of each other.

I hear myself growl, barely recognize the animalistic noise as coming from me, and she whimpers against my lips, a needy sound that has me growing even harder underneath her. She pushes my shirt up, running her fingers over my stomach, and the muscles there jump at her touch. I want those busy hands everywhere. I want her all over me.

My own fingers slip under the hem of her top, tracing the delicate skin on her back, petal-soft. My hands skim over her and it dawns on me that she's not wearing a bra. My entire body hums with approval, but there's a dim, distant voice in my head that insists things are happening too fast. I had things to say to her. Only now everything is hazy, as the blood pounds in my ears, and her tight little body writhes over me, and I can't remember my own name, let alone why I wanted to talk. Why would I want to do anything but this? Why would I think about anything but how right she tastes, how perfect she feels?

Her fingers are on the buttons of my shirt, clumsy with haste as she undoes them, pushing it from my shoulders.

'Oh yes,' she whispers, amusement and lust mingled in her voice, a cocktail I want to get drunk on. 'I'm starting to remember now.'

'I think I still need a refresher,' I huff, tugging at the hem of her shirt. When I pull it over her head and she's laid bare, we're finally skin to skin. The relief is incredible, and I brush my thumb over her nipple. She arches into me with a gasp. I catch her mouth with mine again, and we kiss, slow and filthy.

God, I want to fuck her. I want to take her right now in this trailer.

As she squirms in my lap, starts kissing her way down my neck, I can't think of a single reason not to. I reach for the buttons on her jeans and she gasps her agreement.

There's a knock at the door.

'Cynthie?' Brooke's voice calls. 'Are you in there?'

Cynthie jerks back from me, her eyes wide with shock. Her hair is a tangled mess, her mouth pink and swollen.

'Oh, shit,' I whisper.

'Er, just a minute!' Cynthie calls, as I try and fail to bundle her back in her T-shirt. 'For fuck's sake, Jack.' Her voice holds a hysterical edge of laughter. 'Put your own clothes back on!'

'Right,' I mutter, unable to work out which way my shirt goes, as Cynthie pulls her top on and pushes her fingers hopelessly through her hair, trying to smooth it down.

'Okay?' she asks, after I've finished buttoning myself up.

'Yep,' I say, trying to look casual on the sofa.

Cynthie opens the door with a bright smile, and Brooke's eyes widen in surprise. Unfortunately, the ever-present Declan hovers over her shoulder with his camera.

'Oh, sorry,' Brooke says, 'I didn't mean to interrupt.'

'We were just rehearsing!' Cyn says brightly and then winces, clearly remembering what scene we're shooting today. 'I mean . . .' she trails off looking desperately to me for help.

Which gives me the opportunity to observe that her T-shirt is on inside out.

'We were going over the argument scene,' I say, gamely stepping in. 'We're shooting it later in the week. Big emotional moment. Lots of prep.'

Maybe this will go some way to explaining why our faces are so flushed.

I'm actually feeling pretty pleased with myself until I see Cynthie frantically gesturing to my shirt behind Brooke's back. I look down and realize I've buttoned it wrong. It seems unlikely Brooke, or the camera, will miss it. The more I get to know Brooke, the more I get the feeling she misses very little. Cynthie's eyes close in silent defeat.

'Of course,' Brooke says, her face giving absolutely nothing away. There is only the usual sunshine smile, no hint of twinkle, no knowing glimmer. 'And I really am sorry to interrupt, only, Cynthie, you said you'd sit in for the interview with Nisha, so we could talk about the role of the intimacy co-ordinator together?' She sounds apologetic. 'But obviously if it's not a good time—'

'No, no!' Cynthie says brightly. 'It's a great time. Perfect.'

She shoots me a tortured look.

'Perhaps you could give us a minute alone to debrief,' I say, aiming for professional and realizing the second Cynthie starts choking to cover up a laugh that I've just made the world's worst innuendo.

'Of course.' Brooke nods, serene. 'We'll wait outside.'

Cynthie closes the door behind her and slumps against it.

'Fuck,' she says, her voice low. 'Do you think they know?'

'Your T-shirt is inside out,' I say.

'Fantastic.' Her eyes close again.

'Hey.' I shrug. 'As far as they're concerned, we're in a relationship, so them catching us in a clinch is hardly newsworthy.'

I realize it's the wrong thing to say the second it's out of my mouth. Cynthie's eyes shutter.

'Oh, yes,' she says distantly. 'I suppose you're right.'

'Cynthie,' I start, 'I didn't mean . . . We really need to talk about what just happened.'

'Yeah, I know.' Cynthie rubs her forehead with her fingers. 'Just not now. Can you go out and buy me a couple of minutes to deal with this?' She gestures to herself in a way that encompasses her hair, face and disarrayed clothing.

'Sure,' I agree. 'But I'm serious. We should discuss this.'

'I can't wait,' she murmurs, and then her fingers start undoing the buttons on my shirt, but before I can get too excited, she starts doing them back up correctly.

'Go,' she says. 'I'll see you on set.'

Chapter Thirty-Six

Cynthie

The love scene is being filmed on a closed set. That means Jasmine, Logan and a very small crew, as well as Nisha, the intimacy co-ordinator. Brooke and Declan have been allowed in as well, but they're not permitted to film any footage of Jack and I once the clothes come off, only the process behind the camera.

It feels like an exercise in trust all around.

'Right,' Nisha says, her voice soft and sweet. 'So first we'll run through the scene without removing any clothing. We'll check in at every point to make sure that you're both comfortable. If either of you experience any unease then please say and we'll make adjustments. Okay?'

Jack and I both nod while Logan pipes up. 'Anything at all guys, *anything*. We want this to be a totally safe space, okay? It's important that you know you can talk to us about any concerns, any issues. Particularly you, Cynthie. This is a vulnerable experience and I think it's important that we all acknowledge that, right?' He looks around at everyone.

'Logan, I think they've got it,' Jasmine says wearily. 'Why don't you let Nisha do her job?'

Logan's eyes widen. 'Oh, Nisha! I'm sorry. I certainly don't want my voice to be the only one in the room. It's important to listen, isn't it? I just want to be an active listener. You're the expert here. I defer to you, completely.'

Logan always seems to have a lot to say about active listening, but usually, if left alone, he manages to wind himself down like a toddler wearing themselves out.

'Thank you, Logan,' Nisha says calmly. 'If everyone's ready, we'll begin?'

Jack and I run through the scene, and Nisha takes us through every moment of contact between the two of us. It's not my first time working with an intimacy co-ordinator, but I find myself even more grateful than usual for her presence. After what happened in my trailer, it helps to have an air of calm efficiency to the whole business. I currently have the events of this morning locked up tight in a little box. There isn't time or space to think about it now, despite the fact that my body still hums with pleasure, that I can still taste Jack on my tongue.

If Brooke hadn't interrupted . . . Nope, not thinking about it.

I force myself to focus on Nisha. This is very different from the first sex scene I filmed a decade ago. Intimacy co-ordinators weren't exactly a common presence on set then, and I'd fumbled my way through the thing the best I could, sick with nerves and never totally comfortable with the result.

'And at this point, Jack will remove Cynthie's chemise,' Nisha says. 'Are you happy with that, Cynthie?'

I nod. Funnily enough, despite the heated moment we've just shared, I'd be hard pressed to name someone I feel safer with than Jack. It's not just Nisha who checks in with me at every step; he does too, sometimes with a look, often with words, and I make sure I return the favour.

'So let's get up on the bed,' Nisha says. 'When we're filming, Jack will lift Cynthie up and place her on the mattress, is that right?'

'That's right,' Jasmine jumps in before Logan can get started. 'We want this to feel very tender, romantic. It's been a long time coming for these two. There's passion, but also a lot of feeling, and some nerves too, particularly for Emilia.'

'I don't know,' Jack says, 'I think Edward's probably nervous too. He may not be a virgin, but he's loved Emilia for over a decade. She's the only woman he's ever loved, and now he finally gets to touch her. He'll be worried about hurting her, worried about pleasing her.'

'Good, good,' Jasmine agrees, her voice low. We're all talking in the same hushed tones, like we're in a museum, like this is a solemn occasion.

To his credit, Logan restrains himself from jumping in with explicit directions about tongues and breasts, which I think actually does show some growth on his part. I can only imagine what it would have been like trying to film this the first time around.

We get up on the mattress and run through the rest of the scene. It's impossible for a sex scene not to be awkward. I don't care how professional everyone involved is; you're still performing for an audience without your clothes on. Actors might be more au fait than the general public when it comes to displaying our bodies, but we're still human.

'Perfect,' Nisha says finally. 'So now we'll go through it, and this time we'll take the clothes off and make sure we're all feeling confident about the angles.'

Jack and I move slowly through the scene, and if my hand trembles a little as I undo his cravat, or if his breath catches when he slips my chemise from my shoulders, I tell myself it's because we're in character. It might even be true ... I realize this is what Jack was really trying to say this morning, that what I'm feeling matches what Emilia is feeling so closely that the boundaries are even hazier than usual. Brooke and Declan's presence adds a further complication.

It's nothing like the two of us being all over each other a couple of hours ago. There are people watching us, and they're very interested in the exact angle of our bodies, the perfect, suggestive positioning of the bed sheets. They see us as a collection of photogenic limbs, and the longer the rehearsal drags on, the easier it is to think of my own body with a similar level of detachment.

But we're still skin to skin. He's still running his hands over me, and I still like it.

Jack was right. It's complicated.

By the time we run the scene for real, I'm feeling relaxed enough about the movement to focus more on the actual acting. I sink further into Emilia, her desire, her emotional turmoil.

'Action,' Jasmine calls, and then Jack has me up against the wall, kissing me, kissing my throat, as I tug at his necktie. We move across the room, shedding clothes at carefully planned intervals. When we're down to our Regency appropriate underwear, Jack scoops me up into his arms and I laugh. He places me gently on the bed, on top of the scattering of handwritten love letters that he wrote me thirteen years ago, the ones he just found out I've kept ever since.

The paper crinkles under me as he runs a hand up my calf, pushing the thin white linen of my chemise up and over my thighs. He groans, burying his face in the side of my neck, and I clutch at his hair, my heart beating hard, overwhelmed and yes, a little nervous.

My hand runs tentatively down the muscular line of his bare back. His face comes up, above mine.

'Are you certain, love?' he asks, the words rough with lust and tenderness in equal measure.

I look into his eyes, and it's like the scene wavers, like I'm falling out of it. I'm looking at Jack, and I feel overwhelmed by sensation. The room is hot, the lights so bright. I can feel the eyes on me, the cameras. My breath catches and it's not acting. There's a familiar and dreaded tightening in my chest.

Jack's eyes widen. 'Cynthie?' he says, pulling away from me in an instant, and I think that later I'll be grateful for that, for the way he knew at once that there was something wrong. But for now, all I feel is panic.

Not now, not now, not now, I think as my breathing falters.

'Cut,' Jasmine says crisply.

I push myself up off the bed. Thankfully, I'm still wearing the chemise because I want out of this room as soon as possible.

'I'm sorry,' I manage. 'I feel a bit dizzy. I think I'd better get some air.'

Without waiting for any further conversation I hurry through the door, ducking around people without making eye contact.

When I'm out in the corridor, away from the lights, the temperature feels more bearable. I move into an empty room further down, and sit on the floor, my back against the wall, my knees pulled up to my chest, as I try and ride out the storm raging inside me.

When there's a gentle knock, I expect it to be Jack, but instead, Jasmine walks through the door.

'I'm sorry,' I manage. 'I don't know what happened. It came on so suddenly, just out of nowhere.'

'Sometimes that happens,' she agrees, sliding down to sit on the floor beside me.

We sit quietly for a moment.

'You know if you're not comfortable with shooting the scene then there are a million ways we can work around it,' she says finally. 'We can use a body double, make cuts. No pressure, no judgement, no second guessing. You say the word and that's what we'll do.'

Tears sting my eyes, and something eases off me. I realize I'd been braced for an attack, not empathy. I battle the instinct telling me that abandoning the scene would be a failure, would make *me* a failure.

'I appreciate that,' I say, finally. 'But it's not the scene. It wasn't that I felt unsafe. I've filmed scenes where I was far less comfortable with what was going on.'

'That's not the solid argument you think it is,' Jasmine sighs. 'Being uncomfortable shouldn't be normal. As a director it's my job to make sure that doesn't happen. It's *not* my job to torture a performance out of you.'

Oof. That hits a little close to home.

Jasmine nods like she knows what I'm thinking. 'Can I ask you a question?'

'Of course.'

'Have you been thinking about getting into directing?'

It's the last thing I was expecting her to ask. In fact, it seems so wildly off topic that I give her an unguarded answer. 'Yes.'

She nods. 'I thought so. The way you've been approaching the scenes, your notes. The way you talk to the crew. It feels like you have a more complete vision.'

'Why did you ask that now?' I'm puzzled. 'I haven't mentioned anything about directing to anyone.' *Well, almost anyone.*

'Because directing puts you in a position of power. The dynamics are tricky. For me, it's a priority that you feel safe on set. It shouldn't come as a surprise that we'd want that for you. If you want to direct you need to think about what you'd do with that power, how you'd want to use it.'

Something about the way she says this has the back of my neck prickling. 'Are you . . .' I hesitate, thinking perhaps her roundabout question wasn't that roundabout at all, that she was leading the conversation here. 'Are you talking about Shawn?'

For the first time, she looks away. 'Let's just say that Shawn Hardy has a certain reputation with women in this industry.'

I straighten. 'What?' I stare at her, but she turns back to me, her gaze steady. 'I mean, I know he has a reputation for being difficult to work with,' I continue slowly, 'but are you saying that he's . . .'

'A predator?' Jasmine's mouth pulls up ruefully. 'I'm afraid so. Isn't it hell that there are so many of them out there? And they look just like the good guys, too.'

'You don't have to say it like I've never run into any of them,' I snap, unsettled.

'Of course you have,' she agrees mildly. 'How could you not in this game? It's just that Shawn Hardy is a special sort of manipulative, controlling dirtbag. You probably hadn't heard about it because he tends to target much more junior crew or cast members, the sort who won't dare make a fuss. Plus, there are dozens of NDAs on the go.' She tilts her head, considering me. 'You were something of an anomaly. He almost blew his cover there. Very quick to cast you as the wicked seductress, wasn't he? Really did a bang-up job of turning Hollywood's golden girl into an unreliable narrator.'

Puzzle pieces start to fall horribly into place.

'It wasn't your fault, Cynthie,' Jasmine says quietly. 'Whatever he did. I can guarantee it wasn't your fault. You shouldn't have to carry it around. If you want to talk, then you can talk to me. I actually know a couple of people who've worked with him and had difficult experiences, so maybe you'd prefer to speak with them. It's your call. You know best what you need.'

It's an unexpected offer from a woman who has always seemed remote and self-contained, and I appreciate it, even as I'm not sure if I could ever take her up on it.

'I told Shawn that I was interested in directing,' I say distantly. 'I hadn't mentioned it to anyone else. It was how things started between us. I hoped he'd be a sort of mentor. At first it was like that ... like he really believed in me, then we started sleeping together and things changed. He made me feel foolish that I'd even considered it, like I needed to stay in my lane. By the end, I believed him.'

Jasmine sighs heavily. 'Fucking hell, Cynthie, you run a long con, don't you?'

'What do you mean?' I ask, startled.

She gives me a very small smile. 'Thirteen years ago, I told you I wasn't here to be your mentor or your friend. Now it looks like I might end up being both.'

And then, against all odds, I find myself laughing.

Chapter Thirty-Seven

Jack

In the end, Cynthie comes back on set and we shoot the scene without any further incident. As much as it killed me not to go after her, it looks like Jasmine was right when she said it should be her. When the pair of them finally return to the room, there's a new light in Cynthie's eye, a spark of determination that I recognize.

'Are you sure this is okay?' I ask, quietly. 'If it's not, we can walk away right now, figure something else out?'

'Jasmine already made that offer,' she says, 'but I want to do it now. I have all this energy that I want to send somewhere.' At my questioning look, she squeezes my hand. 'I promise, I'll tell you everything later.'

I guess we'll just add it to the long list of things we need to talk about.

At first I'm hesitant, but it's clear that she means it, that she's glad to be working, that she's fully in the scene again. I'm watching her as closely as any camera. Feeling her start to panic during our first take had taken years off my life. This time when we run through the whole scene, she's totally present, and slowly we manage to fall into it together, the Emilia and Edward of it all.

'Cut,' Jasmine calls after the fourth take. 'I think we got it.'

'That was fucking great.' Logan grins. 'Or should I say—' He cuts himself off abruptly, though the words *great fucking* practically hang in the air. His eyes widen in panic and he clears his throat. 'A moving, consensual scene performed by two professionals.'

He and Jasmine huddle over the monitor, watching the footage back, while Cynthie and I slip into the robes that Nisha offers us.

'That last take was amazing,' Nisha says. 'I got goosebumps.'

'Thanks.' Cynthie nods. 'That one did feel good, right?' She looks to me.

'Yeah,' I agree. 'We really connected.'

'That's it exactly!' Nisha enthuses. 'You could see it, the love between the characters. It was beautiful.' Jasmine calls her over then, and she leaves us alone.

Cynthie absently reaches for one of the prop letters that are strewn across the bed behind us, smoothing the paper with her fingers.

'It's amazing that the prop department made all of these,' she sighs. 'Hundreds of love letters from Edward to Emilia, and they're so romantic. It means something, doesn't it, that she had them for all those years, that she could pull them out and look at them, and see their love story. "My soul aches for you."' She reads, then she looks up at me and grins. 'And what do we get? A string of aubergines in a WhatsApp chat.'

'I happen to be excellent at crafting a romantic WhatsApp message,' I say. 'Full sentences. Not an aubergine in sight.'

'Swoon,' Cynthie laughs. 'I bet you even use Oxford commas.'

'Naturally.'

'Okay, we have it,' Logan calls, grabbing our attention and giving us a thumbs up.

'Moving on,' Jasmine agrees, and the small crew begin the process of clearing out of this set up, on to the next.

Fortunately, Cynthie and I are finished for the day. In fact, we have the whole weekend off, a rare occurrence in such a packed filming schedule. Brooke and Declan are walking behind us as we leave, and I throw a casual arm around Cynthie's shoulder. It's become a habit to touch her whenever we see the documentary crew. Sometimes I want to follow them around, just so I can hold Cynthie's hand.

As she leans into me, yawning, it feels ordinary in a way that thrills me – like it's something we do all the time, like I can touch her because she's mine.

'I'm knackered,' she admits.

'It's been an intense day,' I point out, king of the understatement.

'How about a cup of chamomile tea?' Cynthie suggests.

I grimace. 'No thanks.'

'It's soothing.'

'So is sweet, sweet coffee.'

'Coffee is literally a stimulant, you addict.'

We bicker as we make our way into her trailer, waving goodbye to Brooke and Declan. My arm drops from Cynthie's shoulders, and I feel the cold bite in the air as she steps away from me. This, too, has become habit: shifting in and out of our togetherness based on who's around. Only, this part . . . I don't like. Constantly stepping back from her is starting to feel painful, especially after what happened this morning. It's not like either one of us can claim that was about anything other than what *we* wanted. There was no one to perform for then.

Cynthie boils a kettle, placing a mug of brackish water on the table in front of me. I sniff it dubiously. It doesn't just look like a swamp; it smells like one too.

'I don't see how this can possibly be good for you,' I say. 'You're all falling victim to some sort of scam run by the tea companies.'

'Ah, yes, Big Tea.' Cynthie nods wisely, slipping into the seat across from me. 'Just stop moaning and try it while I text Hannah and tell her the scene went well. She hates when it's a closed set, but at least it gave her the opportunity to sneak off and spend a few days with her parents.'

I take a reluctant sip, and – yep – it tastes exactly like it looks and smells.

'Do you want to tell me what you and Jasmine got into today?' I ask, nudging the cup away from me.

She does, as succinctly as possible.

'I guess it shouldn't be a surprise,' I say when she finishes. 'After what you told me about him. But still ...'

'I know,' Cynthie sighs. 'At first I felt worse, like I'd merrily sailed past even more glaring red flags, but actually in a weird way it helps me to understand it better.' She pauses, cradling her mug in her hands. 'It was so calculated.'

'And how do you feel about that?' I ask.

'Mostly right now I feel mad as hell.' She gives a shaky laugh. 'But that's actually something of an improvement. I'm going to have to think about what I want to do with all this new information.'

I nod. 'That makes sense. It changes things.'

'It does, yes.' She sips her tea, her expression thoughtful.

'So, directing, hey?' I ask after a moment.

Her cheeks pink. 'Do you think I'm delusional?'

'I think you can do anything you set your mind to.'

'Jasmine and I talked about it. She suggested I sit in on looking over some of the dailies with her and Logan. She was ... kind about it.'

Cynthie sounds astonished about this, and I get why – Jasmine being *kind* is a curious concept.

'She sees something in you. She always has. It makes sense.'

'It does?'

'Yes, but it doesn't really matter what I think, or what Jasmine thinks. What do you think?'

She puts her mug down, toys with the string of the tea bag. 'I think it feels like a challenge. A fun one. Or at least it did before all the Shawn stuff.'

I swallow my anger. 'Then it will again,' I say as lightly as I can manage. 'And God knows that the last fun challenge you took on worked out pretty well. Two Golden Globes and an Oscar nom well. You, Cynthie Taylor, are a total badass.'

She looks up at me, and a smile breaks over her face, scrunching her nose. 'Yeah, maybe I am.'

Fuck, she's so cute. 'We should really talk about what happened this morning,' I say.

Cynthie's gaze slips away from mine and she sighs. 'Do we have to? We both got a bit carried away. It was bound to happen, wasn't it?'

'Was it?' I ask, watching her.

She huffs out a breath of frustration. 'We've both admitted there's an . . . attraction between us. And we keep being pushed together, having to pretend to be a couple on and off-screen. The lines are bound to get blurry.' I'm not sure if it's me she's trying to convince, or herself.

I don't know what to say. I don't know if I should tell her how I feel. I don't know if she shares the feelings I'm finding it impossible to ignore, or if – for her – this really is just a physical thing. I don't think that's the case. Whatever this is, she's opened up to me in a way that I know is unusual for her. Perhaps pushing her now would be a mistake.

It's delicate.

'So we've got the weekend off,' she says, changing the subject, and it feels like the moment slips away with it. 'Any fun plans?'

I groan, letting her have her way for now. 'Yes, actually. I've been summoned.'

'Summoned?'

'Lunch at my parents,' I say despondently. 'I'm going to drive down early tomorrow and stay over in town.'

Cynthie looks at me for a long moment. Whatever is in my face has her own expression softening.

'What if ... I could come with ... if you like?' She sounds nervous.

'Come to London with me?' I say blankly. 'Have lunch with my parents?'

She twists her fingers together. 'Only if you wanted me to. If it's not intruding. I thought maybe I could be your moral support for once.'

Something warms in my chest. 'Really?'

Seeing me smile, her expression lightens. 'Of course.'

'I'd love that,' I say, and I remember thirteen years ago when she assumed I didn't want them to meet her because I was embarrassed by her. I hate that she could ever have thought that. 'I'm not even going to do the right thing and tell you that you absolutely shouldn't come because it's going to be a nightmare.' I hesitate. 'Are you happy to stay at my place afterwards? That's where I was going, and I have a spare room.'

'You've stayed at mine,' she says lightly. 'It's only fair.'

'You've got a deal.' I grin. 'I'll pick you up at eight.'

The next morning we set out on the four-hour drive to my parent's house. Cynthie claims control of the playlist, which is my first mistake of the day.

'Please,' I beg. 'No more Julie Andrews. It's giving me traumatic flashbacks.'

'Since Petra started playing her, I've really got into her back catalogue,' Cynthie muses. 'The specials she did with Carol Burnett are brilliant. You just have to detach the music from the overwhelming sense of dread and crippling muscular pain.'

When she sings along to 'I Could Have Danced All Night', I forgive Petra everything. That sweet, husky voice fills the car and I sit back and enjoy it.

'I'd almost forgotten', I say when the song finishes, 'how it is when you sing.'

'How is it?'

'Put it this way, I can't listen to "Black Velvet" without getting painfully aroused.'

She chuckles, bats her eyelids, 'I'm afraid you're not the only person with that problem after seeing me do karaoke.'

'Yeah, I remember Hannah said you started a riot once. I can believe it.'

'I haven't sung it for a long time,' she says. 'She made me swear not to any more. Maybe I could give you a private performance . . .'

My eyes shift over to her and she's grinning, full of mischief. 'Only if you want me to crash the car,' I say, flatly.

'Some other time,' she murmurs, looking out the window, but I can see the edge of her mouth curving up.

I take a few deep, settling breaths as she joins in with Julie on 'The Lusty Month of May'. She's wearing a soft, yellow dress the colour of primroses, and the skirt flares out, stopping just below her knees. I try very hard not to be distracted by her bare legs, as she stretches them out in the seat well.

'So is it just your parents who'll be there today?' she asks as we're battling our way around the M25.

'And Lee,' I reply.

'Tell me a bit about them.' Cynthie leans back in her seat, stretches her arms over her head.

'You probably know most of the broad strokes stuff about my parents. They live for the drama, on and off the stage. My dad is almost twenty years older than my mum, and they met when they were filming a production of *A Midsummer Night's Dream*.'

'They're both very talented,' Cynthie says. 'I never saw either of them live, but I had a DVD of the two of them in a production of *Macbeth* that gave me actual nightmares.'

'Oh, they're incredible actors,' I snort. 'Not that those particular roles were such a stretch for them . . .'

'So keep an eye out for your mum's obsessive hand washing then?'

'I wouldn't put it past her to murder a rival for a part she wanted and call it show business, let's put it that way.'

'Noted.' Cynthie smiles faintly.

'When they met, they were both married to other people.' I nip around the side of a lorry, let the car build up some speed. 'They left their spouses and shacked up together. Within a month or two my mum was pregnant with me. They pushed through their respective divorces and got married, then when I was two, they split up for the first time.'

'The first time? How many times have they split up?'

I wrinkle my forehead, thinking about it. 'Three? No.' I snap my fingers, 'Four. I was forgetting the brief liaison with the Russian Countess.'

'Wow.' She sounds dazed.

'It's certainly been a journey,' I say drily. 'They actually divorced after the first time, then they got back together, remarried and had Lee. Anyway,' I continue, 'they've both had incredible careers. Mum won the Best Supporting Actress Oscar about ten years ago; Dad has one too but his is honorary and it pisses him off, so don't mention it.' I smirk. 'Mum's still working, though not as much, and Dad is supposedly retired. I heard they're trying to talk him into filming *Lear*.'

'But Lee never considered going into the family business?'

I grin. 'No, definitely not. She took a pretty different path. Very academic.'

'Are the two of you close?'

I consider the question as I take the turn off the motorway. 'I mean, I love her, but I wouldn't say we're very close, no,' I say finally. 'She's six years younger than me, which is a big age gap when you're kids, isn't it? And I went away to boarding school when I was twelve and she was six. Then I went straight from school to RADA, so we didn't spend a huge amount of time together. Plus . . .' I hesitate, 'she's not the easiest person to get to know.'

'What does that mean?'

'Just that she's quiet, a bit self-contained. You'll see.'

'It must have been hard for her when you went off to school,' Cynthie says quietly.

'Well, she had Gran,' I reply, defensive because it's a thought that I might have had myself once or twice.

'Ah yes, your granny who buys you handkerchiefs.'

My mouth pulls up again. 'My mum's mother. Thanks to the actual shit show that was our parents' marriage, Gran basically raised us. Lee lives with her now, as her sort of unofficial carer – not that Gran would let you get away with calling her that.'

'Will she be at lunch too?' Cynthie sounds hopeful.

I laugh. 'I doubt it, she has the busiest social life of anyone you've ever met. Also, she can't stand my dad, so to be honest it'd just add one more agent of chaos into the mix if she did turn up.' I glance at her. 'You can't say I didn't warn you.'

'I'm not scared,' Cynthie says with what I can't help but feel is misplaced confidence.

'You say that now—'

'Please.' Cynthie tosses her head. 'You think you're the only one with a dysfunctional family?' She raises her eyebrows. 'Need I remind you, I'm basically my mother's secret love child?'

'I wasn't sure if you remembered telling me all of that,' I admit. 'Have you been in touch with her since?'

'No,' Cynthie sighs. 'I suppose you have to give her credit for not coming out of the woodwork when I got famous.'

'I'm not sure I'd give her credit for anything, actually,' I say sharply, accidentally briefly turning on the windscreen wipers instead of signalling.

'Fair enough,' Cynthie replies, and however offhand she sounds, I know she's been hurt, and badly. 'At least we can take solace in the fact that she has to watch me achieve her dreams from a distance. That's some sweet revenge, right?'

'She never got to know you, Cyn. That's her loss.'

Cynthie's throat bobs. 'I don't know about that – my dad had plenty of opportunities and he didn't take them either.'

'Are you in touch with him?' I ask, worried I already know the answer.

'He died a couple of years ago,' Cynthie says quietly. 'Car accident.'

'Bloody hell,' I exhale.

'I know,' Cynthie nods. 'We hadn't seen each other for ages, three years maybe?' She squints thoughtfully out the window. 'Anyway, I had the house cleared out, and they found this scrapbook, full of clippings all about me.'

She fiddles with her seatbelt. 'And the worst thing was I had no idea what to make of it. Was he proud of me? Had he been all along? Had he collected it all out of a sense of duty? Mild interest? Had someone else given it to him? If I was performing it – I mean, if I was acting the part of Cynthie Taylor finding that book – then the music would swell and I'd play it tearful, a moment of connection, of forgiveness, but in real life it wasn't like that. I had the book and it didn't mean anything at all. Anyway.' She gives a wan smile. 'That's my sad sob story, so at least you *have* a family to have dramatic relationships with. I'm on my own.'

'Come on, Cynthie,' I say sternly, 'don't give me that bullshit.' She looks up, startled, as we wind through the streets of Kensington.

'You know better than anyone that there's more than one way to make a family. You, Hannah, Liam and Patty and Arjun and Priya, you're the tightest unit; you all love each other unconditionally. Every single one of them threatened me with grievous bodily harm if I so much as hurt your feelings . . . and that includes Priya. She was the scariest of the lot.'

'She inherited her mother's thirst for violence.' Cynthie laughs, a slightly watery sound.

'She's a force of nature,' I agree. 'And your fridge is covered in her art. You're not alone. Not even close.'

She looks at me for a long moment. 'You're right,' she says finally. 'I have the family I chose and I wouldn't trade them for anything. They're the most important thing to me. Most people miss that. Not you though. You pay attention.'

I pull into my parents' drive, the gate opening to let us through.

'I pay attention to you,' I say.

Chapter Thirty-Eight

Cynthie

'Bloody hell,' I say, looking up at the gorgeous villa. 'This is where you grew up?'

'Welcome to Mordor,' Jack mutters.

'Sauron is certainly living well.' It's not like I'm a stranger to luxury homes these days (Ask me about the Clooneys' place on Lake Como some time) but the idea of being brought up here still strikes me as bizarre.

The elegant white building in front of us is all understated glamour: deep bay windows, a grand arching doorway flanked by tasteful black iron lamp posts, and immaculately manicured privet hedges. Everything about it screams money. Old money. Lots of money.

'Don't be fooled by the veneer of civility,' Jack warns me. 'Hic sunt dracones.' When I look confused, he smirks. 'Here there be dragons.'

'Warning me off in Latin?' I sigh. 'Poor Little Lord Fauntleroy.'

'Shut up.' He nudges my arm. 'This is your last chance to run screaming.'

'I think I'm made of sterner stuff.'

'Please don't let them scare you off.' He says, softly.

'I'm not going anywhere,' I reply. I can see that he's nervous even if he's trying to hide it. I follow him up the steps to the front door, which he holds open for me.

Taking a deep breath, I try to smooth the creases out the skirt of my pretty silk sundress, and step into a cool entrance hall, tiled in glossy black and white like a marble chess board.

'We're here,' Jack calls.

'In the drawing room,' a man's voice shouts back, and it's the strangest experience, hearing that famous voice, the rich, rolling baritone in real life. I falter.

Of course, Jack picks up on it and lifts his brows. I try to look unmoved, but I know I'm not fooling him one bit.

Jack leads the way through to the drawing room, which turns out to be an enormous, high-ceilinged room, bristling with antique furniture. The tall French doors at the back open onto a terrace overlooking an established leafy green garden – the kind you don't usually find in the middle of the city.

I take this all in in one swift glance before my attention is pinned to the three people in the room. Max Jones has risen to his feet, and – well into his eighties by now – he is still a tall, rugged mountain of a man with a leonine mane of white hair. Blue eyes – Jack's eyes – snap in a lined face that remains handsome though it's hewn in much rougher lines than his son's. He's dressed like Cary Grant in his down-time, a fine-knit grey top with a high neck, tucked into pleated, tan colour slacks. He observes me like a big cat assessing its next meal.

Beside him, sitting on the beautiful silk sofa, his wife doesn't even glance in my direction. At sixty-five, Caroline Turner is still lovely, delicate-looking, with dark hair swept back in an elegant chignon.

'Jack,' Max booms, 'who have you brought us?'

'This is Cynthie,' Jack says.

I notice he and his parents don't greet each other at all, but Max comes forward to shake my hand and kiss my cheeks.

'Of course,' he says. 'Cynthie Taylor, I caught your latest film. A strong performance.'

Despite my best intentions I blush, hopelessly flustered. 'Thank you,' I manage.

'So this is the new girlfriend.' Caroline Turner arches her brows.

The comment is jarring, and I glance towards Jack. We haven't discussed this, I realize. What role we're playing today.

'Cynthie and I are working together at the moment,' Jack says finally, and though I don't know what I wanted him to say, it wasn't that.

'It's lovely to meet you both,' I say into the silence that follows this statement. 'I'm a big fan of your work.'

'Oh, yes?' Caroline looks at me then, her dark eyes amused. 'Which work in particular?'

'Don't be bitchy, darling,' Max chides. 'Forgive my wife, she never can tolerate having another beautiful woman in the room.'

The look Caroline treats him to then is frigid.

'And this is my sister,' Jack says, stepping into the space, taking my arm and guiding me to the sofa opposite his parents where an absolutely stunning blonde sits.

'Hello.' She offers her hand, and her voice is soft, husky. 'I'm Lee.'

Lee is a fascinating mix of contradictions. Her perfect features are pure Grace Kelly, but she's dressed severely in tapered black trousers and a white silk shirt buttoned up tight at her neck. On her feet are a pair of deadly looking black Louboutins, and she sits, her back rigidly straight, as if she's ready for a business meeting. Her blond hair is pulled back in a severe knot, her face serenely blank. It's like she's trying to tone herself down, to fade into the shadows, but if that's her intention, someone should tell her that all this severity only highlights her killer bone structure, the full pouting mouth she inherited from her mother, her father's ice-blue eyes, wide and long-lashed.

Caroline makes a noise of frustration. '*Lee*,' she says with distaste. 'Horrid little name. What's wrong with Ophelia?' Caroline turns to me. 'We named her after the role I was playing when she was conceived.'

'Oh?' I manage, not sure what to do with this information.

Jack winces, and gestures for me to take a seat on the sofa with Lee, while he drops into an armchair beside me. 'Must we start in on the conceptions already?'

'We were going to name Jack the same way,' Caroline sniffs, leaning forward to pick up her drink off the table in front of her. Ice clinks in a glass of amber liquid. 'Only, Max's father died right before the boy was born and Max had a fit of filial obligation.'

'Thank you, Grandpa Jack,' Jack mutters, fervently.

Amusement flickers inside me. I turn to Max. 'What role were you playing at the crucial moment?' I ask.

A smile plays on Max's lips. 'Oberon.'

I choke on a laugh as Jack groans. Lee's lips are firmly pressed together, and I think she's trying not to smile.

'It's a beautiful name,' Caroline says, annoyed. 'Not common, like Jack.'

'I suppose it could have been worse.' Lee leans into me and says in a low voice. 'I could have been conceived then, when Mum was playing Titania.' There's a flash of humour in her eyes. 'Imagine what the kids at school would have made of that.'

'"Ill met by moonlight, proud Titania."' Max's voice projects, filling the room like thunder.

None of his family react.

'Know your Shakespeare, do you?' Max looks at me.

'She's not here to sit an English exam,' Jack says, sounding bored.

'What, jealous, Oberon?' I arch a brow at him, and he laughs.

'You've no classical training?' Max leans forward, resting his elbows on his knees, steepling his fingertips. The weight of his attention is heavy. I feel like I'm at a job interview I haven't properly prepared for.

'No,' I say as calmly as I can manage. 'Actually, my first film was with Jack.'

'I remember,' Caroline says sweetly. 'He was up in arms about it. Didn't you try to get the poor girl sacked?' She turns to Jack.

'Thankfully everyone else knew much better than I did,' he says. 'I was a total twat about it.'

'All worked out in the end though, didn't it?' Max sits back in his seat after grabbing his own glass – it holds the same golden liquid as his wife's. I notice no one has offered us a drink yet. 'For you, at least. In line for another Oscar nom, I heard on the grapevine.' His eyes are shrewd. 'That was good work you did with Hardy – he knows how to wring a performance out of an actor.'

'He was interesting to work with,' is what I settle on.

Caroline scoffs into her glass. 'Oh yes.' Her tone is arch. 'So we hear.'

Jack looks like he's about to start throwing punches, and I put my hand on his knee.

'Hmmmm,' Max continues, 'you haven't done any stage work yet, though?'

'I've considered it,' I admit, 'but it's finding the time. It's such a big commitment.'

'Yes,' Caroline agrees silkily, 'it does require a certain amount of stamina, and of course you don't have the opportunity to do another take if you don't get it right the first time.'

'You've made smart choices.' Max gestures to me with his glass, ignoring his wife's poisonous little jabs. 'Unlike this son of ours who seems very happy to trade in his dignity for a pay check.'

'Give it a rest, Dad,' Jack says on a sigh.

'Someone needs to say it.' Caroline's lip curls. 'Honestly, I don't think you considered at all how it would reflect on your father and me. I hardly know what to say to people when they ask.'

'What do you think, Cynthie?' Max asks me suddenly.

'Sorry,' I say slowly, 'I don't follow.' I actually have no idea what's going on. The two of them are talking like Jack's about to reveal a secret life as a stripper, which actually I would have no problem with – especially if I got a practical demonstration.

'This bloody vampire business,' Max roars, seemingly unaware of the pun. 'Waste of his time and talent.'

I blink. 'You're talking about *Blood/Lust*?'

Caroline grimaces. 'Stupid name.'

'Says the woman who wanted a son called Oberon,' Jack laughs. I turn to him in surprise. Far from looking upset, he seems only amused by his parent's criticism.

'Yes,' Max presses on, ignoring this. 'What do you think about *Blood/Lust*?' He makes sure the name of the show drips with disdain.

'I love it,' I reply, sitting back on the sofa and crossing my legs. I meet Max's look of outrage steadily. 'Never miss an episode.'

'Me neither,' Lee pipes up unexpectedly.

Now that *does* surprise Jack. 'You watch it?' he asks.

'Of course,' Lee shrugs. 'At first I watched it because you were in it, but now I'm deeply invested. If Lucy and Bas don't end up together, I'll riot.' She smiles then, and a dimple appears in each of her cheeks. She is startlingly lovely.

'I can't believe it.' Jack shakes his head.

'Nor can I,' Caroline scoffs. 'Having displayed a total lack of interest in any work of artistic merit your father or I laid before you, now you decide you enjoy this . . . this *paranormal soap opera*?'

Lee's face smoothes out again, and she removes an invisible speck from her trousers. 'I didn't display a lack of interest,' she says, and there's an edge of weariness in her voice as if she's had this conversation many times before. 'I simply told you that I preferred maths.'

'My daughter.' Max shakes his head solemnly. 'An *accountant*.' He says the word heavily, as if it is a synonym for drug dealer.

'After all those lessons too.' Caroline shakes her head. 'She was a beautiful ballet dancer,' she says to me, before remembering that we're not on the same team, and looking away.

'But you can't be serious,' Max presses me. 'There's no need to be polite for our benefit.'

Jack scoffs at this, as well he might, but I keep my smile fixed.

'I'm not being polite. I think it's a great show. Entertaining, fun, it has a huge following. People really love it.'

'*People* meaning the lowest common denominator,' Caroline sniffs.

'Given your daughter and I are both fans, it's clear *you* aren't concerned with being polite.' I lace my tone with sugar.

Beside me, Lee chokes into her water glass. Caroline actually looks briefly thrown. 'I only meant . . . as his father says, it's a waste of Jack's talent,' she says stiffly. 'No serious director will want to work with him now. Only people like that Logan Gallow with his shoot-em-up car explosions.'

'Not a huge number of exploding cars in Regency England,' Jack muses, and it's the lack of frustration on his part that makes my temper leap higher. This is normal, I understand, the way they speak to him, belittling him.

'I guess you haven't actually watched the show.' I press my lips together, trying to keep a hold of my anger. 'Because Jack is doing wonderful work in it. It's a very physical role, yes, and he handles that brilliantly, but he also brings real depth and vulnerability to the character.' Jack's eyes are pinned on me now, the look in them hard to read. 'There was a scene in the last series where he lost his sister. My eyes were swollen from crying for two days afterwards.'

'Oh, yes.' Lee looks more animated. 'It was awful, wasn't it? Imagine watching that and being his actual sister.'

'I still can't believe you watch it, Lee,' Jack says softly.

'I don't know why you'd be so surprised . . . You're the one who took me to see *Twilight* at the cinema.'

Jack groans. 'Longest four hours of my life.'

'The first *Twilight* film is only two hours long,' Lee says primly.

'Didn't seem like it.'

'Don't be a hypocrite. As Cynthie just pointed out, dismissing popular culture is not a good look.'

'Oh.' Jack looks pained. 'But *Twilight*, Lee. They *sparkle* . . .'

The siblings are interrupted then by the appearance of a woman in the doorway.

'Ah, Marie-Therese,' Caroline says. 'Perhaps you could refresh our drinks. And whatever our guests would like,' she adds as an obvious afterthought.

'Of course,' Marie-Therese agrees.

'Hi, Marie-Therese. I'm Jack.' Jack waves from his seat. 'And this is Cynthie. I'd love a sparkling water please, but I know she thinks sparkling water is the creation of mad men.'

'It absolutely is.' I'm surprised he remembers that conversation. 'Just still water for me, thanks.'

'Certainly,' Marie-Therese replies. 'And I wanted to let you know that lunch will be ready in thirty minutes.'

'That's perfect, thank you,' Caroline says airily.

There's a chiming sound, and Caroline's head turns towards the hallway. 'And check who's at the door, will you?'

With that, Marie-Therese slips silently from the room, and Caroline tells Jack he doesn't need to introduce himself to the help every time he's here, and Jack says if she could keep her staff for longer than two weeks he wouldn't have to.

Before they can get into a longer argument, a new person enters the room on a wave of crackling energy, to universal exclamations of delight. Even Caroline unbends enough to smile. It's a man, tall and rangy with a tousled mop of dark curls.

'Nico!' Jack exclaims, leaping to his feet. 'What are you doing here?'

The man in the doorway laughs. 'You said you were coming up, so I thought I'd call on Ma and catch you at the same time.' He and Jack hug, exchanging slaps on the back, and Nico comes forward to greet everyone.

'Caroline.' He kisses her on the cheek. Apparently Nico is important enough to warrant her getting to her feet. 'Looking lovely as always. No Gran today?'

'She had another engagement.'

'Thank God,' Max mutters before shaking Nico's hand.

'Her bowling team are playing in the league finals today,' Lee offers, her voice a little unsteady, and Nico turns to her.

'Hello, Daisy,' he says fondly, hauling her up from her seat, pulling her into a bear hug. When he releases her, there's a wash of pink in her cheeks that wasn't there before.

'Nico,' she says, tugging her shirt back into perfect lines. 'It's been a long time.' Her words are steady as she drops gracefully back into her seat, but the colour in her face remains, her breathing not quite even. I smile, wondering if Jack knows that his sister has a giant crush on his best friend.

Jack introduces us with genuine pleasure.

'Nico and I grew up together,' he says, his arm around his friend's shoulder. 'He and his mum lived in the house next door, and then we were shipped off to the same boarding school.'

'Ma moved back to the States while we were there, so rather than fly out I was here for almost every holiday,' Nico explains. 'Practically part of the furniture.' He grins at me, and I totally get Lee's interest. He's tall and fit, in jeans and a battered leather jacket, the gleam of a tiny gold hoop in his earlobe, but his face belongs to a tortured poet, finely drawn with dark, expressive eyes. There are faint blue smudges under his eyes as if he hasn't slept, and a day or two of scruff covers his jaw.

'It's nice to finally meet you, Cynthie.' He shakes my hand. 'I've heard a lot of good things about you.'

'I'm surprised.' I dart a look at Jack.

He laughs. 'Well, I had to read between the lines a bit. Jack here has had a giant crush on you for thirteen years.'

I grin back at him, as Jack thumps him on the arm hard enough to hurt.

'So your mother is in town, did you say, Nicolas?' Caroline asks once we're all seated again, and Nico is happily sipping a beer, seeming more relaxed here than either Lee or Jack.

'Yes, her latest bloke is something to do with finance and he had a couple of meetings. Ma's going to hang around for fashion week. Chat up all her old mates, you know.'

'Nico's mum was a model,' Jack explains.

'What about you, Nico?' Lee asks, and she has herself firmly back under control now. You'd never guess she had any particular investment in the answer. 'Weren't you just in New Zealand?'

'Yeah, shooting some divers off the Auckland Islands,' he says. 'With my camera,' he clarifies for me with a laugh. 'Got some amazing underwater images of southern right whales. It's a designated sanctuary, and we were able to swim with them. It was incredible.'

'Was that for *National Geographic*?' Jack asks.

Nico nods. 'I'm actually just here for a few days before I fly out to Mexico, so I was happy to catch you.'

'It's good to hear *your* career is going from strength to strength,' Max says heavily, a significant look at Jack, just in case he missed the subtle dig. It seems we aren't over the part of the afternoon where Jack's parents try to make him feel shit about his life choices. Well, not on my watch,

'Nico, you must have some excellent stories about Jack that I can take back to set with me . . .' I lean forward, conspiratorially. 'Tell me everything.'

'Absolutely.' Nico is instantly on board. 'Shall we take Jack's most embarrassing moments chronologically or on a scale of how mortifying they were?'

'Just start at the beginning,' I say, while Jack groans.

Nico tips the rest of his beer back and then he puts the empty bottle down and rubs his hands together. 'Right. So, we're eleven years old and Jack is painfully into magic ...'

'Wait,' I say, holding up my hand. 'I need further details on what "painfully into magic" means.'

'You really don't,' Jack puts in.

'Wore a cape that he never took off.' Nico ticks off on his fingers. 'Insisted we refer to him as The Grand Magneto at all times.'

'The Grand Magneto?' I whisper.

'Oh yeah, he was *also* a comic book nerd,' Nico explains.

'I maintain that it's a very cool name for a magician,' Jack interjects.

'Anyway, he's been practising this trick for ages where he pulls a tablecloth out from under a load of glasses,' Nico continues. 'He's invited all our mates around to my house so that he can do it for them. Always the little performer.' He smirks at Jack who only shakes his head. 'Now, crucially, in the audience is Tansy Bennet, the girl of Jack's dreams.'

'Uh oh,' Lee murmurs, and I get the impression she's never heard this story.

'So Jack sets up the trick, and he invites Tansy to take the prime viewing spot right next to him.' Even Max and Caroline are listening with amusement on their faces at this point. 'And he really piles a lot of stuff up on the table, basically all my mother's breakables. It looks spectacular. Then he pulls the tablecloth out. He's cool and confident; it comes away with no problem ... except that he's pulled it hard enough that he loses his own balance and goes flying backwards ...'

I wince.

'Into my mum's giant aquarium,' Nico finishes.

'Noooooo!' I gasp, my hands flying to my face.

'Yep,' Nico says. 'He tips the whole thing over – it's a miracle it didn't shatter – and gallons of water crash over Jack and Tansy. She's screaming; everyone's screaming. There are tropical fish leaping all over the place. Jack's sliding around trying to scoop up the fish and get them back in the water. Tansy – who looks like a drowned cat at this point – has one leaping about in her hair and she starts crying. Everyone's fucking traumatized.'

'Thankfully no fish perished,' Jack says heavily. 'But the Grand Magneto retired that day. And Tansy Bennet remains the one who got away.'

'Wow,' I say.

'I expect your mother wasn't best pleased,' Max chuckles.

'She actually thought it was pretty funny,' Nico remembers fondly. 'But we were finding those tiny aquarium rocks everywhere for months.'

Marie-Therese comes in then, interrupting the laughter to tell us that lunch is ready.

When we stand up, Jack takes my hand in his, even though he doesn't have to.

I try not to look too happy about it.

Chapter Thirty-Nine

Cynthie

The rest of our visit to Jack's parents is painful. Nico and I are kept busy, running interference every time Max and Caroline try to steer the conversation towards their disappointment in their children (which happens often). While the majority of the disapproval is levelled at Jack, Lee comes in for a fair amount of criticism too – you would think that being an accountant was some sort of capital crime.

I demand anecdotes from Jack's childhood; Nico asks about what's been happening on set and I provide entertaining stories, or he gets Lee to share news of her grandmother's high jinks, drawing her out of her shell. It's like a high-octane game of small-talk ping-pong, and by the time we finish our exquisite chocolate tortes, prepared by the Turner-Jones's chef and served on vintage Sèvres porcelain, I feel like my head is going to explode.

Caroline and Max, having put away a steady flow of alcohol, are most of the way towards drunk and getting less and less passive and more and more aggressive by the minute.

'Of course,' Caroline says, fixing me with a look of naked dislike, 'you've only got so long before you start ageing out of the leading roles. There's a very long and painful wait between thirty-five and *National Treasure* status let me tell you.' She shudders. 'And being a national treasure is bleak enough, in case you wondered. Everyone acts like I'm a hundred years old and a sweet old lady.'

I bury my face in my drink to hide my expression. I'm fairly sure 'sweet old lady' is about the only name Caroline Turner hasn't been called.

'I expect you've already been asked to play the mother to some peppy little nineteen-year-old,' she continues, waving her glass of perfectly pale white wine in the air. 'If you want my advice, start making an investment in your face now. I can put you in touch with my plastic surgeon, I'm sure he could fix . . .' – she gestures at my face – 'things.'

'It's kind of you to show an interest,' I say serenely.

'Fucking hell,' Jack mutters under his breath, and I squeeze his leg. It's supposed to be a reassuring gesture to let him know his mum isn't bothering me, but he flinches dramatically.

'Are you okay?' I ask.

'Fine,' he replies tightly, taking a swig from his water glass.

When I look over at Nico he's watching us with a smirk.

'Of course it's all changed since my day,' Max rumbles. 'Take what happened with Rufus. A few off-colour remarks and now nobody will touch him. Didn't get asked back for your film, did he?' Max shakes his head. 'It comes to something when no one in the business is allowed to have a sense of humour.'

'You know it was a lot more than that with Rufus,' Jack says.

I look to Caroline, thinking she might have something to say about the way women are treated in the industry, but she shrugs. 'Young women today are too sensitive. If I didn't want someone pawing at me, I just told them so.' I think there's a glimmer of something in her eyes, but then she squints down into her glass while Max makes noises of approval.

I'm absolutely certain that's not the real story, that Caroline Turner somehow survived fifty years in the entertainment industry unscathed, but she's entitled to do whatever she likes with those stories, even if it's to pretend they never happened. If I think it's bad now, I can only imagine how it must have been when she was starting out.

'When we made the first film, I was warned never to be left on my own with Rufus,' I say. 'I didn't even question it, but that's not right, is it? You can't have a culture like that. Women on film sets are just trying to do their jobs. We deserve to feel safe.' I think about something Jasmine said to me – that directing could be more than a new creative challenge, that it could be an opportunity to set the tone, to control the culture on a set, to make broader changes in industry standards. It sounded lofty at the time, but maybe she's right.

'You never told me that,' Jack says slowly. 'About Rufus.'

It's my turn to shrug. 'Honestly, it didn't even feel newsworthy. Stuff like that was so common. Still is.'

'One of the journalists I work with is actually writing a story about something similar at the moment,' Nico says, diverting the conversation again, and it flows away onto other subjects.

We limp through the obligatory cups of coffee (glorious, pitch black and flown in from some remote corner of South America. Even in his current mood, Jack can't resist humming with pleasure), and then Nico gets to his feet with a display of reluctance. 'That was amazing, thank you for letting me crash,' he says, 'but I'm afraid I have to get going.'

'Yes.' Jack is up on his feet so fast that his chair scrapes loudly against the floor. 'We have to go, too. We have to go now.' There's something wild in his eyes, and I put a hand on his arm, like I'm trying to steady a horse. I think he might be vibrating.

We say perfunctory goodbyes to Max and Caroline, the two of them already having lost interest in us, and Lee walks us all to the door.

Nico drops a casual kiss on my cheek and then on Lee's.

'Got a date?' Jack asks.

'A gentleman never tells,' Nico says, though his grin reveals the answer clearly enough. My eyes dart to Lee but she shows no emotion at this.

With a cheerful wave Nico takes off for the dilapidated and mud-spattered Land Rover looking extremely out of place on the pristine driveway.

'It was really good to see you,' Jack says to Lee.

'You too,' she replies. 'I'm sorry about them,' she says, nodding her head back towards the house. 'It's nice to see you happy. Don't listen to anything they say.'

'I never do.' Jack's mouth pulls up.

'Can we hug now?' I ask her, and Lee looks surprised but steps tentatively into my arms. The hug is stiff and a bit awkward, but I'm glad we share it. I don't think Lee gets hugged often, and I'm pretty sure she needs one after growing up in that house.

'Maybe I could call you next time I'm in town,' I say. 'We could get lunch.'

'I'd like that,' she replies softly.

Jack opens the car door for me, and before I know it, we're peeling away from the house like we're fleeing the scene of a crime.

Jack's attention is firmly on the road, and he drives in silence, his jaw ticking like mad, his fingers tapping the steering wheel. I can't say I blame him; I feel like I've been through the wringer and I'm not actually related to those people. In the end, we're in the car for about twenty minutes, and Jack pulls up in front of a lovely red-brick, Victorian house near Primrose Hill.

We get out and Jack bounds up the steps to the front door, fishing out a key to open it as I follow behind. He still hasn't said anything and his energy is . . . chaotic.

I wander tentatively inside the house, finding myself in a bright, airy hallway with a staircase curling up one side.

Jack enters a code on a keypad in the wall to disarm the alarm, and then he turns to me with such heat in his gaze that I take a step back.

His hand comes slowly over my shoulder, and he pushes the front door closed behind me with a decisive click. He moves forward, his hand still braced by the side of my head, crowding me until my back hits the door. His eyes never leave mine, and what I see in them has my breath coming in shallow little gasps, each inhale enough to create the tiniest touch of friction between our bodies.

'I need to kiss you now.' His voice is a rumble of thunder, deep in his chest. *Need*, not want. The distinction has butterflies exploding in my stomach.

'Okay,' I whisper, and I barely have time to finish the word before his mouth collides with mine.

I'm trapped firmly between his big, strong body and the door at my back, caged by his arms as he kisses me. His thigh slips between mine, pinning me in place, and one of his hands drifts down, stroking through my hair, absently twisting a long lock around his finger.

I cling to the front of his shirt. His mouth softens, skimming lightly over my lips. His tongue moves lazily, languidly, tasting me, enjoying me, and I barely know what's happening; I'm delirious, lost in the sensation of it all. My hips tilt, and I slide against his thigh. The pressure has me moaning against his mouth.

Finally, he breaks away, pulls his face back, just far enough so that I can blink, unfocussed into his eyes. They're pure wolf now: heavy-lidded and predatory. The look in them sends another violent spike of lust through me. My knees are so weak, he's literally holding me up.

'What was that for?' I manage.

'That', he says, his voice like velvet rubbed against the grain, 'was for being on my side.'

'Oh,' I say, breathless. 'No problem.'

His hands drift down the sides of my body, lightly gripping my waist. He presses a kiss to the corner of my mouth, and then skims his lips across my jaw and down, until his warm mouth finds the pulse hammering madly in my throat. His tongue flicks out and he sucks gently on my skin until I whimper.

'And for being kind to my sister,' he murmurs, his mouth moving lower, across my collarbones as he slips the thin straps of my dress off my shoulders, the trail of his fingertips leaving an electric crackle across my bare skin.

'My pleasure,' I whisper. I curl my fingers into his hair, tugging his face back up to mine, and he leaves a path of soft kisses as he goes, refusing to be rushed.

'And for not pouring a drink on my mother when she said you should change any part of your beautiful, perfect face.' He punctuates his words with kisses to my cheekbone, my eyelids, each touch soft and reverent.

'It crossed my mind.' I barely recognize my own voice.

Jack's hand glides down to my throat, applying the same light pressure that he did that night at the gala, only this time he leans down and catches my hungry little sigh with his mouth.

I'm overwhelmed, surrounded by him. The temperature spikes again, and I clutch desperately at his shirt, clumsy with desire, attempting to undo the buttons with shaking fingers, trying to get my hands on him.

He reaches round my back and finds the zip on my dress, easing it down with slow and torturous care, his fingertips following the line of my spine. Finally, the dress slips away from my body, a pool of sunshine coloured silk against the tiled floor, and I stand in only my underwear, the scraps of lace that I picked out hoping for this, wanting exactly this.

He steps back to look at me for a long, aching moment.

'Holy shit,' he breathes.

Several random buttons on his shirt are open, and he looks wild, a little out of control, and I love it; I love that I did that to him. I lean back, letting him look, luxuriating in the way his eyes rake over my body.

'I like your house,' I manage on a laugh, trying to regain some equilibrium.

He tilts his head. 'You're going to have to wait for a tour. I have other plans for you.' He holds himself back, keeping distance between us, a question in his gaze.

I'm so turned on I can hardly bear it, my whole body hot and tight with need. 'Oh really?' I lick my lips. 'That sounds interesting.'

A flicker of relief crosses his face. 'Love, you have no idea.' The words rumble through me as he steps forward, picking me up with one arm, and my legs wrap around his waist of their own accord. I can feel the hard length of him through his trousers, against the thin lace of my underwear, and I roll my hips, sighing with pleasure.

His mouth captures mine once more, and with my body curled around his, he carries me up the stairs like it's nothing. When we reach the landing, he kicks open one of the doors. Honestly, he could be taking me anywhere, because I'm too interested in his mouth and his arms and his chest pressed hard and firm against mine to care.

I have a brief impression of stormy blue walls and high ceilings, before I'm lowered onto an enormous cloud of a bed.

'I've thought about this a lot,' Jack says conversationally, dropping to his knees beside the bed as I push myself up on my elbows, looking down at him. 'I've thought about this for years.' He picks up my foot and begins to undo the buckle on the strappy sandals I'm still wearing, slipping off one, and then the other, his touch warm and firm.

'I might have thought about it once or twice,' I murmur, falling back and looking blindly up at the ceiling, wondering why the feeling of his hands on the arches of my feet is the most erotic thing to ever happen.

'Mmm,' Jack hums thoughtfully, as his fingers skate up over my calves. 'The last time we did this it was hard and fast.' My breath catches, the mildness in his tone a contrast to the heat of the words as his hands wander higher. 'And I've often found myself wondering what it would be like to do things slowly. What it could be like to really . . . take my time.'

He reaches my hips and yanks me towards him, my legs falling over the edge of the bed.

'Jack,' I gasp, as he hooks his fingers into the sides of my underwear, slipping them down my legs and baring me to him completely.

'So pretty, Cynthie,' he murmurs, pressing a kiss to my inner thigh. 'So pretty everywhere.'

'Jack,' I say again, desperate as his mouth moves over me, as his tongue dips and swirls, a feather-light tease. He's in no hurry at all, and when he blows lightly against my clit I whimper. 'Please,' I moan. 'Please.'

I feel him smile against me and it's so hot. 'Not yet, love,' he murmurs. 'Not for a good while yet.'

And true to his word he teases me, sending me writhing against his cool sheets, bringing me up, up, up, and then pulling back, soothing, running his hands over my quivering limbs, kissing me and tasting me wherever he likes: my hip, my ankle, the back of my knee. He tells me I'm beautiful, perfect, that I was made for him, that he could stay here for hours. Every part of me is treated with exquisite care, and I curse like a sailor and pull at his hair, and chase his touch with my hips, almost sobbing with need and frustration as he brings me to the edge again and again.

When he plunges two fingers inside me, his hand and his mouth working me relentlessly, finally allowing my orgasm to come crashing in, it shudders through my body like an act of delicious violence.

I scream, the world exploding around me. When I finally return to earth, it's to see him getting slowly to his feet. He rubs his thumb along his bottom lip, eyes gleaming, hair a mess, and he's still fully dressed – a situation that cannot be allowed to continue.

'Take your clothes off,' I demand, and the grin that lights his face is wicked. His hands move to his shirt buttons and he follows my instructions, far, far too slowly for my liking. When he is finally, wonderfully naked and he moves towards me, I hold up my hand, halting him in his progress.

'I want to see,' I grind out. He stills, and it's my turn to take my time. I come up onto my knees and run my eyes over him, taking in the perfect, masculine grace of his body, the hard planes of his muscles, the impressive erection that has me rubbing my thighs together, already ready for more of him, much more. I want him with an intensity that I can hardly fathom.

Seeing me squirm, his eyes darken and he grasps the base of his cock, pumping his hand once, slowly, his gaze locked onto mine. I shuffle forward, pressing my palms to his chest, feeling the warmth of him. I rub my thumb gently over the tattoo that wasn't there thirteen years ago, the delicate outline of two twining flames that I first saw during our sweaty workout. I press my mouth against it as I'd imagined doing then, flick my tongue over the sinuous lines of ink. He exhales sharply, and I smile against his skin, trailing my fingers down his stomach, covering his hand with my own.

'God, I want you so much,' he says. 'I always have.'

'I'm here.' I lie back on the bed. 'So take me.'

Our bodies collide, skin against skin, heated, flushed. He's all over me, all around me, pressing me into the mattress, and his clever fingers are between my legs, and I kiss him, put my mouth on him, everywhere I can reach.

'Condom?' I pant, and he moves, fumbling in the drawer of his bedside table. The few seconds his body is away from mine are cold and painful, but then he's back, and I help him put the condom on, only wanting to touch him and tease him as he has done for me, but I can't wait, don't want to wait any longer. We roll over once, twice, until I'm on top of him, straddling him, guiding him inside me with a sigh of pleasure and relief.

He reaches up, undoing the clasp of the bra I had forgotten I was still wearing, throwing it aside. His fingers play across my sensitive flesh as I ride him, taking him deep inside me where I've needed him for so long. I rock against him, delirious with pleasure as he fills me, as he murmurs more praise, as he says my name over and over and over again like a benediction.

'Oh, god.' I squeeze my eyes closed, another orgasm coiling inside me, a glorious tightening, a pressure so intense I find myself bracing for the fall out. 'I'm going to—' I start, but he curves up, pulling my mouth against his, his hand cradling the back of my head, his fingers in my hair, cutting me off as his hips thrust wildly, a frantic, stuttering rhythm that matches my own loss of control. He hits the perfect spot, hits it again, and when his thumb circles my clit it's all I need.

Shuddering, calling his name, drowning in the taste of him, I fall apart. We both do. Together. An intense feeling of joy spreads through me, sunshine running through my limbs, and I laugh, overwhelmed by the pleasure that shudders in waves and waves and waves. My whole world tilts on its axis, like everything I thought I knew is rearranging itself. I have to settle into a new reality now; there's my life before this moment and my life after.

Turns out sex with Jack is basically a religious experience.

'Are you okay?' I croak, several minutes later. The words are muffled against his chest where I have collapsed, draped bonelessly over his body.

There's a moment of thoughtful silence. 'I think I've gone blind,' he says finally.

I lever myself up, far enough to see his face. My discarded bra is draped over his eyes, like a lacy sleep mask. I make the monumental effort to pull it away.

He blinks, his gaze unfocussed. 'Thanks.'

I fall back onto him, snuggling against his chest. 'What do we do now?' I ask, the question slurred.

'We sleep,' he says, rolling us and tucking me tenderly against him. 'And then we do that again.'

'Okay,' I murmur, already more than halfway to unconscious. 'Sounds like a plan.'

Chapter Forty

Jack

When I wake up the next morning it is to the exceptional sight of Cynthie asleep in my bed. The light is filtering in from the curtains I never bothered to close, and sunlight slants over her face, limning her profile in gold. She's lying on her stomach, the sheets thrown back to expose the graceful line of her back. Her face is turned towards me, long lashes forming a crescent-shaped smudge against her skin thanks to the mascara she was wearing yesterday. Her hair is tangled, her expression deeply peaceful.

My heart actually, physically aches while I look at her, and I rub my fingers absently across my chest, as if to ease the pain. I suppose it's time to admit what I've known all along – I'm so painfully in love with Cynthie Taylor; I don't know what to do with myself. And I have no idea how she's going to feel about it.

After we got home from lunch yesterday, I jumped on her like an animal, but I don't have it in me to feel sorry about it, and Cynthie certainly didn't seem to mind. Watching her take on my parents, defending me, so bright and fierce in the face of their disdain, having to restrain myself all damn day while that silk tease of a dress slipped up and down over her bare legs, sitting next to her at the table, wrapped in her perfume, her knee pressed against mine, her long hair brushing across my arm whenever she turned her head . . . I was out of my mind by the time we finally got out of there, barely capable of thought, let alone words. The second the door closed behind us there was only one thing I wanted, and I took it, took everything Cynthie offered, without restraint or concern about the consequences.

Last night was thirteen years in the making, but never in my wildest fantasies have I come close to imagining how it would be between us. We spent the rest of the afternoon and then the whole of the night tangled up in bed together, losing ourselves in one another. Some of what happened was tender and full of soft words, and some of it was a pure, animal need that I didn't know I held inside me.

Now, in the cold light of day I have no regrets. I only hope that she won't either. We still haven't talked about the state of our relationship. It's all very well for my head to be full of fantasies – roses around the door and us, a hundred years old and still together – but she's just come out of a relationship that could be charitably described as traumatic. Her life is in a state of upheaval. She might not be ready for this. My blood runs cold at that thought.

She stirs beside me, her lashes flickering. 'Are you staring at me like a creep?' she murmurs, her voice still rough with sleep.

I smile. 'I might be.' I lean down to kiss her, a sweet, soft 'good morning' that spirals swiftly out of control. Soon enough she's pinned underneath me, panting as I slide inside her once more, the way her body tightens around mine, a gift.

'Feels so good,' she moans.

'That's because you take me so well,' I murmur, kissing my way down the valley between her breasts, pulling one rosy nipple into my mouth, sucking gently while my hips rock and I feel her muscles clench deliciously around my cock. I concentrate on making her feel even better, understanding her body well enough now to know what she needs, what she likes, what exactly will have her fisting the bedsheets and screaming my name.

Afterwards she lies with her head on my chest and I smooth her hair back from her face.

'That's a hell of a way to wake up.' There's laughter in her voice.

'Beats the alarm clock,' I agree, instead of saying 'I could get used to it', which are the words on the tip of my tongue.

'What time is it?' she asks, lifting her head to squint at the clock on the bedside table.

'Almost eleven.' I hear her stomach growl. 'I need to feed you.'

'Yes, you do,' she says, pressing a brief kiss to my mouth as she sits up, clutching the sheets to her chest. 'And you need to find me something to wear – we didn't even get as far as bringing our bags in yesterday. All my stuff is still in the car.'

'I had other priorities.' I run a hand down her arm and she grins, that sunshine-happy smile that scrunches her nose, and tenderness kicks me right in the chest again. I am in so much trouble here.

'I wasn't complaining. But I think now it's time for that tour you promised me.'

'Why don't you take a shower and I'll grab your bag out of the car,' I say, slipping out of bed, ready to hunt out some clothes.

Cynthie gives me a long look from under her lashes. 'Why don't we just start the tour with the bathroom?'

I am powerless to resist, and why would I want to? 'The shower *can* be tricky.'

Her mouth curves. 'Maybe you can show me how it works.'

So I do.

It's another hour before we're sitting downstairs in the kitchen. Cynthie's hair is damp, and because I haven't yet got as far as going out to the car, she's wearing one of my T-shirts while she sits at the table watching me fix her scrambled eggs.

'This house is gorgeous,' she says, looking around the sleek, modern kitchen with interest. She had me show her around every room, picking up objects as she went, turning them over in her hands like they were precious: a framed picture of me and Nico from when we were about fifteen, a packet of playing cards, an old theatre programme from my drama school days, a worn copy of *Middlemarch*. She was quiet and thoughtful as she absorbed all the small details. This is where I live the majority of the time, the place I really consider home, and it feels right to have her here. Every time she goes into a room it's as if she was the single thing that had been missing all along.

'I like it,' I agree now, adding the eggs to the pan where they sizzle. 'I love being in New York, but London definitely feels like home.' Fortunately, Scott has arranged with the cleaning company I use to leave some essentials in the kitchen so we don't have to go anywhere. Most importantly, there's an entire cupboard full of coffee beans, and my expensive machine – the other love of my life – hums contentedly in the corner.

'So this is where you're based when you're not filming?' she asks. 'Do you see much of your parents when you're here?'

'Not really,' I say, gently moving the eggs in the pan. 'I know that it's close to their place, but we don't exactly move in the same circles. To tell you the truth, I avoid seeing them as much as possible.'

Cynthie sighs. 'They really are always like that, then?'

'Now you know why I didn't want you anywhere near them thirteen years ago,' I say. 'They're toxic.'

I watch her absorb this, her eyes widening as she rearranges the memory.

'Honestly?' I continue. 'That was pretty good behaviour for them. That's why Nico turned up ... to play peacekeeper. He's been doing it since we were kids, and he must have known I'd be on edge bringing you there. I only mentioned it to him in passing, but I think he drove straight over from the airport. I noticed he still had his bags in the back seat of the car.'

Cynthie's expression softens at that. 'That's kind of him. I liked him a lot.'

'He's my Hannah, I guess,' I say, turning the heat off on the hob. 'We've been through a lot together. We don't get to see much of each other now – my schedule is bad enough, but his is absolutely wild. If he's not climbing mountains in Nepal or abseiling into glaciers in the Arctic, he's photographing lions in Botswana.' I shrug. 'We stay in touch as much as possible, but it's hard to imagine him being in one place for too long.'

'You miss him,' Cynthie says.

'I do. We used to live in each other's pockets as kids, but things change. He's doing what he loves and I'm proud of him.'

'I figured those were his photographs on the wall in the living room,' she says. 'He's really talented.'

'He is,' I agree, as the toast pops up and I serve our breakfast. I put the plate in front of Cynthie, along with her coffee, and lean down to place a quick kiss on her temple.

'My own personal barista.' She hums with pleasure.

'Scott says at least I've always got a backup career.'

We dig into the food, making easy conversation. Under the table, our feet twine together. It's the sort of Sunday morning I can imagine us having all the time.

We're interrupted by my phone ringing, and I look down at the screen. 'It's my agent,' I say. 'Do you mind if I take it?'

She makes a go-ahead gesture with her fork.

'Hi, Mike,' I pick up the call.

'Jack!' Mike booms. 'I've got great news!'

'Oh?' I raise my eyebrows at Cynthie, who can hear every word Mike is saying, because the only volume he has is eleven.

'Our plan's worked wonders, and the producers have come back with a *very* healthy offer for season six, a full order of twenty-two episodes. Looks like Caleb lives to fight another day!'

'Yes!' I bring my hand down hard on the table. 'That is fucking great.'

'I know.' Mike is just as delighted. 'Apparently all the press you've been getting the last few weeks has viewing figures way up. They're thrilled and they've got big plans for you, more screen time. I don't suppose you'd be up for a conversation about continuing this little arrangement you have going with Cynthie Taylor for a while longer?'

My eyes shift to Cynthie who is no longer looking at me, but down at her plate. 'That wasn't the agreement,' I say carefully.

'I know,' Mike replies, oblivious 'but worth a punt, isn't it? Do you think she'd be up for it? If you ask me, it's got her out of a pretty deep hole, so she should be grateful—'

'I'll talk to Cynthie,' I cut him off.

'Sure, sure.' Mike's tone is airy. 'We'll discuss later. I'll ping all the initial stuff through to Scott now for you to look over.'

'Thanks, Mike,' I reply, before we say our goodbyes.

There's a moment of taut silence.

'Cynthie,' I murmur. 'What's going on?'

She lifts her eyes to mine, smiles brightly. 'Nothing! Congratulations! That's wonderful news, just what you wanted.'

'It is what I wanted,' I agree. 'Which you already knew. But the conversation upset you and I want to know why. Is it what Mike said about continuing our arrangement?'

She doesn't say anything, but her fingers twist together in an anxious gesture that I recognize.

'You know,' I say, leaning back in my chair, 'the first time we slept together we didn't talk afterwards. I've had so much time to think about that night, to replay it in my head . . . not just the good bits,' – I smile, and her hands still, though her expression remains guarded – 'but what happened afterwards. I think that in that moment you needed me to be really clear about how I felt. I think you were scared and vulnerable, and that you didn't have a clue if I liked you or hated you. I think that's why you told me it was a mistake, what happened between us. I think you said it before I could.'

'I couldn't face the rejection,' Cynthie murmurs. 'You'd made it clear so many times that I wasn't good enough for you. I suppose I was used to people feeling like that about me.'

Even though it's what I'd come to suspect, I still feel an awful, hollowing sensation in my stomach. 'Cynthie, I never felt that way, *never*. Not when we were working together, not when we were fighting and you made me want to tear my hair out. I thought you were a fucking firework. I could hardly take my eyes off you. When you told me it was a mistake, I believed that was what you thought and I was crushed; I was just too proud to show it.'

I watch her take in the words.

'You know me better than that now, Cyn,' I say quietly. 'Maybe you can see why I made such a stupid mistake. And I know you now, too. If we'd been able to be honest with each other then, things could have been different. I don't want us to repeat the same mistakes again. Please. Talk to me.'

There's a moment of silence, and I realize I'm holding my breath. It's not often in life that you're aware you're inside one of those big moments, the ones where your entire world can shift, where the story can split into two different directions, but I know in my heart that this is one of them.

I need her to talk to me. This is our chance, and the thought of losing it – of losing her – threatens to break me in half.

'You're right,' she says, finally. 'I know I'm terrible at opening up.' She gives me a wobbly smile. 'It's not like you're the first person to say it. I just find it . . . difficult.'

'I get it,' I say, and I lean across the table, taking her hand in mine. 'But you can talk to me. You can tell me how you feel. I'll listen.'

'When Mike said what he did about our arrangement . . .' she says tentatively, and I nod, 'it made me think about the fact that there's an ulterior motive for both of us to be here, a reason we agreed to pretend in the first place … It makes it hard for me to know what's real between us.'

I want to leap in, to tell her – adamantly – that it's all real, that what I feel for her is more than I ever imagined it was possible to feel for another person, but I know that if I want to be the man who deserves her, rather than the boy who let her down, then this has to be about what *she* needs. So I do what I said I would: I listen.

'It's not that I think what happened last night was wrong or … or some sort of performance,' she carries on, anxiously.

'Well, that's positive,' I say. 'Because I think we can agree I'm not *that* good of an actor.'

It surprises a laugh out of her, has her shoulders coming down. 'You're wonderful at that,' she murmurs, 'at helping people relax. You always make me feel easier.'

It's such a simple compliment, but it hits hard. Perhaps because I know it means I'm giving her something she needs. Ease. Comfort. Safety. I'm starting to realize Cynthie hasn't had a lot of that in her life.

'But the last few weeks,' she continues, and there's some colour back in her face, 'acting for the cameras, for other people. I suppose that's what a lot of my life is … not just the job, but my whole life. Everything has been about appearances, presenting a certain narrative. There's an image of Cynthie Taylor that's been crafted by committee, and that's who I have to be. You and I, we've never been in a relationship, but we've pretended to be in one *twice*. We've pretended to be in love because it benefited us both professionally, so it's all still tied into that Cynthie and her image.'

'And the lines between what's real and what's for public consumption have blurred,' I suggest. 'Again.'

'Exactly.' She nods, relieved that I understand. 'And it's easy to *pretend* to be in love. That's just acting, but I know better than any-one that real-life relationships don't always work out. I'm finding it hard to trust … not you,' she says quickly, seeing something on my face before I can hide it, 'but myself.' Her voice drops again. 'In a way, I think that's worse. I think that's why everything with Shawn hit me so hard … Not because I was in love with him, or because he betrayed me, but because I felt so foolish, so easily manipulated. I lost myself in him.' Her eyes are wide, and it's obvious that she's never said any of this before, that perhaps she hasn't even thought it all through this way before. 'He wasn't what he said he was. And I fell for it. Because … because I was so desperate to be what someone wanted.'

'Cynthie, I get why you would feel that way, but what happened isn't on you. That's all on him.' Underneath the table, my hand is clenched so tightly into a fist that I can feel my fingernails digging into my palm. Whatever else the future holds, I hope to god it in-cludes the chance to knock a few of Shawn Hardy's teeth out.

'I know that.' She smiles. 'Intellectually, I know that. I'm just working on believing it.' She frowns. 'Maybe you were right before, about me finding someone to talk to. I've always been resistant to the idea of therapy because I get so little privacy, but perhaps …'

She looks up at me again and exhales heavily. 'I hate that I'm making this so complicated, so difficult. Honestly, Jack? I can't imagine why you'd think I was worth the effort, all this work. I'm such a mess.'

'You're—' I start, and then I stop myself, force my mouth to slow down, my mind to slow down. 'I'm worried I'm going to get this wrong,' I admit.

'Just tell me the truth,' she says softly. 'You're right, that's what we should have been doing from the start.'

'The truth?' I say wryly. I rub my jaw. 'Okay, but remember you asked for it.'

'I'll bear that in mind.' She smiles, still jittery.

'The truth . . .' I take a breath. 'I think I've been in love with you for thirteen years – from the moment you stormed into my life and I felt like I'd been struck by lightning. I think when I was twenty-four and I met you, I was scared shitless of how you made me feel, and I behaved like an absolute asshole about it. You're smart and beautiful and funny and full of fire. I love arguing with you, just as much as I love not arguing with you. So yes, I think you're worth the effort – whatever the fuck that means – because despite what you seem to think, it's not hard to love you, Cynthie; it's *easy*. It's the easiest thing I've ever done.'

Her lips are parted, her eyes wide. There's a beat, and then another.

'Right,' Cynthie says. 'Okay then.'

I clear my throat. 'Do you have anything you'd like to say?'

She makes a sound somewhere between a laugh and a sob. 'Truth?' I nod. 'I want to kiss you very badly right now.'

'I have no problem with that.'

She holds up her hand to stop me from moving. 'Whoa there. You're not the only one who wants to get this right.'

She closes her eyes for a moment, settling herself.

'I love what you just said. I'd like it on a T-shirt. I want you to record it on my phone so that I can make it my ringtone and listen to it all the time. I don't think you'll ever understand what that meant to me.' She pauses here and blinks. 'I also think . . . I share a lot of your feelings. Maybe I haven't felt this way as long as you say you have, because honestly, thirteen years ago I really did think you were a bit of a dickhead . . . at least most of the time . . .' She drifts off, flustered, and I can't help laughing.

'Shit.' She presses her lips together, her chin trembles. 'It's not fair, because you made this perfect, beautiful speech like you've been scripted by Richard Curtis, and I just called you a dickhead. I *am* messing it up.'

I can't help it, can't stand to see her working herself up, especially when her words make me feel like throwing a parade, and I get to my feet, tugging on her hand until she's up too, then I sit back down and pull her into my lap. She snuggles against me.

'I think you're doing a great job.' I smooth her hair away from her face, tuck her head under my chin. 'Not enough emotional declarations feature calling the other person a dickhead if you ask me. Shakespeare has nothing on you.'

'Okay,' she mumbles into my shirt. 'That's good because I doubt it will be the last time I call you one.'

'Noted.'

She toys with a button on my shirt. 'But I still think what I said is true. We've done everything badly and in the wrong order. We hated each other, we slept together, we had to pretend to be in love, to break up; we didn't see each other for *thirteen years*, pretended to be in love again, became friends, slept together *again*, and now, what? We're supposed to be in a *real* relationship? How can that possibly work?'

'Well, sure, it sounds bad when you say it like that,' I agree mildly, and she pokes me in the chest. 'Would it help if I told you that I have a suggestion?'

'I'm all ears.'

'I understand your worries, and I heard what you said about the place you're in right now.'

'I have a lot of shit to work out,' she says, her voice small.

'Right,' I agree. 'So what I suggest is that we don't break up.'

'*Can* you break up if you're in a pretend relationship?'

'Fair enough,' I amend. 'I think we should start again. For real.'

Her fingers stop fidgeting. 'What exactly does that look like?'

'I have a few ideas.' I smile. 'But essentially, I think we stop performing all together. I think we should date. I think we should do what you do at the start of any relationship and get to know each other. I think we should talk. Constantly. About everything.'

She pulls back, her face clearing. 'That sounds . . . nice,' she says.

'We'll take it slowly. No pressure. And what that looks like in the immediate future is that you go and get dressed and we drive back down to Cornwall and real life. So I'm going to go and get your bag for you.'

Cynthie bites her lip, and then she nods. 'Okay,' she agrees. 'I think this is a good idea. Maybe. Hopefully. But there's just one thing . . .' Her arms come up and wind around my neck. 'Before we start from the beginning, can we pretend for just a few more seconds?'

'I don't see how a few more seconds could hurt.'

And then, she kisses me softly, sweetly.

'Thank you for not giving up on me,' she whispers.

'Never.' It's a promise I know I'll keep. I just hope I can convince her of it.

Chapter Forty-One

Cynthie

The day after we get back from London, I find an envelope with my name scrawled across the front taped to the door of my trailer.

'What's that?' Hannah asks.

'No idea,' I reply, pulling it free. It's been a long day of filming, and honestly, I wouldn't describe my emotional state as particularly calm. The events of the past forty-eight hours have been intense to say the least, and my focus is not on my work the way that it should be. Instead my focus leaps between the hours I spent locked in Jack's bedroom and the conversation we had in his kitchen.

I want to be able to say that I feel nothing but giddy about it, but that's not true.

I *do* feel giddy. The world and everything in it is beautiful. Jack Turner-Jones says he's in love with me. But I also feel terrified. I have this sensation in my stomach like I'm waiting for the other shoe to drop. Seeing Jack on set today, I half expected him to turn around and yell 'psych!' in my face and then high-five the crew as his greatest prank was revealed.

Obviously, that didn't happen. He lit up at the sight of me. He split a cheese toastie with me for lunch, texted me while I was in hair and make-up. He forwarded me a photo of a picture that Nico must have dug up of him aged eleven and dressed as a tiny, earnest magician with a moustache drawn over his lip in eyeliner. It was the most adorable thing I've ever seen and I teased him mercilessly for the rest of the day.

It's delicious; it's easy. So why do I feel like I'm on the edge of a panic attack again?

'Cynthie!' Brooke's voice stops me in my tracks. She's jogging after me, Declan hot on her heels. 'Sorry,' she wheezes when she catches up. 'Phew! I'm definitely not as fit as I thought I was. I wanted to grab you before you went home ... We were going to film a talking head with you today, but I know the shoot ran late, do you still have time?'

'Sorry, Brooke, I totally forgot,' I say, thinking longingly of the sofa in my hotel room and a large glass of wine. I glance at Hannah, who gives a tiny shrug: my call. 'Sure,' I say. I slip the envelope into my pocket.

'Great!' Brooke bounces on her feet. 'We're all set up in Jack's trailer. He finished early today so he said we could use it for a change of scene.'

Inside Jack's trailer Kara and Cooper are waiting, and the four of them flutter around, getting everything ready while I perch in the folding director's chair they've put in the middle of the space.

'How's it all been going?' I ask idly.

'Really well.' Brooke nods, fiddling with the lighting they've brought in. 'The vibe is great, isn't it?'

'It's a good set,' I say. 'It was the first time around, too.'

'Yeah,' Brooke settles into the seat across from me, off camera. 'I get that impression. You're all so close, like a weird, giant family.'

I laugh. 'It's true,' I agree. 'And it's special. It's not always like that.'

'Okay, so we're good to go?' Brooke checks in with the rest of her team, who nod. She settles in, asking me questions about the filming we did today and how I thought it went.

'You and Jack have such incredible chemistry on-screen,' she says.

'It's easy to have chemistry with Jack. He's an extremely charismatic actor.' I grin. 'As I'm sure he's told you himself.'

Brooke laughs. 'The two of you clearly have a strong relationship both on and off-screen.'

I hesitate, thinking about what Jack said, that we should try just telling the truth, being who we are.

'Yes, we do,' I agree. 'It wasn't always so comfortable between us, but he's a brilliant actor and an even better man. I'm so happy we get to make this film together.'

'You and I haven't had a chance yet to talk about the sex scene that you filmed the other day.' She glances down at her notes.

'What would you like to know about it?' I shift uncomfortably. Brooke did catch my meltdown, but I'd been hoping she wasn't going to mention it.

'Is it awkward filming those scenes?' she asks.

'A bit,' I laugh. 'It's very technical, which in some ways makes it more awkward – you know, "Cynthie can you just move your bum a bit to the right" – but in other ways that makes it easier. Everyone's very focussed on getting the shot. It's not titillating.'

Brooke nods. 'And having Nisha there helped?'

'Having Nisha there definitely helped. I'm a huge fan of intimacy co-ordinators and I've worked with some great ones. It's important to make those scenes feel safe.'

'Have you filmed scenes like that where you haven't felt safe?' The question is casual.

I hesitate. 'Yes,' I say finally. 'A lot has changed in our industry in a short time, so even when I was starting out, there weren't the same practices and standards that there are now. It was a bit like the Wild West, and you were at the mercy of your director.'

'And some of those directors didn't prioritise your wellbeing?'

I shift in my seat. 'I wouldn't say that. There were times when

I don't think it occurred to a male director that something might be uncomfortable for me. Often the expectation was that I should get on with things without complaint because to do otherwise was unprofessional.'

'Can we talk about Rufus Tait?' Brooke asks.

'Rufus?' I repeat in surprise.

'You're aware of the accusations surrounding him.' There's a glint in Brooke's eye that I've caught a few times – a hint of steel under the sunshine – and I think it's entirely possible that she's more than happy to let people underestimate her.

'I am.'

'What was your experience of working with him on *A Lady of Quality*?'

'I personally didn't have any trouble with him apart from some off-colour remarks,' I say thoughtfully. 'But that's not to say I don't believe the women who have come forward. I absolutely do. Rufus had a reputation among the female cast and crew on set, and we were warned not to be left alone with him.'

Brooke looks surprised.

'What?' I ask.

She shakes her head. 'I don't know, I just didn't think you'd answer the question.'

I shrug. 'I'm not sure the lawyers will let you use it, but I don't think there's any harm in telling the truth. We have to let the light in on this stuff instead of trying to hide it away. It's not in my interest, or anyone else's interest, for us to cover these things up. That's what creates the problem in the first place.'

It's Brooke's turn to look thoughtful.

'Who exactly warned you about him?'

I furrow my brow. 'I don't remember specifically. I suppose it was one of those whisper networks that so many women have to rely on. You know, *this one's a problem, pass it on*.'

Brooke nods. 'So not Jasmine?'

My eyes narrow. 'No, not Jasmine. For what it's worth, I think if she'd known about him, she wouldn't have had him on the film. You could ask her about it.'

'Oh, I did,' Brooke says airily. 'That's exactly what she said. And I believed her.'

'Good.' The word comes out a little sharp.

'I think Jasmine is actually very concerned about the wellbeing of people on her set,' Brooke continues. 'Is that typical?'

The question feels pointed. 'It varies,' I say, cautiously.

'Have you worked with specific directors who you think have created a problematic culture on set?' Brooke's face is the picture of innocence, but I can see that she's been plotting a careful path through this particular interview.

'Yes,' I answer shortly.

'Would you like to talk about that?' she asks blandly.

My eyes meet hers, and there's something new there now, something that might be sympathy. 'Not at this time,' I say, finally.

'Fair enough.' Her smile is bright and she backs off at once. She asks me another couple of questions and then I get up to leave, unclipping the microphone and handing it back to Kara.

'Thanks for doing that,' Brooke says, walking me to the door to the trailer. She reaches out her hand and lays it tentatively on my arm. 'If there's ever anything else you want to talk about . . . on or off the record. Just let me know.' The words feel heavy, loaded.

I think about her face when she asked me about Rufus. I wonder why she didn't ask about my near panic attack during filming. I have more than a passing suspicion that what she *wants* to ask me about is Shawn Hardy.

Interesting.

'I'll think about it.'

My brain is going about a million miles an hour as I walk away, turning over Brooke's questions in my head. When I get back to my trailer, Hannah's not there. I reach in my pocket for my phone and feel the crinkle of the envelope that I'd forgotten about.

Pulling it free, I tear it open, and when I see what's inside I sit down, right where I am on the floor of the trailer.

Dear Cynthie,

Not so long ago, you and I had a conversation about love letters. You said it meant something to have them, to be able to pull them out and see a love story committed to paper. I want us to have that. I like to imagine you in the future, taking out this letter and remembering how it felt when we were like this – something new and real.

Of course, I haven't written a letter in . . . god, I actually don't know when I last wrote anything except my own name. My handwriting leaves a lot to be desired, and I had to send Scott on a mission for stationery. Do not ask me why he understood this to mean that I needed a professional letterhead, but an hour later I was in receipt of a thousand sheets of tasteful, linen-blend, personalized stationery with Jack Turner-Jones, (PGA) emblazoned across the top. I'm just sorry that your first love letter looks like something I might send to my accountant.

I am writing with a fountain pen, though. It's a gold one that my dad gave me on our first day of filming, thirteen years ago. I don't know if you remember, but I'm pretty sure this pen was the cause of the first of many black marks against me. Truthfully, I used to hate it, too. When he gave it to me, it didn't feel like a gift to commemorate the occasion – it felt like a physical reminder of the weight of his expectations. Maybe that's on me; maybe he was genuinely trying to do something nice and I couldn't see it because I was so scared of disappointing him. Now it doesn't feel so heavy in my hand. Now it just feels like a pen. Time can change a lot, can't it?

I've been thinking about you and me, and time. Last night you slept in my arms, and I found myself wondering . . . if I'd done things differently; if we both had, would we have spent the last thirteen years together? It's hard to realize that you've been in love with someone for over a decade, that the way they fit into your life, your home, your heart, is perfect, and that possibly through your own stupidity you've spent so much time apart.

After a bit of manly brooding on the subject I realized that thinking like that wasn't just unhelpful, it was wrong. In my heart of hearts I know that the versions of us that existed then couldn't have made a relationship work, but now? Now, when I look at you, I see for ever. I think I might need to bring you around on this (you did call me a dickhead yesterday, after all), but I'm pretty confident. I have it on good authority that I'm extremely charming.

You told me yesterday that you're a mess, that you have shit to work out, and I understand that, but I hope you know that if you have growing to do, that you can grow with me. I don't think any of us are ever done changing — I certainly hope I'm not. I'm excited about the us we'll be in ten years, in twenty, in fifty. I can't wait to know every single version of you, if you'll let me.

Remember when I stayed at your place and I was reading Persuasion? *That book was a real kick in the teeth for a man who was going through it, let me tell you. Jane Austen knew her shit. It's hard work, writing a letter to the person you love when you know nothing will ever compare to 'you pierce my soul. I am half agony, half hope.' Captain Wentworth and I have a lot in common.*

I'm going to stop writing now, because I'm sitting in my trailer and Scott is going to come in and rush me over to wardrobe and he'll probably be horrified by the ink stains on my fingers, even if I tell him it adds authenticity.

I love you. (God, what a relief to say it!)

Jack

I'm still on the floor when Hannah finds me a few minutes later. All thoughts of Brooke and our conversation have fled.

'What are you doing down there?' she asks.

'I couldn't stand up anymore,' I say, which is the honest truth. Jack Turner-Jones took me out at the knees. A love letter. I suppose I should have expected it – he did tell me he had some ideas about what should happen next.

'I think I need to talk to you about something,' I tell Hannah, tapping the envelope against my hand, as she placidly ignores the fact I'm sprawled across the carpet, and gathers the stuff she left in here earlier.

Her head snaps up. 'I knew something was going on. You've been so cagey since I got back this morning.'

I take a deep breath and look up at her. 'I slept with Jack.'

'Fucking hell, Cyn!' Hannah plops down onto the sofa. 'Give a girl a warning before you drop a bombshell like that.'

'Yes, it's actually not the first time it's happened,' I continue apologetically.

Her brow furrows. 'When did you sleep with him the first time?'

'Okay. I just need you to be very calm about this.'

'About what?' Her eyes widen. 'Was it when he stayed at your place? That was *weeks* ago.'

'It was thirteen years ago.'

Chapter Forty-Two

Cynthie

'Thirteen years ago?' Hannah repeats blankly. Her eyes do a sort of creepy reptilian blink. I nod.

'You kept a secret from me for thirteen years?' She doesn't sound hurt, just baffled. 'How? You literally tell me everything that happens to you. And not just in real life. You tell me everything that happens to you in your *dreams*. I had to hear all the juicy details about your subconscious marrying you off to Mr Bean, but this slips your mind?'

'It didn't exactly slip my mind. It was very ... memorable.'

'Okay.' Hannah holds up her hand, fishing out her phone. 'Don't say another word, I'm sending out a code red to the group, right now. I'm calling an emergency meeting.' I see her finger smash down repeatedly on the blaring red alarm emoji, then she makes a call.

'Greg,' she barks, when someone picks up on the other end. Greg is our driver, and as far as I know he's been summoned to collect us. 'Are you already here? You did a course in stunt driving, right? How quickly can you get us back to the hotel?' Her brow furrows at the answer. 'Let's see if we can shave another thirty seconds off your personal best, shall we?' She hangs up the phone and fixes me with a look. Her phone is pinging away like mad; she glances at the screen.

'Everyone is mobilized. We rendezvous at the hotel. Let's go. Now.' She's already moving. I half expect her to army roll down the steps.

'You're so scary,' I whisper.

She turns to me with a feral grin. 'Wait till Patty finds out.'

'Shit,' I mutter, hustling after her.

As it turns out, Greg has been looking for an excuse to put his training to use, and we basically squeal into the hotel car park on two wheels. I emerge from the back seat pale and trembling, while Hannah grins and palms Greg an enormous tip. I am one hundred per cent certain that she's enjoying this.

When we get upstairs, Patty, Liam and Arjun are pacing outside the door to my suite like expectant fathers outside the delivery room. These gossip-hungry little gremlins.

'What is it?' Patty demands, before the door is even open. 'What's the big news?'

'Cynthie slept with Jack,' Hannah says, tapping the key card and sailing into the room.

'What?!' Liam and Patty chorus, scrambling in behind her.

'I knew it!' Arjun pipes up, then when we all turn to look at him, he adds, 'Okay, I didn't *know* it know it, but *come on*, is anyone surprised?'

'They also slept together thirteen years ago,' Hannah says.

'WHAT THE FUCK?' Patty explodes.

'Okaaaayyy,' Liam whistles.

'Fair enough.' Arjun scratches his cheek. 'That is actually pretty surprising.'

'Cynthie Taylor, you have some serious explaining to do,' Patty says, flopping down on the sofa. 'Thirteen years you've been sitting on this hot gossip. How did none of us know about this?'

I exhale. 'It's kind of a long story.'

'Our favourite.' Liam sits, his chin propped on his hand. Four pairs of eyes are trained on me, avid and unblinking. If there was popcorn they'd be munching it.

'Do you remember the day we filmed the big kissing in the rain scene?' I start.

'You mean when you and Jack kissed and then you swooned away into his arms?' Hannah perches in a chair.

'As I've said *many times*,' I reply hotly, 'I was hungover and it was very cold and ... you know what, that's not the point. That night I couldn't sleep and I went downstairs to the kitchen and Jack was there and things just ... progressed.'

'In the kitchen?' Patty asks.

'Technically, on the kitchen floor.'

'Fucking hell.' Patty looks awestruck.

Hannah grimaces. 'Not very hygienic, is it?'

'Oh my god,' Liam whispers. 'The *power* that kissing scene has. The MTV thing goes viral like every six months. No wonder you and Jack were powerless to resist.'

'It wasn't the kissing scene,' I say, rubbing my forehead. 'Or it sort of was, but we were both so angry with each other and things got a bit heated, and it just happened.'

'Hate sex.' Patty nods wisely. 'Hot.'

'Was it good?' Arjun asks. 'What?' He says when the others look at him. 'You all want to know.'

'It was the best sex I've ever had, until the night before last.'

They all take a moment to digest this.

'Okay,' Hannah says, after several deep breaths. 'So you had very good, very hot, angry sex thirteen years ago. But what happened afterwards? And what happened this week?'

I fill them in on all the details. It's a messy, meandering story and it contains several segues on my part where I try to explain the shambles that is my mental state, and several more on their part which revolve around questions like 'Why would you say that?',

'Why would you do that?', 'Did he really pick you up with one arm?' (breathless), and '*How* big?!'

'So he said he wants you to be together?' Hannah says slowly. 'To start over?'

'That's right. And then there's the love letter.'

'The love letter?' Patty says blankly. 'Is that slang for something? Is it a sex thing I don't know about?' She pouts. 'I really like to stay up to date on these matters. Oh! Is this like a historical kink thing? They used to call condoms French letters, right?'

'No, he *literally* wrote me a love letter with a pen and a piece of paper so that I can keep it in a box and pull it out when we're old and grey to show our grandchildren.' I'm crying now, sitting cross-legged on the floor in front of them.

'Did he say that?' Hannah asks, dazed.

'No, but I know him; that's what he meant.'

'And just to clarify . . .' Liam says slowly. 'That's . . . bad?'

'No,' I sniffle. 'It's wonderful.'

'Right.' Liam nods wisely before looking to the others in confusion. 'So you're unhappy because . . .' he trails off, obviously hoping I'll finish the sentence.

'I don't know!' I say. 'That's the whole problem. What is wrong with me?'

Hannah gets up from her chair and comes to sit on the floor beside me. She puts her arms around me and holds me like she has many, many times over the years when I've been sad or desperate or heartsick. Only I'm none of those things now. I don't know what I am. Broken, maybe.

'There's nothing wrong with you, Cyn,' she says softly. 'Well, nothing that a qualified therapist couldn't help you with.'

'Yeah, okay, I'll admit it might be time to get some help in that department.'

'Halle-fuckin-lujah!' Patty crows. 'You might be the last resident of LA to enter therapy. I'll give you a list of potential candidates. This is going to be so good for you.'

'But why am I so freaked out over everything that's happening with Jack?' I wipe my eyes with the back of my hand. 'It feels too good to be true, right? There's no way something like this just . . . works out. I know that. You can love romance *in a movie* and know that stuff like that doesn't happen in real life. Love letters and destiny and soulmates. It's just a fantasy.'

My friends exchange another look. That's happening a lot tonight.

'Cyn, it's not like it's a huge mystery . . .' Hannah says, finally. 'You just got out of a . . . I don't even want to call it a *relationship*.'

'More like a hostage situation,' Patty grumbles.

'With someone who massively screwed you over,' Hannah continues. 'With the exception of Theo, you've made fairly consistently awful choices when it comes to romantic partners.'

'God, remember Barry?' Liam says. 'And Josh!'

'Nah, Freddie was the worst,' Arjun says. 'What a wanker.'

'Yes, all right,' I say, nettled. 'I get the point.'

'No, you don't,' Hannah says, shaking her head. She fixes me with her tough-love stare, and I know that whatever is coming next, I'm going to absolutely hate it. 'You've never been out with someone who had the potential to be serious. And I *do* include Theo in that, because neither of you were ever really in that relationship. I know Shawn told you he was getting a divorce, and I don't doubt for a second that you believed him, but don't you think, on some level, that you knew it wasn't going anywhere? That the fact he wasn't actually divorced yet meant there wasn't any real possibility of a future?'

I stare at her, the words bouncing off me like rubber bullets: they might not be fatal, but they sting like a bitch.

'But with Jack,' she says softly, 'it's real, Cynthie. You're in love with him. You have been for ages and we all know it. You're scared.'

'That's not true,' I croak. 'That can't be true. Why would I be scared of that?'

'Babe,' Liam says, getting up to sit next to me on my other side, his arm round my waist. His cheek resting on the top of my head. 'You're like the most stubborn, independent person I know.'

'Now that's *demonstrably* untrue,' I huff. 'Several people have referred to my relationship with Hannah as *almost problematically co-dependent*.' I say this last part a bit too proudly.

'Yeah, because I've been wearing you down practically since the womb.' Hannah rolls her eyes. 'And you still don't let me all the way in, Cyn; you know you don't.'

I wish I could disagree with this, because it makes me feel like shit. How can I possibly be withholding stuff from Hannah, who is as important to me as air? But I know she's right. I know I didn't tell her about Jack. I know I haven't told her about the panic attacks. I know I haven't told her all the details about Shawn – even if she's read between the lines. I've kept those things to myself as much as possible. The only person I've opened up to is Jack . . . and that in itself probably means something.

'I might know a frankly insane amount about what's happening in your life, but you *hate* talking about your feelings,' Hannah continues. 'It's like pulling teeth getting you to admit you're upset about things. You never ask for help, even though we'd all lie down on train tracks for you.'

'I know how to ask for help.'

Patty scoffs, then clambers to her feet and stretches. 'I swear, if you were trapped on a desert island and you had to write a message in the sand for passing planes to see, it would say "no worries if not!"' She comes to sit on the floor and leans against Liam.

'After the stuff with Shawn, you just shut yourself in your house alone,' Liam points out. 'Hannah was performing wellness checks. We had a secret WhatsApp chat with Petra because she was the only one getting near you.'

'What did she say?' I ask, temporarily diverted.

'Let's just say there was a lot of graphic imagery when it came to what she'd like to do to Shawn.' Liam shudders. 'Google translate was having a field day. My search history is a dystopian nightmare. I can't unread that stuff, you know.'

'The Serbs really know what they're doing when it comes to cursing,' I agree.

There's a beat.

'So we're all just sitting on the floor are we?' Arjun asks, sounding resigned, but he comes down to sit next to Hannah anyway.

'The point is,' Hannah says, steely, 'that you're scared of making yourself vulnerable, and you always have been. You have huge abandonment issues. Understandably. You're only comfortable when depending entirely on yourself. But you don't need to get in your own way. It's time to let someone else all the way in.'

'*That's what he said,*' Arjun whispers gleefully, and Patty chokes on a giggle, trying to look sombre.

'I'm sorry,' he adds, instantly contrite. 'I just had to.'

I nod. 'You really did.'

'There was no way we could let that one slide,' Liam agrees.

'It was irresistible,' Hannah sighs.

'So, what?' I ask. 'I just need to find a way to trust that Jack's feelings are real and that he's not going to get me to open up to him and then leave me, and accept that our relationship – which started off as a PR exercise – is now true love, while at the same time overcoming thirty years of abandonment issues, and then everything will be fine?'

'Exactly.' Liam beams proudly.

'I think I might need some help,' I say the words stiffly, but I get a round of applause.

'We'll work something out,' Hannah promises.

'You do know I love you guys, though,' I say, finally.

'Of course we do,' Arjun pipes up.

'And we love you,' Liam adds.

'We're *family*,' Patty insists.

And then they're all hugging me and even though I can't breathe, I think maybe there's something to this whole sharing your feelings business after all, because for the first time today I don't feel worried at all.

'But seriously . . . can we get off the floor now?' Arjun asks.

Chapter Forty-Three

Cynthie

Over the next few days, I amass a collection of love letters, each one as romantic, funny and open-hearted as the first. Jack and I spend a lot of time together, both on set and off. He folds so seamlessly into my life, into my family, that it feels like he's always been there.

With every day that passes I feel some of my anxiety loosen. I even have my first therapy session, online via Zoom with a UK based therapist Clemmie recommends. It looks like this:

Me I just think I'm pretty self-aware and in touch with how I think and feel about things, so I'm not exactly sure what I'm going to get out of this process.

Her Okay.

Me *Sobs hysterically for sixty minutes.*

Her Why don't we schedule another session for tomorrow?

Me Okay.

The problem that I'm facing now is that Jack is being extremely respectful of me and my feelings and he has made no push to do more than spend time with me, talk to me, and write me searingly beautiful letters.

Frankly, it's a nightmare.

'He won't even hold my hand!' I hiss to Hannah.

'Why don't *you* hold *his* hand?' she asks.

Because this is an absolutely valid point, I decide not to dignify it with an answer. The thing is, I know that Jack is waiting for some sort of signal or sign from me, but I don't know what that looks like or even if I'm totally ready for it. The last thing I want to do is mess this up. It's too important. I'm a mess of indecision. I can *see* that I'm sabotaging my own happiness, but somehow I can't stop it.

Even after everything he's done there's still a part of me that can't believe he really feels for me what he says he does. And I have no idea how to fix that.

'Just jump on him,' Patty advises. 'Bang this shit out.'

'My wife, the romantic,' Arjun supplies fondly.

Maybe she's right. After all, the amount of time I spend thinking about getting Jack back into bed … or against a wall … or really on any flat surface is bordering on perverse.

And now he's on a bloody horse.

'I can't believe that Reckless Ed is still going strong,' I say, patting the big, beautiful horse's neck.

'Horses live a long time,' Jack says, 'but I didn't think we'd be reunited like this.'

I might be wearing jeans and a sweater because I'm not filming, but Jack is in full costume and the effect is just as mouth-watering as it was the first time. More so, actually, because I'm even more desperately horny *and* I know exactly what's underneath all that buttoned up regalia.

I'm not the only one who has turned out to watch Jack filming his 'galloping, windswept across the parkland' scenes. I'd say ninety-five per cent of the female cast and crew members (and a significant proportion of the men for that matter) have wandered innocently down for totally legitimate reasons.

'You look very handsome,' I say, a little breathless.

Jack's mouth pulls up in a dangerous half-smile. 'Yeah, I remember you looking at me like that the first time around. A man on horseback really does it for you, hey, Taylor?'

'I think it's you on horseback, more specifically.'

His smile grows. 'Now, that is good to know. How about—' Whatever he's going to say is cut off when Reckless Ed, who has been standing tranquilly, occasionally flicking his ears back and forth, lets out a high-pitched whinny and suddenly swings away from me.

'What the—' I leap backwards, and in his surprise it takes Jack a couple of seconds to get the horse back under control.

'Oh no.' There's laughter in Jack's voice as he calls over his shoulder. 'It looks like Reckless Ed has spotted the one that got away.'

I follow his gaze to find Hannah climbing up the hill towards us. She waves but hesitates when she sees the giant horse. I don't know if horses can actually smile, but Reckless Ed is doing a very good impression of it.

'I didn't know you were here,' Hannah says to me, one eye on the horse who is practically quivering with excitement as Jack moves back towards us.

'Oh.' I frown. 'You didn't come here looking for me?'

She blinks several times. 'Err . . . yes,' she says. 'I mean, no.'

'Well, that clears things up,' I mutter, bemused.

That's when Jack and Hannah share a shifty look. 'What's going on?' I ask suspiciously.

'Nothing!' Hannah says brightly.

'I asked Hannah to come up,' Jack says. 'Sorry, I couldn't resist seeing if Reckless Ed remembered her.'

The horse in question drops his enormous muzzle on top of Hannah's head, huffing happily into her hair. My best friend freezes, a huge, unnatural smile on her face.

'Yep, you got me!' she exclaims, her shoulders up round her ears. 'Anyway, if you don't need me, I'd better be going.'

'Is everything okay?' Jack asks, easily.

'Yep. Yep.' Hannah's head bobs. 'Everything is all good. Just *perfect*.'

'Did you just wink at Jack?' I ask.

'Something in my eye,' Hannah mutters, stepping gingerly away from Reckless Ed.

Jack coughs into his hand, and I think he must be trying to hide a laugh, but I'm distracted by Jasmine's appearance on set.

'Okay, weirdos,' I say. 'I need to go and grab Jasmine really quick. Have a good scene,' I say to Jack. 'I'll be cheering you on from behind the monitors.'

Jasmine looks up when I stomp over. 'That was a good note about the ballroom scene yesterday,' she says. 'I was just talking to Lo and we think we're going to shoot some extra footage to fill the gap, when we're back in the studio.'

'Great.' I feel a little glow of satisfaction. As she promised, Jasmine has let me sit in on the evening meetings when she and Logan go through the day's shooting. Apart from the misery of having to watch myself in uncut, unedited footage, it's been fascinating, and to give Logan his due, he's been just as happy as Jasmine to welcome my input. He even offered to put me in touch with some of his contacts. ('Thrilled to be an ally!' he insisted.)

'I also have those details you were asking about,' Jasmine adds casually.

My gaze sharpens. 'She said yes?'

Jasmine nods, and I exhale. Lilah Meritt was third AD on one of Shawn's films, and someone who Jasmine knew had been pressured into a bad situation with him. I asked Jasmine a couple of days ago if she thought Lilah might be willing to talk to me about it, and it looks like she's agreed.

'She even has another couple of names for us,' Jasmine says.

I press my lips together. 'This thing is really snowballing.' Lilah is actually the second person Jasmine put me on to. The first, Sarah, asked me if I was going to do something about Shawn.

'He needs to be called out,' she said tearfully, over the phone. 'And you're the only one of us with the platform to do it. I know it's not fair, but I hope you'll think about it.'

I have been. A lot.

'Honestly, I wish I was more surprised.' Jasmine squints out over to where Jack is warming Reckless Ed up by putting him through his paces. 'I get the feeling there are plenty of people who have been waiting for an opportunity to talk about this. Have you decided what you want to do yet?'

'I think I'm going to speak to Brooke.'

'Are you sure that's a good idea?'

'No, but I have a feeling she's already interested in the story, and I like her. I know she's green, but the work she's done already is solid.'

Jasmine nods. 'Yeah, I really enjoyed the short she made about book banning. I was surprised she took on this project.'

I smile. 'I think she's genuinely a fan of the first film.'

'And why wouldn't she be?' Jasmine lifts her brows.

'Exactly.'

'Fine, well, if you need anything just let me know,' Jasmine says briskly. 'But right now I'm going to go and make sure my brother has allowed Jack to keep all his clothes on.'

'I'm not going to disagree with him that shirtless Jack on the back of a horse would make for compelling viewing.'

'Philistines,' Jasmine huffs, striding off.

With a grin, I take the seat that Arjun has saved me near the monitors and spend a very enjoyable hour watching Jack look commanding on horseback. Tragically for his audience, he remains fully clothed at all times.

'He's gorgeous,' a voice says from beside me.

'Jack or the horse?' I ask, my eyes glued to the screen.

Brooke laughs. 'Both.'

I turn to her and find Declan filming me. 'Too right,' I agree.

'Is it true that you filmed the kiss scene in the last movie in a single take?' Brooke asks.

'Yeah.' My eyes stray back to Jack, who has finished the current take and is looking down at a gesticulating Logan, laughing. 'We only needed one.'

'That's hot,' Brooke says, matter of fact.

'Do you know what?' I say. 'It really was. But in real life? It's even hotter.'

Brooke is practically fist-pumping at catching that little nugget on camera, and I grin back at her. It feels good just to say what's on my mind.

'I actually wondered if I could have a word with you?' I ask her. 'In private.'

'Sure,' Brooke agrees easily. 'Dec can shoot some B roll of Jack, right?'

'No worries,' Dec agrees.

I get to my feet and catch Jack's eye, waving to let him know I'm leaving.

'Hang on,' he calls, trotting over to the two of us. 'I needed to ask you something.' He's not wearing a hat and his hair is wind-tumbled, his cheeks pink. He looks so handsome that I find it difficult to focus on what he's actually saying. 'Are you free tomorrow night?' he asks.

It takes a moment for me to process the words when my brain is busy chanting KISS HIM, KISS HIM, KISS HIM. 'I think so, why?'

He flashes me a grin. 'Because I'm taking you on a date.' He treats Brooke to a little wink, and she practically dissolves on the spot. On that note, he wheels the horse around and the two of them thunder away.

Next to me, Brooke gives a small, lovelorn sigh. 'You're right. He is even better in real life.'

'Annoying, isn't it?' I say, my eyes still on Jack, then I give myself a little shake. 'Come on then, let's go and see if Pam in craft services has anything on offer. I'm starving.'

Brooke and I make our way down to base in companionable silence, and I try not to worry too much about the conversation we're about to have. It's only a first step, I remind myself. I'm not committing to anything.

We park up at a small wooden table in front of Pam's food truck, tucking into ham sandwiches made with doorstop thick slices of bread.

'So, what's up?' Brooke asks.

'I've been thinking about our last interview,' I say, blowing on my scalding-hot cup of tea. 'When you asked me about Rufus.'

Brooke sits up straighter, unable to hide her interest.

I treat her to a long measuring look. 'I watched some of your other work, you know,' I say. 'Before we started filming. I wanted to know who was going to be following us around.'

There's a hint of colour in Brooke's face. 'What did you think?'

'I thought it was good. You have a great eye, and a skill for crafting a compelling narrative. I liked the work you did on the women's shelter in New York.'

'That was my student thesis,' she says, surprised.

'I like to be thorough.' I put my cup down. 'And I'm glad they booked you for this. I think you'll make something more interesting than the puff piece the studio is after.'

'I hope so. It's been a lot of fun so far.'

'So what I wanted to ask you about was your next project.'

Brooke's expression is guarded. 'What about it?'

I run my finger around the top of my mug. 'I suppose I wondered if your question about Rufus had something to do with it. We both know the studio isn't going to let you put anything about him in the documentary, so I wasn't sure why you'd even ask. Plus, there was the other thing.'

'What other thing?'

I lift my eyes to hers. 'I'm pretty sure you were trying to get me to talk about Shawn Hardy, and I want to know why.'

It's my turn to be measured. Brooke's lips purse thoughtfully as she considers me. 'I'm working on something about women in the entertainment industry post MeToo,' she says finally.

'And you think there's something to be said about Shawn?' I steady my tone as I ask the question, though my heart thumps.

'I know there is,' she says, just as steady.

There's a beat of silence then. To give myself something to do, I take a sip of my tea which is still too hot.

'Okay,' I say softly, more to myself than to her. 'I think you and I should have a conversation.'

'On the record?' Cheerful, sunny Brooke is gone; now she looks more like a shark scenting blood. I can appreciate that killer instinct. It tells me I was right about her.

My shoulders relax. 'Let's see how we get on.'

It's a start.

Chapter Forty-Four

Jack

I knock on the door to the hotel room and wait.

'That's not the knock we agreed on,' a voice comes from behind the door.

'You were serious about that?' I ask.

There's no reply. With a sigh, I rap my knuckles in a vague approximation of the chorus to 'Shake it Off' by Taylor Swift.

The door swings open and Arjun beams at me. 'Nice,' he says. 'Welcome to the secret headquarters.'

'You've all been very cryptic,' I say, moving past him into Hannah's room. 'What's this about?'

Hannah looks up from her desk which is covered in papers, and are those . . . blueprints?

'Are we heisting something?' I ask, interested. 'I've always fancied being in on a heist.'

'If Hannah wanted to plan a heist, she'd plan a heist,' Patty says from the sofa, where she is sprawled, eating a bag of gummy worms. 'And no one would ever know about it. For all we know she's sitting on the real Mona Lisa and the one in the Louvre is a clever forgery.' Patty bites the head off a worm with obvious relish.

'I'm more of a diamond girl,' Hannah murmurs, still scrawling on the notepad in front of her.

'Babe, you really need to clean your make-up brushes.' Liam emerges from the bathroom and beams at me. 'Jack! You made it.'

'Yeah,' I agree, bemused. 'But I still don't know why. What's going on, guys?'

Hannah gets to her feet. 'First of all,' she points at me, 'did you invite Cynthie on a date tomorrow like I told you to?'

'Yes.'

'And she agreed to it?' Hannah looks pleased.

'Honestly, I didn't exactly give her time to disagree,' I say.

'He ran away,' Arjun puts in, flopping down next to Patty and pinching one of her gummy worms.

'I didn't *run away*!' I protest. 'I rode away. On a horse. Manfully.'

'Smart,' Liam nods. 'Can't give her time to talk herself out of things.'

I'm not sure that's a flattering interpretation of events, but it's not exactly wrong.

'So I take it there's a reason you wanted me to ask her,' I say. 'Not that I'm complaining. I wanted to do it anyway; I just wasn't sure about the timing.'

'That's precisely why you're here.' Hannah nods. 'Please, take a seat.'

Patty and Arjun leap up from the sofa so that I can sit there, and Liam disappears back into the bathroom and then re-emerges, rolling a whiteboard into the room.

'Oh my god,' I whisper.

'Pretty cool, hey?' Arjun says proudly.

In the middle of the whiteboard are blurry photos of me and Cynthie, and surrounding the pictures are a web of strings leading to words and phrases like: 9:15 LEAVES WARDROBE ON HUNT FOR COFFEE and CONTACT DOVE GUY??? And HOT LIBRARI-ANS!!!!!!! (that one is underlined three times.)

'Are you ... planning to murder us?' I ask.

Arjun laughs loudly and then squints at the board. 'Huh,' he says. 'Now you mention it, I guess the vibe *is* a little murder-y.'

'If you'll all turn to page one of your handout,' Hannah sails on, ignoring this.

'There's a handout?' I ask weakly, but Patty is already thrusting it at me. It's been professionally bound and the title on the cover is 'Operation Grand Gesture'.

'On the first page you'll find a word cloud of Cynthie's interests,' Hannah continues. 'The bigger the word, the greater the frequency with which she references it.'

I'm gratified to see my name is only slightly smaller than Hannah's.

'You want to help me plan a grand gesture?' I ask, weirdly touched by how invested they all are.

'Of course we do!' Arjun says.

'Well, I'm grateful,' I say, 'but I don't really understand why you're doing this.'

Hannah looks down at me. 'Jack, are you in love with Cynthie?'

'Yes,' I reply without hesitation. 'Deeply, irrevocably, embarrassingly in love with her.'

Her face softens. 'Yeah. That's what we thought.'

'But it's still nice to hear it.' Liam sniffles a bit.

'You're perfect for each other,' Patty agrees.

'But with Cynthie.' Hannah shifts on her feet. 'It's ... complicated. She wants to trust you, but it doesn't come easily to her.'

'I know that,' I say softly. 'I'll earn it. I'm not going anywhere.'

Liam's hand goes to his heart. Arjun is doing some pretty hard blinking.

'The thing is,' Patty cuts in, 'Cynthie's getting in her own way. She thinks it's all too good to be true, and you need to do something to show her that you mean business.'

'She needs an intervention,' Hannah says firmly.

'And we promised we'd help her,' Liam adds.

'Hence the grand gesture,' I murmur, running my hand across my jaw as the truth dawns on me. 'Cynthie thinks that the love we see in the movies doesn't exist in real life,' I muse. 'So we should show her that it really does. That life can be grand and romantic. That she *deserves* that – the time and the trouble and the thought, she deserves someone who loves her ... epically.'

When I look up all four of them are watching me, wide-eyed. Hannah is smiling.

'That's exactly right,' she nods approvingly. 'Cynthie *wants* the big splashy happily-ever-after moment, but she's been let down too often. She *wants* to believe that you're in love with her, but she's holding herself back.'

'It's like she needs proof,' Arjun sighs, his eyes flicking to the murder board. 'Hard evidence.'

There's a pause as we absorb that.

'We could have a trial.' He perks up. 'A love trial! I could wear a judge's wig. We could prove the case beyond reasonable doubt.'

'That doesn't sound very romantic,' Liam puts in doubtfully. 'It sounds more like a bad episode of Judge Judy.'

'Well,' Arjun says with a shrug, 'I already told you I've got a dove guy—'

'Arjun!' Patty huffs, 'Stop banging on about the dove guy. There's nothing romantic about a load of fancy pigeons crapping everywhere.' She hesitates. 'But I'm not against the idea of seeing you in one of those wigs.'

Arjun's eyes widen and his grin threatens to split his face in half. 'I'll bear that in mind.'

'*Once again*, can we not get distracted by your role-playing kink,' Liam groans. 'I cannot believe how often I have to say that.'

'Actually, I think Arjun might be on to something,' I say thoughtfully.

'Yes!' Arjun pumps his fist. 'Vindication! You want me to call my guy right now? I can get you a great deal. We can have *so many doves* here in the next hour.' His expression is gleeful, bordering on manic.

'No, no,' I cut him off with a wave of my hand, frankly starting to feel a bit worried about this avian obsession. 'Not the doves. The proof. I think I have an idea.' My eyes meet Hannah's. 'But it's a ton of work and we'd need a lot of help to pull it off by tomorrow.'

Hannah's smile widens. 'What I'm hearing is that you require the help of an organizational whizz.'

'And her ragtag crew of loveable misfits,' Arjun adds.

'We're totally here for you,' Liam nods. 'Whatever you need.'

'I want it to be perfect for her,' I say. 'I want it to be something she'll never forget.'

'We know you do,' Hannah says. 'That's why we're here. Do you think we'd trust anyone who wanted anything less with our girl?'

I look at them, at all the work they've already put in, and I can *feel* the love coming off them. And it's not just for Cynthie, I realize. Somehow, miraculously, they're here for me, too. I've become a part of this family, this painfully loyal, close-knit, ride-or-die group. This ragtag crew of loveable misfits.

I'm exactly where I'm supposed to be.

'Okay.' I grin, rubbing my hands together. 'In that case, let's get down to business.'

Chapter Forty-Five

Cynthie

The next day I find myself fluttering about with nerves over my date with Jack. He's been very tight-lipped about the whole thing, refusing to tell me where we're going or what we're doing.

'I just need to know what to wear,' I whine while he makes me a cup of coffee in his trailer. 'Ball gown? Swimming costume? Inflatable minion suit?'

'Do you *have* an inflatable minion suit?' He looks up, interested.

I nod. 'We all did for Halloween last year. Priya was Gru.'

'Okay, I definitely need to see those pictures.' He laughs, expertly topping my cup with foamed milk. 'And also, yes, absolutely you should wear that.'

I stretch. 'Damn. You've called my bluff. I don't tend to travel with it.'

'Disappointing.' He shakes his head, handing me my coffee. 'But anything will do. It's casual. No need to dust off the ball gown.'

'Casual?' I think about it. 'No, it still doesn't give me anything to go on. I've got no idea what we're doing.'

The door to Jack's trailer bursts open and Arjun sticks his head in. 'Hey, Jack, I have everything set up ready to go to the ...' – he catches sight of me and falters – 'dry cleaners,' he finishes weakly.

'Why are you doing Jack's dry cleaning?' I ask, puzzled.

'Yes, Arjun,' Jack says, and it looks like he's trying not to laugh, 'why are you doing my dry cleaning?'

'Hmmm?' Arjun looks innocent. 'What?'

'You're being weird,' I say.

'Well, you know me,' Arjun says brightly. 'Anyway, I have to go. Now that I've told you the news. About the dry cleaners.' He leaves, closing the door firmly behind him.

'What was that about?' I ask.

Jack shakes his head. 'With Arjun? Who knows.'

Almost immediately, there's a knock at the door. 'Come in,' Jack yells.

This time Hannah stands in the doorway, and when she sees me her eyes widen. She's clutching a clipboard. 'Oh. Hi, Cynthie!' The words come out in a bright staccato.

'Hi?' I reply. Then Hannah says nothing, just smiles at me. 'Did you need me for something?'

'Nope,' she says, then, seeming to collect herself. 'I mean yes, obviously.' She looks from Jack, back to me. 'Can I get you anything to drink?' she asks, finally.

I look down at the coffee cup in my hand. 'Er, no, I'm fine thanks.'

'Great!' Hannah says and then she whirrs back out the door.

'Okay, *something* strange is going on,' I say. 'Why is everyone behaving like they're on drugs?' I look more closely at Jack, 'And why is your eye twitching?'

His smile looks a bit more pained now. 'I have no idea. Maybe you were right and the caffeine is finally catching up with me.'

'If you say so,' I reply, dubious. I think about it for a moment. 'Are you going to prank me?'

'What?' His surprise looks genuine, but I remain suspicious.

'There's a lot of big prank energy in the air,' I say, waving my index finger in a circle. 'And I'll remind you, that's not something you want to start with me.'

He laughs, looking delighted. 'I solemnly swear no one is pranking you.'

'Fine,' I grumble, sipping my coffee. 'Whatever is going on, I'll get it out of Hannah later.'

'So, finish telling me about Brooke,' he says, changing the subject and slipping into the seat across from me. 'Do you think you'll talk to her on camera?'

'I don't know.' I frown. 'I need to know a bit more and speak to a few more people first, but it seems like she could be a good person to trust with the story. Don't you think?'

He nods. 'Yeah, actually, I do. I think she's smart and her work is strong. She's using the documentary here to boost her profile and make contacts. It also might be better to explore Shawn's behaviour in the context of a wider problem.'

'That's what I think too,' I agree. 'So it doesn't come off as some sort of personal vendetta. And either way, her project sounds interesting. She's already managed to get interviews with some high-profile people. I was thinking maybe I could come on board in a production role . . .'

'Wow.' He leans back in his seat. 'That's a big step.'

'I know, but I've been talking about setting up a production company for years. It would be the perfect thing for Hannah to run – she's the most capable person on the planet, and she knows everyone. The assistant network is no joke.'

'Oh god, you're right. She'd be brilliant at that,' Jack exhales.

I tap my fingers against the side of my coffee cup. 'Plus, she shouldn't be my assistant for ever, no matter how much I love having her around. She's got way too much talent.'

'It would be hard on both of you, though. Not to be together so much,' Jack says gently.

'Yeah, it would,' I agree with a pang. 'But I don't ever want our relationship to hold her back. She's outgrown the job, and I know her – she needs a challenge.' I take a sip of my drink. 'And it feels like . . .' I hesitate.

'What?' Jack prompts after a moment.

I look at him and think again how strange this is. It's not just that I can tell him what I think or how I feel; it's so obvious that he *wants* to know. It's in every line of him. I'm like his favourite book, the one he can't put down.

'I don't know, it feels like things are changing. Like the timing is right somehow.'

Jack nods wisely. 'You're both thirty-three,' he says. 'That's a year of transformation.'

I laugh. 'You sound like Liam.'

'Don't knock it,' he says with a shrug. 'It's a whole thing apparently.'

'What did you do when you were thirty-three?' I ask, settling my chin in my hand. He's not the only one who's fascinated. I want to roll around in his thoughts; I want to own every secret he has and hoard them with my own.

He rubs his hand across his jaw, thinking. 'I decided I was going to stop caring what my parents thought about my career.'

'Just like that?'

'Pretty much. It had been coming on for a long time, but I was working on *Blood/Lust*.' He sits back in his chair. 'I hadn't had the best offers coming in and I took that part against their advice. My own hopes for it hadn't exactly been high, but, fuck, I loved it pretty much straightaway. The cast and crew are fantastic, and we got really tight; the writing is great; the opportunity to work on a single character for so long and really get to know him, the *fandom*.' He exhales a chuckle. 'Being part of that is wild.'

I grin at him, at the enthusiasm coming off him.

'I'd finished the first season and I was having a ball. I realized I wasn't going to be able to stop my mum and dad from making their comments, but I didn't have to listen to them. I'd made something without them, and I liked it. They didn't approve, and it didn't matter. It was liberating.'

'I bet,' I murmur. 'You know, it's impressive all the work you've done since we met.'

'I'm a very impressive man.'

'I'm serious,' I insist. 'You've grown and changed so much over the last thirteen years.'

'So why do you sound sad about it?'

'I'm not sad about it. I'm happy for you. I'm actually weirdly proud of you.'

'But . . .' He watches me steadily.

I sigh. 'I suppose I can't help comparing the two of us. You're happier, steadier. You *found* something, but I feel like . . . I don't know, like maybe I lost something along the way.'

He's quiet. 'You know, that year I also let Nico drag me along to get my tattoo,' he says after a moment, and the turn in the conversation throws me.

'Oh, yes.' My eyes flick to his beautiful torso, currently hidden by his T-shirt. Unfortunately. 'I meant to ask you about that.'

'It's a bonfire,' he says, mischief in his face now.

'A bonfire?'

'Mmm.' He rubs his fingers against his chest, over the spot where I know the tattoo is. The one I traced with my tongue only days ago. I blink. *Focus, Cynthie.*

'It's a reminder of that decision, to find the fun in my work, to do what makes me happy. Just like you told me that night by the bonfire.'

'Like I—' I give an incredulous laugh, but his expression is serene. 'You're serious? Wow. You weren't kidding about that conversation being important to you.'

'Everything about you is important to me,' Jack says simply.

'That's . . .' I trail off, my heart too full to find words.

'I don't think you lost anything, Cynthie,' he says quietly. 'I think you're full of joy and light and you always have been.'

'Oh,' I manage, eloquently. Fuck, he's so good at this. All this emotional intelligence, it's driving me crazy. 'You're just going to make me feel safe and cared for and heard until I start believing in true love and fairytales and happy endings, aren't you?' I grumble.

'That's pretty much my evil plan, yeah.' He grins. 'Thirty-three, Cyn. The year of transformation. Let's make a romantic of you.'

'A romantic of me and a producer of Hannah,' I sigh, steering the subject back to safer ground. 'Not sure who's going to be a bigger challenge.'

'You'll both find your way,' Jack says with an awful lot of certainty. I wish this self-assured, confident thing of his wasn't doing it for me, but it really is.

'I just need to convince her, I guess.'

'You will,' he says cheerfully. 'No one can resist Cynthie Taylor for long.'

'You put up a pretty good fight.'

'Nah, I was a goner on day one; I'm just an excellent actor.' He gets to his feet. 'Speaking of which, I need to go and get into costume. I'll see you later. The car will pick you up at eight.'

'Okay,' I say. 'I'll see you wherever we're going in my cowboy hat and daisy dukes.'

'Can't wait,' he replies, leaving on a laugh.

I hang around set for a bit longer, though I don't have any further scenes scheduled for the day, and I don't think it's my imagination that everyone is behaving strangely towards me. Barry, the key grip on set and one of my favourite gossip buddies, turns around and walks off in the opposite direction when he sees me coming, even though I've been waiting all day to catch up about the latest episode of our favourite reality TV show.

'Hope you're looking forward to tonight,' Hilary from the costume department calls as I'm leaving, and then Greg, the driver, digs her in the ribs and says 'Shhhhh!' Even Logan goes out of his way to avoid me, muttering something about a health and safety meeting that definitely isn't happening. Brooke treats me to a cheery thumbs up for no apparent reason and looks startled by her own hands. I don't think she's ever given anyone a thumbs up in her life.

It's deeply weird.

Still, I have other things to think about, and my nerves pick up again as I get ready for my date.

A date.

A real date.

With Jack.

I wonder what it will be like. I wonder if he'll finally put his hands on me. *God*, I hope he puts his hands on me.

As promised the car picks me up at eight sharp, and I have no idea what's going on when it starts taking the road back to Darlcot. 'Are we picking Jack up from set?' I ask Greg as we bump up the drive.

'Yes?' Greg says, sounding troublingly uncertain.

When we reach the house, Jack is waiting outside. He's wearing jeans, a mossy green jumper and a nervous expression. He comes round to open the car door for me.

'What's going on?' I ask, confused. 'I thought you wanted to go on a date?'

'We are,' he says. 'The date is here.'

Greg is beaming at us.

'Here?' I repeat, no wiser. 'At work?'

'Do you trust me?' He's smiling, but there's something in his voice, something in his eyes, that tells me the question isn't light-hearted.

'Yes,' I say, and the word comes easily.

He looks relieved as he holds out his hand to me. 'Come on, then.' His fingers tangle with mine, and it's the first time we've touched in almost a week. It's the tiniest taste of what I've been craving, a drop in the ocean. I wonder how quickly I could get him naked. His outfit has a reassuring lack of buttons, so I'm thinking it wouldn't take me too long. I'm so distracted by my own thirsty schemes that I barely register where we're going.

He guides me around the side of the house and there, on the edge of the formal lawn, I find my friends waiting for us.

Chapter Forty-Six

Cynthie

'What . . .' I begin, trailing off as I take in the scene in front of me.

It's an outdoor cinema. And it absolutely wasn't here a few hours ago. The entire cast and crew are milling around, drinking champagne and chatting. When they catch sight of me, a cheer goes up.

I lift my hand in greeting, bewildered. 'What is going on?' I whisper.

There are picnic blankets with cushions strewn across them, arranged in neat rows on the grass. Tall glass lanterns with white candles inside them are clustered around the edges of the lawn. Pam is there, running a makeshift bar out the side of her van. Overhead there's an enormous metal rigging frame from which hundreds of fairy lights have been suspended around an extremely serious looking projector. There's a screen – a professional set up with a load of substantial sound equipment.

'How did you . . . ?' I start again, still dazed.

'The whole crew pitched in,' Jack replies, tugging me forward to where Hannah is holding out a glass of champagne to me.

'I still don't understand,' I say. 'This is incredible. Are we going to watch a film?'

'What on earth gave you that idea?' Patty says drily.

I narrow my eyes. 'What are you all doing here on my date? Is this why you've been acting like lunatics?'

'Well, truthfully, it's less of a date and more of an intervention,' Hannah warns me.

'A romantic intervention,' Jack says quickly.

'Yeah,' I say after a pause, 'I think I need more information than that.'

'You asked us for our help,' Patty reminds me. 'So we're delivering.'

'Just take your champagne and go and sit down,' Liam says soothingly.

'We got you popcorn, too,' Arjun says. Priya is sitting on his shoulders and she beams at me.

'Hi, Auntie Cyn,' she sings. 'Do you like your party?'

'I love it,' I reply, taking the bag of popcorn she holds out.

'No reason an intervention can't be comfortable,' Arjun adds.

'*Romantic* intervention,' Jack says again a bit desperately.

'I'm not sure saying the word romantic makes it any better,' I murmur faintly, thoroughly confused.

'We saved you a blanket down at the front,' Hannah says, bossily. 'Off you go.'

'Just tell me what's going on,' I plead with her.

She takes my free hand in hers and squeezes it, smiling at me with so much affection in her face. 'Just trust us.' It seems there's a lot of trust involved in tonight's proceedings. 'We've got you.'

'Okay,' I agree reluctantly, because at this point what else can I do?

'Oh, and hand over your phone,' Hannah says. 'I'll put it with the others.'

'The others?' I ask.

In response she gestures to a colourful sign in Priya's handwriting. It says,

BY ORDER OF MANIJMENT! NO FONES. NO KAMERAS. NO EGGSEPSHUNS!

I guess there's no arguing with that, so I hand over my phone and let Jack tug me through the crowd. Along the way people keep stopping to hug me. It feels like it's my birthday, and I don't hate it; I just wish I knew why it was happening. I also can't help but feel that this audience is going to interfere with my get-Jack-naked scheme. Maybe we'll be able to sneak off to my trailer at some point.

'You two are down here at the front.' Brooke appears in front of me. 'I hope you understand what a sacrifice it is that I'm not filming any of this,' she whispers to me.

'Honestly, I haven't got a clue what's happening.'

She only smiles mysteriously, and then points to a blanket that has a reserved sign on it. It's right at the front. The night is warm, and the lights sparkle in an intricate web above us.

'This is so beautiful. Did the crew really do all of this to surprise me?' I ask doubtfully.

'Turns out you're pretty beloved,' Jack says, pulling me down beside him.

'Oh.' I glance back over my shoulder to where everyone else is getting comfortable. I spy Hattie sitting with Simon and she winks at me. Logan gives me a cheerful wave from beside Nisha the intimacy co-ordinator. I can't help noticing that the two of them look pretty cozy. Jasmine is here too. She's drinking champagne straight from the neck of the bottle and lifts it in my direction in a knowing salute. I see Lucy the horse trainer and half expect to find Reckless Ed somewhere in attendance. There are people here from wardrobe and props and every single other department, and the air is full of happy anticipation. I don't know what is going on, but I already love it.

'Okay, this is amazing.' I turn to Jack. 'But I have to admit, I didn't think you'd invite quite so many people on our first date.'

He laughs. 'Let's just say our original idea spiralled a little bit. People wanted to get involved.'

I glance around at the outdoor festival that he and my friends have thrown together. 'No kidding.' I shift closer to him, lean in. 'Are you going to tell me what's going on?' I sound nervous because I am.

He takes my hand again. 'I know you said life isn't a fairytale, and that's true. But it can still be magic. Not every relationship ends in disaster. Look at Patty and Arjun.' He gestures to where the two of them stand. Priya is still on Arjun's shoulders, bent over with her skinny arms around his neck so that her head rests on top of his. Patty feeds him popcorn and he nibbles at her fingers, making her laugh. My heart melts.

'Yeah, they're pretty good,' I agree.

'Liam and David, Hannah's parents,' Jack says, 'Clemmie and Theo. All excellent love stories.'

'Hmmm.' I tilt my chin. 'I suppose so.'

'And I know that you're having trouble believing in this, in us. I know that you've been let down, badly, by people you loved, by the people who were supposed to stay.' His voice is soft, his words earnest. 'But Cynthie, I won't hurt you. I won't lie.' He looks me in the eyes. 'And I won't leave. I will choose you every day, and I need you to know that. I need you to *see* that. That's what's going on.'

My eyes are swimming with tears, but before I can say anything, Brooke steps up in front of the crowd, to rowdy applause.

'Hello, everyone,' she says brightly. 'And thank you for coming to this very special screening. When Jack and Hannah came to me with this idea, I thought the two of them were mad, but the truth is' – her eyes land on me and I blink the tears back, force a smile even as my heart is beating almost out my chest – 'they both just love Cynthie a lot. Normally I wouldn't dream of sharing footage part way through a project, but once I heard their story, I got on board pretty quick. I want to thank my team and Jasmine and Logan for helping me put this together in record time, and everyone else who helped with the set up. So, without further ado, I give you: a love story, thirteen years in the making.'

'Oh my god,' I whisper, as the projector whirrs to life.

The screen fills with an image of Jack and me. It's thirteen years ago. The quality isn't the best and we're doing the chemistry read together. I've never seen this before. It's the first time we ever met and we look so young. Straight away I can see it – the spark between us, all that heat simmering under every line. This is why I got my big break – because the chemistry between Jack and me really is electric.

After a couple of minutes, Logan's voice yells, 'Cut!'

On the screen, I blink like I'm coming out of a dream. I look up at Jack and grin. I'm smiling so hard; I can feel my own joy vibrating across the years. Sitting here now, I remember that moment so well, the moment of pure undiluted pleasure at performing well, of performing with Jack for the first time.

The Cynthie on-screen throws her arms around Jack and hugs him, looking up at him with stars in her eyes. 'That was fun.'

'Thanks so much, Cynthie,' Jasmine's formal voice comes from the speakers. 'We'll be in touch.'

'Great.' I gather up my bag and walk across in front of the camera. 'Thanks for seeing me.'

As Marion talks to me for a moment off-screen, the camera remains trained on Jack, who is looking over to where I'm standing, with such naked longing in his face that my breath catches in my throat. He lifts his hand slowly to his chest and rubs his fingers over his heart, as if it's aching. It's a gesture I've seen him make a few times.

'That was the moment,' Jack says low in my ear, here in the real world, right beside me. 'That was the moment I fell for you, Cynthie. I told you it had been thirteen years, and I meant it. That's how you can know. You can see it right there for yourself.'

The image on the screen cuts to show Logan and Jasmine sitting side by side.

'After the chemistry read, it was really a no-brainer,' Jasmine says. 'It's not often you actually get to watch two people fall in love in front of you,' Logan says with a grin, 'but with those two, it was like . . . destiny.'

Music starts playing from the speakers, and there's a compilation of footage from the original film – times when the cameras must have been left rolling. They caught so much, I realize, more than I had ever thought possible.

There's me and Jack bickering while we walk uphill in our coats, our bodies curved in towards each other. There's Jack laughing with Simon, while I watch him in the background, something like yearning in my face. Me trying to blow a stray hair from my wig out of my face, and Jack reaching over and tucking it behind my ear. Me laughing myself silly while Reckless Ed charges around with Jack on his back. Jack kissing me in the rain, and the way we look after cut is called, like we want to jump each other there and then. Him catching me in his arms when I faint, his face a mask of anger and worry as he cradles me to his chest, yelling for help. There's some shaky footage of dubious quality of me singing karaoke, that has everyone in the crowd wolf-whistling, especially when it catches Jack's face for a moment, his eyes glued to me with a hungry intensity that can't be denied.

'They were so determined not to get along,' Hattie's voice comes through the speakers, 'but it was clear as day that the pair of them were mad for each other from the start.'

Now the film cuts to face after face in quick succession.

'Totally into each other,' says Liam.

'Jack was out of his mind in love with Cynthie from the beginning,' Arjun laughs.

'The two of them lit up the screen.' Mark, the cinematographer nods. 'It was mad to watch. We all knew it was special.'

'You could always tell they were going to end up together,' Hilary from wardrobe sighs. 'It was so romantic.'

'You can't fake chemistry like that,' Logan says.

'They really challenged each other,' Hannah says thoughtfully. 'It was the most alive I'd ever seen Cyn.'

'The attraction between them was intense.' Patty smirks. 'The air was basically buzzing with pheromones whenever they were near each other. You couldn't miss it.'

'I think they were the only ones who didn't see it.' It cuts back to Hannah.

'Those dummies,' Arjun laughs.

Then, the footage gets a bit shaky, and it takes me a second to recognize that it's from the charity gala. Jack and I posing for pictures. He looks down at me, and I know that's the moment he noticed the necklace I was wearing, but all anyone else sees is the way we stare at each other, a slow, dawning recognition. My cheeks go pink; Jack's throat bobs. It's almost painfully intimate.

And then it's time for another compilation, only this time Brooke had cameras following us so there's so much more. Dozens of clips flicker across the screen. Of Jack sitting off camera watching me perform with a smile on his face. Of me with my chin in my hand nodding at something he says. Of Jack running lines with my feet in his lap. Of me gazing with such naked lust at the sight of him on the back of a horse that the crowd laughs. Our hands touching at any opportunity. My head on his shoulder. Laughing and joking with Patty and Liam. Jack giving me a piggyback through the mud so my shoes don't get ruined. Me handing him a coffee while he looks like I've saved his life. Jack twirling me into an impromptu slow dance. Him watching me. Me watching him. Him watching me. Me watching him.

It goes on and on.

Then I'm there on camera.

'What part of working with Jack do you enjoy the most?' Brooke asks. It's from an interview we did only this morning.

I watch the smile curl on my lips, finding it hard to believe that

I ever thought I could hide the way I feel about Jack from anyone, let alone myself. I smile like I have the best secret in the world. 'Honestly?' I laugh. 'It's everything. He's fantastic at his job, but he's so much more than that. Working with him is . . . the most fun I've ever had. I just love being around him.'

Now Jack's face replaces mine and Brooke asks him the same question.

He blows out a slow breath. 'I don't know where you start,' he says. 'Her passion, her intelligence, her dedication. The way her skill pushes everyone around her to be better. Mostly though, it's the pure joy of it. Working with her, knowing her, has changed my life for ever, for the better in every way.'

'It sounds like you're really in love with her.' I can hear the smile in Brooke's voice.

Jack's own smile grows. 'Oh, yeah,' he says, sincerity in every line of his beautiful face. 'I'm so in love with her it's ridiculous. You know, people think Edward and Emilia's story is the height of romance, but they have no idea, none at all.' He shakes his head. 'What you all saw on-screen doesn't hold a candle to what happened behind the scenes. Me and Cynthie? That's the real love story.'

The screen goes black, and Jack's words hang in the still, warm air. I don't even realize that I'm crying until I feel Jack's thumb come up to my cheek, brushing the tears away.

'Don't cry, love,' he murmurs.

I look at him, and the rest of the world simply disappears. It's just the two of us, and he's looking at me with so much emotion in his eyes that it hurts – it physically hurts – like something inside my chest is cracking wide open.

Transformation.

'It is real, isn't it?' I whisper. 'This thing. *Us*. It was always real.'

'Always was.' Jack's voice is steady. 'Always will be.'

And like a key turning smooth in a lock, I hear the words, and

I believe them.

'I love you, Jack.'

'I know.' He tucks a strand of hair tenderly behind my ear.

'Did you just quote *Star Wars* during our big romantic climax, you dic—' I don't get any further because then his mouth is on mine, and somehow I'm kissing him and laughing and crying all at once, and my hands are around his neck and he's pulling me in tight against his body. I can feel his heart beating, can hear my own in my ears, perfectly in sync. He kisses me like I'm the most precious thing in the world, and distantly, dimly, I'm aware that the crowd is cheering for us but none of that matters now. There's no need to perform anymore.

Right now, there's no one but us.

And this isn't the happily ever after moment. It isn't the perfect ending to our story at all. It's the perfect beginning.

Epilogue

Cynthie

Two Years Later

'And Jack,' the moderator says from behind his podium, 'how are you feeling about season seven?'

I watch from the side of the stage as Jack leans forward in his seat, grinning wide. 'I'm feeling great about it. We've got a lot of fun stuff coming up.'

The enormous Comic Con crowd cheers. They're so loud that the floor shakes, and Jack's expression is gleeful. He looks unbearably handsome, so I'm not surprised it sounds like he's about to cause some sort of riot.

'And is there any truth to the rumour that there might be a musical episode?' the moderator presses. 'I know a lot of fans would be excited to see that.'

The screaming crowd reaches a higher pitch at this and Jack laughs. 'I'm pretty sure my wife started this rumour,' he says, and it's my turn to smile as I twist the gold band on my ring finger. Jack's turned into an even bigger *my-wife* guy than Theo. Clemmie and I have had to call off our drinking game for the time being now that she's pregnant, but the last few times we played the pair of us got totally smashed because the two of them together are utterly out of control. 'She just likes to see me tap dance,' Jack continues.

'And not all of us have been off over the summer starring in West End musicals,' Emily, one of Jack's co-stars teases him. 'Trust me, no one wants to hear Phil belting out show tunes.'

Phil, who plays Jack's uncle in the show, grimaces. 'That is . . . accurate.'

I linger in the shadows for another couple of minutes, enjoying myself. Jack is happy and relaxed as the questions continue. He laughs with his friends, charms the audience, and I know he's fired up about starting shooting on the series in a few weeks.

When it looks like things are wrapping up, I slip away, following the directions of the helpful assistant towards Jack's dressing room. After I close the door behind me, I take a second to check my reflection in the mirror and spot the photos he's tucked around the edge. They're the same ones that graced his dressing room every night that he performed in *Singin' in the Rain* at the theatre on Drury Lane: there's one of the two of us windswept and beaming into the camera, my hand – adorned with a giant diamond ring – cradling his cheek; there's one of Priya dressed as Gru surrounded by six inflatable minions; there's a battered polaroid of me and Jack from all those years ago. I'm wearing a wig, a ballgown and a pair of sunglasses, and I'm looking down at my phone. Jack is dressed in full Regency get up, clutching a cup of coffee.

He's looking at me.

I touch my finger to the photograph and feel a familiar rush of affection for those two dummies who didn't know what was right in front of them. Fortunately, we got there in the end. Turns out Jack was right: we were the real love story all along.

Voices reach me from outside the door, and I turn, leaning back against the dressing table as it swings open and my husband steps in. His eyes fall on me, and happiness knocks all the air out of my lungs when I catch the look of delight on his face.

'What—' he starts, but he doesn't get very far, because I'm already running for him, leaping up into his open arms.

My legs go round his waist and my mouth crashes into his. He stumbles back, kicks out blindly with his foot to slam the door behind him, and with a growl that I feel deep in my core, he returns my kiss. Enthusiastically.

Jack

I pull back from Cynthie, looking down into her beautiful, flushed face. 'I thought you and Hannah were still in New York for your meeting?' I manage, and then – before she can answer – I drop my mouth to hers again, pulling her tighter against me.

I don't care when she got here, or how, all I care about is this: her hands, her mouth, the delicate skin on her neck. I bury my face there, drinking in the scent of her perfume, pressing open-mouthed kisses against her throat.

'We finished up early and I flew straight out,' she replies, breathless. 'I caught the end of your panel. You were great.'

I press another soft kiss to her lips, and reluctantly release her so that she's standing on her own feet. She stays close, her fingers toying with the buttons on my waistcoat.

'How did it go?' I ask.

Her face lights up, and seeing her happy is my drug of choice. My bloodstream buzzes with the hit. 'It was great. She loved our pitch, and we're going to option the book. It's going to make an amazing movie.'

'It will with you directing it.' I kiss her again. 'I knew you guys had it in the bag.'

'Hannah did all the hard work,' Cynthie insists, but I know my wife. No one can resist her. Cynthie's been looking for her first solo directing gig for a while, and this second-chance rom-com is the perfect fit. Even Jasmine agreed.

Plus, with Hannah in charge, their production company has been going from strength to strength. It doesn't hurt that their first film – Brooke's documentary about women in the film industry – won a raft of awards, including an Independent Spirit Award back in February. Personally, I think the biggest prize was the immaculate takedown of Shawn Hardy. His clever ex-wife even managed to get in a good slap to his face that went viral. Sometimes I watch it when I need to unwind.

'We have to celebrate,' I say now. 'Let me take you out for dinner.'

Cynthie steps back, boosting herself up onto my dressing table. She runs her gaze over me, slowly.

'I have a better idea,' she says.

I step between her thighs, already dizzy with how much I want her. I'll never get enough of this, never get enough of the two of us together.

'Oh, really?' I murmur, leaning forward, my hands coming down either side of her hips, caging her in.

'Mmm.' Her head tips back as she looks at me, and she sinks her teeth into her bottom lip. 'I've just had to spend the last hour watching you on stage dressed in your sexy librarian costume.'

I huff a laugh and glance down at the tweed waistcoat over the white shirt, with the sleeves rolled up to the elbows. My wife and her hot-librarian kink.

I reach out and run my hand up her bare calf, pushing the hem of her skirt over her knees. Her breath catches, and I want to bottle the sound. My mouth comes down over hers and I deepen the kiss, as my fingers drift higher.

'Jack,' she whispers against my mouth, her lips curved into my favourite smile.

'Yes, Cynthie?'

'Leave the glasses on.'

Acknowledgements

When I wrote the acknowledgements for *Under Your Spell* it was very early on, and at the time I had no possible conception of just how grateful I would be to so many people. This book is already long and I'm mindful that I can't write another hundred pages of gushing thanks to all of you individually, but to every single person who has shared about, posted about, sold, loaned, gifted and reviewed my books, THANK YOU from the bottom of my heart. Thank you for the posts and the videos and the messages – every single one of them means so much to me and delivered a glorious hit of serotonin.

Thank you, as always, to my agent, Louise – *Blood/Lust*'s number one fan, and my friend and biggest supporter. I am grateful every single day that I won her in a competition.

To my US agent, Jess – I'm so happy we finally got to meet in person. I wish you nothing but un-spilled matcha lattes and Hear-me-out Balto cakes.

I'm so grateful to my wonderful editor, Molly, who I just want to hang out with all the time. To the whole brilliant, brilliant team at Simon & Schuster, but particularly to my Romance House Party girl gang: SJV, Sabah, Sarah, Gen, Harriett, Laurie, Maddie and Kate. I'm sure you have friends! Thank you to Misha for keeping me so beautifully organized, and to Pip for not one, but two PERFECT covers.

Thanks to my whole team at Atria, especially my so kind and clever editor Melanie. Being able to hug you in person made my whole year. Every single person at Atria has been incredibly generous towards me, but I have to especially shout out Elizabeth, Dayna, Morgan, Megan and Falon. Thank you for making me feel so seen and understood and for caring as deeply as I do about the people I made up. I hope there are many more glorious, gossipy lunches to come.

Thank you to ALL my incredible publishers and translators – in seventeen languages and counting – who have treated my books with such care and respect. I am so grateful to you for taking a chance on me and for bringing my stories to readers all over the world.

This is the second time I have thanked Emma Thompson – who I tragically do not know – in my acknowledgements, but I am spectacularly grateful for her *The Sense and Sensibility Screenplay & Diaries* which helped me so much in understanding what filming *A Lady of Quality* might look like. (Read them! A huge joy!)

There are so many writers I admire who have been generous with their time and their support. Thanks to my friends and hand-holders and cheerleaders: Sarra Manning, Kate Young, Wren James, Keris Fox, Ella McLeod, Sarah Chamberlain, Hux, Kirsty Greenwood, Ella Risbridger, Catherine Walsh, Lucy Vine, Cressida McLaughlin, Anna James, Louise O'Neill and Jo Clarke. Thank you a million Marian Keyes, Hannah Grace, Julia Quinn and Christina Lauren for saying such kind things about my book when I have spent so many happy hours enjoying yours. Special thanks to Lindsey Kelk who helped me to plan the perfect LA ice cream date.

There have been TOO MANY people who have made a lot of noise about *Under Your Spell* and given me the greatest boost, but in particular I want to thank Jesse (@exercise_read_repeat), Kelly (@nuclearfiction), Cindy Burnett (@thoughtsfromapage), Jodi (@more.time.2read),

Claire (@theauthorslounge), Kerry (@bookbeforeuleap), Becki (@bookswithbecki), Randi (@randireads), Megan (@megs_bookblog), @bookbruin, Elizabeth (@briony2181), Rachel (@abookishmum) and Courtney (@thebooklifeofcat), who have been incredibly kind.

The best book club in the whole world, my kindred spirits, Reading Between the Wines PEI. Thank you for making me an honorary member.

To my pals at Mr B's, but especially to Hannah, Lottie and Liv.

To Emily Dayton for her book recommendations and general cheerleading.

Thank you to my friends and family who get lumped in at the end, but who I would be lost without. I love you all so much.

The biggest thanks I have in a foolishly grateful heart will always go to Paul and Bea, my little family and my safe place. I love you and I like you.

Discover more from
Laura Wood

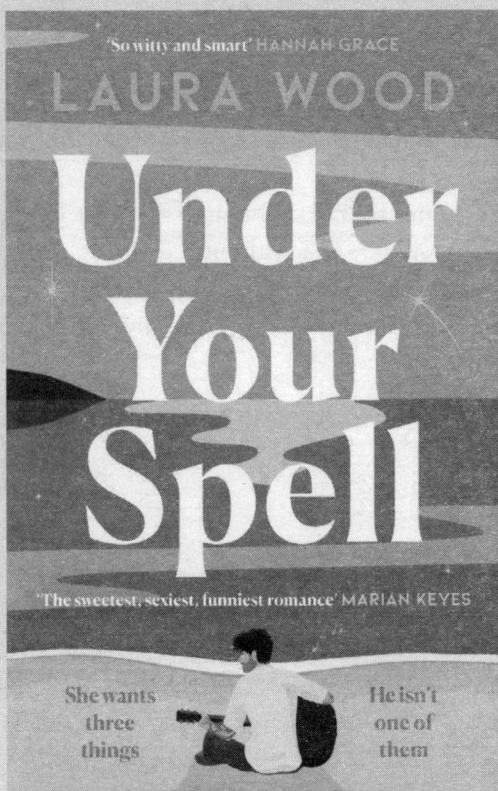

Available now

Simon & Schuster

booksandthecity.co.uk
the home of female fiction

NEWS & EVENTS | BOOKS | FEATURES | COMPETITIONS

Follow us online to be the first to hear from
your favourite authors

bc
booksandthecity.co.uk

X
@TeamBATC

Join our mailing list for the latest news, events and
exclusive competitions

Sign up at
booksandthecity.co.uk